CHAPTER & HEARSE

Lorna Barrett

BERKLEY PRIME CRIME, NEW YORK

THE BERKLEY PUBLISHING GROUP
Published by the Penguin Group
Penguin Group (USA) Inc.
375 Hudson Street, New York, New York 10014, USA

Penguin Group (Canada), 90 Eglinton Avenue East, Suite 700, Toronto, Ontario M4P 2Y3, Canada
(a division of Pearson Penguin Canada Inc.)
Penguin Books Ltd., 80 Strand, London WC2R 0RL, England
Penguin Group Ireland, 25 St. Stephen's Green, Dublin 2, Ireland (a division of Penguin Books Ltd.)
Penguin Group (Australia), 250 Camberwell Road, Camberwell, Victoria 3124, Australia
(a division of Pearson Australia Group Pty. Ltd.)
Penguin Books India Pvt. Ltd., 11 Community Centre, Panchsheel Park, New Delhi—110 017, India
Penguin Group (NZ), 67 Apollo Drive, Rosedale, North Shore 0632, New Zealand
(a division of Pearson New Zealand Ltd.)
Penguin Books (South Africa) (Pty.) Ltd., 24 Sturdee Avenue, Rosebank, Johannesburg 2196,
South Africa

Penguin Books Ltd., Registered Offices: 80 Strand, London WC2R 0RL, England

This is a work of fiction. Names, characters, places, and incidents either are the product of the author's imagination or are used fictitiously, and any resemblance to actual persons, living or dead, business establishments, events, or locales is entirely coincidental. The publisher does not have any control over and does not assume any responsibility for author or third-party websites or their content.

PUBLISHER'S NOTE: The recipes contained in this book are to be followed exactly as written. The publisher is not responsible for your specific health or allergy needs that may require medical supervision. The publisher is not responsible for any adverse reactions to the recipes contained in this book.

CHAPTER & HEARSE

A Berkley Prime Crime Book / published by arrangement with the author

PRINTING HISTORY
Berkley Prime Crime mass-market edition / August 2010

Copyright © 2010 by Penguin Group (USA) Inc.
Excerpt from *A Crafty Killing* by Lorraine Bartlett copyright © by Penguin Group (USA) Inc.
Cover illustration by Teresa Fasolino.
Cover design by Diana Kolsky.
Interior text design by Laura K. Corless.

ISBN: 978-0-425-23601-7

BERKLEY® PRIME CRIME
Berkley Prime Crime Books are published by The Berkley Publishing Group,
a division of Penguin Group (USA) Inc.,
375 Hudson Street, New York, New York 10014.
BERKLEY® PRIME CRIME and the PRIME CRIME logo are trademarks of Penguin Group (USA) Inc.

PRINTED IN THE UNITED STATES OF AMERICA

10 9 8 7 6 5 4 3 2 1

ACKNOWLEDGMENTS

Writing a book can be a lonely process—but when you've got friends cheering you on, you never feel completely isolated. I owe many thanks to my critique partner, Sheila Connolly; my Guppy Sisters in Crime: Krista Davis, Janet Koch, and the always generous Sharon Wildwind, who is a virtual font of useful information. My friend Michelle Sampson, director of the Wadleigh Memorial Library in Milford, New Hampshire, is always available when I have a "local color" question. And, of course, my ever-faithful cheerleaders, Gwen Nelson and Liz Eng.

Thanks also go to all the terrific people at Berkley Prime Crime who've worked so hard on my behalf, including my wonderful editor, Tom Colgan; his assistant, Niti Bagchi; and the publicist, Megan Swartz. Thanks also go to Teresa Fasolino for the amazing paintings she does for my covers. I sometimes think she's reading my mind, because the covers are exactly how I picture the streets of Stoneham. Thanks, too, to my agent, Jacky Sach, for none of this would have been possible without her.

I love to hear from my readers. I hope you'll visit my website, www.LornaBarrett.com, for updates and to join my newsletter mailing list.

ONE

The poster on the Cookery's display window had advertised the book signing for at least a month. Throngs of people were supposed to be in evidence. A temporary cook station had been assembled, and ramekins filled with diced vegetables, chopped chicken, and spices were lined up like props in a stage play.

Tricia Miles forced a smile and tried not to glance at her watch. "Everything looks perfect," she said with a cheerfulness in her voice she didn't quite feel.

The "guest" author, her sister Angelica, stood behind the cook station, head held high, although her eyes were watery and her mouth trembled ever so slightly. Next to her stood a larger-than-life-size photo cutout of . . . herself! The real Angelica was maybe five foot six in her stocking feet—the cutout was six feet tall, dressed in dark slacks and a white blouse covered by a buff-colored, full-front apron with her name emblazoned across the front: ANGELICA MILES, and beneath that: author of EASY-DOES-IT COOKING.

Tricia tried to concentrate on the living Angelica, but her gaze kept wandering to the cutout. It wasn't a good likeness, but somehow Angelica had missed that when she'd purchased the thing as an aid for promotion. Her rather demented expression was one of perpetual surprise—either that, or one of a victim of bad plastic surgery. With her fingers splayed, the cutout reminded Tricia of a bird spreading its bony wings. Yes, that was it—Angelica looked like she'd been goosed. Either that, or the photographer had coached her into an uncanny imitation of a constipated blue heron.

The real Angelica spoke, her voice sounding wobbly. "Nobody's going to come. Not one person."

"I'm here," said a smiling Ginny Wilson, Tricia's twenty-something assistant at her mystery bookstore, Haven't Got a Clue.

"And I," said elderly Mr. Everett, Tricia's other part-time employee.

"Don't forget me," Frannie May Armstrong said in her Texas twang. Angelica owned the Cookery, Stoneham's cookbook store, and Frannie managed it for her. Angelica also owned Booked for Lunch, a retro café across the street. Writing cookbooks was just another entry on her colorful résumé.

Unfortunately, the village of Stoneham, known locally as "Booktown," was more a tourist destination not far from the New Hampshire/Massachusetts state line. Not many of the locals supported the booksellers, who'd been recruited to save what had been a dying village. And shops filled with used, rare, and antiquarian books had done it, too, as evidenced by new prosperity and a much-needed influx of tax revenue.

"Wasn't a busload of gourmands supposed to arrive for the signing?" Mr. Everett whispered to Frannie.

"I got a call about an hour ago," she whispered in reply. "They canceled, but asked for a rain check. They may come up sometime in the fall."

Tricia refrained from commenting. Thanks to the Internet, Angelica had cultivated a relationship with the "Gamboling Gourmets," who traveled New England throughout the summer, tasting the local cuisines. Tonight's signing was to be their first outing of the year, and Angelica's launch party. She'd spent days preparing a table full of desserts—all from her newly published book, *Easy-Does-It Cooking*, which had been officially available all of two days.

Angelica's cutout notwithstanding, Tricia had expected at least a few more *warm* bodies to attend the signing. Mr. Everett's bride of eight months had come down with a cold, which explained her absence, but surely the employees at Angelica's café—Jake Masters, the cook, and Darcy Gebhard, the waitress—might have made an effort to be there. And someone else was conspicuous by his absence.

"Anybody know where Bob is?" Frannie asked.

Bob Kelly, owner of Kelly Real Estate and the president of the local Chamber of Commerce, had been Angelica's significant other for the past eighteen months—ever since she'd come to live in Stoneham.

"I'm sure he'll have a perfectly reasonable explanation for being late," Tricia lied. She and Bob weren't exactly best friends, but she tried to overlook his many shortcomings for her sister's sake.

"I saw his car parked down the street, near History Repeats Itself," Ginny volunteered. "It's been there awhile."

Angelica pouted. "He said he'd be here."

"There's still time," Tricia reassured her.

Angelica nodded, resigned, and tucked a lock of her short, blonde hair behind her left ear. "Business hasn't been good lately, and he's been preoccupied. It probably just slipped his mind."

"I'm sure you're right," Tricia said, and hoped her nose hadn't just grown an inch. For weeks, Angelica had done nothing but talk about the event.

Frannie straightened the stack of unsigned books on the side table, and everyone tried not to make eye contact with Angelica as they waited in awkward silence for someone—anyone—else to arrive. Finally, Ginny suggested Angelica go ahead with her cooking demonstration.

"What's the point?" Angelica asked, defeat coloring her voice.

"Well, it's almost seven thirty, and none of us has had dinner. I can't be the only one eager to try your Hacienda Tacos."

"Good old Tex-Mex—the best food on Earth," Frannie piped up, then sighed. "Next to a luau, that is." It was Frannie's dream to retire to the fiftieth state.

Angelica gave a careless shrug and turned on the electric skillet.

Across the street, the newly installed gas lamps glowed. The Board of Selectmen had approved the installation of the old-fashioned streetlights in an effort to capitalize on the town's history and its new lease on life. Tourists ate up that kind of stuff, and the Board of Selectmen was eager to do all it could to encourage their visits. Unfortunately, when the bookstores closed, the visitors disappeared, leaving no one to appreciate them.

Within minutes, Angelica had prepared the filling, spooned it into corn tortillas, and passed them out to her small—and hungry—audience. The desserts were then sampled, and everyone sipped complimentary coffee, not making a dent in the contents of the five-gallon urn borrowed from Angelica's café.

As Angelica served Mr. Everett another portion of coconut cake, Tricia gave Ginny a nudge. "Buy a book," she whispered.

Ginny's eyes nearly popped. "They're thirty-four dollars," she hissed. "I can't afford it."

"Use your charge card, and I'll credit your account tomorrow morning. I want Ange to make at least a couple of sales tonight."

Ginny shrugged. "If you insist." She set down her paper cup, grabbed a copy of the coffee-table-sized book filled with glossy photos, and marched up to the cash desk where Angelica stood wringing her hands. "I don't know about the rest of you, but I'm proud to be the first to get my signed copy of *Easy-Does-It Cooking*."

Mr. Everett's nervous gaze shifted to Tricia. She mouthed the words *Buy one—I'll pay you back*.

"Uh, uh—let me be the second," Mr. Everett said.

Luckily, Angelica hadn't noticed Tricia's prompting. She pressed a clenched hand to her lips, fighting back tears. "You guys are just the best. Frannie, grab the camera, will you?" she said. Next, she played director, carefully positioning Ginny with her back to the camera, posed to her satisfaction. She shook Ginny's hand. She raised a finger to make a point. She looked surprised—then serious, and, ultimately, very silly. At last, Angelica reached for her pen, wrote a few words on the flyleaf of Ginny's copy, and signed her name with such a flourish that it was completely illegible. Frannie kept snapping pictures as Angelica handed the book to Ginny.

Ginny frowned. "Live free or diet?" Was Angelica mocking the state motto?

"Yes, don't you think that's clever?" Angelica said. "I'm going to sign that in all the books."

Though Ginny forced a smile, her voice was flat. "Go for it."

As Mr. Everett stepped up to have his book signed, Tricia moved to look out the large display window that faced Main Street. As Ginny had said, Bob's car was parked near History Repeats Itself. Tricia's anger smoldered. How inconsiderate of Bob to ignore Angelica's very first signing. He had to know how much it meant to her.

Tricia glanced back at her sister and Mr. Everett, still posing for Frannie. In a fit of pique, she decided it was time for action. She'd go find Bob and, if necessary, drag him back to the Cookery by this thinning hair. Besides, Angelica's photographic self was beginning to creep her out.

Tricia took a Zen moment to calm herself before she spoke. "I think I'll run out and see if I can find Bob," she told Angelica. "If his car is parked down the road, he can't be very far away."

"I suppose," Angelica said. "But please hurry back to help us pack up some of these desserts." She shook her head, taking in the amount of leftover food. "I can't serve all this at the café. Would you like to take some home, Ginny?"

"Would I? Hand me the plastic wrap, will you?"

"Be right back," Tricia called and headed out the door.

The village was practically deserted, and Bob's car was the only vehicle parked on the west side of Main Street. Tricia crossed the street and started down the sidewalk. Upon consideration, she decided she wouldn't berate Bob, at least not in front of Jim Roth, owner of History Repeats Itself. It wouldn't do to go ballistic with him as an audience. Instead, her plan was to poke her head inside the door and cheerfully ask if Bob hadn't forgotten another engagement—and probably do it through gritted teeth.

The glowing gas lamps really did lend a quaint, old-fashioned charm to the already picturesque storefronts. Although an expensive indulgence, they added to the village's ambience—especially outside of Haven't Got a Clue. It went right along with the atmosphere she'd created, emulating 221B Baker Street in London.

Tricia was within two doors of History Repeats Itself when she paused to look inside Booked for Lunch. Angelica had done a wonderful job decorating the café. Heck, she'd done a terrific job managing two businesses *and* starting a writing career. Not that Tricia had ever mentioned to Angelica how proud she was of Angelica's accomplishments. As it was, her swelled head could barely fit through a standard doorway.

As Tricia took a step forward, she heard a *phoomph*. The Earth shook as a shower of glass exploded onto the street, and a rush of hot air enveloped her, the shock of it knocking her to the ground.

Then everything went black.

TWO

 The first thing that registered was the muffled sound of sirens. Lots of them. Tricia realized she was sitting on her backside on the cooling pavement, wondering what had just shaken her world into senselessness. In addition to the glass shards that littered the sidewalk around her, scraps of singed paper—the remains of hundreds of books?—floated to the ground in a blizzard-like fashion.

A Stoneham Fire Rescue squad screeched to a halt some ten feet ahead of her. One of the firefighters jumped from the rig and raced to Tricia. "Are you hurt, ma'am?"

"What?" Tricia asked. Couldn't this guy speak louder?

"Are you hurt?"

Tricia shook her head, then wished she hadn't, as the world seemed to tilt crazily around her.

More firefighters spilled from the truck. The man helped Tricia to her feet and then pulled her farther down the sidewalk, away from what had once been History Repeats Itself.

Two firefighters dragged the limp form of a man away from the shop. Tricia instantly recognized the tattered kelly green jacket covered in dust. Rivulets of blood cascaded down his face. "Bob!" she called, frantically trying to escape the hold the firefighter had on her arm. Her next thought was *Angelica!* and how upset she'd be. How could this happen—and just a day before Angelica was to leave on her self-financed book tour of New England?

Another firefighter blocked Tricia's way. "Ma'am, please stand back. There may still be gas leaking from somewhere in the vicinity."

Ma'am! Tricia would never get used to being called that.

On the other side of the street, Tricia saw Angelica hurrying frantically down the sidewalk. "Tricia—are you all right?" she called, her expression filled with worry. She crossed the street, threw her arms around Tricia, and drew her into a tight hug.

"Ange, Bob's been hurt."

Angelica pulled back, sudden fear drawing lines on her face. "How bad?"

"There was blood on his temple, and his jacket was pretty torn."

"Where is he?"

"I don't know. The firemen brought him out of the building. I think they took him over to that ambulance." She pointed the way.

Angelica clasped Tricia's hand, dragging her forward, and the women hustled around the firefighters as they made their way to the back of the ambulance. Bob was inside. When Angelica reached for a handhold to enter, one of the EMTs barred her. "Ma'am, are you next of kin?"

"Well, no, but Bob and I—"

"Sorry," the beefy woman apologized, "but I'm going to have to ask you to move away. This man deserves his privacy."

"He's my boyfriend. He's—"

The paramedic raised an eyebrow.

"I know that sounds stupid at our ages, but honestly, Bob really is my—"

The paramedic stood taller, suddenly looking menacing. "I'm not going to ask you again, ma'am."

Tricia pulled her sister's arm. "Come on, Ange. Let them take care of Bob. We'll catch up with him at the hospital." She turned back to the EMT. "Will you be taking him to Milford or Nashua?"

"Probably Nashua."

"Can you at least tell me how he's doing?" Angelica pleaded.

"Privacy laws prevent me from—"

"Yeah, yeah, yeah," a scowling Angelica interrupted her.

"But I don't want to go to the hospital," they heard Bob call out. If he had the lungs for that, he would, no doubt, soon be on the mend.

They crossed the street once more, moving to stand before Haven't Got a Clue. With light bars blazing, another Sheriff's Department cruiser pulled up to the curb. By now most of Main Street was blocked—not that there was much traffic along the village's main thoroughfare once all the shops had closed for the day.

Captain Grant Baker got out of the cruiser, noted Tricia standing in front of her store, and nodded to her before crossing the street to converse with the fire chief.

Angelica nudged her sister. "Go on. Go see if Captain

Baker shakes some information out of those paramedics and can tell you how Bob's doing."

"He only just got here," Tricia protested. "Besides, why would he go out of his way to give us any peace of mind?"

"Bitter—bitter," Angelica cautioned.

"I'm not bitter." Ha! Of course she was bitter. She and Grant Baker had just started dating—were having fun getting to know each other—when his ex-wife popped out of the woodwork with a serious disease. Not that they'd reconciled. But Mandy Baker needed a "friend" to help her through the worst of her illness. Captain Baker had promised to call Tricia once he felt Mandy was stabilized. That was more than six months ago. A long, lonely six months. Not that Russ Smith, owner of the *Stoneham Weekly News* and Tricia's ex, hadn't tried to worm his way back into her affections. So far, she had resisted his overtures. She remembered too many evenings spent in the company of Russ and his beloved police scanner—being alone was actually preferable. And besides, it had given her a chance to catch up on some of her reading.

Angelica clutched her sister's arm. "Trish, please— please go over and ask Captain Baker to get us some information on Bob."

"Okay." Tricia took a breath to steel herself before she stepped off the sidewalk. That's when she caught sight of Russ—his camera slung around his neck—hurrying down the sidewalk. She ignored him and headed toward the captain.

Baker was in deep conversation with the fire chief. Tricia crept forward, relieved that no one had tried to make her move back to the opposite side of the street.

At last the chief nodded and stepped away. Tricia

reached out and touched Baker's arm. "Grant? Can you get us some news on Bob Kelly? My sister is—"

He faced her, and she fell under the spell of his mesmerizing green eyes. She had a thing for green eyes. Her ex-husband had had them, too.

"I'll let you know as soon as I get any information. Why don't you wait by your store?" Not exactly a brush-off, but not all that welcoming, either.

"Thank you."

Baker nodded, and Tricia went back to where Angelica stood twisting her hands with worry as she spoke to Russ—or, rather, was being grilled by him. They both went silent at Tricia's return.

"Captain Baker will be over in a few minutes," Tricia said.

"Angelica tells me you witnessed the explosion," Russ said.

"Yes—I guess."

"Well?" he demanded.

"I heard a *phoomph* and was blown off my feet. That's all I know."

Russ capped his pen and scowled.

Mr. Everett and Ginny joined the growing crowd on the sidewalk, and quickly moved to stand beside the sisters. "Is anybody hurt?" Ginny asked.

"Bob," Angelica said, her voice cracking. She turned to Tricia. "I never even thought to ask—what happened to Jim?"

Tricia realized the firemen hadn't brought anyone else out of the shattered building. "I haven't seen him. Do you suppose he . . . might not have made it?"

Ginny's hand flew to cover her mouth. "Oh, no."

Russ uncapped his pen and scribbled on his ever-present steno pad.

"What was it? An explosion?" Mr. Everett asked.

"I think so. One of the firemen said there might still be gas leaking."

"Do you think it was from the new gas lamps? Shouldn't they evacuate the whole block?" Ginny asked.

"I don't know," Tricia said, answering both questions.

Frannie closed and locked the Cookery's door, then hurried over to join the group outside Haven't Got a Clue. "What happened?" she cried, staring at the police and fire equipment blocking the view of the buildings across the street.

"History Repeats Itself blew up—with Jim Roth and Bob Kelly inside," Ginny said.

"Jim!" Frannie cried. She nearly jumped off the sidewalk, but Tricia grabbed her arm to stop her.

"You can't do anything to help. Angelica and I have already been warned off."

"Are they okay? How badly are they hurt?"

"They're taking care of Bob in the ambulance," Angelica said, her voice filled with worry. "We haven't seen Jim yet. Tricia thinks he might've—" She didn't finish the sentence.

Frannie's mouth dropped open, and then her face crumpled into a mask of grief. "No!" she wailed, wrapped her arms around herself, stumbled backward, and dropped down to sit on the curb. Tears streamed down her face as she began to rock back and forth.

Not knowing what to do, Tricia stared at the others, then reached down to put a hand on Frannie's shoulder. "Frannie, were you and Jim . . . friends?"

Frannie nodded frantically. "I met him . . . when he became . . . a member of the . . . Chamber," she managed between gulping breaths. Frannie had been the Chamber of Commerce's receptionist for ten years before taking the manager's job at the Cookery.

Tricia exchanged a glance with Angelica. For this kind of reaction, Frannie and Jim had to have been more than just friends, but now was not the time to pry.

One of the paramedics closed the door to the ambulance, ran to the front, and jumped in the passenger side, and the vehicle slowly pulled away from the curb. Captain Baker nodded to the fire chief and made his way to Haven't Got a Clue.

Russ waved his pen in the air. "Captain Baker—can you give me a statement?"

Frannie's wails had subsided into gulping sobs. Baker nodded toward her. "Is she okay?" he asked Tricia.

"She was a friend of Jim Roth's. Is he—?" Tricia was afraid to voice the word.

"They found no other bodies. But Mr. Kelly told us Mr. Roth had gone out back for a cigarette. It appears his cigarette lighter ignited the fumes. There'll be a full investigation, and they'll do tests to identify any—" He paused, and Tricia finished the sentence for him

"Human remains?"

Baker cleared his throat. "Whatever they can scrape up," he said quietly, sending Frannie into another fit of howling.

"How's Bob?" Angelica asked anxiously.

"Looks like some second-degree burns. He asked me to tell you not to worry. And not to bother to come to the hospital."

"Like I'm going to hang around my store and twiddle my thumbs," Angelica said sarcastically. "Of course I'm going to the hospital." Her tone changed as she looked at Tricia. "Will you come with me?"

"Of course."

Angelica turned back to the captain. "How could such a terrible accident have happened?"

"Accident?" he repeated. "We don't know yet if this was an accident."

"What do you mean? It must have been the new gas lamps," Tricia said.

Baker frowned, and jerked a thumb over his shoulder, indicating the still-lit lamps across the way. "This explosion had nothing to do with the gas lamps."

"Then what happened?"

"I'll need to speak to Mr. Kelly to find that out." He glanced back at the building and shook his head. "The damage is pretty severe. They'll probably have to knock the whole thing down in the next day or so."

"What about the books?" Tricia asked.

Baker frowned. "What about them?"

"The building might be dicey, but there could be many salvageable books inside."

"It's not safe."

"The firemen are inside," Tricia pressed. "Can't some of us—?"

"We can't allow civilians inside. It's too dangerous. But I'll ask Chief Farrar about it. The firefighters often try to salvage property after a fire."

"Thank you," Tricia said.

"If you ladies will excuse me. . . ." Baker tipped his hat in their direction, turned, and stepped off the curb.

"We've got to save those books," Tricia murmured.

"What for?" Angelica groused. "Jim's dead."

"He must have heirs."

"Okay, but will they want to take a load of books? Who's going to store them until an heir can be found?"

"Maybe the booksellers could pitch in," Mr. Everett said. "Perhaps they could hire a storage unit for a few weeks—just until other arrangements could be made. I'd be glad to make some phone calls," he volunteered.

Sudden tears filled Tricia's eyes. "You're a treasure, Mr. Everett."

He blushed in embarrassment.

"Tricia, we should follow the ambulance to the hospital," Angelica insisted.

"What about the Cookery?" Tricia lowered her voice. "Frannie's obviously in no shape to close the store, and it might be hours before we return."

Angelica looked torn.

"It'll take only a few minutes," Tricia insisted.

"If you'll trust me with the keys, Angelica, I'll take care of it. And I'll make sure Frannie gets home okay," Ginny said. She had worked at the Cookery before Angelica bought it.

"Thank you so much, Ginny. I'll make it up to you," Angelica promised.

"You don't need to. Now, you grab your purses and go!" Ginny gave Tricia a gentle push.

Angelica didn't need to be told twice.

It was after eleven when Bob was finally transferred from the emergency room to a semiprivate room in the hospital. By then Angelica had badgered at least seven nurses and three doctors for information on Bob's condition. "No can do," was the answer from all, and more than one quoted the HIPA Privacy Rule of 2003. Once a bandage-swathed Bob was in his own room, though, he was free to answer their questions for himself. Only he didn't.

"I'll be okay," he insisted after Angelica had fussed around his bed, adjusting the covers for the fifth time.

"I just want you to be comfortable."

"Right now I'm comfortable. Although when those pain meds wear off. . . ." He let the sentence trail off, and closed his eyes.

"Can you tell us what happened?" Tricia asked.

"Jim and I were talking. He went out back for a smoke. There was a loud *whoosh,* and then the next thing I knew, I was lying on the sidewalk outside his shop, surrounded by firemen and a lot of glass," Bob said, not opening his eyes.

"What were the two of you talking about just before all that happened?" Tricia asked.

"Nothing much," he said, without inflection. Bob didn't seem very disturbed by the death of his friend.

"Did you smell gas before the place blew?"

Bob sniffed. "Not with my allergies. Look, I'm really tired. Why don't you girls go on home? I'll talk to you tomorrow."

"But Angelica won't be here tomorrow," Tricia said. "She'll be starting the first leg of her book tour."

"Of course I won't," Angelica declared, and then lowered her voice, placing her hand gently on Bob's shoulder. "I'm staying right here with Bob until he's fully recovered."

He opened his eyes. "No, you're not. You've worked too hard to get all the publicity this tour will give your book. You can't afford to cancel—especially at this late hour. And I'm speaking literally and figuratively. I will manage." His tone indicated he was finished with that subject.

"When did the doctor say you could leave, Bob?" Tricia asked.

"Probably tomorrow or the next day. I'll have to arrange for a ride home. Perhaps a cab."

"Don't be silly. I'd be glad to take you home whenever you're released," Tricia said.

"Yes, and I'll stop by your place and pack a bag for you," Angelica said. "You can't go home wearing a hospital gown, and your clothes are ruined."

"No," Tricia agreed solemnly, "Captain Baker would probably arrest you for mooning all of Stoneham."

Bob made no comment. He lacked a sense of humor at the best of times, and no doubt whatever painkillers they'd given him had also dulled his senses.

"I'll just leave you two alone to say good night. Ange, I'll get the car and meet you at the front entrance," Tricia said, and backed out of the room. "I hope you feel better, Bob."

He didn't answer.

Tricia did not like hospitals, and neither did she like traversing a dark parking lot to find her car. But in minutes she'd retrieved her Lexus and pulled around to the hospital's front entrance to await Angelica. Ten minutes later, she was still waiting. A security guard approached her car. She rolled down the window.

"Didn't you see the sign?" He jerked a thumb toward a white sign with red lettering: NO PARKING OR STANDING.

"I have to pick up my sister," Tricia protested.

The guard shook his head. "You can't tie up the lane in front of the entrance. You'll have to keep circling until she comes out."

Tricia exhaled a loud sigh, started the car, and pulled away. She'd circled three times before she saw Angelica waiting on the sidewalk.

Another car stood at the curb. Where was that security guard now? Tricia pulled over, out of the fire lane, stopped her car, and shifted into PARK. As Angelica stepped off the sidewalk to cross the drive, Tricia heard the roar of an engine. She turned to see the high beams of a car come bar-reling up from behind.

Angelica froze, the car's bright headlights illuminat-ing her. At the last second, she seemed to come alive and jumped out of the zooming car's path. Tricia heard the thud as her sister landed on the hood of her Lexus. In seconds, she was out of the car.

"Ange! Are you all right?"

Angelica did not move. Terrified, Tricia reached for her sister's limp arm, checking for a pulse. It was there—racing.

Angelica groaned, braced her arms on the hood, and pushed herself up. "What was that?"

"A car!"

"I know it was a car," Angelica growled. She looked around, dazed. "Where's my purse?"

Her giant handbag had gone sailing into the air just before she'd hit the Lexus. Tricia glanced around, found the leather purse and its contents scattered across the asphalt. She stooped to pick up all the odds and ends. "Are you okay?"

"Bruised only," Angelica said, gently touching the skin under her left eye.

"We should call the police."

"What for?"

"Someone just tried to kill you!"

"Don't be silly. It was probably just a teenager on a joy ride."

"At a hospital?" Tricia asked, incredulous.

Angelica waved away her concerns. "And anyway, what would we tell the cops? Did you see what kind of car it was—or even the color?"

"No," Tricia admitted, handing over Angelica's purse. "But we should at least tell hospital security."

Angelica reached for the passenger-side door handle. "Forget it. I'm tired. And we've still got to stop at Bob's house so I can pack that bag for him." She got in the car, buckled her seat belt, and leaned back against the headrest. Tricia got in, and with shaking hands turned the key once more and pulled away from the hospital's now silent entrance.

Angelica made small talk all the way home, mostly on the subject of her upcoming book tour. Tricia kept glancing up at the rearview mirror, worried those bright headlights might zoom up behind her once again.

THREE

 Angelica closed the zipper on her large, shocking pink, Pierre Cardin suitcase. A mere nine hours after her scare at the hospital, the skin under her left eye was puffy, but makeup had done a good job of covering the purple bruise.

Tricia had shown up early on her sister's doorstep, still worried about what had happened the night before. "I think you should reconsider going."

Angelica placed her hands on her hips and frowned. "Every time the subject of my book tour comes up, you give me the impression you don't approve."

Tricia crossed her arms over her chest. "I didn't think my opinion would be well received."

"By who? Me?"

"Yes, you."

"You think I'm wasting my time?" Angelica asked, and checked the zippered pocket of her makeup case.

Tricia didn't answer.

Angelica raised an eyebrow. "Or maybe you're jealous."

"Jealous? Of what?"

"That I'm published and you're not."

Tricia's mouth dropped. "I've never aspired to be published. I'm perfectly happy selling other people's books."

Angelica raised the other eyebrow. "Oh, really?"

"Yes, really. Really great authors."

"Then you must be moping about next week."

"Me, mope? I don't know what you're talking about."

"Yes, you do. You're upset because Mother and Daddy canceled their trip to visit in time for your birthday."

"I am not." Of course she was, but she hadn't been surprised by their announcement the previous week, either. No, they'd come back from wintering in Rio in time for Angelica's birthday, but for more years than Tricia could count, they'd been unavailable for Tricia's natal day. Their father had often traveled for business during Tricia's childhood, and their mother had volunteered for a number of charities. More than once her birthday celebration had been rescheduled to suit other people's convenience. This year was to be no different.

"I told you," Angelica continued, "when my book tour is over, I'll bake you a cake, fix a nice dinner, and the three of us will celebrate your birthday."

"The three of us?" Tricia asked.

"Sure, you, me, and Bob."

"That won't be necessary."

"Of course it is."

"I appreciate the offer, but I really don't want to celebrate *my* birthday with *your* boyfriend."

Angelica glared at her, then shrugged. "Suit yourself."

Tricia felt her cheeks grow hot. Angelica could have protested at least a little bit.

"Getting back to the subject at hand," Angelica said, hauling her suitcase from the bed and heading for the door and the stairs that led to the Cookery below. Tricia picked up the other two suitcases and followed. Angelica *never* traveled light. "Why do you think this book tour is such a bad idea?"

"I didn't say it was a bad idea. I just wonder if it's a fiscally prudent idea. You've got your hands full with the Cookery and Booked for Lunch. The publicist you hired costs more than your advance—"

"That may be," Angelica interrupted, "but she also arranged all these lovely book signings. And I'm going to be on the radio and interviewed on some cable access channels, too."

"But will you ever see a royalty check? You sell a lot of hardcover remainders at the Cookery—which tells me there are an awful lot of cookbooks out there that the authors never see a dime from. You're making only a couple of bucks per book. Your gas alone on this book tour will wipe out any potential profit."

Angelica turned and paused. "Listen, Paula Deen didn't start out with an award-winning TV show and a monthly magazine—she started with one cookbook. I've got to get my name out there if I'm ever going to reach her level of success."

Tricia controlled the urge to scream. Nobody in the Miles family had ever had an ego as big as Angelica's. Where had she acquired it? Maybe she was adopted and nobody had told Tricia—or the rest of the family. If she took a few hairs from Angelica's brush, maybe she could have her DNA checked.

"Actually, after what happened at the hospital last night—" Tricia began.

"Don't be ridiculous. It was a stupid accident. Nothing is going to stop me from taking this trip." And with that, Angelica took the larger of the suitcases Tricia held, stuffed it and the bigger case in the dumbwaiter, closed the door, and sent it to the Cookery below. "Now, I'll try to call the store and the café at least a couple of times a day, but if Frannie or Jake or Darcy needs direction, I've told them to come to you. Okay?"

"I don't know what good I'm going to be to Jake or Darcy, but—okay."

"I've e-mailed you a copy of my itinerary and a list of emergency numbers."

"Emergency numbers?" Tricia repeated.

"My employees' home numbers, my agent, my editor—"

Why not the butcher, the baker, and the candlestick maker, too? Tricia thought.

"Frannie and Darcy will bring the day's receipts over to you after closing. You *will* take them to the bank with your own deposits, won't you?"

"Yes," Tricia said, and sighed. They'd been over this at least a dozen times.

"And I want you to do everything you can to help Bob. I can't be here for him this week, and he's going to need someone to cheer him up."

"Angelica—I have a business to run. And now you want me to run both of yours, too?"

"My employees can handle most things that come up, but they still might need some guidance. And you've said so yourself; Ginny is the best assistant in all of Stoneham.

I'm sure she can handle anything that comes up on your end, too. Besides, I'll only be gone a few days."

"And be back a day or so before you take off again."

Angelica shrugged. "That's the price of success." With a wave of her hand, she ushered Tricia to take the stairs, then turned, locked her apartment door, and started after her sister.

After helping Angelica load her car, Tricia waved goodbye and returned to Haven't Got a Clue. Miss Marple waited behind the door and immediately scolded Tricia for leaving her alone. "You're getting as snarky as Angelica," Tricia warned the cat. She raised the blinds and was once again confronted with the gaping hole across the street, what had once been History Repeats Itself. Yellow crime scene tape fluttered in the slight breeze. A man had died in what was now just the shell of a building.

Miss Marple jumped onto the shelf in front of the display window and meowed for attention. Tricia absently petted the cat and tried to remember the last time she'd actually spoken to Jim Roth. It must have been months earlier at a Chamber of Commerce breakfast meeting. They'd compared notes about their stores' holiday receipts. Haven't Got a Clue not only had held its own but had done exceptional business, but Jim's store hadn't been as fortunate. Like many of the shop owners, he'd kept his expenses to a minimum—hiring no staff. Tricia often wondered if that contributed to the decline of a business. Working alone, could an owner get so burned out he'd lose the passion that inspired him to become an entrepreneur in the first place?

The shop door opened and Ginny barreled in. "Morning!" Since her breakup with her boyfriend, she'd been on time to work every day, and often, like today, she'd come in early to share a cup of coffee and trade village gossip with Tricia. She was vivacious, the customers loved her, and Tricia was fond of her, as well.

"Is the coffee on?" Ginny asked, heading for the coffee station.

"I didn't get around to making it. I had to make sure Angelica got off all right."

"Oh, yeah," Ginny said, and popped a filter into the restaurant-sized coffeemaker.

Tricia's gaze returned to the gaping hole in the storefronts across the street. It was lucky none of the other businesses had suffered more than broken glass and stock knocked from the shelves. It was also fortunate that the explosion had happened after hours, when the tourists had left for the day—otherwise the body count could've been much worse. She thought about Mr. Everett's offer the night before, and wondered if he'd been successful in his efforts to save the books inside History Repeats Itself.

After a few moments, Ginny joined her. She reached into her pocket and withdrew a ring of keys. "I wanted to return these to you. They're Angelica's."

"Thanks." Tricia stowed them under the counter, intending to put them in a more secure place when time permitted.

"The electricity was still out when I got over to Booked for Lunch, but PSNH had restored it by ten o'clock, so everything is okay—nothing spoiled. A few items got knocked off the walls from the blast, but I cleaned up, and put as much of the launch party leftovers as I could in the fridge.

The rest went into the freezer. I found another dome for the torte and left it on the counter for Angelica's customers."

"Why not put that in the fridge, too?"

Ginny shrugged. "Cakes go stale faster if they're kept cold. Something I picked up when I worked for Doris Gleason. She used to lecture me about stuff like that. But it's come in handy—or least it did last night."

"Thanks for helping Ange. I'll make sure she knows all that you've done."

Ginny shrugged away the praise, and rested her elbows on the glass display case. "The fire chief said they'd probably have to come in today and knock down the rest of the building. It's a safety hazard as it stands."

"That won't cheer Bob Kelly."

Ginny shrugged. "Knowing him, it was probably insured to the hilt. He'll make out okay."

Yes, he probably would.

"You should have seen Mr. Everett in action last night—you would have been proud of him. He got ten or twelve volunteers to save a bunch of Jim Roth's books."

"Oh, good. That had me worried."

Ginny laughed. "It was like a bucket brigade. The firemen handed out the books and the volunteers loaded them into their pickups and vans. Mr. Everett even got Harvey Carson at the Stoneham Mini Storage to open up for him—and to give him a month's rent for half price."

A lump of emotion rose in Tricia's throat. "Do I tell you two enough how glad I am that you work for me?"

Ginny laughed. "Not nearly!" But her merriment was fleeting, and her expression quickly sobered. "For a minute there, we were so caught up in saving the books, we almost forgot that Jim had died." She was quiet for a few moments, and Tricia glanced out the window at the destruction of what had been her neighbor's store.

"To make matters worse," Ginny continued, "I got more bad news when I collected my mail last night." She reached into the pocket of her slacks and handed Tricia a wrinkled envelope. "This is the end of the road—at least for my little cottage in the woods."

The return address was Bank of Stoneham. Tricia withdrew the creased letter and skimmed the wording. Imminent foreclosure on the house Ginny had put so much time and effort into, and had loved so much.

"I didn't think it would happen this fast," Ginny said wistfully, and sighed.

"When was the last time you made a payment?"

"A full payment? November. I've been paying what I could, but I'm still months behind. Without Brian, there's no way I can make the full payments on my own. And I really don't want to wait for Captain Baker or some other sheriff's deputy to show up on my doorstep with an eviction notice, so I've already started packing."

"Why didn't you put it on the market?"

"I owe more than the market value. And the house is still all torn apart. Who'd be crazy enough to buy it as is?"

"Did you consult Bob Kelly?"

"I didn't want him knowing my business."

When the bank foreclosed, everybody—and especially Bob—would know about it. "Do you have enough money put aside to rent an apartment?"

Ginny sighed. "I think so. I've already started looking and have a few prospects. I might be able to sign the paperwork in a day or two. The problem is, I don't know how I'm going to move all my stuff. All Brian's friends with pickup trucks think I should've stood by him."

Tricia wasn't among that crowd. "How about if I paid for a rental truck? Do you have enough friends to help you fill it and move you?"

"Oh, I couldn't let you do that."

"Yes, you could. Now please answer my question."

"Maybe," Ginny said, with a grateful smile. "Then all I'd have to do is find someone to store Brian's stuff for him. So far, none of his friends have volunteered. I can't afford to pay for a storage unit for him—and why should I? But if I leave it at the house, the bank will probably just toss it."

"You've tried to do the right thing."

"Yes. And look what it got me. My credit rating will take a beating for years."

"But at least you won't have to declare bankruptcy."

Ginny shrugged. "I guess."

The aroma of fresh-brewed coffee filled the bookstore. Ginny retrieved their ceramic mugs, filled them, and joined Tricia at the window.

Tricia gave her employee a weak smile, and they both gazed at the ruin across the street. There had to be something Tricia could do to help Ginny, something better than just paying for a rental truck to move her possessions into some crummy apartment. The pickings in Stoneham weren't that great.

Then it hit her. There *was* something she could do. She could pay off Ginny's mortgage. Her divorce settlement had been extremely generous, and her grandmother had left the bulk of her estate to both Tricia and Angelica. It wasn't something she ever talked about, but, quite frankly, she was filthy rich. And though she made many charitable contributions throughout the year, nothing would give her as much pleasure as helping someone she truly cared about.

If . . . it could be arranged. She'd have to visit the manager at the Bank of Stoneham, and wondered if she'd be able to fit that into her busy day.

"Poor Jim," Ginny said, interrupting Tricia's musings. "What a terrible thing. Here one minute—gone the next."

"I wonder if he had any family," Tricia said aloud, and thought again about Frannie's reaction to his death.

"Someone told me he lived at home—with his *mother*. That's kind of strange for a man his age, isn't it?"

Tricia had to agree. Then again . . . "That poor woman. Does she live in the village?"

Ginny nodded. "I think she lives on Poplar Street."

"Maybe I should pay her a visit to express my condolences. She must be beside herself."

"You might want to pay a visit to Frannie, too. You saw how she reacted to Jim's death. Don't you think they had to be lovers or something?" Ginny asked, with a gleam in her eyes.

"It certainly came as a surprise to me."

"They must have been discreet, since no one seemed to know about it."

"Or maybe it was over a long time ago?" Tricia suggested.

Ginny shook her head. "Not the way she cried last night. Let's keep an eye out for her. As soon as she walks by to open the Cookery, you can pounce on her."

"I'll do nothing of the kind."

"Damn, you're no fun," Ginny teased.

The shop door opened, admitting their first customer of the day. Immediately after, the telephone rang. Tricia stepped over to the counter and picked it up. "Haven't Got a Clue, this is Tricia. How can I help you?"

"Tricia, it's Darcy from Booked for Lunch. The poultry

guy is here, but Angelica didn't leave any money to pay him."

Tricia glanced out the window. She hadn't noticed the Jefferson Poultry truck that was parked in front of Angelica's café. "Is this your regular delivery?" she asked. Angelica was usually on top of these things. Then again, she'd been distracted by all the prep for her launch party and book tour.

"I guess," Darcy said, not sounding at all certain. "I'm not usually here when deliveries are made. Angelica asked me to put in more time while she's away—to kind of look after things."

Yes. She had.

"All right. I'll be right over with a check."

"Thanks."

Tricia hung up the phone and pulled the store's checkbook from under the counter. "I've got to solve a problem over at the café," she told Ginny.

Ginny nodded, and went back to helping the customer.

Tricia crossed the street and entered Booked for Lunch. Although the café wasn't yet open, the truck driver sat at the counter, nursing a cup of what was no doubt free coffee, with a fat slice of Angelica's coconut cake in front of him. Tricia knew that Angelica had reprimanded Darcy at least once for giving away the store.

Darcy Gebhard stood behind the counter, looking subdued. Something about her bugged Tricia. Dumpy was the word that best seemed to describe her. Maybe it was the ill-fitting clothes she wore, or the color of her dyed hair—red, bordering on magenta. Angelica had mentioned that she was the same age as Tricia, but for some reason she looked older—harder. But then if Tricia had worked only at minimum-wage jobs most of her adult life, she might make the same clothing and grooming choices. Only the woman's perfectly manicured nails and the silver rings gracing each finger seemed to hint that she might aspire to more in life than waiting tables.

Tricia faced the deliveryman, noticing his grubby pants and shirt, the dirt under his fingernails, and made a note to herself never again to order the grilled chicken sandwich. "Hello, I'm Tricia. I understand you've just made a delivery."

"Yeah. It's already in the freezer. That's not part of my job, you know. I just did it because I'm a nice guy."

Hence, the free coffee and cake.

"Thank you. May I see the invoice?" He reached for a piece of paper on the counter and handed it to her. She inspected the items and the total at the bottom of the page. Everything looked in order. She noticed that Jake, the cook, along with his perpetual sneer, had appeared behind the half doors that separated the dining room from the kitchen. He didn't bother to acknowledge her presence, and she ignored him as well. For some reason, Angelica thought the world of her short-order cook. Tricia didn't share the sentiment.

She set the invoice and her checkbook on the counter, wrote out the check, tore it out, and handed it to the deliveryman. "Thank you for your patience."

He pocketed the check. "Not a problem."

Tricia's teeth involuntarily clenched. She hated that phrase. Why couldn't people just say, "You're welcome"? She forced a smile and said it for him. Miss Manners wouldn't approve—she chastised her readers who brought bad behavior to light, but so be it.

"May I have a receipt?"

The deliveryman looked to Darcy. "Just mark the invoice

Paid in Full," she suggested, scooped it up, and handed it to him. He complied, and handed it back to Tricia.

The deliveryman made no move to leave, and Jake and Darcy continued to stare at Tricia, making her feel uncomfortable. She forced another smile. "I'll just be on my way—and I'll see you later, Darcy." She turned, and headed for the door.

"Thanks," Darcy halfheartedly called after her.

Tricia took her time crossing the street to return to her own store. Something definitely hadn't been right about her visit to Booked for Lunch. She'd have to talk to Angelica about it.

The bell over the door tinkled cheerfully as Tricia entered Haven't Got a Clue, making her feel a little better. That is, until Ginny said, "Bob Kelly called while you were gone. He's ready to come home from the hospital—and he needs some clothes." She giggled. "I keep imagining him sitting in his hospital room, buck naked."

Tricia wasn't amused. "I can see I'm not going to get much done today." She grabbed the overnight bag Angelica had left for Bob, gathered up her purse, found her keys, and headed for the door. "I don't know when I'll be back."

"Don't worry—we're open until seven," Ginny called brightly, and waved a cheerful good-bye.

Bob wasn't naked when Tricia arrived at his hospital room, but he was waiting impatiently. She handed him the overnight bag. "Angelica packed a sweat suit. She thought you'd be more comfortable in it."

"I'll be more comfortable when I get out of here. I need to stop at a pharmacy and get a prescription for pain pills filled. That is, if you don't mind."

"Of course not. Should I call for a nurse and a wheelchair?"

Bob shook his head. "I'm walking out of here on my own power." He got up from the room's only chair, held the back of his hospital gown to cover his rear end, and hobbled across the floor to the bathroom. It took him some time to get dressed, but he didn't ask for help, and Tricia wasn't sure she'd have felt comfortable helping him. When he emerged some ten minutes later, she noticed his pallor, and felt ashamed for worrying about her own convenience.

"Let's go," she said cheerfully, and carried his overnight bag.

Bob waited on a bench outside the hospital while Tricia brought the car around. She parked it, and got out to help him into the passenger seat. His face looked ashen in the bright sunlight. Was he really in any shape to be left alone?

Tricia put the car in gear and pulled away from the curb. Bob stared out the passenger window—not the best company. Tricia struggled to make small talk. "What about those Red Sox?"

"I hate baseball," Bob muttered.

Okay.

Tricia pressed the brake for a red light. "Are you going to be able to change your dressings by yourself?"

"Yes."

Usually you couldn't shut Bob up, but suddenly he had nothing to say. She tried again. "Have you spoken to Captain Baker yet?"

"Yes."

"And?" she prompted.

"I told him I didn't have anything to say without an attorney present."

Startled, Tricia tore her eyes from the road. "Bob! Why in the world would you need an attorney present? Do you have something to hide?"

"No."

Tricia was getting tired of his blunt, single-syllable answers. "Then why—?"

"I really don't want to talk about it, Tricia."

Tricia clenched the steering wheel, squelching the urge to wrap her fingers around Bob's throat. "Have you got an attorney?" she tried again.

"No."

He really *didn't* want to talk about it.

They drove in silence for several miles down Route 101. Tricia's gaze was riveted on the road; Bob's gaze was fixed out the passenger-side window. When Bob finally spoke, it was to direct Tricia to stop at the grocery store's pharmacy in Milford. It took twenty minutes for Bob's prescription to be filled. Bob waited in the car; Tricia waited in the store. After all, she'd promised to help Bob, not babysit or keep him company.

It was lunchtime when Tricia pulled into Bob's driveway. Parked at the curb was a Draper Security Systems truck. Tricia raised an eyebrow. "Having some work done, Bob?"

"Yes." Yet another succinct answer. Tricia wasn't sure if she was irritated by this new behavior or if she should celebrate it.

"Did you arrange for this while you were in the hospital?"

He glared at her. "No."

Tricia leaned forward for a better look at the security company's van. "Feeling insecure?"

His glare intensified. "No!"

His refusal to give a decent answer to any question was maddening. Tricia shifted her gaze once again. If he hadn't ordered the work during his hospital stay, he must have arranged for it before then. Okay, so a couple of people had been killed—all right, murdered—during the past eight months. And there'd been a particularly vicious attack—but other than that, Stoneham was no more dangerous than East Los Angeles on a hot summer night, she thought facetiously.

Bob opened the passenger-side door, swung his legs out of the car, and paused. Just that slight movement brought a bead of sweat to his brow. "Thank you for the ride, Tricia."

"You're welcome." Tricia gathered her purse and the pharmacy bag, got out of the car, and retrieved Bob's overnight bag from the trunk.

Bob waited for her. "I'll take that."

"I'll carry it to the house for you. It's no trouble," Tricia said.

"No," he said firmly, "I'll take it."

Behind him, Tricia noticed the security guy waiting for Bob on the home's small porch, and she realized Bob didn't want her to hear the conversation he was about to have with the stranger. "I guess I'd better get going."

"Thanks for the ride."

"I'll check up on you later. Angelica—"

"—worries too much. I'll be fine."

"Would you like me to get you some lunch, or—"

"No," Bob said, firmly. "I'm fine. I'll see you later, Tricia."

She'd definitely been dismissed. She tried not to take it personally. After all, it got her off the hook for playing nursemaid to him for the next couple of days.

"Fine. I guess I'll see you around, Bob."

He said nothing. Just stood there.

Tricia turned, and walked back to her car.

Bob was still staring at her as she drove away.

FOUR

Tricia parked her car and glanced at her watch. She still had nearly half an hour before Ginny's lunch break, and wondered if she should walk over to the Bank of Stoneham to ask about paying off Ginny's mortgage. It would probably be a waste of time. No doubt the manager would be away from her office during the noon hour. Still . . . .

A minute later, she walked into the bank and asked the receptionist if she could speak to someone about a mortgage.

"Sure. I'll tell Billie you're here. She'll be glad to talk to you." Tricia watched as the woman headed for a cubicle at the back of the bank.

It was said that Billie Hanson, manager of the Bank of Stoneham, was named after Billie Burke, the actress who played Glinda the Good Witch in *The Wizard of Oz*. Not that she looked like that icon of the silver screen. She didn't have long, frizzy red hair, nor was she tall. In fact, Billie, short and squat, reminded Tricia of a fireplug. And her close-cropped blonde hair and brusque demeanor had earned her the label of dyke from more than a few of the locals. Tricia didn't know—nor care about—her sexual orientation. Billie had proven to be an apt businesswoman, and was a fellow member of the Chamber of Commerce.

Not a minute later, the receptionist waved for Tricia to follow her.

Billie stood behind her desk. "Tricia, good to see you. I hope you're well."

"I am, thanks. And I'm glad you could see me on such short notice."

Billie ushered Tricia to one of the seats before her desk. "Always glad to talk to one of Stoneham's best success stories."

"Me?" Tricia asked.

"It's no secret that you and your sister are probably the best businesswomen in town. And I'm pleased you've chosen to bank with us rather than one of the national banks in Nashua."

Tricia liked to do business locally. The fact that the Bank of Stoneham was extremely convenient didn't hurt, either.

Billie leaned forward on the desk, folding her hands and looking very businesslike. "What can I do for you today, Tricia?"

"I'd like to buy a mortgage."

"Oh, you've found a home in the village? The stairs to that loft finally got to you, right?"

"Uh, no, actually. I don't want to buy a house. I want to buy the mortgage of someone who has a house that's about to go into foreclosure."

Billie frowned. "That's not a very sound business decision. If the person is in foreclosure, it's not likely they'll be able to pay you any more than they can pay us."

"This person has had an unfortunate string of bad luck. I want to help her—not make money off of her."

Billie frowned. "Mixing business with friendship is seldom a good idea. Usually one party grows dissatisfied. The friendship is often the first casualty—not to mention the investment."

"I have thought of that. I'm prepared to walk away from the deal with a complete loss."

Billie mulled that over for a few moments. "Let me take a guess. You'd like to save your employee, Ginny Wilson, from losing her home."

"She really loves it. And she's worked so hard to make that house a home. I'd like to do all I can to help her keep it."

"Have you spoken to her about this?"

"Not yet. I wanted to see if it was possible before I brought up the subject. I don't want to buy the house outright. Ginny isn't one to take charity. But I thought if we could set up a manageable repayment schedule—something that she's able to live with—in the long run it would benefit both of us."

Billie exhaled a long breath. "Before you do anything, I think you should talk to Ms. Wilson. Make sure you're on the same page. She may not want to feel beholden to you."

"I thought I would surprise her."

Billie shook her head. "That's not a good idea. Talk to her. If she agrees, you may pay off the mortgage, including penalties, and I'd advise you to consult a real estate lawyer to set up a new mortgage for you, with terms you both can agree to."

It wasn't what Tricia wanted to hear, but it was sensible. She stood. "I'll do that." She offered Billie her hand. "Thank you for seeing me on such short notice."

"Not a problem," Billie said and smiled, missing Tricia's cringe at her choice of words.

With Angelica away, Tricia felt uncomfortable going over to Booked for Lunch to take her midday meal, and instead raided her own refrigerator. Funny, in times past, she and Angelica had gone for years without speaking. Now, she found she missed her sister after only a few hours' absence. Missed their daily bickering sessions. Missed Angelica's company. And though she almost always ate the café's tuna salad plate, she liked the convenience of slipping across the street and being served, as well as not having to clean up. The only one happy about her finding her own lunch was Miss Marple, who begged for and got an extra kitty snack.

Fifteen minutes and a container of lemon yogurt later, Tricia was back behind the counter at Haven't Got a Clue. Ginny was with a customer, and Miss Marple had resumed her post on the shelf above the register to keep a careful watch on things and/or sleep the afternoon away.

The black Art Deco phone on Tricia's cash desk jangled loudly. Tricia picked up the monstrously heavy receiver. "Haven't Got a Clue, Tri—"

"Tricia?" said a tearful voice that she instantly recognized as Frannie's.

"What's wrong?"

"I . . . I—" She seemed to choke on the words.

"Do you need someone to talk to?" Tricia asked, resigned.

"Do you mind?" Frannie had always appeared so strong; to hear the vulnerability in her voice was heart-wrenching.

"I'll be right over." Tricia hung up the phone.

"Don't tell me," Ginny said, and sighed. "Another crisis. This time I'm betting you'll head for the Cookery."

"Right in one. Angelica picked the wrong week to reach for bestsellerdom. Sorry."

"Hey, I'm fine. And Mr. Everett will be here by one, so we're covered."

"Unless we get a couple of buses of tourists," Tricia said.

"One can only hope," Ginny chirped.

Tricia forced a smile and sailed out the shop door. Ah, youth. Ginny was remarkably chipper for someone in her circumstances. At that moment, Tricia envied her optimism. She had a feeling that for the foreseeable future, she'd be bouncing back and forth between her sister's businesses like a Ping-Pong ball. Maybe she'd chart the time on a spreadsheet and present Angelica with an invoice. The thought made her smile—not that she'd follow through with it.

Tricia was startled to find Angelica's larger-than-life cutout standing outside the Cookery. Frannie had taped a note between the photographed Angelica's hands that read Get Your Signed Copy of *Easy-Does-It Cooking* Inside! As she reached for the door handle, Tricia wondered if the cutout would discourage—instead of encourage—customers to enter the Cookery.

There were no browsers inside the store. Frannie stood behind the cash desk. All traces of Angelica's aborted book launch party were gone, as evidenced by the fresh vacuum tracks on the carpet. And it looked like the Cookery was having as slow a day as Haven't Got a Clue.

As always, Frannie was dressed in one of her cheerful aloha shirts—this one turquoise with white hibiscus flowers in full bloom. Her face, however, was anything but jovial. Bloodshot eyes looked out from under her fringe of bangs, and her nose was crimson.

"Do you need a hug?" Tricia asked.

Frannie nodded, and burst into tears. She clung to Tricia as sobs wracked her slim body. Tricia patted her back as one would a small child. "What's wrong?"

"My heart is broken forever," Frannie wailed.

Tricia pulled back. "Come and sit down," she said, and led Frannie to the only upholstered chair in the store. Angelica had no reader's nook, saying it took up valuable retail space. Idly, Tricia wondered if she should have flipped the Cookery's OPEN sign to CLOSED.

"Can I get you a glass of water or something?" she asked Frannie.

Frannie shook her head, and pulled a damp tissue from the pocket of her slacks to wipe her nose.

"Now, tell me all about it," Tricia said.

"I've never told anyone before, but—" Frannie took a breath, exhaled it loudly, as though trying to steel herself. "Jim Roth and I were more than just casual friends."

No surprise there. Tricia waited for more.

"In fact we were . . . lllllooov—" She couldn't seem to say the word.

"Lovers?" Tricia supplied.

Frannie blushed, hung her head in shame, and nodded.

"Forgive me, Frannie, but you and Jim were two mature, single adults. What was wrong with the two of you seeing each other?"

"His mama didn't approve."

"But why?"

Frannie shrugged. She sniffled, and pressed another damp tissue to her nose.

"Bob still won't say what he was doing at Jim's store last night. Do you have any idea?" Tricia asked.

"Probably hounding him for the rent. History Repeats Itself hadn't been doing so well, what with the economy and all, and Jim was a little bit behind."

"How much is a little?"

Frannie winced. "Six months."

No wonder Bob didn't want to talk about it. He probably didn't want it to seem like he had a motive for murder. It wasn't like Bob to let someone slide for so long—and maybe his reticence was due to the fact he didn't want others who owed back rent to find out.

"How long had Jim had the store?" Tricia asked.

"He was the first bookseller Bob lined up to open a shop here in Stoneham."

"Had they been friends?"

Frannie nodded. "But Jim and I never really talked about Bob—we had so little time together, thanks to Jim's mother," she added bitterly.

"I suppose it was really quite sweet that he had his mother come to live with him."

"That's not exactly the way it was. He *always* lived with his mother," Frannie reluctantly admitted.

"He'd never lived away from home?" Tricia asked, astounded. After all, Jim *was* in his fifties.

Frannie shook her head, clearly embarrassed for him. "I invited him to come live with me, but he said he couldn't leave the old lady, even though he would've been only two blocks away. She'd come to depend on him. I mean, she *is* in her eighties."

Had Jim, the man obsessed with warfare, been a spineless mama's boy?

"I hadn't talked to Jim in a few months. Am I remembering that he hadn't been feeling well?"

Frannie nodded. "He had stomach problems that came and went. Never anything too alarming—just enough to make him cancel the few dates we made."

Tricia frowned. "Did he see a doctor about it?"

"No. Like I said, it wasn't anything he worried about. And the next day he usually felt fine. He really was strong as a horse."

Tricia knew from experience—ten years of riding lessons—that horses were actually quite delicate creatures. "I wonder why Jim didn't smell the gas."

"He had terrible allergies, and with everything coming into bloom, he probably couldn't smell a thing." Frannie wiped at a tear.

Tricia laid a hand on Frannie's thin shoulder. "I'm so sorry, Frannie."

"I thought I was doing okay until I called the Baker Funeral Home to see what arrangements had been made for Jim." She took a couple of gasping breaths.

"And?" Tricia prompted.

"Since there's no body, Mr. Baker said Jim's mother has decided against a wake or service."

"Nothing?"

Frannie shook her head. No wonder she was so upset. Those rituals made acceptance of death easier on the loved ones left behind.

"I'm so sorry," Tricia said again, knowing the words were inadequate. "But you know, there's no reason Jim's friends and colleagues can't celebrate his life."

"What do you mean?"

"We could hold a memorial service for him."

Frannie's eyes widened, and she sat up straighter. "Yes, we could."

"We could invite the Chamber members and any other friends or relatives."

"No other relatives," Frannie said. "Jim was an only child—and so were both his parents."

Tricia nodded.

"I think I should be the one to arrange it," Frannie said, her voice suddenly stronger. "Jim wasn't religious, so I don't think it should be held in a church. I'll call Eleanor at the Brookview Inn to see if I can book the function room for Sunday morning, when all the shops in town are closed—that way the other bookstore owners can come."

"That's a wonderful idea." Planning the service would keep Frannie from dwelling too much on her grief—at least for a few days. Only time would dull her long-term pain.

Frannie stood, suddenly all business—there was a reason Angelica's store had thrived under her management. "I have lots to do—and you've got your own store to tend to."

Tricia gave her friend a smile. "I promised Angelica I'd be available if you or Darcy or Jake needed me, so don't hesitate to call."

"You have no idea how much you've already helped." Frannie headed for the cash desk, found a legal pad and a pen, and quickly jotted down a few notes.

Tricia wished all life's problems could be solved so easily.

"I'll just let myself out," Tricia said, and headed for the door. Then she paused, and turned to face Frannie. "Just one more question: What's Angelica's cutout doing outside the shop door?"

Frannie rolled her eyes. "It kept staring at me. It was like having Angelica looking over my shoulder all morning. I finally couldn't stand it, and put it outside. Don't worry, I'll bring it in if it looks like rain."

Tricia nodded, but secretly hoped someone would steal the cutout. Much as she loved her sister, Tricia couldn't stand looking at the thing, either.

It was well after one by the time Tricia returned to her store, and Ginny had disappeared up the stairs to Haven't Got a Clue's second-floor employee break room. Mr. Everett stood behind the sales counter, helping a customer, while Miss Marple looked on. She was always interested in promoting good customer relations.

Mr. Everett finished ringing up the sale and wished his customer good-bye before greeting Tricia. "Hello, Ms. Miles. Isn't it a lovely day?" he said without much enthusiasm. He swept a hand toward the front display window and the sunny street beyond.

She glanced around the empty store. "Looks like another slow day," she observed.

"Yes, but the economy has picked up, and good weather brings tour buses," he said, but his voice lacked its usual cheerfulness.

"I want to thank you for saving those books last night. Ginny told me all about it."

Mr. Everett shrugged. "It was the right thing to do."

Tricia nodded. "How's Grace? Has her cold improved?"

He nodded. "Her sniffles have abated and she is her smiling self once more."

"And where is your smile?"

Mr. Everett's frown deepened.

Perhaps it was time to open a more candid dialogue. "Mr. Everett, you've seemed preoccupied for several weeks. Is something wrong?"

"You're very perceptive, Ms. Miles. But I don't like to burden my friends with my petty troubles."

"Maybe I could help."

He seemed to wrestle with the idea. "Perhaps. You see, it's . . . it's Grace."

"Oh, dear, I hope her cold hasn't gotten worse."

"Oh, no. As I said, her sniffles have almost disappeared." His expression grew more solemn. "It's her . . . her . . . her generosity."

Generosity a problem? "I don't understand."

"When Grace and I married, I had some outstanding debts—all tied to the closing of my grocery store. However, when my statements arrived this last month, I found that she'd paid off all my creditors." His cheeks colored, and he avoided her gaze. "I'm afraid we had words over it."

"Oh, dear."

He nodded, his gaze heavy with . . . disappointment?

"I'm sure she had the very best of intentions," Tricia said.

"Oh, no doubt. But . . . my pride, you see."

Tricia nodded. *Pride goeth before a fall*, she repeated silently to herself. "You can't let this come between you. The two of you have been so happy together."

"Yes. And I'm sure we shall be again. Although I'm afraid desperate measures may be necessary to alleviate this situation."

"Desperate?" Tricia repeated. She didn't like the sound of this.

"I may have to take out a loan," Mr. Everett said and gave a heavy sigh; and suddenly Tricia felt just as weary.

The day was barely half over, and already she felt wiped out. It also seemed as though she'd started a new career—personal counselor to half of Stoneham.

Before she could give a word of advice or comfort, the shop door opened. A woman customer entered, and Mr. Everett sprang into action, as though grateful for the opportunity to end their conversation.

Tricia headed for the coffee station. She needed a strong jolt of caffeine to jump-start her afternoon. But the pot held only dregs. She poured them out and started a fresh pot, working on automatic pilot.

She thought again how used she'd gotten used to having Angelica around during the past year and a half, and now that she was gone—albeit for only a couple of days—Tricia felt oddly isolated. Poor Mrs. Roth must be feeling terribly alone. Since Jim was an only child, and had been recruited by Bob to relocate to Stoneham, the poor woman might have no one to reach out to. And it was obvious Frannie wouldn't extend a hand of friendship to her anytime soon.

On impulse, Tricia crossed the store and grabbed the slim phone book from behind the cash desk, hoping the Roth home still had a landline. In less than a minute, she found the number and dialed it. Someone picked up on the second ring.

"Hello," said a wavering voice.

"Mrs. Roth? My name is Tricia Miles. I own the mystery bookstore here in Stoneham. I was a friend of Jim's. I'm so sorry for your loss. Is there anything I can do for you?"

"How kind of you to ask," said the old woman, with more than a hint of an English accent. "As it happens, I could use some help. James had the family car. I'm sure it's probably still parked in the municipal lot, but I have no way to get there to retrieve it. I'm afraid my knees couldn't handle a hike that far."

"I'd be happy to pick you up and take you to the car."

"If it wouldn't be an inconvenience," she said.

"Not in the least. When would you like to go?"

"Is an hour from now too soon?"

"Not at all."

"Thank you, dear." She gave Tricia the address. "I'll look forward to meeting you. James never did introduce me to any of his lady friends."

Tricia choked back a laugh. "Jim and I were members of the Chamber of Commerce. Sadly, I didn't know him all that well."

"I see," said the old lady, her voice cool. "Well, I'll see you in an hour, then."

Tricia heard a click, and the line went silent. She frowned at the receiver, feeling a bit dismayed. Had Mrs. Roth been expecting Frannie to call? Had she believed Tricia that she and Jim had only been acquaintances?

As she replaced the receiver in its cradle, Tricia wasn't at all sure she should have made the call.

FIVE

Tricia parked her car at the curb outside 44 Poplar Street at precisely two o'clock. The outside of the Roth home looked like something out of a travel brochure for Merrie Olde England. The house was not at all in keeping with its Victorian neighbors, but instead looked like a whitewashed country cottage, sans thatched roof. A white picket fence surrounded the property, reining in what would, in weeks, no doubt be a magnificent cottage garden. The perennials hadn't yet burst into flower, but a few strategically planted annuals already made a cheerful welcome.

Tricia unlocked the gate, making sure the latch closed behind her. If Mrs. Roth had a canine friend, she wouldn't want to be responsible for its getting loose. She followed the flagstone path to the fire-engine red front door, which sported a glossy black medallion from which the white house number seemed to jump out at her. A brass knocker below it was in the shape of a lion's head, reminding her of the one described in Dickens's *A Christmas Carol*. She knocked, and seconds later the door opened.

Mrs. Roth, a stooped, elderly woman—probably in her late seventies or early eighties—was dressed in a floral housedress and a maroon cardigan sweater. Her snowy hair was neatly coiffed—perhaps she went to the same hairdresser as Grace Everett.

"Hello, Mrs. Roth. I'm Tricia Miles."

"Thank you for coming, Miss Miles."

"Please, call me Tricia."

"Won't you come in?" The older woman stood back, and beckoned Tricia through the entryway and into a small living room. Tricia's nose twitched at the odor of stale cigarette smoke. The inside of the home did not match its outward appearance. Instead of having white walls, the interior was dark. Framed pictures of military planes and uniformed soldiers dotted the walls. A gleaming silver sword with a gold hilt and a red tassel hung over the faux brick fireplace. Taking up one whole corner of the room was a large plasma TV. A leather club chair sat before it, with an oak side table and a large, empty ashtray beside it. The rest of the room housed bookshelves and display cases with swastika-covered war souvenirs. At least one shelf had been emptied, its books neatly stacked in several cardboard cartons.

"Won't you step this way?" the old lady asked, and directed Tricia to the dining room. "Do you have time to join me in a pot of tea?"

"Oh, please, I don't want to inconvenience you."

"To be quite honest, I'd welcome the company."

Tricia managed a smile. "Thank you. I'd enjoy that."

Mrs. Roth's eyes brightened. "Please make yourself at home. I'll only be a moment." And she tottered off to the kitchen.

Tricia glanced around the immaculate dining room. Not so much as a speck of dust marred any surface. Unlike the living room, this room was definitely a woman's territory—full of knickknacks and doilies, glassware and china. An assortment of brown transferware dishes decorated the buff-colored walls. Dinner plates, luncheon plates, cake plates, and even saucers hung high on the walls, just below the ceiling, making an attractive border. The antique china cabinet, filled with an assortment of bone china tea services, stood against the north wall. Sitting atop the oak and glass cabinet were three soapstone vases and two Russian tea glasses. Above them hung a bashed and battered pewter platter—no doubt a family heirloom. Another cabinet held an assortment of chintz china—not a whole set, but the mismatched pieces made a cheerful floral garden. Cups and saucers, sugar and creamer sets, and several small pieces that Tricia couldn't identify.

Mrs. Roth entered the dining room and set a polished silver tray with teapot, sugar and creamer, a plate of bar cookies, and a bowl of sliced lemons onto the table. "I hope you like Earl Grey. I find it a soothing treat in the middle of the afternoon."

"That would be lovely, thank you."

"Would you like to select a cup?" Mrs. Roth asked, waving a hand at the oak cup shelf on the east wall.

"Oh, I couldn't. They're all so lovely. I'd be afraid of breaking it."

"Don't be silly, dear. I use all my treasures. What good

is having them if they don't get used? And each of my cups has a story."

Tricia moved to stand in front of the shelf. Flowers graced most of the cups; violets, bluebells—daffodils appeared to be a favorite—and every cup had a unique shape. She chose one with a bold pattern of pink and blue flowers that stood out against a black background and gold rim.

Mrs. Roth smiled. "I thought you might choose that one. It's one of my favorites."

"And its story?" Tricia prompted.

"It was given to me by my late mother. A wedding gift." Her smile waned. "I didn't get many, you see. Mr. Roth and I were married at the Registrar's office. A week later, I left England for good."

"Did you ever return?"

Mrs. Roth's wrinkled mouth quavered. "Not for many years. I'd always hoped to go back there to live—after my husband died, of course. But by then all my family was gone, and all my friends had either died or moved away."

"How sad for you."

Mrs. Roth nodded. "I've certainly had my share of heart-ache. And now dear James is gone." She sank into one of the chairs at the dining table and sighed. Her lips trembled as she spoke. "Now I'm all alone in this world."

So, no dog after all.

Tricia moved closer, hesitant to rest a comforting hand on the elderly woman's shoulder. "I'm so sorry. I didn't know him well, but Jim seemed like a wonderful person. Everyone seems to have loved him."

"Oh, yes, he was well loved." Was there a bit of anger in her voice?

Mrs. Roth squeezed her eyes shut, pulled a floral hankie

from the sleeve of her sweater, and dabbed at her nose. "My poor, poor James. For years I begged him to quit smoking. I knew it would kill him one day."

"Kill him?" Tricia asked.

"That nice man from the Sheriff's Department said it appeared Jim's cigarette lighter touched off the explosion."

Tricia wasn't sure what to say in reply, and cast about the room, her gaze landing on the teapot. "Should I pour?"

Mrs. Roth's head bobbed.

Grateful for something to do, Tricia chose another cup from the shelf, set it in front of the old lady, lifted the heavy silver pot, and poured the tea. Setting the pot down, she took a seat at the table and waited for Mrs. Roth to compose herself. When the old lady raised her cup to her lips, her hands had stopped shaking. She reached for one of the bar cookies.

Tricia cleared her throat. "You have a lovely home. It looks like Jim had quite a diverse collection of war memorabilia."

"Disgusting, isn't it?" the old lady said. "Too many people glorify violence, and James's collection has overrun the house. My only havens have been this room"—her gaze wandered around the dining room—"my bedroom, and my garden."

"I'm looking forward to seeing your garden in full bloom."

"It's taken me five years to achieve. James wouldn't help." Her voice dripped with disapproval. "But then he spent so much time at the shop—and with his other activities—that sometimes I'd spend less than ten minutes a day with him."

"It must have been very lonely for you."

"Only in the winter, when I couldn't be in my garden.

But I have my books"—she indicated a small stack of library books on the sideboard—"and they're a great comfort to me."

Tricia sipped her tea and was pleased to seé they were all mysteries by the great mistresses: Allingham, Christie, Sayers, and Tey.

"Since there was no body to bury, I've decided not to hold any kind of service for James," Mrs. Roth volunteered.

"Yes, I heard."

Mrs. Roth frowned. "Oh?"

Tricia backpedaled. "One of Jim's friends contacted the Baker Funeral Home to find out if any arrangements had been made."

"Of course," Mrs. Roth said, but there was something in her tone that conveyed her disapproval. She sighed. "I see no need for a service. We have no family. And the expense—"

"But, surely Jim's friends—"

Again, Mrs. Roth shook her head. "I simply can't afford it. The shop hadn't been doing well, and now my income has—" Her voice broke, and again she dabbed the hankie at her nose. "All that is beside the point. My family had no history of burials, anyway."

"I don't understand," Tricia said.

"In England, there are very few new burial sites. Or at least that was how it was when I lived there. You can rent a grave for a term—say, one hundred years, and then—"

"They dig you up?" Tricia asked, aghast.

Mrs. Roth nodded. "That's what happened to my grandmother. That's why cremation is so popular. My parents, my friends, and their husbands were all cremated, and their ashes spread in a garden of remembrance. If you liked, you could buy a rosebush in someone's memory, and they'd put the ashes under or nearby."

Good God, Tricia thought, *a loved one reduced to plant fertilizer!*

"Of course, poor James was . . . was—" Mrs. Roth swallowed the catch in her voice and continued. "I think I shall plant a rosebush in my garden to remember James by. It'll be pretty, and—" She stared at the dining table, shook her head, but did not continue the sentence.

Tricia waited until the old lady composed herself once again. "Would you be opposed to some of Jim's friends setting up a memorial service?" Tricia asked, crossing her fingers, since Frannie was already planning such an event.

Mrs. Roth looked up, the barest hint of annoyance shadowing her eyes. "I don't know. I suppose that would be all right. But—"

"I'd be glad to let you know when the arrangements have been completed." Tricia decided not to mention Frannie at this point. The poor woman had enough on her mind.

Mrs. Roth reached across the table and placed her hand on Tricia's. "Thank you, dear. You're so very kind." She looked around the table, cleared her throat, and reached for the plate of bar cookies. "Won't you have a lemon square? They were James's favorite treat. I often made them for him."

Tricia hesitated. She wasn't a big sweets fan, and the bright yellow color was a bit off-putting. It reminded her of the radiator fluid that had leaked from her last car. She remembered something Frannie had said about Jim becoming ill just before their dates. If Mrs. Roth hadn't approved of Jim dating, might a few drops of coolant put him out of commission for a few hours? She hesitated, told herself she was being foolish, and reached for one of the cookies, took a bite, chewed, and swallowed. "Mmm, it's delicious."

Mrs. Roth's eyes narrowed, her mouth quirking into a crooked smile. A shiver ran through Tricia. She wasn't at all sure she liked Mrs. Roth.

SIX

 It was nearly three o'clock when Ginny said, "Mail call!" and dumped a pile of envelopes and packages on Haven't Got a Clue's glass display case, startling Tricia. Awash in order forms to restock the coffee station, she hadn't heard the door open and the mail-man come in.

"Bills, bills, bills," Ginny said with a laugh. "Makes me feel like I'm at home."

The door opened again, and a customer walked in. "Can I help you?" Ginny asked, and left Tricia to deal with the mail. She sorted through the envelopes, separating them into piles.

Among the bills and circulars was a squat package. Tricia scrutinized the return address. There was only one person she knew in Colorado—her ex-husband, Christopher. They hadn't spoken in at least eighteen months, not since she'd called him, needing to hear a friendly voice after Doris Gleason's murder. Since they'd parted, she hadn't received so much as a Christmas card from him, and now this—whatever it was. A birthday gift, perhaps? If so, jewelry, most likely. He'd bought her rings, earrings, necklaces, and bracelets for birthdays and Christmases, and after he'd left her, she'd found it unbearable to wear any of his presents. They now resided in her jewelry box, stuffed in the back of her closet. She'd gone to a discount store and chosen an inexpensive—but dependable—Timex watch as her only piece of adornment—that and a few pairs of post earrings.

Tricia turned the box over and shook it, but nothing rattled inside. Christopher hadn't insured it, so whatever was inside probably wasn't valuable. And if it was meant as a birthday gift, was she supposed to wait until next Wednesday to open it?

The heck with that! She fumbled for the box cutter she kept under the counter and slit the tape that sealed the box. Inside the cardboard, nestled between two layers of foam peanuts and wrapped in a protective sheet of bubble wrap, was a red-velvet-covered box. Yup. Jewelry. At least Christopher always had good taste. She extracted the box and opened it. Inside was a lovely oval locket engraved with calla lilies—her favorite flower. Christopher hadn't forgotten. She opened the locket and found he'd inserted a picture of Miss Marple. She frowned. She'd half expected he'd put a picture of himself inside. That maybe he was thinking of her. That maybe he'd gotten over his midlife crisis and was thinking of *returning* to her.

She searched the box. Sure enough, on the bottom was a small white envelope. The flap had been tucked inside. She removed the card, which had a watercolor of calla lilies on the front, and opened it. It was Christopher's familiar handwriting, all right. She read the lines:

To remind you of the one you love the most.

Love,

Christopher

Tricia frowned at the words, puzzled and hurt. Yes, she loved Miss Marple, but did he think she was incapable of loving a person as much? She had loved him with her heart and soul, and he had left her for a life of solitude in the Colorado mountains.

She was fighting back tears when an out-of-breath Darcy Gebhard pushed through Haven't Got a Clue's front door. "Tricia!"

Tricia wiped her tearing eyes, stuffed the box under the counter, and tried to keep her voice level. "What can I do for you, Darcy?"

Darcy brandished a blue banking pouch. "I've brought over the day's receipts."

Tricia cringed. Ginny and her customer both looked up. Did Darcy have to announce it to the world at large?

She handed over the pouch, and Tricia quickly stowed it under the counter. She lowered her voice. "Perhaps tomorrow you could bring it over in a plain paper bag so as not to draw it to my customers' attention."

"Oh, sure." Darcy laughed. "Oh, I get it. You don't want me to make myself a mugging target. Good thinking."

Was the woman completely clueless? Tricia consulted the clock once again. It usually took Angelica more than an hour to wind things down at the café; she was a stickler for cleanliness. However, Jake was probably long gone, and Tricia wondered if Darcy had been as thorough in her end-of-day tasks. "You seem like you're in a hurry."

Darcy raked a hand through her too-long bangs. "Yeah, I gotta get moving. I'm helping a friend get her garden in shape. Don't want to be late." With her brightly lacquered nails and fingers full of silver rings, she hardly seemed the gardening type.

"Gotta run," she said, making an abrupt about-face. "See you tomorrow." And out the door she went.

Ginny and her customer approached the cash desk. "I'll just ring that up for you," Ginny said.

Tricia stepped aside and bagged the order, tossing in a copy of store's latest newsletter as well as a couple of bookmarks she'd received from current mystery authors, and handed the bag to the customer before she glanced out the front display window. Darcy was heading in the direction of the municipal parking lot. Who wanted to garden at the hottest part of the day? Tricia shook her head.

"What's up?" Ginny asked, once the customer had departed.

"Darcy. She's an odd duck."

"Yeah. She's either overly friendly or just plain ignores you."

"I didn't think you'd eaten at Booked for Lunch all that often."

"I haven't. But I've run into her a few times around town. She's almost as obnoxious as Angelica's cook. The few times I've run into him and said hello, he's sneered and ignored me."

"Good." At Ginny's startled expression, Tricia explained. "I mean I'm glad I'm not the only one who feels that way about him. Angelica thinks the world of him."

"There's no accounting for taste," Ginny commented. "I'm going to straighten the shelves in back. Call me if you need me."

Tricia nodded. Once Ginny was out of sight, she brought out Christopher's gift. Miss Marple jumped down to the counter from her perch on the wall behind Tricia. *Brrrrrp!*

"Christopher thinks I love you best."

Miss Marple rubbed her head against Tricia's arm, as though to say, "Well, of course you do!"

Tricia held the locket in her fist, wondering what she should do with it. Should she throw it away or . . . wear it?

Throw it away, the hurt, angry part of her said.

Keep it, the part of her that still ached for Christopher begged.

Tricia grasped the chain and opened the clasp, fumbling to fasten it around her neck. But instead of wearing it outside her sweater, she tucked it inside. She didn't want to talk about it or show it to Ginny. This would be her secret. And if she never wore it after today, that was okay, too.

Tossing the box and packaging in the wastebasket, she sorted through the rest of the mail. Nothing too pressing; nothing very interesting. Miss Marple soon became bored and returned to her perch above and behind the sales counter.

The bell over the door rang, and two elderly women entered Haven't Got a Clue. That alone wouldn't have startled Tricia, but the fact that the ladies were dressed alike, in matching tennis shoes, dark slacks, and floral tops, and wore the same hairstyle, made them look like they'd been stamped out with a cookie cutter. How old could they be? In their seventies? Perhaps eighties?

"Good morning. My name is Midge Dexter, and this is my sister Muriel," said the first of the women.

"We're twins!" Muriel chimed in, and then giggled. "I'm the baby. I was born fourteen minutes after Midge."

Midge gave her sister a look that said she'd heard that line a little too often.

Tricia fought to keep from smirking, and cleared her throat. "Very nice to meet you, ladies. What can I do for you?"

"We'd like you to sign our petition," Midge said, indicating the clipboard she held under one arm. "We want to reestablish a police force here in Stoneham."

"We've been without one for almost eighteen years," Muriel piped up.

"The Sheriff's Department isn't really equipped to keep the law in a village like ours. Did you know the average response time for a 9-1-1 call is almost twenty minutes? And thanks to the influx of tax revenue, we feel the time is right to resubmit our request to the Board of Selectmen."

"You've made this request before?" Tricia asked.

Midge nodded. "For the past four years. Why is the village spending money on foolish things like gas lamps when we should be protecting our citizens from murderers?"

"Yes," Muriel continued for her sister, "we've had four murders in less than two years. It had been years—"

"Decades," Midge interrupted.

"—since anyone was killed here in Stoneham, and since the booksellers moved here—" Muriel slapped a hand across her mouth to cut herself off.

"You think the booksellers are responsible for an increase in crime?" Tricia asked.

"No, dear," Midge said, "just you."

"Me?" Tricia cried. Oh, boy, here came that same "village jinx" label she'd been stuck with since Doris Gleason had been murdered some eighteen months before.

"Well, you do seem to be falling over corpses every few months," Muriel said.

"I did not fall over Jim Roth's corpse. In fact, there was no corpse," Tricia said, a bit more emphatically than she'd planned.

"But you were on your way to his store when the explosion happened," Midge said.

"You must've been born under an unlucky star," Muriel added, nodding sagely.

Tricia wasn't sure how to reply to that.

"Now," Midge said, pushing her clipboard forward, "we need at least two hundred and fifty signatures. Won't you be the first merchant on Main Street to sign our petition?"

"Yes, it would be symbolic," Muriel agreed. "And I'm sure if you signed it, the rest of the booksellers would be more inclined to sign it, too."

"How much is this likely to cost taxpayers?" Tricia asked, playing devil's advocate.

"Thousands," Muriel said.

"Oh, no, dear, millions," Midge corrected. "Over the long haul, that is. But I'm sure everyone in the village will sleep better at night knowing we have our own officers patrolling the streets and keeping us safe. I know I will."

"Me, too," Muriel agreed.

With no sales or income taxes, property taxes paid for all that was needed in New Hampshire—from filling the potholes to paying the state's public servants. As far as Tricia knew, all of the booksellers leased the properties that housed their stores, but the landowners—Bob Kelly in particular—passed the property tax expense on to their leaseholders.

"Let me guess," Tricia said, "I'll bet you ladies rent your home."

"How did you know?" Muriel asked with a smile.

"Just a lucky guess.

"Why couldn't the Milford police just patrol Stoneham, too? They already take care of Amherst and other surrounding towns," Tricia pointed out.

"That wouldn't do," Midge said, "not when Stoneham is such a large tourist draw. People come to visit from all over New England and the mid-Atlantic states."

"Yes, but those people aren't paying property taxes," Tricia pointed out.

"Well, why should they? They don't live here."

"That's exactly my point," Tricia said.

"Do you need a pen, dear?" Muriel asked. Had she even been following this last portion of the conversation?

Tricia shook her head and grabbed a pen from the mug by the side of the register, and signed the petition. She handed the clipboard back to Midge.

"Thank you so much," Muriel gushed. "Come, sister, we must go next door to the Cookery. I want to buy that cookbook by that local author named Angelica Miles. They say she's going to be the next Paula Deen."

"Wait, don't you want my employees to sign your petition?" Tricia asked.

Midge giggled. "Dear, they already have." The sisters gave Tricia a smile and a wave, and headed out the door.

Ginny was behind the coffee station, tidying up, and Tricia called her over. "You signed a petition to restore a Stoneham police department?"

"Yeah, the Dexter sisters nailed me at the convenience store early this morning. They got Mr. Everett in the parking lot before he came in."

"Did you know they consider me the cause of most of the crime in Stoneham?"

"Um . . . yes, they may have mentioned that. I defended you, of course."

"And what did they say?" Tricia asked.

"That you're . . . a jinx."

Tricia's hands clenched and she winced. "Am I never going to live that down?"

"Tricia, you're in New England. People around here have long memories."

"But I never caused anyone's death," she protested.

"I know . . . that's why they only consider you a jinx, not a murderer. Look at it this way," Ginny said, "if Stoneham has its own police force, you'll never have to meet up with Sheriff Adams ever again."

"As it is, I've been lucky not to meet up with her for months."

"It's a win-win situation," Ginny said.

"As a homeowner, how much do you think your taxes will go up?"

It was Ginny's turn to wince. "Oh. I hadn't thought of that. But then, I'm losing my house to foreclosure. Why did you sign the petition?"

"It was a reasonable request. I know several times I haven't called the Sheriff's Department to report things because I didn't want to wait for a deputy to show up. Maybe with a police presence, crime will go down. Not that it's really a problem. Most of our shoplifters aren't from Stoneham—they're visitors to the village."

"That's right," Ginny said. "But the taxpayers won't pass the measure, anyway. I mean, they've turned it down the last four years. I wouldn't worry about it."

"Oh, I'm not worried," Tricia said. But then another thought crossed her mind. If Stoneham had its own force, was she likely to see Captain Baker again?

It was a disconcerting thought. They weren't an item, and probably never would be. But she liked him. She enjoyed seeing him on an irregular basis.

With their conversation at an end, Ginny returned to the coffee station to tidy up.

Tricia fingered the chain around her neck. So she might never see Grant Baker again. All things came to an end—just like her relationship with Christopher.

That didn't mean she had to like it.

SEVEN

The day wore on. Customers came—and customers went. Finally, the hands on the clock crept toward closing time. Although sunset was still almost two hours away, the east side of Main Street had retreated into the shadow of its western neighbor. Tricia tidied the already orderly sales desk for the fourth time, and Miss Marple stirred from her nap, unhappy that the solar heat she'd enjoyed most of the afternoon had disappeared.

The shop door opened, but it wasn't a customer. Instead, Grace Harris-Everett, Mr. Everett's bride, entered Haven't Got a Clue. "Hello, Tricia!"

"Grace, what brings you here this evening?"

"William's car is in the shop. I'm here to give him a ride—and perhaps convince him to take me to dinner in Nashua."

"Sounds like a date to me."

Grace actually giggled. "Marrying William has given me such joy. I do wish we'd done it sooner. You should try it."

"I still might—but right now there are no likely candidates."

Grace's smile faded. "I was so sorry when you and Russ Smith broke up. Do you think there's a chance you might get back together? I know he hasn't given up hope."

Had Russ been confiding in Grace? "I'm afraid not." Not when she still thought about Grant Baker on a regular basis. Not that she was pining for Baker, either.

It was time to change the subject. "Grace, do you know Jim Roth's mother?"

She shook her head. "I'm afraid I don't. She and Jim only moved to Stoneham about five years ago, when he opened the store."

Tricia frowned. For some reason, she had the impression—especially after seeing the inside of the Roth home and the wonderful garden—that they had been citizens of Stoneham for a lot longer.

"Mrs. Roth told me she couldn't afford a funeral for Jim. Frannie's planning a memorial service. Apparently Mrs. Roth depended on Jim's income. I wonder if the other booksellers would contribute to a fund for her."

"I didn't know Jim well, but I'd be willing to contribute."

"That's very kind of you."

Grace opened her purse and took out her checkbook. Using the display case as a desk, she wrote out a check and handed it to Tricia. "I've left the pay-to portion blank in case you want to cash it and give Mrs. Roth the donations in a lump sum."

Tricia looked at the check, and her mouth dropped. One

thousand dollars. "Oh, Grace, that's extremely generous of you."

Grace shrugged. "My first husband left me well off. I have no one to leave it to. If it can help Jim's mother, I'm happy to give it."

On impulse, Tricia gathered Grace into a careful hug. "I'm so glad you're my friend."

Grace patted Tricia's back and chuckled. After a few moments, Grace pulled back, craned her neck, and looked for her beloved. "Where is William?"

"He went up to the storeroom to look for a copy of *The Zero Clue* by Rex Stout."

"Oh, that's one of my favorites."

"We got a request for it on our Website. He should be down any moment."

As if on cue, the door to the stairway at the back of the store, marked PRIVATE, opened and both Mr. Everett and Ginny appeared. "Grace, my dear. Is it time to go already?"

"I'm a few minutes early," Grace admitted, standing on tiptoe to give Mr. Everett a demure peck on the cheek. He blushed as he handed Tricia the book.

"Why don't you two run along?" Tricia said. "Ginny and I can close up."

"That wouldn't be fair to either of you," Mr. Everett said.

"It's not like we've got anyone waiting for us at home," Ginny said, rubbing salt into Tricia's figurative wound.

Grace smiled, and tweaked her husband's collar. "I hope you realize how lucky you are, William, to work with two such lovely women."

"Indeed I do," he said solemnly.

Tricia felt a burst of affection for the old man. She'd never known either of her grandfathers, but she hoped they'd been as sweet as her elderly employee.

"Mr. Everett, I hate to ask, but for the next couple of weeks I'm really going to depend on you and Ginny while Angelica's away on her book tour. I might be called upon to take care of the café. Luckily, Frannie seems able to manage alone at the Cookery."

"We have no plans for the next month or so. I'd be glad to fill in as needed," the old man said.

"Thank you."

"William, what do you think about a nice steak at Eddie's Chop House?" Grace asked hopefully.

Mr. Everett's mouth pursed in disapproval. "Now, dear, you know it's not in our budget."

"It's in *my* budget," she said, her voice tinged with strain. Grace clasped her husband's hand, brandishing a forced smile. "Why don't we talk about it in the car?" She led him to the exit. "See you soon," she called. A dour Mr. Everett waved good-bye and closed the door behind them.

"Hmm—think there's an argument brewing?" Ginny asked.

"It's none of our business," Tricia said. She wasn't about to gossip about her favorite married couple—especially when Mr. Everett had confided his feelings about money to her. She tucked the check Grace had given her into the bottom of the register's cash drawer. It looked like she was now officially the one to collect money in Jim's name. Another thing to add to her to-do list.

"You may as well take off, too," Tricia told Ginny as she gazed around the empty store. "You've got things to do as well."

Ginny's expression soured. "Packing isn't my favorite thing. I've got an appointment to see another apartment tonight. Who knows—this might be the one." She grabbed her purse from under the counter, and called a good-bye.

"Wait," Tricia called, and Ginny turned. "There's something I want to talk to you about."

Ginny paused, her expression changing from cheerful to wary in a heartbeat. "What is it?"

Tricia laughed. "Don't look so worried. This is good news, not bad."

"Oh?"

"Yes. I wondered if you'd like to hear a business proposition I've been thinking about."

"Business?" Ginny repeated. That perked her up.

"Yes. I've been mulling over your situation, and I really don't want to see you lose your little cottage in the woods. What would you think about me holding the mortgage?"

Ginny blinked. "Come again?"

"I could pay off your mortgage, and then we could come to an agreement about repayment. This way you wouldn't lose your house to foreclosure."

Ginny was still blinking. "You'd do that for me?"

"I would. I will."

Ginny's gaze dipped, and she let out a breath, looking shell-shocked. "Wow. I can't believe it. I might actually get to *keep* my little house." She looked up. "Oh, Tricia, I don't know how to thank you." Ginny rushed forward and gave Tricia an enthusiastic hug. Then she pulled back, and actually jumped up and down couple of times. "Oh, wow!"

Tricia laughed. "I was hoping you'd like the idea."

"I get to keep my house, I get to keep my house!" Ginny sang. Then, just as suddenly, she stood stock still and covered her mouth, as her eyes welled with tears. "Nobody's ever done anything this nice for me in my whole life. Thank you, Tricia. Thank you so much."

"I'll have to speak to Roger Livingston—my lawyer— but according to Billie Hanson at the bank, we could iron out the details in no time."

"You've already been to the bank?"

Tricia nodded.

"Oh, wow," Ginny said again, and wiped at her eyes.

"Why don't you go home—and start unpacking?" Tricia suggested.

"You don't know how huge a weight has been lifted off me. Thank you, Tricia. I've said it before, and I'll say it again: You're the best boss in the world."

"Go home," Tricia said and pushed Ginny toward the door.

Again Ginny smiled and sang, "I get to keep my house, I get to keep my house," as she went through the door.

Miss Marple jumped down from her perch behind the cash desk, and daintily walked across the glass top of the showcase, unmoved by Ginny's euphoria. She had more important matters to consider, and looked hopefully at Tricia. Tricia looked at the clock and sighed. "Yes, it *is* almost your dinnertime." Miss Marple allowed Tricia to smooth her fur, and began to purr. "Well, at least I've been able to make two people happy today."

The little bell above the door rang and Tricia straightened, eager to welcome a last-minute customer, but it was only Russ Smith. Her shoulders slumped, her good mood gone. "Oh, it's you."

"What's wrong with that?"

She sighed. "Nothing. What can I do for you, Russ?"

He sauntered up to the cash desk and petted Miss Marple, who eyed him warily. "I wondered if you were free for dinner tonight."

"In case it's escaped your attention, we are no longer an item."

"It has not escaped my attention. But you're alone—I'm alone. We're not lovers, but I hope we're still friends. And why can't friends share a table at the Bookshelf Diner once in a while? We can even share the check." Tricia was about to refuse when he spoke again. "Tonight's special is chicken and biscuits," he called in a singsong cadence.

"Which, if you'd paid attention in the past, you'd know would never entice me."

"Okay, then, we can talk about the explosion at History Repeats Itself. I'll tell you what I know, and you can share what you know."

"What makes you think I know anything?"

Russ laughed. "Because I know you. You can't help yourself when it comes to sleuthing. You're like a heroin addict or something. All those mysteries you read have you thinking you're Stoneham's own Miss Marple."

At the sound of her name, Tricia's cat gave a spirited "*Yow!*"

"I am *not* that old."

"But you *are* that smart."

Tricia shrugged. She wasn't about to argue with the truth. She eyed him warily. With Angelica gone, she was feeling a tad lonely, and, as her grumbling stomach reminded her, she was hungry, too.

"All right. But don't think we're going to make a habit of this. And I can't leave right now. The shop is officially open for another ten minutes. And I have to feed Miss Marple before I can go anywhere."

"Feed her now. I'll mind the store."

Again she shrugged. He'd done it before.

Ten minutes later, Tricia locked the door to Haven't Got a Clue, and she and Russ crossed the street, heading for the diner. They didn't speak again until they'd been seated. Except for curt exchanges, Eugenia Hirt, the night waitress, hadn't spoken with Tricia since the unpleasant situation the previous fall, nor would she make eye contact. At first it had bothered Tricia, but now she just ignored the silly girl.

"Bring us a couple of glasses of house red, and give us a few minutes, will you, Eugenia?" Russ asked.

She nodded, and pivoted to make a fast escape.

Tricia perused the menu. Same old, same old.

Russ rested his arms on the table and leaned forward. "Now, what has Bob Kelly told Angelica about the night of the explosion?"

Tricia didn't look up, and considered the Cobb salad. "Nothing."

"Oh come on, it's me, Russ. You can tell me."

"I can't tell you, because Bob isn't talking—to Angelica, to me, and, as far as I know, he's not talking to anyone else, like Captain Baker, either."

Russ frowned. "I've received the same cold shoulder."

Speaking of which, Eugenia returned with their drinks, plunking them on the table and nearly spilling them. "Ready to order?" she asked.

She'd gone back to wearing the studs in her nose and eyebrow. *It must drive her mother crazy,* Tricia thought. "I'll have the Cobb salad, with poppy seed dressing on the side."

"Chicken and biscuits for me," Russ said.

Eugenia nodded and again escaped.

Tricia picked up her glass and took a sip. "So, who dishes first—you or me?"

"Ladies first," Russ said, and picked up his glass.

"Jim Roth's mother didn't see the point of holding a funeral service, since there's no body to bury. So Frannie Armstrong is planning a memorial service for him on Sunday at the Brookside Inn."

"Why Frannie?"

"Apparently they were friends." That wasn't a lie—it just wasn't the whole truth. Besides, it was bound to come out eventually, anyway. Russ was a reporter. If he wanted more information on the subject, he would have to dig for it himself.

Tricia sipped her wine. "Have you started Jim's obituary?"

He shook his head. "I've got an appointment to talk to his mother. She said she might be able to dig up some photographs. To tell you the truth, she didn't sound all that interested in talking about her son. She didn't even sound all that sad."

"People express their grief in different ways," Tricia offered, even though she'd wondered about Mrs. Roth's true feelings toward her son. Should she bring the subject of radiator fluid into the conversation? Probably not. After all, she couldn't even say she had suspicions . . . just . . . a funny feeling.

"I might get a few of the other booksellers to say something. Jim was well liked, but it doesn't look like he was particularly close to anyone in town."

Tricia thought about Frannie and bit her tongue. Mrs. Roth had mentioned that Jim was involved in other activities. What could she have meant?

"If his mother's no help," Russ continued, "I may forget the whole thing and just run a short piece about the explosion."

"You'll do what you have to," Tricia said, and smoothed the curling edge on her paper placemat.

Before the lack of meaningful conversation could get awkward, Eugenia brought their food, carefully setting Russ's down in front of him, and then nearly tossing the salad at Tricia. A grape tomato bounced from the bowl and onto the table.

"Hey!" Russ protested.

"Sorry," Eugenia mumbled, sounding anything but, and took off again.

Tricia unwrapped her cutlery from the paper napkin that surrounded it. "Apparently she hasn't forgiven me for what happened last fall."

"That wasn't your fault."

Tricia stabbed at a piece of lettuce. "No, it wasn't."

"Eugenia was lucky to get a sympathetic judge who gave her only probation and community service, or she might be in jail like her boyfriend," Russ said, and dug into his chicken. "Back to Jim," he said, and shoveled in a mouthful. Tricia waited impatiently until he had chewed and swallowed, and could speak again. "Now that it looks like his death may not have been accidental, who do you think did it?"

"Who said it wasn't an accident?" Tricia asked.

"I'm a newspaperman. I don't reveal my sources."

Tricia glared at him.

"You didn't answer my question. Do you think Bob Kelly might've offed old Jim?"

"Of course not. Angelica would never allow it."

Russ laughed. "You're probably right. But it's been said Jim was behind on all his bills—his biggest creditor being Bob."

"And if he wanted his money, I'm sure Bob wouldn't go

around killing anyone—much less destroy his own building. That would be a sure way of never seeing what was owed him. Bob is simply too cheap to kill when he can go to small claims court to get what's owed him. Besides, they were supposedly friends."

Again, Russ laughed. "Look at you—defending Bob Kelly. I never thought I'd see the day."

Neither did Tricia. She dipped a piece of green pepper into her dressing. "Do you think there's a viable suspect—besides Bob, I mean?"

Russ shook his head. "Nothing that's come to light. But then it's not quite twenty-four hours since it happened."

Tricia leaned forward. "The way you spoke at my store, I thought you actually had something interesting to tell me."

"You don't find our conversation interesting?"

She turned her attention back to her salad. "I'd find it more interesting if I didn't feel like you'd lured me here under false pretenses."

"What pretenses? You're hungry—I'm hungry. And we're talking about Jim's death. That doesn't mean it has to be the only topic of discussion. For instance—why don't we talk about us?"

Tricia put her fork down. "There is no *us*. You made that quite plain last fall."

"I also told you I was wrong."

He had. But by then, she was already interested in Grant Baker—and that had gone nowhere, too.

"Let's get back to Jim," Tricia said. "Do you know what caused the explosion? Captain Baker didn't seem to think the gas lamps were involved."

"No. The firemen, sheriff's deputies, and utility people were out back of the shop until late last night, checking things out. They spent an awful long time looking at the area where the meter had been. I'll bet you dinner someone tampered with it. The flash point was at the back of the building."

This wasn't going to be much of an information exchange if that was all he could come up with. "No bet. The deal was, I pay for my dinner and you pay for yours. Bob wouldn't risk destroying his own building—eviction is the easiest way to force a deadbeat out."

"I'm told Jim never smoked in his shop, but he did out back. He lit a cigarette and—*kaboom*—the walls came tumbling down," Russ said.

Tricia chewed and swallowed. "So Mrs. Roth said, and Captain Baker confirmed a cigarette lighter was responsible," she said, and stabbed another piece of lettuce. "Who knew Jim's habits? His customers? Fellow businessmen? How about the mailman or any of the delivery guys?"

"As far as I know," Russ continued, "Jim had no enemies. In fact, outside of the shop and the occasional Chamber meeting, I don't think he had much of a life. He lived with his mother, for chrissakes. I don't think he'd ever lived on his own—or, God forbid, with someone of the opposite sex."

"Why do you say that?" Tricia asked, again thinking about Frannie. Apparently she and Jim had been extremely discreet.

"You know how guys talk about sex. Jim never joined in."

"Maybe he was a gentleman. Or do you think he was gay?"

"Not necessarily. Maybe he was just missing the romance chip."

That was rich—coming from Mister I-never-turn-off-my-police-scanner-for-anything-or-anybody. Tricia turned her attention back to her food.

"I've spoken to a number of Chamber members, but the story's pretty much the same," Russ went on. "None of you booksellers have much of a social life, so no one seems to know much about their neighbors."

Was that last an insult against Tricia, or did he really believe what he said? She chose to ignore it.

"It's pretty hard to keep tabs on each other when we're dealing with busloads of people on and off all day," Tricia admitted. "Then again, some of us *are* keeping tabs on our neighbors, or at least I am while Angelica's off on her book tour. I've already had to solve one crisis at Booked for Lunch. I have a feeling it won't be the last."

"Lucky you." Russ had never been overly fond of Angelica, and the feeling had been mutual. "So where does that leave us? With just Bob as a key player?"

"I suppose."

"There's speculation he won't rebuild," Russ said.

Tricia dropped her fork. "What do you mean? There's a gaping hole in the street. He *has* to rebuild."

"My guess is he'll take the insurance money and put the property up for sale."

"Who'd buy it?"

"You've got a point. Rebuilding in a historic district will be prohibitively expensive. But if I know Bob, he'll want to cut his losses."

"It would be a shame." And the view from Haven't Got a Clue would be ruined forever—not that Tricia voiced that opinion.

Russ shrugged. "Then again, I've heard talk of a developer poking around, looking for investments here in Stoneham."

"Really? Who?"

"I don't have a name. I just heard a rumor."

"From whom?"

Elbows on the table, Russ laced his fingers together and stared at Tricia. "I haven't got a clue."

Tricia refrained from commenting on that. "Would Bob sell to a developer? I didn't think he'd even consider it. He sure wasn't interested in talking about selling when I broached the subject with him prior to opening Haven't Got a Clue."

"Times, and people, change," Russ said, and dived back into his chicken and biscuits.

Maybe so. But Russ hadn't changed, and because of that, Tricia knew she'd be going home alone.

EIGHT

Tricia stared at the calculator's digital readout and frowned. Three times she'd added up the figures, and three times they hadn't matched the cash she'd counted out of Booked for Lunch's bank pouch. That there was more cash than receipts didn't make her feel better. A few dollars here and there wouldn't have worried her—but the pouch had contained thirteen dollars more than the total of the receipts. Had someone lost or disposed of several of the grease-stained table receipts? The receipts were numbered, and sure enough, four of them were missing from the stack.

Maybe you're jumping to conclusions, she told herself. Just because the numbers didn't jibe didn't mean someone—Darcy or Jake—had been light-fingered with the till. Maybe Darcy had messed up a few of them, had tossed them away, and rewritten the orders on a new order blank. If Tricia was the suspicious type, and it wasn't so god-awful late, she might be inclined to check the café's trash to look for missing order receipts. As she'd learned in the not-too-distant past, you could learn a lot about a business by going through its garbage. At least Darcy had brought over the day's receipts. Frannie was supposed to do the same, and hadn't. Still, that didn't ring alarm bells. Tricia knew and trusted Frannie. Darcy had been working for Angelica for only three or four months.

Tricia filled out the bank deposit slip, put a rubber band around it and the day's cash, and stowed it back in the bank pouch. She'd deposit it along with her own receipts in the morning.

Tricia glanced at the clock. It was already after eleven. Like an expectant parent, she'd hoped Angelica would call long before this.

Turning off the kitchen lights was the signal that bedtime had come, and Miss Marple roused herself from the stool where she'd been napping and jumped to the floor, stretching before trotting off toward the bedroom.

Tricia started to follow when at last the phone shattered the quiet. She grabbed it before it could ring again. "Angelica?"

"Yes, at last!" came the voice she'd been waiting for. "You wouldn't believe the day I've had."

"Me, either," Tricia said. "Why are you calling so late?"

"I only got to the hotel about half an hour ago. I jumped in the shower, and then into my jammies. I didn't even get anything to eat tonight. If this place had a mini bar, I'd be raiding it now."

Tricia carried the wireless phone over to the kitchen counter and sat down on the stool she'd abandoned only a minute before. She had a feeling this could be a marathon call. "Tell me all about it."

And Angelica did—from the road trip to the north end of the state, down to the problem she'd encountered when she'd gone to fetch her car after her second signing of the day.

"Someone slashed your tires?" Tricia repeated in disbelief.

"All four of them," Angelica said, not disguising her disgust. "The bookstore manager was terribly embarrassed, although not enough to offer to pay anything toward replacing them."

"Who's to say it was one of her customers?"

"Exactly. It took forever for Triple A to tow it to their garage. It should be ready for me by nine o'clock tomorrow, which gives me just enough time to drive to Conway for tomorrow's lunchtime signing."

"I'm sorry you had such a bad day. It wasn't that great here, either."

"How's Bob?" Angelica asked, ignoring Tricia's hint that maybe she needed to vent as well.

Tricia sighed. "Grumpy."

"I suppose that's only natural after what he went through last night. I tried calling him several times, but all I got was voice mail. Do you think he could've been sleeping the whole day?"

"Could be. Did you know he'd ordered a security system to be installed at his house?"

"No. He never mentioned it."

"The firm was finishing up when I dropped him off this morning. I asked him about it, but, like last night, he wasn't talking."

"That's not like Bob." Angelica sighed. "I hope he calls before I have to take off tomorrow morning."

"I'm sure he will," Tricia lied. She thought about what Russ had said. "There's a rumor Bob won't rebuild on Main Street—that he'll sell the land Jim's store stood on. Russ heard there's a developer looking for investment properties in Stoneham. Do you think Bob would sell?"

"It's possible," Angelica said, but she didn't sound very sure. "Anything else new?"

"I've been thinking about helping Ginny with her mortgage."

Silence greeted that statement. And then, "Please tell me I just heard wrong. You're going to—?"

"Help Ginny with her mortgage," Tricia repeated.

"Help how?"

"I'm going to pay it off, and then I'll have Roger Livingston set up a repayment schedule on terms Ginny can actually afford."

"On what you pay her?"

"Hey, I pay her more than the going rate."

"I know, but it's still not enough to make mortgage payments."

Tricia took a burn to that remark.

"I've got another question: Why?" Angelica asked.

"So she doesn't lose her house."

Angelica sighed. "Let me tell you, as a cookbook author, this idea of yours is a recipe for disaster."

"Why do you say that?"

"Because Ginny's your subordinate. Now she'll feel beholden to you. Friction will build up. One day it'll explode—taking whatever friendship the two of you have with it. And don't you dare give me that look."

Tricia felt anger boiling within her. "What look?" she

asked through clenched teeth, knowing her sister couldn't see her through the phone.

"The one that says, 'I won't believe you simply because I don't want to.' If you really think about it, you'll agree with me. And is losing Ginny's friendship something you really want to risk?"

First Billie Hanson and now Angelica. Didn't anyone have faith in the power of kindness and friendship anymore?

Tricia heard Angelica heave another sigh, and wished she hadn't brought up the subject. Time to change it. "By the way, Ange, you owe me two hundred and forty-five dollars and sixty-three cents."

"What for?"

"Chicken. Just after you left this morning, the poultry man made a delivery to the café and demanded a check before he'd leave it."

"There must be some mistake. I don't use that much chicken in a month."

"That was the amount on the invoice."

Tricia could picture her sister frowning. "Well, okay. You know I'm good for it."

"Yes, I do. Just out of curiosity, how close do the café's cash and order receipts add up on an average day?"

"Within a dollar or two. You know how it is—take a penny, leave a penny. Why?"

"The café's cash didn't match the orders. It was thirteen dollars over."

"Better over than under."

"Mmm," Tricia halfheartedly agreed.

"Did Frannie bring over the Cookery's receipts?" Angelica asked.

"No. She probably just forgot. And I'm not surprised,

either. She was extremely upset about Jim Roth's death. In fact, this morning she admitted to me that she and Jim had been lovers."

"You're kidding!" Angelica gushed.

"Nope. His mother decided not to hold a funeral, so Frannie's planning a memorial service. It'll be Sunday morning so that the booksellers don't have to close shop."

"Poor Frannie. And damn, I can't be there. I've got a signing in Bennington."

"Poor Frannie? Don't you mean poor Jim? He's the one who was pulverized," Tricia reminded her sister.

"Of course. But I didn't think Frannie had ever even been with anyone . . . if you know what I mean. Now to find out she's been having an illicit love affair—well. . . ."

"Not that illicit. They were two unencumbered, consenting adults."

"Mmm. If I get a chance, I'll give her a call tomorrow morning to get all the dirt firsthand. And find out what happened to today's banking."

Tricia looked at the clock. "It's late. I'd better let you go."

"Thanks for taking care of the café for me. I'll make it up to you somehow." She paused. "I know, I'll buy you a nice big present. You deserve something deliciously girly and sweet for your birthday. That is, if I ever get any time to myself in the next couple of days and can shop."

Tricia frowned. Girly and sweet? She made no comment. "Remind me—just when will you be coming home?"

"Next Friday."

Which seemed a million years from right then, Tricia decided. Still, she tried to sound upbeat. "Okay, see you then. Call me when you can, and you take care, now."

"Good night, Trish. And think about what I said about

Ginny. If you go through with this plan, you might lose a good employee, and a friend."

"Good night!" Tricia said and hung up the phone.

An annoyed Miss Marple had reappeared and sat at her feet. "*Yow!*" she said.

"Don't you take Angelica's side," Tricia warned, but later, as she lay in bed staring at the ceiling, all she could think about was the threat of Ginny one day hating her, and Angelica saying, "I told you so."

Tricia was up with the birds the next morning. After showering and dressing, she spied the locket Christopher had sent her, still lying on the dresser where she'd left it the night before. It was time to make a decision—banish it to the back of the closet, or wear it.

She decided to wear it, once again tucking it inside her sweater. After all, it was likely to be the only birthday gift she would receive.

Tricia fingered the chain next to her skin. Birthdays were meant to be special, she'd decided at a very early age. The fact that hers hadn't been as special as Angelica's had been a source of great hurt and puzzlement. That's why, as an adult, she used to plan to be somewhere special, doing something special, on her special day. Paris, Rome, San Francisco . . . and until the last year of her marriage, her husband had bought into that idea, too.

Tricia tightly held the chain at her neck and thought wistfully of those days.

Since nobody else was interested in her birthday, maybe she should do something to treat herself. There were day spas in Nashua, but that wasn't really her thing. She wasn't a clotheshorse, so a day trip to Boston for shopping wasn't something she'd aspire to, either. She couldn't really cook—and though Angelica had promised her what would probably be a gourmet meal, she did not want to celebrate her birthday with Bob Kelly. She needed nothing—any book she wanted she got as stock for her store, read it, and then it put on the sales floor. She needed nothing material, like jewelry or furniture.

If she was honest with herself, besides her parents and Angelica, there were only two people on the planet she would care to spend her special day with: her grandmother, who'd been dead for over twenty years, and . . . Christopher . . . neither of whom was available.

Birthdays were probably overrated, anyway. A baby emerged from the womb, and it was the mother who had suffered through pregnancy (an extremely difficult one, Tricia had always been told). Shouldn't it be the mother who was honored with cake, flowers, and gifts? Of course, the year Tricia had done just that, it hadn't been well received. For some reason, the unexpected child had never been able to please her parents the way that Angelica had charmed them.

Tricia let go of the chain, and the urge to discard the gift again surfaced—and yet she didn't rip it from around her neck. Something had spurred Christopher to send it. Maybe it was only guilt, but it had been the first contact he'd initiated since their split. She would not disregard that, but neither could she give it too much credence. It was what it was—only a locket and chain—but at least Christopher had thought fondly of her, and she could accept that at face value.

Tricia shook herself. She was getting maudlin in her old—or should she accept it as just middle?—age.

Never mind. She had two errands to run that morning—with both venues opening at nine o'clock. That gave her only an hour before Haven't Got a Clue opened at ten. She'd have to hurry. And she'd have to find time during the next day or so to canvass the Chamber of Commerce members to collect money in Jim's honor for his mother. Yet another chore: Tricia needed to get a card for them to sign, too. One more stop to put on her places-to-go list.

Tricia and Miss Marple descended the stairs to Haven't Got a Clue. Miss Marple deigned to check out the large square table in the reader's nook while Tricia opened the blinds that covered the large display window overlooking Main Street. She noted that a Sheriff's Department cruiser sat outside History Repeats Itself, with a deputy inside—probably guarding the site to keep rubberneckers away. Crime scene tape fluttered in the slight morning breeze. It surrounded not only what was left of Jim Roth's store, but was still tied to the buildings on either side of it. Booked for Lunch hadn't been affected, thank goodness. Angelica didn't need that headache on top of all her other worries.

The bank was Tricia's first stop that morning, where she deposited cash and checks for Haven't Got a Clue and Booked for Lunch. She'd have to make another run tomorrow for the Cookery. Or maybe she'd wait until Monday, to save wear and tear on the soles of her shoes. Next up was a stop at the Stoneham Library.

Tricia parked her car and retrieved a box of books from her trunk. Was it her imagination, or had they gained ten pounds since she'd put them in there the week before? Somehow she managed to close the trunk lid, and staggered up to the library entrance. Jabbing the Handicapped door opener, she swung around and entered the library.

Head librarian Lois Kerr caught sight of her and met her

halfway to the checkout desk. "My goodness, Tricia, is that another batch of books you're donating for our quarterly sale?"

"Yes. They came in a box lot from an auction I attended last week. Nothing very valuable, I'm afraid, but there are at least a dozen mainstreams by bestselling authors, as well as some big-name romances, so you should be able to sell them with no problem."

Lois smiled and shook her head. "If all the booksellers were as generous as you, we wouldn't have to worry about donations for these book sales, which wouldn't even be necessary if the Board of Selectmen would stop slashing our budget. Here, let me help you carry them to the conference room." She grabbed one side of the box, and the women did an awkward sideways shuffle to the book sale dumping ground.

They set the box on the floor next to several other cartons. The library had a long way to go until there were enough books to hold a sale. Tricia decided she'd ask Angelica if she could spare anything, and maybe she'd hit up Deborah Black at the Happy Domestic as well. And what was going to happen to the stock salvaged from Jim Roth's store?

"It's a shame what happened to Jim Roth," Lois said, as though reading Tricia's mind.

"Yes. I shudder every time I look out my store window. That big gap in the street reminds me of a front tooth missing from a beautiful smile."

"I'm sad to say I met Mr. Roth only a couple of times," Lois went on, "although his mother comes in quite frequently. I've spoken to her on a number of occasions, and helped her find new authors. Like you, she likes to read mysteries. Although. . . ." Lois frowned. "Several months ago, she asked me about poisons."

"Poisons?" Tricia repeated, taken aback.

"She said she'd seen something on television about cats and dogs dying because they found antifreeze and lapped it up. I helped her look up information on ethylene glycol."

Tricia had seen the same report. The chemical had a sweet taste, which attracted animals and small children—and the results were almost always fatal. An uncomfortable wariness swept through her as she thought about the bright yellow color of the lemon bar cookies Mrs. Roth had served her the day before. Mrs. Roth had mentioned that they were Jim's favorite treat.

Sanity prevailed, and Tricia again dismissed the notion. Jim had died from an explosion, not from ethylene glycol poisoning. But then . . . Mrs. Roth had said a few things that didn't quite feel right. She'd have to think about all this.

"I heard once the Sheriff's Department is finished investigating on site, they'll have to knock down whatever is left of the store," Lois went on.

"It's a shame," Tricia agreed. "It had one of the prettiest facades on Main Street. But it is dangerous to leave it as is. I heard several crashes during the night. I figured they were falling bricks or rafters or something."

Lois shook her head in sympathy.

Tricia glanced at her watch. "I'm sorry, Lois, but I'd best be on my way. I have just enough time to get a condolence card at the convenience store. I'm collecting money for Jim Roth's mother."

Lois beamed. "You are a dear. Will you let me contribute?"

"That would be very nice, thank you."

Lois stepped into her office, and came back a few moments later with a ten-dollar bill. "Will you sign my name on the card?"

"I'd be happy to," Tricia said, and tucked the money into the side pocket on her purse.

Lois walked her to the exit. "Thank you again for your generosity."

"It's my pleasure." Tricia gave a farewell wave as she headed for her car. She did have time to get that condolence card. But where would she find the time to contact all the Chamber of Commerce members?

One thing at a time, she told herself . . . *one thing at a time*.

NINE

 After a stop at the convenience store to pick up a condolence card, Tricia made it back to the municipal parking lot with a full ten minutes before she needed to open her store. While she'd been gone, the Sheriff's Department cruiser had departed, and a large Dumpster had appeared outside of History Repeats Itself, taking up almost three parking spaces, while the neck of a tall wrecking crane towered over the back of the building. Construction workers in hard hats tossed bricks and other rubble into the Dumpster, making a terrible clatter. She sighed. The sound of demolition was sure to put off more than just her customers, and she wondered how soon the wreckers could complete their task.

The lights were on in the Cookery, and the photographic version of Angelica was once again outside the shop door. This time, however, it was wearing a sombrero and a colorful serape. The note telling customers they could find Angelica's book inside was now pinned to the fabric.

Tricia knocked on the door. Stationed at the cash desk, Frannie looked up, gave her a wave, and rounded the counter to open the door. "Hi, Tricia, what brings you over so early?" The words were cheerful, but her expression was anything but. Frannie's eyes were swollen and bloodshot, no doubt from crying. And she wore her least cheerful aloha shirt—the black one with the solemn white calla lilies. Someone had once told Tricia the calla lily was a flower of death. Despite that, it was still her favorite.

Frannie didn't look like she needed another problem, but Tricia's first loyalty was to her sister. "Was there something you forgot to do yesterday?"

Frannie frowned, her brow furrowed in concentration. "I don't think so."

Tricia nodded toward the register.

"Oh, my goodness! I was supposed to give you yesterday's receipts, wasn't I?"

Tricia nodded.

"I'm so sorry. I locked them in the safe last night, and then just opened as usual this morning. Does Angelica know?"

"She did ask."

Frannie winced. "Am I in big trouble?"

Tricia shook her head. "No. But could you have them separated for me this evening? I'll need to go to the bank tomorrow."

"But won't Angelica be back on Friday?"

"Next Friday, but I don't think she'll have time to do much of anything, besides laundry, before she has to go back on the road. It's going to be a rough month, I'm afraid—for her and for us." By "us," she also meant Darcy and Jake. "I take it you haven't heard from Angelica? She did say she was going to call this morning."

"The phone hasn't rung yet."

Hmm. Angelica had said her car would be ready by nine. Perhaps she'd forgotten . . . .

Tricia jerked a thumb behind her, toward the door. "What happened to the cutout of Angelica?"

Frannie managed a laugh. "That's how I found it when I went to bring it in last night. Someone thought it was funny, I guess. But Angelica's book does feature some Tex-Mex and Mexican recipes, so I thought I'd just leave it as is. Do you want me to take them off now?"

Tricia sighed. "I wouldn't want it to offend anyone."

"Ah, good idea," Frannie said. "As soon as I get a chance, I'll put it back the way it was. But maybe I'll take a picture of it first," she said, with just the hint of mirth in her eyes.

"How're the plans for the memorial service going?" Tricia asked.

"Fine. I've booked the conference room at the Brookside Inn. Did you know they're in financial trouble? They've shut down the restaurant—at least part of the time."

"I hope you're kidding," Tricia said, remembering many fine meals she'd eaten there, and the excellent room service when she'd stayed at the inn prior to moving into her loft.

Frannie shook her head. "Nope."

"But where will we have our Chamber breakfasts?"

"They'll have to go back to the Bookshelf Diner, I guess." Which they both knew was really too small to accommodate the entire group.

"I convinced the inn to let us bring in the food for Jim's send-off, but they'll supply the tables, chairs, and linens and let us make coffee and tea. Of course, I had to sign a waiver in case anyone gets sick so the inn can't be sued, but I'm not worried about that. I've already asked Nikki Brimfield, and she said she'd bring a cake and maybe some fresh Danish. Do you think you could bring something—maybe a coffee cake?"

Tricia bake? "Um . . . sure." She'd have to see if she could order something from Nikki's Patisserie. She hadn't actually baked anything since earning her Girl Scout cooking badge way too many years before. "What time?"

"Ten. I asked Bob Kelly to speak, since he knew Jim the best—except for me, of course, but I don't think that would be fitting. Don't you agree?"

"Well, I—"

"But Bob turned me down flat. I don't understand it. I know he was angry about Jim's back rent, and now he's lost his building—but insurance should cover that."

What was the value of a historic building in the middle of a thriving business section, Tricia wondered.

"So who's going to speak?"

"I've asked Chauncey Porter from the Armchair Tourist. He used to talk to Jim at Chamber meetings, and they were next-door neighbors."

"Did he agree?"

Frannie nodded. "And he said he'd call all the other Chamber members to see if anyone had anecdotes. I'm afraid anything I'd have to say wouldn't be appropriate." For a brief second Frannie smiled, and then her eyes filled with tears. She grabbed a tissue from the box behind the counter. "I can't believe I'll never see Jim again."

The shop door opened, and a couple of middle-aged women entered the Cookery. Frannie turned away, struggling to regain her composure. She cleared her throat, opened her eyes wide, and plastered on a grin that would frighten a circus clown. "Welcome to the Cookery. Please let me know if you need any help." Her voice was high and tight, and for a moment Tricia was afraid the customers would flee. But then they turned and escaped to the anonymity of the parallel bookshelves.

"I'd better get going. I'll see you tonight, right?" Tricia said.

"Yes, of course." The phone rang, and Frannie picked it up. "The Cookery, Frannie speaking. How may I help you?"

Tricia gave a wave as she exited the shop and headed for her own store.

She walked slowly, remembering she hadn't yet called her attorney to talk about setting up a new mortgage for Ginny. She also wondered what Mr. Everett would think when he heard she was helping Ginny. Would he see it as favoritism, or perhaps expect some kind of equal treatment?

Tricia unlocked Haven't Got a Clue, turning the sign on the door to OPEN. Miss Marple jumped down from her vigil on the readers' nook's large, square coffee table and trotted across the shop to join her, jumping onto the display case's glass top. "*Yow,*" she announced.

"You said a mouthful," Tricia agreed as she petted the cat.

The door rattled, and Ginny entered. "Sorry I'm late," she called, and then looked at the clock, which said nine fifty-eight. "Almost late," she amended.

"You're just in time," Tricia said. "I was about to call my attorney about the mortgage."

Ginny stood there, mouth open, and then shook herself. "Good idea. Um, I have to get my apron," she said, and scooted for the back of the store.

"*Yow!*" Miss Marple exclaimed.

Again Tricia petted the cat. "No, she didn't seem very enthusiastic." Tricia shrugged it off. Maybe Ginny had had a bad night. The door opened once more, letting in the day's first customer. Ginny was still tying her apron, and intercepted the man before Tricia had a chance to greet him. It was just as well, as a Sheriff's Department cruiser slowed in front of Haven't Got a Clue, then pulled into an empty space in front of the Cookery. Captain Baker got out and looked toward what was left of History Repeats Itself before he turned back and walked toward Tricia's store.

"Well, well, well. Looks like we're about to have company," Tricia told the cat. Miss Marple just yawned. Tricia moved from behind the counter to stand in front of the big display window as she waited for Baker.

The little bell over the door tinkled cheerfully as Captain Baker entered, but his expression was anything but happy.

Tricia straightened—so much that her spine hurt. "What can I do for you today, Captain?"

"You could call me Grant," he said, removing his flat-brimmed hat. "You did for a while there."

The rod up her spine seemed to grow in girth. "Yes, well, times were different then, weren't they?" Why did she have to sound so . . . prissy?

"I wasn't happy with the way things ended between us," Baker said, his voice softening.

"I wasn't all that happy about it, myself." Good grief, if she looked in a mirror right now, she'd probably see Margaret Hamilton's green witch face from *The Wizard of Oz*.

"There's no chance Mandy and I will ever be together again, but until she fully recovers, I need to be there for her."

Tricia felt her fists clench and her jaw tighten. "That's very commendable of you."

Baker's eyes wandered, and he noticed Ginny was eavesdropping. He leaned in and lowered his voice. "Look, can we go somewhere and have coffee or something? I'd like to talk to you"—he shot a glance in Ginny's direction—"without an audience."

Tricia shrugged. "I suppose. The café across the street isn't open yet. How about the diner?"

"I was thinking of something a little more private. How about we get something from the Coffee Bean and take it to the park? It's a beautiful day—what do you say?"

Again, Tricia shrugged. She turned. "Ginny, I'm going out for a few minutes."

"Okay," she said brightly, and waggled her eyebrows. No doubt she'd pump Tricia for information the minute she returned.

Tricia felt the blush creep over her cheeks, and turned away before Captain Baker could notice.

They exited the store, crossed the street, and entered the Coffee Bean. The aroma of freshly ground—and brewed—coffee was heavenly. Captain Baker ordered for them, remembering exactly how Tricia liked hers, and paid for it. Then they left, heading for the park on the edge of town. On the way, their conversation was polite but halfhearted. As they passed the *Stoneham Weekly News*, Tricia surreptitiously glanced into the big display window. Russ was at his desk, on the phone. He looked up and caught her eye; she quickly looked away.

Captain Baker led her toward the grand gazebo, a large,

freestanding edifice of white-painted wood on a granite base. Its copper roof had gone a mellow green with age. Nearby was an empty forest green bench, where they sat.

"How's your investigation going?" Tricia asked.

"Not as well as I'd hoped, which is one reason I wanted to talk to you. I can't convince Bob Kelly to talk candidly. You know him well, and I hoped you could help me out."

She didn't know him all that well, but she wasn't up to denying it. "What's he not saying?"

"When I've tried to pin him down about the night of the explosion, he's been evasive. I want to know exactly what happened in the minutes before all hell broke loose."

"He hasn't exactly been candid with me or my sister, either. Frankly, she's worried. I know Jim was behind in his rent. Bob isn't the most forgiving landlord—not that I can speak from actual experience. I've always paid my rent on time."

"Do you know of anyone who held a grudge against Jim Roth?"

Tricia shook her head. "Why do you ask?"

"The gas meter behind the building may have been tampered with. I'm waiting to receive a detailed report from PSNH."

Tricia shook her head. The idea that Jim's death could have been premeditated was . . . well, rather shocking.

"What do you know about explosions?" Baker asked.

Tricia shrugged. "*Boom!* Destruction. That's about it."

Baker frowned. "There are several zones associated with an explosion. First is the pink zone. That's where Mr. Roth was virtually vaporized: the flash point. No one in the pink zone survives."

That wasn't news to Tricia. "Go on," she urged.

"Next is the yellow zone. Oddly enough, one can be

killed in this zone but the body may not have a mark on it."

"Why?"

"Because it's the shock wave from the explosion that kills them. Next up, the white zone, which contains a strong obstacle—in this case, a brick wall. The area behind it may or may not be safe, depending on how much falling debris there is. With multiple obstacles, you get multiple shock waves, going in all directions. But in this instance, the shock wave moved down the building, straight as a strike from a bowling ball."

"And that's why the building had to be taken down? This shock wave took out the load-bearing walls and the second and third floors?" Tricia asked.

Baker nodded. "After that is the blue zone. Bob Kelly was standing at the front of the store, at the far end of this zone, which is what saved him."

"Lucky Bob."

"Did Roth have an enemy—someone who might have been angry with him for any reason?" Baker asked.

"Well, sort of," Tricia hedged; she thought it over, and shook her head again.

"What? Tell me."

Tricia sighed, feeling like a rat for what she was about to say. "It seems Jim had a . . . girlfriend. Sort of."

"Sort of?" Baker asked.

"Frannie Armstrong. She manages the Cookery for my sister. But she loved Jim—I'm sure of it. It was his mother she held a grudge against."

"Why?"

"Because Jim wouldn't leave his mother to be with her."

"That could be a motive for murder," Baker agreed.

"Only if Frannie was that kind of person—which she isn't. And if she was, wouldn't she be more likely to go after his mother—not Jim?"

"People make stupid, impulsive mistakes—especially when there's passion involved."

Passion? Frannie and Jim? Somehow, Tricia couldn't imagine that. "Yes, but Frannie was at the Cookery, with three witnesses, at the time of the explosion."

"There was a buildup of gas before the explosion. Was Ms. Armstrong at the bookstore all day?"

Tricia opened her mouth to answer, but then stopped. "I couldn't say. When Angelica's not in the store, Frannie holds the fort. She's usually there from opening until closing. I sometimes wonder if she even takes bathroom breaks."

"Was your sister in the store on Wednesday?"

Tricia shrugged. "I know she was working on the food for her launch party, probably in her loft apartment. I don't know if she spent much time in the store that day."

Baker nodded. "Looks like I need to talk to your sister—and Ms. Armstrong."

"Please don't tell Frannie I told you about her relationship with Jim. Though she didn't actually tell me not to say anything, I don't think she expected me to sic the law on her."

Baker sipped his coffee. "It would've probably come up during the course of the investigation, anyway. Secrets rarely stay secret for long."

A young mother pushed a stroller down the sidewalk while her toddler waved and called "Bye-bye." Tricia waved back. Baker looked uncomfortable.

"Have you met Jim's mother? She seems like a charming lady—" Except for that rather nasty smile she'd flashed when she'd offered Tricia a lemon bar. Still, Tricia tried to be charitable. "And she's all alone in the world right now."

"I spoke to her, too. She was very cooperative, but she didn't mention her son had a lady friend."

"She may not have known," Tricia said, then remembered Frannie's comment on Jim becoming ill when they were supposed to have a date.

"I take it you weren't well acquainted with Jim Roth."

"No. I saw him at Chamber meetings, but I don't go all that often, and whenever we spoke, it was mostly small talk."

"Can you tell me *anything* about him?"

Tricia thought about it, then sighed. "He used to run parlays."

"Give me a for instance."

"When Deborah Black had her baby, Jim ran a parlay. You know those grid things—choose a date and put down a dollar. My sister had been in town only a week, and she won. I think he did them for sports events, too. You know— the Super Bowl, the Final Four. I never paid much attention because I don't like to gamble—even when it's only a couple of dollars. It seems like such a waste—unless you win, of course."

"Do you know when Roth ran the last one?"

Tricia shook her head. "My employee, Ginny, might. It seemed like she always entered. Do you think that could have had something to do with Jim's death?"

"Right now I'm open to any possibility." Baker drained his cup, got up, and tossed it into one of the park's trash cans.

Tricia stood to follow him.

"You've been very helpful, Tricia."

"If someone deliberately tampered with Jim's gas meter, I want you to catch whoever did it."

"Yes," Baker agreed. "There's always a chance Mr. Roth might not be the killer's only victim."

TEN

Ginny waited behind the door of Haven't Got a Clue. "Well, well?" she asked as Tricia entered.

"Well, what?"

"Captain Baker took you for coffee. Was it a date? Are you two getting back together?" she asked excitedly.

"It was not a date. Captain Baker was on duty. We talked about Jim's death. And I now know more about explosions than I ever cared to."

"Bummer," Ginny said, her shoulders slumping.

"Miss," came a voice from the cash desk. "I'm ready to check out now."

Tricia pushed up her sweater sleeves and headed for the register. The customer had made some good choices. Tess Gerritsen and P.D. James. As Tricia placed the customer's twenty into the cash drawer, she caught sight of Grace's check meant for Mrs. Roth. Jim's memorial was only two days away. If Tricia was going to solicit funds for his aged mother, she'd have to get started.

She bid her customer good-bye, told Ginny her plan, and struck out with her list of Chamber of Commerce members. Her first stop: the Armchair Tourist.

Chauncey Porter had been the second or third bookseller to come to Stoneham, and though Tricia had once loved to travel—before she owned a bookstore and was now unable to leave it for more than a day or so—she couldn't understand how Chauncey had kept afloat selling old atlases, maps, and Fodor guides. Or was it books by the likes of Bill Bryson, who mixed travel with observations on life, that sold the most? After all, the name of the store was the Armchair Tourist. Then again, it was probably Chauncey's amazing ability to spin a yarn and keep an audience entertained. He'd be perfect for reminding the mourners at Sunday's gathering what a great guy Jim was.

The Armchair Tourist was located next to what had been History Repeats Itself, and Tricia wondered how it had fared during and after the explosion. The crime scene tape was now gone, and she opened the door, greeted by the sound of an annoying buzz, not as friendly as the little bell that tinkled when a customer entered Haven't Got a Clue. Chauncey, a portly gent with a full head of white hair and somewhere on the high side of sixty, sat behind the main counter on a padded stool. He turned his gaze to check out his visitor, peering over the tops of his reading glasses. "Ah, Miss Tricia, always lovely to see you."

"It's good to see you, too, Chauncey. How's business?"

Chauncey looked around his empty shop. "Fair to middling. Of course, it didn't help that I lost a full day while they dismantled History Repeats Itself. But I suppose it could have been a lot worse."

Tricia looked around, but didn't see much in the way of damage. "Everything looks fine."

"It does, now. When they finally let me in yesterday, I found all the bookshelves against the south wall had toppled. Worse, I lost most of my back outside wall—and quite a bit of inventory. It's boarded over until the insurance company figures out what the settlement will be. Thank goodness I never let my insurance lapse when times were even leaner." He looked around his shop, which was not graced with customers. "Business will pick up once the children are out of school and their families go on vacation."

Tricia nodded. "I wish I could say I'm just here to visit, but I'm afraid it's on a more serious note."

"Yes, I wondered when you might come 'round to visit. I understand you're collecting for Jim Roth's elderly mother."

Word certainly got around. "Do you know her?"

"As a matter of fact, I met her only last week. She came in looking for information on Caribbean cruises. As it happened, I had just the book for her. A little dated, but the basic information is still viable. And I told her about my very first cruise—to the Greek Islands. It was back in seventy-eight, when I was a tour guide. There was this gaggle of giggling nuns who—"

"Yes, yes," Tricia interrupted, hoping to stave off an entire review of his decades-old vacation. "I wish I could hear all about it, but I really must—"

"I completely understand, my dear." Chauncey pushed a button on his cash register, and the drawer popped open. He pulled out a crisp ten-dollar bill and handed it to Tricia. "I'm sorry it couldn't be more, but with the way business is—"

Tricia added the money to her envelope. "I'm pleased

you're willing to help Mrs. Roth. I'm sure she'll be grateful, as well."

"Glad to be of help."

"I've got a card to sign," she said, and handed it to Chauncey. He read the sparse lines of text, and then picked out a pen from a holder on the counter, signing his name, and that of his shop, with a flourish before handing it back to Tricia.

"Will you be at the memorial service on Sunday?" Tricia asked.

"Miss Frannie has asked me to give the eulogy."

Oops! Tricia had forgotten that. "Then I'll see you there," she said, and sketched a wave.

Chauncey gave Tricia a smile and a return wave, and resumed his reading as she backed out the door.

One down, more than ten to go. It was going to be a long morning.

Tricia visited all the shops on the west side of Main Street, save for the Happy Domestic, which seemed to be inundated with customers. She'd try that later. The morning was quickly evaporating, so she also skipped the *Stoneham Weekly News*, the Chamber of Commerce office, and Kelly Realty. She'd catch up with them later.

Crossing the street, she made the Stoneham Patisserie her next stop on her whirlwind charity tour of Stoneham. So far, the standard donation was ten dollars. She'd thought the other Chamber members would have been more generous—but then she was hesitant to judge. She didn't know what difficulties they were experiencing nor what their bottom lines could stand to lose.

Tricia entered Stoneham's only bakery, inhaling deeply of the aroma of fresh-baked bread, which was almost strong enough to lift her off her feet. Nikki Brimfield, the Patisserie's owner, gave Tricia a quick wave as she finished waiting on a customer, and Tricia turned her attention to the delights in Nikki's glass showcases. She was an artist with a pastry bag: cupcakes that looked like frogs—for boys?—and sunflowers—for girls and their moms. Scones, apple turnovers, chocolate and coconut cakes, and at least ten different kinds of cookies were enough to keep anyone chained to their treadmills and exercise bikes for the rest of their lives.

Nikki bid her customer adieu and turned to Tricia. "Great to see you, Trish. What can I get you today? Raspberry thumbprint cookies? Chocolate chips? Our oatmeal raisin cookies are made with whole wheat flour—extra good for you."

"How about a dozen—four of each of those you mentioned?"

"Coming right up." Nikki took a partially put together bakery box from a stack on the shelf.

"We haven't had a chance to speak since History Repeats Itself blew up the other night," Tricia said.

"Wasn't that awful? Poor Jim," Nikki said, grabbing a piece of baker's tissue and placing four oatmeal cookies into the box.

"I'm collecting money to help out Jim's elderly mother. She's all alone, and she depended on Jim's income."

"Oh, dear," Nikki said, and finished filling the box. She tucked in the lid and then grabbed a piece of string from the holder that hung from the ceiling. With a few quick moves, she tied the box and broke the string, pushing the box toward Tricia, who already had her wallet out. She handed Nikki a ten.

Nikki rang up the sale, handed Tricia the change, and then she dipped back into the cash drawer and withdrew Tricia's ten, handing it back to her. "This is for Jim."

"Thank you. Would you like to sign the card?"

"Sure." Nikki took the card, scribbled her name and the Patisserie on it, and handed it back to Tricia.

"I hope you'll make it to the gathering on Sunday at the Brookview."

"I wouldn't miss it—even if it is my only day off," Nikki said. "Besides, I have to deliver and set up the cake that Frannie ordered."

Tricia frowned. Set up a cake? That sounded pretty elaborate for a memorial service, but she decided not to question it. "I'll see you there. And thank you for helping Mrs. Roth."

"Not a problem," Nikki said cheerfully, and missed Tricia's wince at that expression.

Tricia made one more stop, at Have a Heart, the home of used and out-of-print romance novels, where the owner, Joyce Widman, made yet another ten-dollar donation to the cause.

Tricia tiptoed past the Cookery, grateful Frannie was fully occupied. It wasn't likely she would want to contribute to Mrs. Roth's fund, and Tricia wasn't sure how she was going to break the news to her that she'd been collecting for someone Frannie considered an archenemy.

Feet dragging, Tricia made it back to Haven't Got a Clue. Ginny had gone to lunch, and Mr. Everett was helping a customer when Tricia stowed the collected money and signed card under the cash drawer, deciding she'd call the last three prospects on her list. If they were interested in donating, she'd make a point to get over to collect the cash. If they weren't . . . .

Tricia timed her call to the *Stoneham Weekly News* for when she knew Russ would be out to lunch. She'd let his office manager/stringer/custodian pass along the news. She tried Bob's realty office, and wasn't surprised to get his answering machine. She left a message, but didn't expect a reply. Bob wasn't likely to contribute to a fund for Mrs. Roth when her son had owed him thousands of dollars in back rent, although maybe there was a chance he'd forgive that bad debt and not go after the estate to collect it. Then again, Bob hadn't become the most successful business-man in Stoneham by being softhearted.

Ever efficient, Betsy Dittmeyer, secretary/reception-ist at the Chamber of Commerce, answered the phone on the second ring. "Hi, Betsy. It's Tricia Miles from Haven't Got a Clue. I'm collecting money for Jim Roth's elderly mother. As Jim was a Chamber member—"

"He was not," Betsy said, her voice hard.

"I beg your pardon?" Tricia asked.

"Mr. Roth failed to pay his dues in January. At the time of his death, he was not a member of the Stoneham Cham-ber of Commerce."

"Oh, well—"

"May I remind you that the Chamber is not a charity, and we don't make donations frivolously."

"I believe Jim was the first bookseller to join the Cham-ber. He was a member in good standing for at least four years. Doesn't that make a difference?"

"As I said, the Chamber is not a charity. *Rules* are *rules*."

If Frannie was still the face of the Chamber, she wouldn't have been so coldhearted. She would have found some way to find the funds. Then again, Frannie hated Jim's mother and would probably be upset if she'd been asked to do so.

Goodness, what a tangled web . . . .

It was with relief that Tricia put down the phone and went back to the business of bookselling. As she rang up

yet another sale, she noted the titles and decided the day
was turning out to be some kind of Travis McGee love fest.
She'd already sold five or six copies of John D. MacDon-
ald's most popular books. That the author had been dead at
least two decades was a testament to the popularity of his
writing. She made a mental note to check the storeroom for
more copies of his work, and would do it once Ginny got
back from her lunch break.

"Thanks for shopping with us," she told her customer,
and handed her the sturdy paper shopping bag. Before the
woman made it out the door, the phone rang. Tricia picked
up the receiver. "Haven't Got a Clue, this is Tricia. How
can I—?"

"Tricia, this is Frannie. Did you tell that guy from the
Sheriff's Department about Jim and me?"

Oh, dear. "Um . . . it may have come up in conversation.
Why?"

"He came into the store a couple of hours ago. I've been
so busy, this is the first chance I've had to call and ask you
about it." And, from the sound of it, she'd been stewing
about it ever since.

"I'm sorry, Frannie. He asked me to tell him everything
I knew about Jim. You wouldn't have wanted me to lie,
would you?"

"Of course not. But did you have to volunteer *that* piece
of information?"

"Yes, I did. But I also told him you're practically chained
to the store, and that I didn't believe for a moment you
were capable of hurting anyone."

"You're darn right." Tricia heard the bell over the Cookery's door go off. "Gotta go," Frannie said, and hung up.

No sooner had Tricia put the receiver down than the phone
rang again. "Haven't Got a Clue, this is Tricia, how—?"

"Jake's already left for the day," Darcy cried. "I'm all alone with a bunch of customers screaming for their food!"

Tricia glanced at the clock. "But it's only one thirty. Booked for Lunch is open until at least two."

"I know. What do I do? I can't cook *and* wait on tables. If you can come over and take care of customers, I think I can handle the food for half an hour. Will you? Please, Tricia, please!"

Tricia glanced around her store filled with customers. Ginny was still at lunch, but luckily Mr. Everett was working that afternoon. She sighed. "I'll be right over." It took all her self-control not to slam the phone into its cradle. Damn that Jake!

"Another emergency over at Booked for Lunch?" Mr. Everett guessed.

"It doesn't seem to stop."

"Go on. We'll be fine," he assured her.

Tricia ditched her Haven't Got a Clue name tag and headed for the door. "I'll be back when I can."

No wonder Darcy was in a panic—the café was packed. As soon as Tricia entered, Darcy practically threw her order pad at Tricia and fled into the kitchen.

Tricia made a quick circuit around the dining room, verifying orders and refilling coffee cups. The patrons' mood was impatient, but no one seemed on the verge of exploding into a rage—yet. Tricia pushed open the double doors to the kitchen. "What can I do?"

Wielding a wicked-looking knife, Darcy sliced a lettuce-filled sandwich in half, tossed a pickle spear and a handful of chips onto the plate, and shoved it forward on the counter, where it joined another sandwich-filled plate. "These are for table four." She plunged a ladle into a large pot of soup. "We usually serve the soup first, but I need to be in Nashua by three—let's get these people fed and out of here!"

Tricia eased the bowls and plates onto a large plastic tray, hefted it, and backed out of the kitchen—and straight into one of the disgruntled customers. The tray went flying, sending scalding soup, bread, lettuce, tuna, and pastrami sailing into the air to splatter the walls and floor.

"Was that my lunch?" an overweight man demanded, his mustard-stained shirt straining at the seams.

Darcy began to wail.

"Sir, we're shorthanded and we're doing the best we can. Please sit down."

"I've been waiting fifteen minutes for my sandwich. I demand to see the manager."

"You're looking at her. Or at least the acting manager," Darcy said with a nod toward Tricia.

"I'm sorry you had to wait," Tricia said, trying to keep an edge from rising in her voice. "If you'll let us get back to work, we'll have your meal to you as soon as we can."

Darcy abandoned her work space and grabbed a mop, tears still streaming down her cheeks.

"I want my lunch comped," the man demanded.

"I'll ask you again nicely, sir, please take your seat."

He straightened, his jaw jutting forward. "And if I don't?"

"Then I'll ask you to leave."

"Don't bother." He turned to face the other customers. "I'm not waiting another minute for my food. Come on, Mabel, let's get out of this dump!"

Tricia pushed though the door to watch the man depart, his red-faced companion slinking out behind him.

Darcy scooped up the bread and sandwich meat, and tossed it into the trash.

"Wash your hands and start over again," Tricia said kindly.

Darcy nodded. "What table was that guy at?"

Tricia looked out at the dining room. "Four."

"That *was* his lunch," Darcy said, and went back to work.

Within fifteen minutes, all the customers had been served. The clock was edging toward two, and Darcy was looking antsy. "Now that things are under control, can you please tell me what happened and why Jake left in a huff?" Tricia asked.

Darcy looked away, squirming as she covered what was left of a head of lettuce with plastic wrap. "We kind of had a little tiff."

"About what? And I sure hope it wasn't loud enough to be heard by the customers."

"We're not *that* dumb," Darcy countered. She opened the fridge and placed the lettuce and luncheon meats inside. "It was *all* Jake's fault. He took at least four smoke breaks in two hours. The orders were piling up and the customers were getting cranky. I had to keep apologizing. I sure didn't want them to think it was *me* goofing up."

Tricia found herself grinding her teeth. Something about Jake had always rubbed her the wrong way. Was he deliberately acting up just because Angelica was away?

Darcy scraped a plate of uneaten food into a slop bucket. "You know, I have to give Angelica a lot of credit for giving people second chances."

"Oh?" Tricia said, handing Darcy another stack of dirty dishes.

"I'm talking about Jake, of course," Darcy said nonchalantly, and the gleam in her eye told Tricia she was ready to dish.

"Jake?" Tricia repeated. She didn't have to play innocent.

"He was convicted of a felony. He's not even allowed to vote, but Angelica depends on him to cook for her customers. That's what I call real trust."

"Why? Do you think he'd tamper with the food?"

"Oh, no. It's just. . . ." She leaned in, and lowered her voice. "If he's capable of breaking the law—what else is he capable of?"

"I guess that would depend on what he was convicted of. Do you know?"

Darcy shook her head. "Jake didn't actually tell me this. I heard him on the phone talking to his parole officer."

"Angelica has an eye for detail. I'm sure if she hired Jake, she knows all about his background." *And why didn't she tell me?* Probably because Tricia read too many mysteries, and not only would worry, but probably would have tried to talk Angelica out of hiring Jake. After all, these days the unemployment pool had plenty of acceptable candidates who didn't have criminal records. Then again, it was commendable that she'd help someone down on his luck. Angelica hadn't always had that reputation.

Darcy was still talking, and Tricia picked up on the word "explosion." She hadn't been paying attention. "I'm sorry. I must have zoned out for a second."

"I was saying that it's too bad about the guy who got killed. What was his name?"

"Jim Roth," Tricia supplied.

"Yeah, him. They say he was killed immediately. That he didn't suffer."

"Mmm," Tricia agreed.

"But man, what a way to go," Darcy said. She didn't sound at all sorry for poor Jim. But then, she probably hadn't even seen, let alone met, the man. Darcy didn't seem like a read-for-pleasure kind of person—and certainly didn't seem the type to visit a history store that specialized in military nonfiction.

"Have you heard from Angelica?" Darcy asked.

"Yes, last night. She said she'd been calling the café for updates."

"Yeah, I talked to her a couple of times. She hasn't been real chatty, though."

"She has a lot on her mind," Tricia said.

Darcy glanced at the clock as she pushed the slop bucket to one side. "I'm outta here."

"Wait—I don't know what to do. I mean, I can clean up—but I don't know where anything goes. And what about the rest of the dishes and all the pots and pans?"

"I'm sorry, Tricia," Darcy said, already untying her apron, "but I really need to leave. I'll finish busing the tables, and clear off the counter. The rest is common sense."

"Can you at least show up early tomorrow to make sure things are set up properly?"

"I'll try."

"And what about Jake? Is he likely to show at all?"

"I sure hope so. I don't know how to make soup. Usually Angelica starts it and Jake finishes. Without either of them—there goes half our menu." Soup and a scoop—of egg, tuna, or crab salad—and soup and half a sandwich were the core of Angelica's lunchtime offerings.

Darcy sidled past Tricia and entered the dining room.

Tricia surveyed the tiny kitchen. She'd need to mop the floor and wash the walls, wash all the dishes, then start on the dining room. She looked down at her pretty peach sweater and felt like crying. It was already stained with mustard and soup. Goodness knows how many more splotches would dot it before she was done. And it would take hours for her to tackle this mess alone.

She marched over to the wall phone, punched in a number, and waited for someone to answer.

"Haven't Got a Clue, this is Ginny. How can I help you?"

"Have you ever aspired to have dishpan hands?" Tricia asked hopefully.

ELEVEN

The first thing Tricia did upon returning to Haven't Got a Clue was to hunt down the list of emergency numbers Angelica had left for her. Naturally, Jake's number immediately rolled over to voice mail. He did, after all, leave Booked for Lunch for his regular job at a French bistro in Nashua. It took all her willpower to remain calm as she left a message asking him to call her at his earliest convenience. She couldn't afford to alienate him—not with Angelica out of town and Darcy unable to cope in the kitchen. But knowing he had a criminal record had really upset her, and she needed to know what the man had done—and, as Darcy had hinted—might be capable of.

The shop door opened, the little bell above it ringing cheerfully, but instead of a customer, Tricia's friend and fellow bookseller Deborah Black, owner of the Happy Domestic, stepped inside. "Hi, Tricia. I hear you've become a collections officer," she said, waving a piece of paper. She slapped it down on the glass display case. A check.

"Hello, yourself. And what are you talking about?" Tricia asked.

Deborah batted at the ends of her long, dark hair, tossing it over her left shoulder. "Grace Harris stopped by my store this morning. Oops, I mean Grace Everett. I keep forgetting she remarried. Anyway, she said you were taking up a collection for Jim Roth's mother, and I wanted to contribute."

"That's very sweet of you," Tricia said, and instantly felt guilty. For a moment she'd almost forgotten she was spearheading the campaign. And worried what Frannie would say when she found out. "I canvassed the other shopkeepers, but you looked inundated when I was making my rounds."

"I had a great morning. Wish they were all like that. So tell me, how did you get roped into becoming a collections officer?"

"I feel so sorry for the old lady—all alone in the world."

"Have you met her?" Deborah asked.

"Yes, yesterday, in fact," Tricia said, without elaborating. She was still a bit unnerved by the visit.

"I heard she didn't have enough money for a funeral, the poor dear. Maybe this will help."

"I'm sure she'll be very grateful." Time to change the subject. "What are you doing out of harness?"

"Sometimes I think I'll go crazy if I have to spend another whole day at the store. Luckily, my mother helps out now and then. Today's one of those days. Except she has to bring Davey"— Deborah's toddler son—"with her. He's napping right now, or else I'd be trapped. Would you believe David"—Deborah's husband—"wants to talk about having more kids? Not with me!" Deborah had been more than a little stressed since Davey's birth, as evidenced by the perpetual dark circles under her eyes. When the economy took a downturn, she'd had to let go her part-time employee, which made her a virtual slave to her store. Tricia didn't envy her.

"Would you like a cup of coffee? Maybe that'll perk you up," Tricia suggested.

Deborah laughed. "It's only caffeine that keeps me going." Her smile wavered, and then her face crumpled and she began to sob.

Tricia hurried around the counter and gave her friend a hug. "What's wrong? Can I help?" Deborah cried even louder.

Tricia pulled back and guided Deborah to the readers' nook, where they sat.

Ginny appeared. "Can I help?' she asked, concerned.

"Please get Deborah some coffee," Tricia whispered. "And a tissue."

Ginny nodded, and took off.

Deborah's sniffling had begun to slow, and she wiped a hand at her eyes. "I'm sorry to dump on you like this, Tricia. I didn't mean to." Deborah looked around the store, and seemed relieved her meltdown hadn't been witnessed by a crowd of customers.

"Don't worry about it. Now, tell me all about it."

"I don't think I can handle it much longer. David won't help at the store. My mother sees more of my child than I do. I'm a complete and utter failure," she managed before the tears began again.

"That isn't true," Tricia said. "Is your store in the red?"

Deborah shook her head. "No. But—"

"You're going through a rough time right now. We all are—"

"*You* managed to hold on to your employees," Deborah accused.

Tricia leaned in and lowered her voice. "I've had to dip into my savings." Well, that wasn't exactly true, but Deborah didn't need to know the details of Tricia's financial situation.

Ginny reappeared with a large Haven't Got a Clue cardboard coffee cup, a couple of cookies, and a wad of napkins. "Here, Deborah. You need to eat something, then you'll feel better. They're Nikki's famous raspberry thumbprints."

"Thank you, Ginny." Deborah blew her nose on one of the napkins, took a sip of coffee, and nibbled on a cookie.

"Maybe this is a problem we should bring up at the next Chamber meeting," Tricia suggested. "You're not the only shopkeeper in Stoneham who's had to let an employee go."

"That's right," Ginny piped up. "I feel lucky to still have a job, and I know Mr. Everett feels the same."

Now there was an idea. Mr. Everett was looking for more hours, and Deborah needed help but had no money. Maybe Tricia could do a labor loan—pay Mr. Everett to give Deborah a few hours of help a week. That sounded good, but Tricia also knew Deborah was proud—and stubborn, like Mr. Everett—and might not accept what she considered to be charity. Tricia would have to figure out a way to make it happen. In the meantime, all she could do was listen as Deborah vented her frustration with her husband, the paperwork running a business entailed, and the fear she was missing the best years of motherhood.

By the time Deborah left Haven't Got a Clue, she'd calmed down, and promised not to have another sobfest the next time she and Tricia met.

"Gosh, maybe it's lucky I haven't had the time or money to open my own store," Ginny said, her voice hushed. "I didn't realize it could be so overwhelming." She faced Tricia. "You and Angelica always manage to meet all your obligations, whether it's family or business. With everything that's happened in the past eighteen months, you two don't let things get you down."

Tricia managed a weak laugh. She wasn't about to discuss the pitiable state of her love life with Ginny. "I don't know about Angelica, but I'm a good actress."

Ginny chewed at her lip, looking pensive.

"It's a balancing act, Ginny. Some days are easier—less hectic—than others." This was not one of those easy days. To prove that, an Apollo tour bus drove down Main Street. "Why don't you check the coffeepot. Look's like we're about to get hit with another crowd of customers."

The rest of the day alternated between customer overload and nothing to do. But Tricia knew that when it came time to tally the day's receipts, she'd be one very happy shopkeeper.

"See you tomorrow," Ginny said, and headed out the door. As she left, Frannie entered, carrying a small Cookery shopping bag with handles. "Here're the receipts for yesterday and today, along with the register tapes."

"Thanks, Frannie," Tricia said, and took the bag. Thankfully, Frannie seemed to have gotten over her snit about Tricia's conversation with Captain Baker.

"I heard you're collecting money for Jim's mother," Frannie said, her voice tinged with scorn.

Then again . . . .

Tricia let out a guilty laugh. "It was a kind of spur-of-the-moment thing. I mentioned to Grace Everett how Mrs. Roth told me she needed Jim's income to survive, and Grace kind of set the ball rolling."

"Grace is a nice person, but she has no clue about the *real* Olivia Roth." Frannie leaned in closer, her eyes narrowing. "It turns out Mrs. Roth had a very big insurance policy on Jim."

"How did you find that out?"

"I'm not at liberty to tell. Suffice to say someone overheard her conversation with Billie Hanson over at the Bank of Stoneham. Mrs. Roth arranged to have the money deposited directly into her account and to have Billie call her when it arrived."

"That's interesting."

Frannie's eyes narrowed. "*Very* interesting. Especially since the old biddy has been going around town telling everyone how destitute she is."

Tricia sighed. She'd never heard Frannie speak with such spite. "It can take months before the insurance company releases the death benefits. How is she supposed to live?" she asked, reasonably.

"She's got her husband's Social Security and some investments. If she was really hard up, she could put the house up for sale. It's in her name."

Tricia frowned, remembering Mrs. Roth's living room. "I got the impression the house belonged to Jim."

Frannie shook her head. "Poor Jim never had a pot to piss in. He was a terrible money manager, which is one of the reasons his store was in trouble. He wanted his mother to take out a home equity loan so he could pay off his creditors, but she refused. He said they'd argued about it more than once."

Did repeated disagreements over money give Mrs. Roth a motive for murder? No, Tricia refused to believe that little old lady could hurt a fly, let alone kill her only child—and her only living relative. At least, not in such a violent manner.

Not when poisoned lemon bars could do the trick.

"I know what you're thinking, Tricia, and you're wrong. Mrs. Roth is not a nice person. She kept Jim under her thumb his entire life. Until he started his own business, he never really had a life."

"Where did he get the money to open History Repeats Itself?"

Frannie exhaled a deep breath. "His mother."

"So she was one of his creditors?"

"His biggest," Frannie sheepishly admitted.

"Then why didn't she bail him out? Keeping the store afloat would've been in her best interest."

"Not as long as I was in the picture. Jim as much as said so."

Or was that what Frannie wanted to believe?

"I wonder if I should give Captain Baker a call and tell him about that insurance policy," Frannie said.

Tricia swallowed. "If you feel you must."

Frannie nodded, and changed the subject—for which Tricia was truly grateful. "I heard from Angelica. She's very worried about Bob. She wants me to offer to help him with whatever he might need. I haven't so far. He'd turn me down flat."

"You worked closely with him for over ten years," Tricia pointed out. "Angelica probably thinks you can read his mind."

"Sometimes I believed I could. But we were hardly

friends. And I can't say I hold any warm feelings for him after the way he treated me at my job at the Chamber. And especially after the threats he made against Jim."

"Threats?" Tricia asked.

Frannie's cheeks colored. "I didn't mean physical threats—but to evict him from his store. That probably would've killed Jim in itself," she said bitterly.

"Then you don't think he's responsible for Jim's death?"

"Of course not. Bob never dirties his hands on anything. And he definitely wouldn't do anything where he might actually get hurt, like cause an explosion. He used to whine when he got a paper cut, so second-degree burns must've really put a twist in his boxers."

"Did Captain Baker ask you about Bob?"

Frannie nodded. "Of course."

"Did you tell him everything you just told me?"

"Maybe not everything," Frannie admitted. "If he thinks Bob might've killed Jim, then he won't be considering me as a suspect."

Until that moment, Tricia wouldn't have thought so, either. But now . . . she wasn't so sure.

Once Frannie had left, Tricia emptied her cash register, counted the day's receipts, and put the receipts from Booked for Lunch into the sack along with those from the Cookery. Should she do bookwork, or have a bite to eat and read for a couple of hours? Yes, she had Julia Spencer-Fleming's new Clare Fergusson mystery sitting on her nightstand, just begging to be started. She stowed the money in the safe under the cash desk and spun the lock, intending to take care of it in the morning.

"Come on, Miss Marple—we can always do the paper-work in the morning, right?"

Miss Marple rose and stretched, then jumped down from the shelf behind the cash desk, where she'd spent the bulk of her day. Tricia was heading for the stairs that led to her loft when the phone rang. She wasn't going to answer it, but then considered that it might be Angelica calling, and headed back for the cash desk and picked up the receiver. "Haven't Got a Clue—"

"Tricia? It's Russ. I was just listening to my police scanner—"

Tricia winced. His scanner had been the main reason for the lack of a reconciliation between them. Okay, him dumping her had been the main reason—but it had been her main reason for not missing him all that much.

"There's a break-in in progress at Bob Kelly's house," he continued. "Are you interested?"

"Am I!"

"Lock up and meet me in the municipal parking lot." The line went silent. Tricia slammed the phone down, grabbed her keys and sweater. "Sorry, Miss Marple, but dinner will be a little late tonight."

Tricia flew for the exit, fumbled with the lock, then yanked the door shut behind her. Up ahead, Russ was already dashing across Main Street, heading for the munici-pal lot, and she jogged up the sidewalk, wishing she'd had time to change into running shoes.

Russ had already started his truck by the time Tricia caught up and jumped into the passenger seat. Her teeth nearly rattled as Russ shoved the vehicle in gear and took off with a squeal of tires. "Why are you so interested in Bob's house being broken into?" she asked.

"So far he's the only viable suspect in the Roth murder.

And if it wasn't him—" The pickup rounded the corner at a dangerous speed.

"You think the real killer's going after Bob?" Tricia asked.

"It's possible. Either that, or Bob's just a wuss scared by what happened and is taking no chances."

"How do you know it was Bob who called in?"

"I don't."

Bob's house loomed into view. Every light—inside and out—seemed to be switched on. Bob, clad in boxers and a T-shirt, stood on his front porch, shotgun in hand, looking down the darkened road. Behind him, a window gaped, its glass missing.

Russ's truck bounced to a halt at the curb. He opened his door and jumped out, with Tricia only seconds behind him.

"Did you see him?" Bob shouted.

"See who?"

"Someone was trying to break into my house." Bob pointed north. "He ran in that direction."

"Are you sure it was a guy?" Russ asked.

Bob hesitated. "Pretty sure."

"Are you okay?" Tricia asked.

Bob nodded. He had removed his bandages, and the skin on his arms was tight, red, and shiny. Beads of sweat covered his forehead, and he seemed to wince every time he moved.

They all turned as the sound of a wailing police siren broke the twilight calm. "Better late than never," Bob groused.

A Sheriff's Department cruiser rounded the corner and screeched to a halt just inches from Russ's bumper, arriving much quicker than the average twenty minutes the Dexter twins had mentioned in their pitch for a Stoneham police force. Captain Baker bounded out of the vehicle, his hand resting on his open pistol holster. "What's going on?"

"The bad guy got away," Tricia said, crossing her arms to ward off the encroaching night's chill.

"Someone tried to break into my house," Bob said, indicating the broken window.

Several of Bob's neighbors had turned on their porch lights, and a few of them had gathered on their lawns to see what the trouble was.

"How tall was he? What was he wearing?" Baker asked.

"I couldn't say how tall. Jeans and a black leather jacket. A black motorcycle helmet, too."

Russ, pen in hand, was madly scribbling in his steno notebook.

"But you said he took off on foot?" Baker looked at all of them. "Did you hear a motorcycle start up?"

They all shook their heads. "I'm going to call it in," Baker said, and headed back to his cruiser.

"I'm going to talk to the neighbors," Russ said, and took off at a trot.

Bob had taken a seat on one of the white wicker chairs on his porch. His upper lip was beaded with sweat. Tricia couldn't help but feel sorry for him. "Is there anything I can do for you, Bob?"

"No! And I wish everybody would stop asking me that. If I wanted help, I'd ask."

Tricia's mouth dropped in shock.

Bob looked panicky. "I'm sorry, Tricia. I didn't mean to take it out on you. It's just—" He sighed. "Please don't tell Angelica. About this attempted break-in or that I yelled at you. She's not very happy with me right now, and I don't want to make her even angrier."

"She's just worried about you. We all are."

"Thank you," he said grudgingly.

Baker returned from his cruiser, looking annoyed. He nodded toward Russ, who was still talking to one of Bob's neighbors. "I thought you two broke up."

"We did, but that doesn't mean we can't talk to each other. Besides, why do you care? It's not like you and I are going out." *Or ever will*, she stopped herself from saying aloud. "How come you showed up instead of one of your deputies?"

"I should be asking you what business you've got being here."

"I'm a citizen. Bob is a friend. I was concerned."

"And how did you know he needed a friend right now?"

Tricia tossed her head in Russ's direction. "Russ has a police scanner. He called to tell me. Your turn to answer my question."

Baker frowned. "I like to take on a patrol now and then. Especially after there's been trouble. Seems like Stoneham has had more than its fair share this last year or so."

"Well, don't blame me."

"I wasn't going to," he snapped back.

"No, but I'll bet Sheriff Adams would like to try."

"She hasn't even mentioned your name—at least not lately."

"I suppose I should be thankful for that."

Look at them—two adults acting like kids bickering on the playground. Did that mean they still had some feelings for each other? Hard to believe—they'd barely had time to develop feelings before the captain had called a halt to their budding friendship.

Russ walked across the dewy lawn and rejoined them.

"None of the neighbors seem to have seen anything," he told Bob, ignoring Captain Baker.

"Are you questioning my word?" Bob accused.

"Not at all—just stating what I was told."

Bob had the grace to look embarrassed. "Sorry, Russ. It's been one hell of a few days."

Russ waved a hand in dismissal. "Not a problem."

Tricia's fists clenched, and she felt like bashing Russ. He turned to her. "You about ready to leave?"

Tricia turned to Captain Baker. "May I go?"

"I wasn't keeping you."

She frowned. "No, you weren't." She turned to Bob. "See you later, Bob." He didn't bother to answer.

Another Sheriff's Department cruiser pulled up next to Baker's, and the captain followed Russ and Tricia across the street.

Russ climbed in the truck, yanking his door shut with a bang. Judging by his expression, he was annoyed that she'd taken time to speak with Baker. That didn't please Tricia. No way did she want him to feel proprietary toward her. Those days were gone. For good.

Tricia got in the passenger side, pulled the door shut, and grabbed her seat belt.

Russ glared at her. "Getting chummy with Captain Baker again?" he asked coldly.

"No. Not that it's any of your business."

He stabbed the key into the ignition, then let his hand fall to his lap. "Look, I'm sorry. I didn't mean to sound so—"

"Possessive?" Tricia offered, still ticked.

"Yes."

Tricia let out a breath. "You're forgiven." *This time*.

"I guess old habits die hard," he said quietly.

She forced herself to look at him. He really did look sorry, but she wanted to avoid talking about their old relationship or the possibility of starting over again. "Did you learn anything from the neighbors?"

"Like I said, no one seems to have seen a thing. Bob's next-door neighbor was inside with the TV blaring—she didn't hear any glass breaking. They say they heard Bob shouting, but didn't see anyone running away."

"What are you thinking? That Bob staged this break-in?"

"It's a possibility. If Baker thinks he's a suspect, it might be a way of deflecting suspicion."

"Suspicion of what? Jim's death?"

Russ nodded.

Tricia shook her head. "If he wanted to do that, wouldn't he have waited until it was full dark outside?"

"If he's still on pain meds, he might not be thinking clearly," Russ countered.

That was a possibility. Still . . . .

The other deputy got out of his car and walked up to the nearest neighbor's house, while Captain Baker crossed the street, heading back for Bob's.

Russ touched Tricia's arm, startling her. "Tricia, isn't there any way I can make things right between us?"

Tricia exhaled a breath and looked out the passenger-side window. Captain Baker was talking to Bob once again. If she was honest, she *was* lonely. But she wasn't lonely enough to settle for just anyone, and Russ was definitely a settle-for candidate.

"I'm sorry, Russ, we just weren't meant to be together. It would be easier on both of us if you accepted that."

Russ pursed his lips, grasped the key, and started the engine. "Be that way."

They didn't speak again until Russ had pulled up in front of Haven't Got a Clue. "I'm not giving up on you, Tricia. I think you're worth the heartache you've caused me."

Tricia opened her mouth to reply, then shut it. Apparently there was nothing she could say to deter him. She unbuckled her seat belt, opened the door, and got out of the truck. "Good night, Russ."

Without a backward glance, she entered her store and closed and locked the door. It was only then that she heard the sounds of the engine rev and tires squealing as Russ peeled off.

TWELVE

Tricia had finished totaling receipts for Haven't Got a Clue, Booked for Lunch, and the Cookery hours ago, and once again the café's receipts didn't match the cash in the register. She'd have to bring it up to Angelica again, and hope her sister would take the news more seriously. Her conversation with Russ had left her too unsettled for sleep. *She'd* caused *him* heartache? The man was absolutely clueless.

Miss Marple watched with a distinct lack of interest as Tricia paced her living room for the hundredth time. She'd hoped to find a message from Angelica on her voice mail when she'd returned from Bob's house, but there was none. She could have called Angelica's cell phone, or even the hotel, she supposed, but she didn't. Tricia's news about Bob would only upset Angelica—and so would her news about Russ.

She made another circuit of the room. Her encounter

with Russ had left her too rattled even to read, and reading had always been her escape. Another strike against the man.

There must be something she could do to occupy herself until she felt sleepy.

She wandered from the living room into the bedroom that overlooked Main Street. From this vantage point, she could see the empty shell of what had been History Repeats Itself. The construction guys had made quick work of deconstructing the building.

Poor Jim. Now all that was left for him was the memorial service Frannie had planned for Sunday. Tricia straightened. Frannie had asked for a contribution of food, and she hadn't thought to order something when she'd spoken to Nikki at the Patisserie. Too bad Angelica was away. Maybe the two of them could've come up with something.

Tricia frowned at the thought. Did she really need Angelica to help her with something as simple as baking? After all, baking wasn't rocket science. It didn't require any real knowledge of food prep. And, as Angelica had often said, "If you can follow directions, you can cook."

Tricia searched her bookshelves until she came up with *The Nero Wolfe Cookbook*. There was sure to be something in it that she could bring to Jim's wake. She flipped through the pages until she came to the segment on breakfast foods. Ah, blueberry muffins. Everybody loved blueberry muffins. It would be perfect. Of course, she needed a few ingredients—blueberries, for one. And perhaps it might be a good idea to test the recipe first.

Tricia marched into her kitchen, Miss Marple trotting along behind her.

"We are going to make muffins. You like muffins," she told the cat.

Miss Marple agreed with a hearty *"Yow!"* She jumped up on one of the stools at the kitchen island and watched as Tricia assembled her ingredients. Tricia was delightfully surprised she had so many on hand. She retrieved a small bag of flour from the fridge. Since she didn't use it often, Angelica had warned her it might pick up weevils if she left it in the cupboard. Tricia had baking soda, vegetable oil, and eggs. No blueberries, but she'd substitute Craisins for this particular batch. And if she couldn't get fresh blueberries (too early in the season?), she'd try to find canned or frozen. And since she didn't actually have a mixing bowl, she took out a large salad bowl.

Tricia consulted the recipe again. Butter. Butter was fattening. She'd replace it with her low-cal spread. Hmm . . . she didn't have any baking powder. But weren't baking powder and baking soda pretty much interchangeable? And she didn't actually have a muffin tin. She could just plop the dough (or was it batter?) onto a cookie sheet. That would probably be okay.

"Angelica thinks she's the only good cook in this family," Tricia told Miss Marple. "Well, we'll prove her wrong, won't we?"

Again Miss Marple agreed with a loud *"Yow!"*

Twice Tricia plunged her cup measure into the flour, sending plumes of powder into the air. Both were a little more than full, but if a cup was good, surely a bit extra would be better. Next she added the baking soda. The dry ingredients were supposed to be sifted together, but since she didn't have a sifter, she stirred the mixture with a spoon.

She consulted the recipe again. It called for two large eggs. Eggs had cholesterol, right? She'd use one. And two-thirds of a cup of sugar seemed a lot. The fruit was naturally sweet. She'd cut that in half, too.

After finding another large bowl, Tricia combined the sugar, the spread, and the egg, beating the mixture with a wooden spoon until it was nicely blended. The recipe said to alternately combine the milk and the butter mixture with the dry ingredients, but that seemed counterproductive. She mixed the milk with the spread, then added it to the flour. The dough was stiffer than she would have thought, and there seemed to be a lot of lumps, so she kept mixing until the dough was completely smooth—building her biceps as she went.

Oops! She had forgotten to preheat the oven. She turned it on and searched for the aluminum foil to cover the cookie sheet. Next, she found her ice cream scoop. Since she didn't have a muffin tin, she wanted the muffins at least to have a rounded shape. She scooped out twelve mounds of dough, setting them on the cookie sheet. The recipe said it made twelve muffins, but she still had plenty of dough left, so she kept scooping, adding some to each mound until the salad bowl was empty.

The oven wasn't quite up to speed, but she popped the tray into the oven anyway and set the timer, giving the muffins an extra few minutes.

Now that the action was over, Miss Marple settled down on the stool to doze while Tricia tidied up the kitchen. Soon the aroma of baking filled the entire loft. "Who says baking is so tough?" she asked Miss Marple, who didn't react.

Eventually the timer went off, and Tricia grabbed her pot holder, removing the cookie sheet from the oven. The muffins weren't exactly beautiful. She'd get some of those little paper cups from the baking aisle next time she went to

the grocery store. And if they had a muffin pan, she'd buy
that, too. Maybe Angelica sold them in her store—Tricia
wasn't really sure what stock her sister handled besides
new and used books.

She left the muffins on the counter to cool, and headed
for her bedroom to get ready for bed. Ten minutes later,
she was back in the kitchen. Miss Marple was nowhere to
be found, and one of the muffins lay on the floor. "Miss
Marple," she called, but the cat refused to come out. Tricia
picked up the muffin, which had obviously been nibbled,
and sniffed it. Not wonderful, but not horrible, either.

Tricia removed the rest of the muffins from the cookie
sheet, piled them on a plate, placed a clean dish towel over
them, and put them in the microwave, out of harm's way.

It was with a feeling of accomplishment that Tricia
climbed into bed. Together, she and Rex Stout—or should
she credit Nero Wolfe?—had done it. As she drifted off to
sleep, Tricia looked forward to the morning and providing
her employees with a wonderful breakfast treat.

Tricia and Miss Marple made it down to Haven't Got a
Clue early the next morning. Tricia wanted to be ready for
Ginny and Mr. Everett to arrive, and set the coffee to brewing. As she opened the shop blinds, Tricia was surprised to
see a ladder standing against the gas lamp outside her store.
A pickup truck was parked at the curb, its cargo bay filled
with hanging baskets holding gorgeous salmon-colored
geraniums.

A young woman removed one of the baskets and turned
toward the ladder. Tricia left her shop to investigate. "Hi,"
she called.

The woman—who looked to be about college age—smiled. "Hi. Beautiful day, isn't it?"

"Yes, and it looks like you're about to make it prettier," Tricia said, indicating the flowers. She introduced herself.

"Amy Schram. Pleased to meet you," the woman responded.

"What's with the flowers?" Tricia asked.

"Part two of the Beautify Main Street campaign of the Stoneham Board of Selectmen. My family owns Milford Nursery. We were hired to hang and maintain the flowers over the summer," she said as she climbed the ladder and hung the basket from a bar on the gas lamp. "Come Christmastime, they'll hang banners."

Tricia hadn't heard about these plans, and decided she ought to make more of an effort to get to Board of Selectmen meetings. She admired the robust basket. "I recognize geraniums, but what are the other plants?"

Amy stepped down from the ladder and folded it. "Each basket has a spike and a trailing vinca. They should look even nicer in a couple of weeks when it all bushes out."

Tricia glanced down the street, noting Amy had already hung five or six baskets. They added a lovely accent to the already picturesque street. Too bad they couldn't dress up the empty lot where History Repeats Itself had been.

"You'll be seeing a lot of me over the summer," Amy said and hefted the ladder, carrying it to the next lamppost.

"Well, I won't keep you from your work now. It was nice meeting you."

"Likewise," Amy called, and continued with her work.

Tricia retreated to Haven't Got a Clue. She'd just counted out the money for the till when Ginny arrived.

"Hey, did you see all those pretty flower baskets hanging from the gas lamps?" she called, and stepped up to the cash desk.

"Yes, they're gorgeous."

"Sure makes me wish I had a store here on Main Street," Ginny said wistfully.

"You'll have your store one day."

"Yeah, a million years from now," she groused. "You know, you ought to have postcards made showing Haven't Got a Clue's facade—especially with the flowers looking so pretty right now. You could give them away to tourists."

"That's a great idea. Thanks."

The door opened, and Mr. Everett entered. "Good morning, ladies. Have you seen the lovely flowers hanging outside?"

"Yes," Tricia said, "we were just admiring them. And I have another surprise for you two." She directed her employees to follow her to the coffee station, where the muffins she'd made sat on the counter, still covered by the dish towel.

"What's going on?" Ginny asked suspiciously.

"Just a little surprise," Tricia said, finding it hard to keep the Cheshire cat grin from her face. She pulled off the towel. "Voilà!"

Ginny leaned in close and scrutinized the plate. "What are they?" she asked, with the hint of a curled lip.

"Blueberry muffins," Tricia answered, taken aback. I made them myself."

Ginny bent lower to examine the "goodies." She pointed to one of the colored protrusions. "Blueberry? Then what are those red things?"

"Well, they're actually not blueberries. I didn't have any, so I substituted Craisins."

Ginny shot a look at Mr. Everett, whose eyes seemed unnaturally large in his wrinkled face. "And why are these . . . muffins . . . here?" Ginny asked with wariness.

"To sample. Frannie asked me to bring something to Jim's wake tomorrow, and I figured I'd better do a trial run before then. I haven't done all that much baking," Tricia admitted.

Mr. Everett swallowed, looking like he'd just been goosed.

Tricia picked up one of the muffins. "Go on," she urged, "try one."

"Have you eaten any of them?"

"This is my first," Tricia admitted. She wasn't about to say only Miss Marple had done a taste test.

Ginny hesitated before plucking one of the muffins from the plate.

"Why don't I pour the coffee?" Mr. Everett volunteered, and escaped to the other side of the coffee station.

Ginny stared at the muffin in her hand. "It feels a little damp."

"They may have still been a bit warm when I put them in the microwave last night. I didn't want Miss Marple to get into them."

"I can see why," Ginny said. She swallowed, closed her eyes, and bit into the muffin. She chewed, and chewed, and chewed, but didn't seem to swallow.

Throwing caution to the wind, Tricia bit into her own muffin—and nearly gagged. She grabbed a napkin and spat the gummy mass into it. "Forgive me," she said, embarrassed.

Ginny had stopped chewing. She'd opened her eyes, but they seemed stuck in a permanent wince.

"Oh, Ginny—get rid of it!" Tricia handed her assistant a handful of the paper napkins, and she, too, spat out what was left of the masticated muffin.

"That was dreadful," Tricia admitted.

"Did you follow the recipe?" Ginny asked, her voice sounding strangled.

"Of course. Well, I did make a few substitutions," Tricia admitted.

"Such as?"

"I used Craisins instead of blueberries, and I didn't have any baking powder, so I used baking soda instead."

Ginny shuddered, still grimacing, and smacked her lips.

"Quick, you'd better drink this," Mr. Everett advised, handing Ginny her coffee mug. She gulped the hot brew, and gasped.

Tricia, too, took her coffee and downed a mouthful, hoping to obliterate the lingering taste of the muffin. They'd smelled delicious while baking—how had they mutated into such a vile-tasting, rubbery mass?

Tricia walked around the counter, grabbed the plate, and dumped the rest of the offending muffins into the trash. Mr. Everett and Ginny seemed to be looking anywhere but in Tricia's direction. Thankfully, the phone rang. "I'll get it," Tricia said, and hightailed it for the cash desk and the Art Deco phone. She picked up the receiver. "Haven't Got a Clue; this is Tricia. How may I help you?"

"Hello, Tricia, this is Livvie Roth—James's mother. Am I calling at a bad time?"

"Not at all. What can I do for you?"

"You were so kind to help me the other day. I was wondering if you could spare me a few minutes today."

"I'd be glad to. What do you need?"

"One of the booksellers brought over some boxes of memorabilia Jim had at the shop. I wanted to go through them to determine if anything was worth saving. I've done that now. Do you think you could help me move the cartons from the house into the garage? It would probably only take a few minutes."

"I'd be glad to come over. Would this evening be all right?"

"Oh, dear. I've promised to have dinner with a friend."

"That's okay, I can make it this afternoon. How about two o'clock?"

"That would be fine. Thank you, dear. I'll see you then. Good-bye."

Tricia hung up the phone and frowned.

"Something wrong, Ms. Miles?" Mr. Everett asked.

"That was Jim Roth's mother. She said a bookseller had brought some boxes of rescued items from Jim's store. I thought everything had gone into the storage unit."

"I took them over," Mr. Everett admitted. "They were rather fragile fabric items, and I was worried they might be damaged."

"That was very thoughtful of you."

Ever too bashful to accept a compliment, Mr. Everett merely shrugged.

"Ginny and I have an errand to run later this afternoon. Would you mind taking care of Haven't Got a Clue while we're gone? It should only take an hour."

"It would be my pleasure."

"Thank you. And I have another favor to ask. Would you be open to helping out over at the Happy Domestic for an hour or so during lunch hour a couple of days a week? Since she lost her only employee, I'm afraid Deborah's been pretty frazzled. Of course I'll pay you for your time."

Mr. Everett chewed his lip for a moment. "I could use the money." He looked around to make sure Ginny was out of earshot. "I'm determined to repay Grace."

Tricia's frown returned. "Are you sure you want to make an issue of it? I believe she thought she'd be easing your financial burden."

"*I* believe a person should make their *own* way in this world. A man should provide for his family—not the other way around."

Tricia wasn't up to arguing about outdated chivalry, and she was glad she'd asked Ginny not to say anything about her refinanced mortgage. No doubt Mr. Everett wouldn't approve of that, either.

"Have you spoken to Ms. Black about my helping out?" Mr. Everett asked.

"Not yet. I'll let you know what she says and when she can use you."

"Very good."

The shop door opened and a lone customer entered. Mr. Everett perked up. "May I help you, sir?"

"Yes. I'm looking to fill several gaps in my collection." The slight, older gent withdrew a folded piece of paper from the breast pocket of his sports shirt and handed it to Mr. Everett, who studied it for a moment.

"I believe we can help you with at least a few of these. Let me show you where you can find the John Dickson Carr titles."

Tricia smiled after them, then happened to glance out the window. It was already after ten, and there was Jake Masters casually strolling down the sidewalk, heading for Booked for Lunch. He should've arrived long before this to start the soup of the day.

Tricia signaled to Ginny, who was refilling the sugar at

the coffee station. "I've got to step out for a minute. I'll be right back."

Ginny nodded, and returned to her task.

Tricia waited until it was safe and then crossed the street, intercepting Jake right outside Booked for Lunch. She could see Darcy inside, standing at the counter as she refilled saltshakers. Hands thrust into the pockets of his denim jacket, Jake halted in front of her.

"Shouldn't you have been here long before now?" Tricia accused.

"We don't open until eleven—I've got plenty of time to get things ready."

"What about the soup?"

"Soup?" he asked, confused.

"Darcy says it needs to be started hours before Booked for Lunch opens. It's the mainstay of Angelica's menu."

"Yeah, and I started it yesterday. It just needs to heat through. You got any other worries? You want to know how fine I dice the carrots or thin I slice the onions?"

Tricia crossed her arms over her chest. "Darcy tells me you were convicted of a felony."

"That's none of her damn business," Jake grated.

"Angelica gave you this job. She deserves to know," Tricia said.

"We've talked about it. And she doesn't have a problem with my past."

"What were you arrested for?" Tricia pressed.

"Jaywalking."

"That's not a felony."

"And neither is keeping my business to myself. Look, you'd be better off talking to Angelica about the café—not Darcy. Maybe Angelica will be glad to answer any of your questions—because I sure as hell won't. Now, you're keeping me from that soup you're so worried about. If you'll excuse me." He pushed past her and entered Booked for Lunch. Tricia watched as he confronted Darcy, who immediately went into defensive mode. They both turned to the window, Jake gesticulating wildly. Since discretion was the better part of valor, Tricia hightailed it out of there before Jake threw another hissy fit and stormed out of the café for a second day in a row—and maybe forever.

THIRTEEN

Tricia couldn't remember such a slow Saturday in Stoneham. Okay, it wasn't yet high tourist season, but surely there had to be people out there needing to find something new—or old—to read. The day continued to drag on. While Mr. Everett dusted the shelves, and Ginny was dispatched to the storeroom to update the inventory, Tricia called Billie Hanson at the bank and persuaded her to stay after hours to see her and Ginny about the mortgage. Why not move forward on the project now that Ginny had accepted her offer of financial assistance?

A stack of books awaited reshelving, but Tricia felt too lazy for real work. And besides, Jim Roth's memorial service was the next day, and Frannie was expecting her to bake something to bring to it. Obviously, for this next attempt, she'd need the right ingredients and the proper tools. And she knew just where to get the latter.

After telling Mr. Everett she had to run an errand, Tricia

grabbed her purse, left Haven't Got a Clue, and walked over to the Cookery. The cutout of Angelica was once again outside the entrance. This time, someone had attached a pair of novelty Groucho Marx glasses, complete with funny nose and mustache, and between the splayed fingers was a cat's cradle of string. Someone's idea of a joke? Angelica certainly would not be pleased.

Tricia entered the store. Unlike Haven't Got a Clue, the Cookery at least had one shopper. Frannie, who was helping the customer, waved and called out "Howdy," letting Tricia know they'd talk when convenient. And since the manager-customer ratio could change in a heartbeat should a bus full of tourists arrive, Tricia figured she might as well look around and try to find what she needed to make a decent muffin recipe. First up, a cookbook dedicated to baking. Next, she selected what looked like a rubber muffin pan, new measuring spoons, a can of Maine blueberries, and a tin of baking power. She figured she could find the rest of the ingredients at the grocery store in Milford.

Once Frannie's customer left the store, Tricia stepped up to the sales counter, her arms filled with books and other products.

"My, my—are you actually going to bake?" Frannie asked, inspecting the items Tricia placed on the counter.

"Yes. And why is everyone so amazed? Lots of people bake."

"Not you."

"Well, I do now. Or I will, as soon as I install this muffin pan in my kitchen. Do these rubber ones actually work? I mean—it won't melt in my oven, will it?"

"Of course not. And it's not rubber. This flexible silicone cookware is great. Easy cleanup, and it can withstand high oven temps—even up to five hundred degrees. All the chefs on the Food Network use them."

"If you say so."

Frannie totaled up the items. "It's rumored that Livvie Roth has been seen in Milford—with a man."

"Oh?"

Frannie nodded. "Imagine that, cavorting around at her age."

Cavorting? Mrs. Roth? Then again, she did say she had dinner plans with a friend. "Where was she seen?"

"At the Milford Travel Agency, for one. Word is she's booked a cruise—*for two*."

"To where?"

"The Caribbean. She got one of those sell-out deals." Frannie's voice dripped with disapproval.

No surprise there. Chauncey Porter had said Mrs. Roth bought a book on cruises. "And did your spy tell you when she's to depart?" Tricia asked.

"In two weeks. I hope they stick her below the waterline on a very rough sea."

"Frannie," Tricia scolded.

"I'm sorry, Tricia. I can't help but feel a bit catty. That woman kept her son and me apart."

"Are you absolutely sure it was Mrs. Roth, not Jim, who did that?"

Frannie gaped. "Are you suggesting that Jim would lie to me?"

"He wouldn't be the first man to look for any excuse to avoid commitment."

Frannie stared at the baking book in her hands, her mouth trembling. "Jim wasn't like that. He—he wanted to be with me. He said so many times."

"But?" Tricia prompted.

Frannie swallowed. She continued processing Tricia's order, and didn't answer. "That'll be thirty-seven seventy-eight, please."

Tricia sighed, and handed Frannie her credit card. She processed the rest of the sale without comment. Tricia changed the subject. "How are the plans for the memorial service coming along?"

"Pretty good," Frannie said, weariness now coloring her tone. "I ordered a poster-sized print of a picture I took of Jim last fall—from the same place Angelica got her cutout. I'll pick that up this evening. The Chamber of Commerce has an easel I can borrow—that is, if Bob doesn't find out. I used Angelica's name to get it. That Betsy Dittmeyer is a real stickler for rules. She shows about as much compassion as a worm would."

"I'm sure Angelica won't mind," Tricia said, ignoring the slur—however truthful—on Betsy's character. "Now, about that cutout—"

Frannie looked out the large display window, saw the most recent alteration to the cutout, and cringed. "Not again."

"I don't think Angelica would approve of her likeness being mocked."

"I'll take care of it as soon as you leave. I promise."

"Maybe you should just put it in the back of the store, out of sight."

"No can do. Angelica specifically told me to place it where the customers could see it."

Tricia shrugged. "Okay."

"Getting back to Jim," Frannie continued, as though grateful to leave the subject of Angelica's cutout. "I think he should have a good turnout. He *was* loved by just about everyone in town."

And especially you, Tricia thought.

The credit card machine spit out a piece of paper. Tricia signed it, and handed it back to Frannie. With their transaction completed, Frannie handed Tricia her shopping bag and receipt.

"Will I be seeing you later this afternoon?" Tricia asked.

Frannie frowned. "What for?"

"The day's receipts," Tricia reminded her.

"Oh, yes. Of course." Frannie gave a nervous laugh. "I wouldn't have forgotten today. See?" She pointed to a pink Post-It attached to the register. "I made myself a reminder."

The tense moment seemed to have passed, for which Tricia was grateful. The door opened, and several giggling women shoppers bustled inside. Hopefully, they had friends who'd just entered Haven't Got a Clue.

"Okay, I'll see you later this afternoon," Tricia said, picked up her bag, gave a wave, and headed for the door.

The morning sun had defied the weatherman's prediction of rain. Of course, everyone said they needed rain, and it was true that in retail, inclement weather encouraged the bored to go forth and shop, but too many rainy days weren't good for the soul.

And then Tricia stopped dead. Since she'd left Haven't Got a Clue, a Kelly Realty FOR SALE sign had gone up in front of the empty lot where History Repeats Itself had been only four days before. Her fine-weather good feelings were instantly obliterated. Was it Jim Roth's death due to a cigarette addiction, or the death of a building, that bothered her more? That structure had been a part of Stoneham during the good days and the bad—and it had been repurposed during the village's current revitalization, outliving how many of its former owners and tenants.

Tricia turned away from the site and entered Haven't Got a Clue. Ginny was at the cash desk, checking out a customer, while Mr. Everett helped someone in the back of the store. Tricia braved a smiled and joined Ginny, stowing her purchases behind the glass display case and bagging the books, adding a copy of the latest newsletter before handing the shopping bag to their customer. "Thanks for shopping with us," she said, and let out a weary sigh as the customer exited the store.

"What's wrong?" Ginny asked.

"Bob Kelly must be in a hurry to unload his empty lot."

Ginny looked confused until Tricia pointed toward the large green sign across the street. "Oh, dear."

Tricia shook herself. "I don't want to think about it. In fact, let's think of something much more pleasant. I made an appointment for you and me to go to the bank to talk to Billie Hanson today. She said she'd stay after closing, so we could go about one o'clock. I've already asked Mr. Everett to cover for us."

Ginny looked away, her frown deepening. "Oh, well . . . I promised to have lunch with my friend Rhonda today. She's only in town until tomorrow morning." Ginny gave a nervous laugh. "She didn't see any future in staying in Stoneham and moved away right out of high school. Maybe we could go to the bank on Monday or Tuesday?"

"Okay," Tricia said, managing yet another counterfeit smile. "As soon as we have the figures, I'll talk to my attorney about setting up a mortgage. You'll want to consult your own attorney, as well."

"Oh, I hadn't thought about that."

"You know I wouldn't cheat you, but it would be in your best interest."

"Yes, I suppose it would. I wonder what that would cost," Ginny said, frowning.

"You do want to do this, don't you?" Tricia asked.

"I'd be crazy to turn down an opportunity like this. Thousands of people across the country haven't been so lucky."

Then why are you dragging your feet on this? Tricia felt tempted to ask. Instead, she gave Ginny a hopeful smile. "Well, let me know when you're available."

Ginny's return smile was halfhearted. "I will. Oh, I left my inventory sheets upstairs. I'd better go get them before they get lost." And off she went.

Tricia frowned. The day had taken on a decidedly sour cast. First Jake, now Ginny.

Thinking of Jake reminded her about a call she needed to make. She picked up the old-fashioned receiver and dialed Captain Baker's number. For once, she was glad voice mail picked up, directing her to another number should this be an emergency—yada, yada, yada. Finally, she got the beep to leave a message. "Grant, this is Tricia Miles. First of all, I apologize for last night. I didn't mean to get testy with you. I let Bob Kelly's bad mood influence my own, and that wasn't fair to you." *Or me*, she thought. "Could you give me a call? I kind of need a favor, too. Thanks." She hung up the phone and wondered if she'd just made a big mistake.

Lunch, such as it was—yogurt again—came and went, and all too soon it was time for Tricia to head over to Livvie Roth's little cottage.

As Tricia pulled up the drive, she was surprised to find stacks of cartons, along with large black plastic trash bags, at the curb. Jim had been dead not quite four days. Could his mother already be going through all of his belongings and throwing them away?

With trepidation Tricia opened the gate and entered the garden that was the front yard. Before she had a chance to climb the steps, the front door opened. "Tricia, dear. Thank you so much for coming," Mrs. Roth said. "Won't you come in?" Decked out in a pink floral housedress, Mrs. Roth had covered her head with a faded bandana. From the looks of her grubby hands, she'd been doing some serious cleaning.

Once again, Mrs. Roth gestured her to go ahead, and Tricia entered the little home's living room, which had undergone quite a transformation. The tobacco-stained walls had been scrubbed. Gone were the military pictures that had once decorated them, replaced with still-life prints and oil paintings of roses, most of them in heavily gilded frames and in various sizes. The club chair and oversized plasma TV were also gone, replaced by a chintz-slipcovered love seat and chair. A white wicker table sat before them, with the silver tea set upon it. The ashtray was gone, and the side table, now doily covered, held Mrs. Roth's library books and a milk glass bud vase with a single pink rose. A floor lamp sat close to the love seat, making a perfect little reading nook. Jim's wartime display cases were gone, too, and in their place were little shelves filled with books and knickknacks—more of Mrs. Roth's treasures.

"You've been redecorating," Tricia said.

"Not really. I've just moved things around a bit."

"You did this all yourself?"

"I had some help this morning," she said, as evidenced by the two tea-stained cups still sitting on the silver tray.

Mrs. Roth gazed at one of the rose paintings and sighed. "I'm so glad I never threw these away. They've been in storage for ages. Aren't they pretty?"

"Yes, very," Tricia agreed.

Mrs. Roth studied Tricia's face and frowned. "You must think me a terrible mother, erasing James's presence so quickly. I can assure you, I haven't done so entirely. It was quite painful, but I went through his things, weeded out what couldn't be donated or sold, and kept those that were most dear to him. They're in his bedroom, which I think I'll keep as a shrine to remember him by."

That was a little morbid, but Tricia did have to admit that with even these small changes, the house now seemed more like a home than a war museum.

"Did you know the booksellers rescued as many of the books as they could from Jim's store?"

"Yes. A William Everett called to tell me that. He's the one who brought the boxes of items for me to sort through. He could have tossed them in a Dumpster, for all I care."

"They could be worth quite a bit of money."

"I don't have the means to sell them to the highest bidder. And sitting in a storage unit, they'll just be another drain on my finances. I do wish someone had consulted me before they took that on."

"I'm afraid that was my fault. I suggested they try to rescue them."

Mrs. Roth's lips pursed, but she didn't comment.

"Would you consider donating them to a worthy charity?"

"Such as?"

"If nothing else, the Stoneham Library's next used-book sale. Lois Kerr is always looking for donations."

Mrs. Roth thought about it for a few moments. "That would be acceptable. Would you be willing to make the arrangements?"

"I'd be happy to."

"Will you also pay the fee on the storage unit?"

Tricia hesitated, then forced a smile. "Of course."

"I don't want to keep you from your shop, dear," Mrs. Roth said, and pointed to the cartons that were stacked along one wall. "Do be careful when you lift them. Some of them are quite heavy."

She wasn't kidding. Tricia struggled to pick up the top box, and carried it from the living room, through the kitchen, and into the attached garage. Mrs. Roth followed her like a puppy. "Where would you like me to put it?"

"Just make a new pile over there," Mrs. Roth directed.

Mrs. Roth certainly had been clearing house, as evidenced by the stack of boxes and bags. Tricia wondered if there was anything left to put in Jim's room to remember him by.

"I've got a man coming on Monday to make an offer on some of the books and memorabilia. From what I understand, some of it's quite valuable." Mrs. Roth wrinkled her nose. "I never did like having it in the house."

The phone rang inside the house. "I'll just go get that," Mrs. Roth said, and hurried inside.

Tricia took a look around the garage, grateful the door was up and light was spilling into the dusty room. Like the rest of the house, it was neat, with plastic shelves that held household cleaning products, garden tools, motor oil, and . . . a gallon jug of antifreeze in a bright yellow container. Yellow—the color of Mrs. Roth's lemon bars. Antifreeze, made of ethylene glycol. Poison to man and beast.

For some reason, the sight of it bothered Tricia, especially as she remembered the look on Mrs. Roth's face when she'd mentioned that the lemon bars had been Jim's favorite. Tricia looked back through the screen door and into the kitchen, where Mrs. Roth conversed on the phone. In only three days the old lady had practically erased all traces of her son from her home. Could she have wanted him gone? Could she have planned to help him leave this world?

Tricia shuddered, and in the next second berated herself for being foolish. Jim had been killed in an explosion, not by poison. But what if the explosion hadn't happened? How long would he have lived otherwise?

FOURTEEN

 With Ginny and Mr. Everett already gone for the day, Tricia was ready to pack it in herself. The bell over the door rang, and Tricia looked up, expecting a last-minute customer, but instead Grant Baker stood in the doorway. "Oh, I was expecting a return phone call, not a visit," she said. He was out of uniform, dressed in a dark green golf shirt and tan Dockers, looking tall, tanned, and tantalizing.

"I happened to be in the neighborhood and thought I'd drop by."

That was a lie. He lived closer to Manchester than Milford.

"How's Mandy?" Tricia almost managed to keep the bitterness out of her voice.

"Still in remission, still doing well," Baker answered.

But not well enough for him to resume a life without her.

Stop it! Tricia told herself. She didn't want their conversation to follow the previous night's course.

"You called," Baker reminded Tricia. "You said you needed a favor."

"Yes. It turns out my sister has hired a convicted felon."

"Convicted of what?" Baker asked, interested.

"That's what worries me. He wouldn't tell me."

"Did you ask your sister?"

"She's out of town on a book tour."

"Oh, yes, *Easy-Does-It Cooking* by Angelica Miles. From Penguin. Published June first."

Tricia laughed. "How did you remember all that?"

Baker scowled. "Because your sister has recited that little speech just about every time I've seen her. She's like a broken record, but I suppose that's good for sales."

"Yes, I guess it is."

"Now, what about this employee? Do you have a name?" Baker asked.

"Jake Masters. He's her short-order cook, and he also works evenings as a sous-chef at La Parisienne in Nashua. I'm not sure where he lives."

"That's not much to go on. Have you got a license plate number?"

"I've never seen his car."

"With all the mysteries you read, you of all people should know what a cop needs to track someone down."

"Well, I'm hardly in a position to give you his Social Security number." Ouch! That was no way to win friends and influence people. "I'm sorry. I guess I'm a little on edge. I haven't had a very good day."

"You could tell me about it over dinner."

Tricia blinked. "I could?"

"That is, if you're not otherwise occupied."

Tricia gazed around the empty store. Miss Marple sat

on the readers' nook coffee table. She yawned. "I suppose I could change my plans for the evening."

"And what were you planning on doing?"

"Baking."

Baker snorted a laugh, then caught himself.

"That was not meant to be funny."

"I'm sorry, but your gastronomic reputation precedes you."

She decided to ignore the slur on her cooking abilities. "What did you have in mind?"

"The Bookshelf Diner, if you don't mind."

Safe. Secure. And decidedly unromantic. Well, they were, after all, *just friends.* "Sure. Let me feed my cat, and I'll be right with you."

"Fine."

Leaving Miss Marple in the apartment, Tricia grabbed a heavier sweater and headed back down to Haven't Got a Clue. Baker was perusing a book, which he put back on the shelf at her arrival.

"Would you like to borrow it?" Tricia asked.

He shook his head. "I barely have time to read the newspaper. Shall we go?"

Baker waited as Tricia locked the door, then ushered her down the sidewalk. "We'll want to cross at the corner," he said. "I wouldn't want to break the law by jaywalking."

Tricia tried not to smile. She'd admonished him for doing just that soon after they'd met. "Who'd know? I've heard the response time for a Sheriff's Department cruiser for a 9-1-1 call averages twenty minutes."

Baker frowned. "It's a sad fact. This is a big county, and our resources only stretch so far."

"The other day I signed a petition to reestablish a police force in Stoneham. Do you think that's a good idea?"

They paused at the corner. "I do. The Sheriff's Department wasn't eager to take on patrolling this area when the village nearly went bankrupt almost two decades ago."

"Were you here at the time?"

"Little more than a raw recruit. I've got nineteen years in. I can retire next year—that is, if the rules don't change. A lot of police forces are calling for longer periods of service. Soon officers will need more than just twenty years on the job before taking retirement."

"Isn't that fiscally sound?"

"A forty- or fifty-year-old officer can't run after a suspect like he did fresh out of the academy."

They crossed the empty street and entered the diner, where they were seated in its front booth for the entire world to see—and in exactly the same seat Tricia had occupied for dinner with Russ just two nights before. Oh, well, Tricia reminded herself, this wasn't really a date. It was a shared meal with a *friend*.

Why did that word have to leave a sour taste in her mouth?

Eugenia, the weeknight waitress, was not on duty, which meant Tricia might actually enjoy her meal. Then again, as she perused the uninspiring menu, she decided she might be wrong. It never changed. And the specials always seemed to be the same, too. Couldn't they offer entrées that didn't require a deep-fat fryer?

Out of the corner of her eye, Tricia saw a familiar figure walk past the diner's window: Russ. She looked back down at her menu, hoping he hadn't noticed her. What was he doing in town? His office had been dark when Tricia and Baker had walked past it.

"The fried chicken looks good," Baker said, eyes glued to the colored photograph on the menu before him.

"Not if you're on statins." She let her gaze stray to the window. Good. No sign of Russ.

"Are you going to live forever?" Baker asked.

"That's my plan."

He folded his menu. "I predict you'll order the Cobb salad."

"And why's that?"

"Because you always order the Cobb salad."

"I order plenty of other things."

"Such as?"

"The spinach salad. The tuna plate. . . ."

"Why don't you order dessert? In fact, why don't you order two of them?"

"Life is short—eat dessert first, because you never know what might happen?" she asked, trying not to smile.

Baker grinned. "Something like that."

Tricia glanced up at the window. Still no Russ. She turned her gaze back to the menu. Too bad she wasn't a fan of sweets. Then again, she didn't want Baker to think he could read her mind.

Janice, the weekend night waitress, came over to the table, her order pad at the ready. "What can I get you folks?"

Baker nodded in Tricia's direction. She gave him a chagrined smile, and looked up at the waitress. "I think I'd like—"

But before she could finish the sentence, a blur at the edge of her peripheral vision shouted, "Is this what we pay our taxes for? Public servants dithering in diners while a killer is on the loose?"

Tricia looked up, and there, not five feet from their table, stood Russ Smith, his face twisted into an ugly snarl. She hadn't noticed him enter. The diner had gone deadly quiet, with all eyes on their table. Janice backed up a few steps, looking uneasy.

Tricia's gaze darted to Baker's face. For a moment he seemed oblivious of the interruption, his expression a study in tranquillity. Then he turned to Russ and said in a low voice, "Excuse me?"

"You're in charge of the Jim Roth murder investigation. Why aren't you out there looking for his killer—keeping the citizens of Stoneham safe?"

"I'm off duty. My men are following every lead. Now, if you'll excuse me. . . ."

"No, I won't. What the hell are you doing here with my girl?"

"Russ!" Tricia admonished with a scowl.

Baker didn't bother to look up. "I'm attempting to order my dinner. You're making that extremely difficult. I suggest you leave before you embarrass yourself any more."

"Russ, please!" Tricia implored, but before she could say more, Russ launched himself at Baker, grabbing him by the collar of his shirt, yanking him up and out of the booth. Baker's eyes blazed and his arms came up, smashing at Russ's, and the two of them went tumbling to the floor.

Tricia struggled to get out of the booth. "Stop it! Stop it!"

"I'm calling 9-1-1," Janice hollered, and ran up the aisle.

"I *am* 9-1-1!" Baker yelled, or tried to, as he dodged Russ's ineffective blows. Giving up, he hauled off and slugged Russ, sending him sprawling backward. "Pal, you made a big mistake coming here tonight." Baker got to his feet and then bent down to grab a groggy Russ by his shirt, pulling him onto his feet. Russ's legs were rubbery, and he had a hard time standing.

"You picked the wrong person to hassle, pal. You're going down for assault and battery," Baker said.

"Grant, please don't press charges. It was just Russ being"—she sighed, frustrated—"Russ."

"Yes, I will press charges. Look, Tricia, I've seen this happen far too often. No charges leveled, and the next thing you know, you're a statistic of domestic violence."

Tricia met Baker's level green gaze. She knew he was right. How many true crime books had she read chronicling the same pattern of abuse, stalking, and murder? But this was Russ Smith they were talking about.

"Besides," Baker continued, "it's me who'll be pressing charges, not you. That way he's more likely to take his spite out on me instead of you."

A Sheriff's Department cruiser pulled up outside the diner—again beating the twenty-minute response time—and a uniformed deputy got out, putting on his flat-brimmed hat. Tricia recognized the man: Deputy Placer. He came into the diner and eyed the three of them still standing there, with the rest of the patrons staring. "What have we got here, Captain?"

"Mr. Smith attacked me. I've got a diner full of witnesses." Several people nodded in agreement. "He'll be taking a trip down to the county lockup. Assault and battery. I'm sure you can take care of him until I can get there to finish the paperwork."

"Not a problem," Placer said, while Tricia ground her teeth. Placer had already taken out his handcuffs. Seconds later, he had locked them around Russ's wrists, grabbed the now-submissive man by the arm, and hauled him out of the diner. Everyone watched as he loaded Russ into the cruiser's backseat, climbed into the driver's seat, and drove off.

Tricia and Baker resumed their seats. It took a few moments for the low murmur of voices to fill the diner once again. Tricia was afraid to look up and see the number of faces she'd recognize. This wasn't how she'd expected the evening to turn out.

Baker picked up his menu once again, turning back to the picture of crispy chicken and whipped potatoes.

Tricia was the first to speak. "I don't understand why Russ is acting like this. *He* dumped *me*," she hissed. "And it's not as if you and I even have a relationship."

Baker didn't take his eyes off the menu. "I think of friendship as a relationship. And who knows what the future will bring?"

Tricia felt a flush creeping up her neck to burn her cheeks. Did Baker expect her to put her life on hold while she waited for him to make up his mind to leave his ex-wife behind and make a new life? And wasn't that more or less what Jim Roth had expected of Frannie?

It wasn't a question Tricia was willing to ask, at least not in front of a diner full of people.

Janice came back to the table. "Do you want to try ordering now?" If she was trying to be funny, she'd missed the mark.

"I think I've lost my appetite," Tricia said.

"I'll have the fried chicken, the salad with poppy seed dressing, and a Geary's." Baker closed his menu. "My friend here will have a glass of chardonnay and a hot fudge sundae, heavy on the fudge."

"Grant," Tricia protested.

"Better keep one waiting in the wings, too. Just in case," he said, handed Janice his menu, and winked.

"Got it," Janice said with a smile, collected Tricia's menu, and turned away.

"I don't even *like* hot fudge sundaes," Tricia said.

"Of course you do. That is, you would if you'd *let* yourself like them. I'm sure there are lots of other good things in life you'd enjoy if you'd only let yourself."

"What's that supposed to mean?"

"Have you ever noticed all the nice things you do for people? How many of them do nice things in return?"

"I don't know what you're talking about."

"You're collecting money for the dead guy's mother. You pay your employees almost double what the other shopkeepers pay theirs—"

"How do you know—?"

"You've been playing nursemaid to a man you can't stand."

"You know perfectly well I'm only doing it because Bob is my sister's boyfriend."

"Tricia," he said softly, and reached across the table to take her hands in his. "You've been especially kind to me, letting me put this stuff with Mandy behind me. I don't think I've met another woman who would've done that."

"I'm not pining for you, if that's what you think."

He shook his head. "Not at all. If you met someone you cared about, I wouldn't stand in your way. Not like Mr. Smith. For now I'll take friendship. It's all I can expect, and more than I deserve."

Tricia was afraid to look up at him, to get caught up in those mesmerizing green eyes. And this subject was getting far too uncomfortable to talk about. "What am I going to do about Russ? The last few days he's gotten more and more possessive."

Baker withdrew his hands from hers. "Sometimes a restraining order works. Sometimes it just makes a person more cantankerous, and things can escalate."

"He hasn't really done anything to me—*except* annoy me."

"If he bothers you, call the Sheriff's Department—any time of day or night. I mean it."

Tricia nodded.

Janice returned with Baker's beer and Tricia's wine, setting them on plain white cocktail napkins. "Be right back with your entrées."

Baker lifted the bottle and poured a generous amount into the pilsner glass. "Here's hoping Mr. Smith learns from his mistakes."

Tricia did not raise her glass. "And if he doesn't?"

Baker shrugged. "We'll just have to wait and see."

FIFTEEN

Tricia put down her book after realizing she'd read the same page three or four times and none of it had registered. The evening's events had a stranglehold on her thoughts. Too wound up to sleep, she'd tried watching TV and reading, and had even contemplated baking, but couldn't seem to concentrate on anything. Meanwhile, the clock kept ticking.

It was ten thirty-six when the telephone rang, and Tricia eagerly picked up the receiver, hoping it would be Angelica. "Trish?" It was.

"Where are you tonight?"

"At this very moment, I'm sitting in my car in the municipal parking lot."

"Here in Stoneham? But I thought you were supposed to be in Portland, Maine, tonight."

"I was. But I figured I was only two hours from home—

and I want to sleep in my own bed tonight. I just picked up a pizza. Are you hungry?"

"Sure. Come on up."

Three minutes later, Angelica let herself into Tricia's loft apartment. "You're a sight for sore eyes," Tricia said and threw her arms around her sister—only slightly hampered by the pizza box between them.

"Whoa! That's an enthusiastic welcome. I may just go out and come back in." Angelica set the pizza box on the kitchen island and flopped onto a stool. Miss Marple jumped up and greeted her with a curious *"Yow?"*

Angelica addressed the cat, petting her on the head. "Yes, sweetie. I'm glad to see you, too." They'd made their peace last fall, and since then, Miss Marple seemed to enjoy Angelica's visits, although she knew better than to sit on her lap and shed cat hair.

Tricia got plates from the cupboard and snatched a spatula from the crock on the counter. "Want some wine with that?"

"I was hoping you'd ask."

Tricia snagged a couple of glasses and an unopened bottle of chardonnay from the refrigerator.

"I have a confession to make," Angelica said, and slipped off her shoes. "You weren't my first choice of companion."

"Bob?" Tricia asked.

"Yes. I stopped off at his house with my lovely Mario's pizza, and he turned me down flat," she said, aggrieved. "He said he'd taken his pain pills and was too sleepy for company. It hurt my feelings."

"I'd be more sympathetic toward Bob if he hadn't been so secretive since the night of the explosion," Tricia said, testing the warmth of the pizza and finding it lacking. "I'll just pop this into the oven for ten minutes, okay?"

"Oh, sure," Angelica agreed, grabbed the bottle, opened it, and poured them each a glass of wine.

Tricia turned on the oven, put the pizza—sans box—into it, and set the timer for ten minutes.

"I don't know what to make of Bob," Angelica said, and sipped her wine. "The truth is, he hasn't been all that chummy for the past month or two. I attributed it to stress. He took a hard hit during the real estate crisis. And Jim wasn't the only one of his tenants late with the rent, which has hampered his cash flow."

"And now?" Tricia asked.

"Now I'm not so sure. He's acting guilty—and that's something he's never done before."

"Do you think he's cheating on you?"

Angelica frowned, and suddenly looked all of her forty-seven years. "I don't know. I hope not. Way too many men have betrayed me in the past. That's one of the reasons I haven't pushed my relationship with Bob too far, too fast." She swirled the wine in her glass, and stared into space for several moments before she shook herself and sat straighter. "Let's change the subject," Angelica said, and abruptly emptied her glass with one large gulp. "What's been happening in your world?"

It was about time she asked. "It seems I've got a stalker."

"A stalker!" Angelica was on her feet in an instant. "Why didn't you say something? Have you called the Sheriff's Department? Are you getting nasty phone calls?"

"Whoa—whoa!" Tricia said, making a T with her hands for a time-out. "It's Russ."

"Russ? Give me a break." Angelica sat back down, grabbed her glass, and poured more wine.

"Maybe stalker is too strong a word, but he's gotten awfully possessive the past few days. I was having dinner with Captain Baker tonight, and—"

Angelica smiled lasciviously. "Now the story's getting interesting."

"Just as friends," Tricia said, then continued. "Then Russ came in and attacked him."

"And, and?" Angelica pressed, her eyes wide.

"Grant had him arrested."

"My, my, little Tricia part of a lovers' triangle. I didn't think you had it in you."

"I don't."

"It's all much more exciting than my book tour, let me tell you," Angelica said, and sighed. "I feel like I'm living in my car. And those hotel beds range from rock hard to squishy soft. I'll be glad when it's all over."

"And you were so looking forward to it. How many more weeks will you be on the road?"

Angela's frown grew deeper. "Three, off and on."

"The perils of being published," Tricia said without sympathy. Her gaze lit on the shopping bag from the Cookery that still sat on her counter. It was time to change the subject. "I had a rather bad experience last night." She paused, embarrassed to admit it. "I baked."

Angelica actually giggled. "You? Baked? That's priceless. I only wish I could've witnessed it."

"I'll thank you not to mock my efforts."

"Did you save any for me to try?"

Tricia hesitated. "No."

"I'm sorry. I'm sure they were just *delicious*," Angelica said, failing to stifle a smirk. She didn't sound one bit sorry, either.

"I was wondering if you could you give me a few tips. I have to bake some muffins for Jim's wake tomorrow."

"It's tomorrow already? Where does the time go?" When it came to cookery, Angelica was all business.

"First off, have you got the ingredients and the appropriate tools?"

"Yes. I visited the Cookery and bought everything I need."

"You visited my store? Oh, Trish, that was sweet of you. Thank you."

"Yes, and I have your receipts down in my safe. I'll bank them for you on Monday."

"Great. Now, let's eat this pizza and get to baking."

"You have to get up early in the morning. And besides, you must be exhausted after being on the road for three days."

"Darling Trish, I *live* to bake. After being away from my kitchen for three days, I'm going through cooking withdrawal. The oven's already up to speed—there's nothing to stop us."

"Okay, but only because you insist."

The timer went off, and Angelica got up. She took the pizza out of the oven, returning it to its cardboard box. She set it on a trivet, then grabbed a slice and a plate. "Anything else happen while I've been gone?"

"All is not happiness and light at Booked for Lunch," Tricia said as she reached for the wine and topped up their glasses. "You've got a problem."

"So I gather."

"The receipts just don't match the cash—we're talking every day," Tricia said. "I don't want to accuse anyone of anything, but I want you to have a look before you take off again."

"I don't have time, but I'll be back on Friday and stay for the weekend. I'll figure out what the problem is then." Angelica took a bite of pizza, chewed, and swallowed.

"Darcy and Jake just don't get along. It may not have been a good idea to hire her."

"Are you sure it's not Jake who's the problem?" Tricia asked.

"Jake? He's fabulous. Mark my words, in a couple of years I'll lose him when he opens his own restaurant and becomes the toast of Nashua . . . or did he say Manchester?" She shook her head and took another bite.

"He was quite rude to me this morning."

"Jake, rude?" Angelica laughed.

"Did you know he was convicted of a felony? That he's done jail time?"

"Of course I knew." Angelica's eyes narrowed. "How did you find out?"

"Darcy told me. Jake wouldn't say what he was put away for."

Angelica stared at Tricia, frowning.

"Well?" Tricia pressed.

Angelica looked away and picked a rogue piece of green pepper out of the box, putting it on her pizza. "It's really none of your business."

"What?" Tricia demanded. "You're my sister, and you've got a convicted felon working for you. Of course it's my business."

"Somebody's got to hire former prisoners, or else they'll have to continue to lead lives of crime. You of all people should understand that. Most of the bad guys get put away in all those mysteries you read. They have to get out of jail at some point, and then they need jobs to keep a roof over their heads and food on the table. I suppose even Russ will need someone to give him a break once he's out of the pokey."

"I'm sure he made bail."

"Whatever," Angelica said with a wave of her hand.

"You're really not going to tell me Jake's crime?" Tricia asked, feeling hurt.

"No, I'm not. And don't you go asking that wannabe boyfriend of yours to dig up dirt on my employees, either."

"Wannabe boyfriend? What are you talking about?" Tricia wasn't about to admit she'd already asked Captain Baker about Jake.

"Oh, the way Captain Baker looks at you, like a lovesick teenager."

"He does not. In fact, he's the one who wanted to cool things between us."

"Well, he's got a sick ex-wife, hasn't he? It just proves there are *some* men still out there who feel loyalty, or at least compassion, for someone they were once in love with."

That shut Tricia up. She pushed away the plate with the half-eaten slice of pizza.

Angelica closed the lid on the pizza box, picked it up, and put it into the refrigerator. Then she spied the shopping bag on the counter and emptied it. "Why didn't you buy my cookbook?" she demanded. "It's got recipes for muffins in it."

"I didn't think about it."

Angelica frowned. "How am I supposed to become a fabulously rich and famous author if my own family doesn't buy my book?"

"I'll buy it tomorrow."

"You promise?"

"Yes."

"Thank you."

If they were any more civil, the kitchen's temperature might plummet to downright frigid. Angelica broke the ice.

Shall we get going on those muffins? You can make them, and I'll correct you as you go along."

Tricia sighed. It was going to be difficult not to strangle Angelica, but she was sure she'd somehow find the will-power. Tricia collected her ingredients and placed them in a row on the counter, then gathered up her tools.

"Aren't you going to wash that muffin pan?" Angelica asked.

Tricia sighed, squirted some dishwashing liquid on the pan, and ran it under the tap.

"Make sure it's totally dry. You don't want the muffins to stick to the cups."

Tricia ground her teeth as she dried each and every muffin cup with meticulous care.

"Okay, first you measure the flour. Have you ever done that before?" Angelica asked.

"Yes."

"Where's your sifter?" Angelica asked, opening a cupboard.

"I don't have one."

"You don't have one? Everybody has at least one."

"Not me." Maybe asking Angelica for help hadn't been such a good idea.

Angelica closed the cupboard. "Since your birthday is coming up, I'll get you one."

"Don't bother. I don't plan to make baking a hobby."

"Ah, that's what they all say—until the baking bug hits." Angelica leaned closer and squinted. "Tricia—I do believe you're wearing a necklace."

"I am?" Tricia said, playing dumb.

"Yes. I can see the chain around your neck."

Tricia lifted a portion of the chain with her left thumb. "Oh, this? Yes, I guess I am wearing a necklace."

"But you don't wear jewelry."

"I don't?"

"Well, you haven't since I've been living here i
Stoneham—maybe longer."

"I'm sure you're wrong," Tricia said and tugged on he
right earlobe, which was decorated with a gemstone stud.

"I'm not talking about earrings or a watch—they'r
givens."

"Are they?" Tricia asked, skeptical.

"Was it a birthday gift? Did Captain Baker give it t
you?"

Tricia didn't answer the first question. "No, Grant didn'
give it to me. It's just something I had lying around an
decided to put on."

"Oh." Angelica sounded disappointed.

"Now, can we get going with this baking? You've got t
hit the road early tomorrow."

Angelica sighed. "Don't remind me. Okay, first, let m
go home and get my sifter. If we're going to make thes
muffins and expect people to eat them, we're going to mak
them right."

"Aw, but Ange—"

"No buts. It's what our grandmother would have done."

Tricia winced. Pulling the grandmother card was no fai
"Fine. Go get your sifter."

"I'll be right back," Angelica said, grabbed her key
and headed for the door.

Tricia grabbed her wine glass and emptied its contents
At least she'd sidestepped the question about her ne
necklace.

Four more days and she'd be a year older, which wa
absurd. She grew older every day—but it was the anniver

sary of birth that aged you another year, not the interven-
ing days.

Four more days. And then it would be over. No one to
celebrate with. No one to share the joys and sorrows of the
day with.

As though reading her mind, Miss Marple said "*Yow!*"

"Oh, yes, I forgot. According to Christopher, you're the
one I love best."

"*Yow!*" Miss Marple replied.

"And I know you love me best."

Again, Miss Marple agreed.

"Then we'll spend my birthday together. Just the two
of us."

And didn't that sound like loads of fun?

Tricia fingered the chain around her neck. It was long
past time to stop thinking about the past—and hoping for
a future with someone who had made the choice of a life
of solitude. Except for the note that came with the locket,
she hadn't heard from Christopher in eighteen months. He
might have moved on and found someone else, and sending the locket was his final message, telling her to move
on as well.

That decided, she reached for the clasp on the chain—
then thought better of it. The locket was meant to be a
birthday gift. She'd wear it until Wednesday, then put it
away with the rest of Christopher's gifts in the back of her
closet.

Again she fingered the chain, felt the weight of the
locket that hung between her breasts—close to her heart.
Was that the reason Christopher had chosen such a gift?
She much preferred it to a sifter. But then, she wasn't likely
to get any other gifts on her birthday.

"Come Wednesday, we will *not* have a pity party. Maybe I'll buy a precooked lobster and one of Nikki's mini cakes. You like lobster and frosting," Tricia told Miss Marple, who agreed by purring.

"Then it's decided," Tricia said, with just the slightest catch in her voice. The plan sounded good—but she had a feeling that despite her resolve, a pity party might still be on the agenda. She would just have to resist the temptation.

The door rattled and Angelica returned, clutching a battered and discolored metal sifter that had obviously seen heavy use. "Look, Trish, it belonged to Grandma Miles," she said, handing it over.

Tricia examined the sifter and smiled, remembering how she'd watched her grandmother use it when making cakes.

"I want you to have it," Angelica said.

"Oh, no, I couldn't," Tricia said and tried to hand the sifter back. "I know how much it means to you."

Angelica refused to take it. "You don't know how much it means to me to know you're interested in baking. I want to encourage that in you."

Tricia swallowed a lump in her throat and gazed at the worn red wooden handle. "Thank you, Ange. This is the nicest gift you could have given me." A sentiment she would not have believed five minutes earlier.

Angelica beamed. "Let's get to baking!"

And for the first time in her adult life, Tricia enjoyed it.

SIXTEEN

Tricia was up early the next morning, but when she called to wish Angelica a safe trip, she found her sister had already hit the road for her next round of book signings.

After her usual stint on the treadmill, a leisurely shower, and a cup of coffee, Tricia gathered her purse and the plate of big, beautiful muffins covered in plastic wrap, and headed down to Haven't Got a Clue, with Miss Marple following her. Although it was only nine thirty, she decided to get to Jim Roth's wake early, figuring Frannie might need help to get things set up. "I'll be back in a couple of hours," she told the cat, backed out the door, and locked it.

As she turned around, Tricia saw a SALE PENDING sticker had been plastered across the Kelly Realty FOR SALE sign. She turned right around, unlocked the door, and reentered Haven't Got a Clue. Miss Marple still sat where

Tricia had left her mere seconds before, and gazed at Tricia quizzically.

"I know, I know—but I've got to make a call," she said, put her purse and the muffins on the counter, picked up the receiver, and dialed the old-fashioned rotary phone.

Bob Kelly answered on the fourth ring. "Hello," he barked.

Tricia put on her sunniest voice. "Hi, Bob, it's Tricia. I thought I'd give you a call to see how you're feeling."

"Fine," he said succinctly.

"Do you need anything?" Tricia asked.

"No, thank you." The man was positively infuriating.

"Will you be coming to Jim Roth's memorial service this morning?"

"No. I'm not feeling well."

He'd just said he was feeling fine. Tricia plowed ahead. "I see you've put a Sale Pending sign up on the lot on Main Street. I'm surprised it sold so fast. You put the For Sale sign up only yesterday. That was rather quick, wasn't it?"

"Yes."

Tricia ground her teeth to keep her anger from seething. "Do you mind if I ask who bought it?"

"Some development company. I never heard of them before."

"And they are?"

He sighed. "An outfit called Nigela Ricita Associates. Their representative contacted me last night. They want to sign the paperwork as soon as possible."

"Sounds like a woman-owned business," Tricia said.

"I don't care who owns it, just as long as they pay me so I can dump the property. I don't want to be associated with it."

"Why not? It wasn't your fault someone tampered with

the gas meter." She decided to push in the knife—just a little. "Was it?"

"Of course not."

"Then why are you being so coy about what you were doing at History Repeats Itself the night of the explosion?"

"I'm not being coy. I was there to collect the rent. Period."

"And did Jim pay you?"

"We hadn't gotten that far."

"Witnesses put you at the store for some time before the explosion."

"What witnesses?" Bob demanded.

Okay, just one witness—Ginny. But Tricia wasn't about to tell him that. "You'll have to ask Captain Baker about that. But, come on, Bob, you know that keeping mum on what you were doing there just makes you look bad. You can't afford a tarnished reputation."

"My reputation is sterling."

"Well, it won't stay that way if it looks like you have something to hide."

"This conversation is going nowhere," Bob said. "Good-bye, Tricia." Tricia heard a click, and then the line went dead. She replaced the receiver in its cradle.

"*Yow!*" Miss Marple said.

"Yes, he *is* being a big pill! I don't know how Angelica can stand him."

"*Brrrrp!*" Miss Marple agreed.

Tricia glanced at her watch. If she was lucky, she could make it to the inn in time for the . . . service? That didn't seem the right word. Perhaps celebration of Jim's life was a better description. "You're in charge, Miss Marple," she told the cat, collected her purse and the muffins once again, and struck out for the Brookview Inn.

It was exactly nine fifty-five when Tricia pulled into the Brookview Inn's already full parking lot. Parked in a tow-away zone was a Sheriff's Department cruiser. Had Captain Baker decided to attend the gathering—or had he sent one of his underlings to scope out the mourners?

There was one vehicle parked in the lot that Tricia had hoped she wouldn't see: Russ's junky old pickup truck. She'd been right: he'd made bail. *I am not going to let his presence bother me. I won't,* Tricia told herself, but she didn't feel all that confident. Still, perhaps he wouldn't behave like a horse's ass at what was supposed to be a solemn occasion.

Tricia grabbed the plate of muffins, closed the car door, and walked around to the front of the inn. The Robert Paige Memorial Dialysis Center was under construction across the street. The lovely, peaceful woods had been bulldozed, and only the bones of the new building stood in the morning sunshine. It was hard to believe the gutted landscape would ever look like the attractive architectural drawing on the sign out front.

As Tricia walked up the flagstone path that led to the inn's entrance, she noticed there were no flowers. The previous spring, pink begonias had welcomed the inn's visitors. No window boxes full of geraniums brightened the long porch, and it looked like the paint was beginning to peel along some of the clapboards.

Tricia entered the lobby and headed for the reception desk. Thankfully, everything around her looked as lovely as usual, and she could hear the buzz of voices coming from the conference room.

"Tricia, it's good to see you," called Eleanor, the inn's receptionist. "It's been too long."

"Yes, it has. I've been busy. I thought I'd stop and say

hello before I joined the rest of the group." Gosh, that made it sound like she was attending some kind of business meeting—not a memorial.

"It's terrible about poor Mr. Roth," Eleanor said. "I didn't know him well, but we spoke sometimes when he'd arrive early for Chamber meetings." Eleanor leaned in. "Although sad as the occasion is, we're happy to have the business. Things haven't been good lately. Bookings are down. We're seeing less trade in the dining room. We've had to let one of the maids go, and even the weekend sous-chef. That's why we've dropped our Sunday breakfast buffet."

No wonder they had allowed Frannie to bring food to Jim's wake. "I'm so sorry to hear that," Tricia said sympathetically.

"There's even talk the inn may go up for sale," Eleanor said with a catch in her voice.

Tricia's mouth dropped. "I had no idea things were this bad."

Eleanor nodded. "In the past, we've been able to weather these things—but this time. . . ." Her voice trailed off.

Stoneham without the Brookview Inn? The thought was too painful to contemplate. "Can't you hang on until the new dialysis center is built?" Tricia asked.

"It's one of the reasons we're doing so badly. The construction is very noisy. Guests come to the inn for peace and quiet. The sound of cement mixers and dump trucks starting at seven in the morning has been a real turnoff for our guests. The construction is due to last all summer and into the fall. The only saving grace is they don't work weekends. To add another nail in the inn's coffin, there's talk a low-cost motel chain is interested in buying the Full Moon Nudist Camp to build a hundred-unit structure."

"Do you think they'd sell the camp? I mean, after all the hoops they jumped through to develop that property?"

"Money talks," Eleanor said. "If a motel is built, it would absolutely kill us."

Tricia shook her head. "There will always be people interested in more than just low cost when it comes to travel. And I've heard there's a developer looking into buying properties here in Stoneham," she said. "Maybe they'd be interested in investing in the inn."

"I hadn't heard about that," Eleanor said. "I'll mention it to my boss. Do you know the name of the developer?"

"Nigela Ricita Associates, but I don't know how you'd contact them."

"Don't worry—I'll find out. Thanks for the tip." Eleanor leaned closer and lowered her voice. "Did you hear the latest? The convenience store up by the highway sold the winning Powerball lottery ticket, and the prize was twenty million dollars."

"That's terrific news. Maybe that'll bring some welcome relief to the local economy. Who won?" Tricia asked.

"I hope it's me—but my tickets are at home. I'll have to wait until my lunch break to check them."

"Good luck," Tricia said, giving Eleanor a thumbs-up.

Eleanor smiled hopefully, and waved a hand in the direction of the inn's large conference room. "You can go straight in."

Tricia nodded and headed in that direction. The murmur of voices grew louder as she approached. Since the parking lot had been full, she guessed it had been filled with Jim's friends and not the inn's guests. Clutching her plate of muffins, Tricia entered the conference room. A large easel stood just inside the door with a poster-sized print of Jim's smiling face set up to greet the mourners. Talk about disconcerting! Her gaze immediately zeroed in on Russ. He didn't notice her, since he was busy talking with Joyce Widman from the romance bookstore and jotting notes in his ever-present steno notebook. The puffy mouse below his left eye was an off-putting shade of purple. Served him right for being such a jerk the night before. Now, if he would just behave himself during the next hour—and not cross paths with Captain Baker.

Dressed in civvies, Baker stood at the sidelines along with a uniformed Deputy Henderson, watching the crowd. Had Baker brought along backup in case Russ stepped out of line? Baker caught sight of Tricia and nodded in her direction, but his face remained impassive. She acknowledged him, too, then caught sight of the elderly Dexter twins, again dressed identically—this time somber black dresses, dark hose, and dark shoes. They wore little pillbox hats with veils that had been popular nearly fifty years before. Could they have known Jim Roth, or were they looking for more signatures for their petition? Tricia looked closer, and sure enough, Midge was holding her clipboard. How rude of them to crash Jim's memorial. Then again, what better place to make their case?

Tricia stepped over to the refreshment table to drop off her contribution. The assembled pastries, muffins, and fruit trays rivaled the best the inn had ever offered. But the pièce de résistance was the multilayered cake frosted in pastel yellow. It looked like . . . a wedding cake, complete with basket weave design, plastic pillars supporting each layer, and a fresh flower garnish. The only thing missing was the bride and groom topper.

Several sprays of flowers stood to one side. Tricia checked the cards. Several booksellers had gone in on each, and the bouquet of yellow roses from the staff at Haven't

Got a Clue was simple yet dignified. Conspicuously absent was an official remembrance from the Stoneham Chamber of Commerce. Did that mean Frannie's replacement wasn't on top of things, or that because of her "rules are rules" attitude, she—and Bob Kelly—had withheld such a gesture out of pure spite?

The room was quite crowded, with knots of people Tricia didn't know. They didn't seem to be mingling with the other booksellers and Chamber members. Most of the booksellers had little time for social lives. Perhaps they were friends of Jim's from out of town.

Tricia caught sight of her friend Deborah Black, clad in a floral dress made tight by the fact that she hadn't quite lost all of her pregnancy weight. Tricia waggled her fingers in a wave, and Deborah broke away from the group she'd been chatting with, meeting Tricia halfway. "Good turnout, huh?" she said.

"Yes. Jim would've been proud," Tricia agreed.

Deborah searched the faces in the room. "Is Angelica coming?"

"No, she had to go back on the road promoting her book. She should be back on Friday."

"Good. I've ordered ten copies of her cookbook, and I'd like to have her sign them for my customers."

"I'm sure she'd love to."

Deborah nodded in the direction of the crowd she'd just left. "What's with Frannie and that outfit?"

Had Frannie attended the wake in her usual dark slacks and a colorful aloha shirt? Tricia craned her neck, but all she could see was the back of Frannie's dark head.

"I know black is no longer a funeral requirement, but surely that outfit she's wearing is more appropriate for a wedding—in fact, more suited for the mature bride."

Tricia frowned. Frannie *had* hoped to be Jim's bride. She wouldn't have worn—she couldn't . . . .

She had.

Frannie stepped away from the others, revealing white shoes and a white linen dress with a pink carnation pinned to the lapel of the matching jacket.

"And did you get a load of that cake?" Deborah said under her breath.

Tricia braved a smile. "It's lovely."

"I'll bet it's white cake under that frosting," Deborah muttered. "What's going on?"

"I really don't know," Tricia lied.

"And what's *he* doing here?" Deborah asked.

Tricia followed her gaze to Captain Baker, who now stood alone at the side of the room. Since she'd entered the room, he'd lost the deputy and acquired a glass of punch and a plate of pastries. He looked uncomfortable. Was he off duty, or just trying to blend in with the crowd?

Tricia looked away. "I've been thinking a lot about our conversation the other day, and I've got a business proposition for you, Deb."

"That sounds interesting," Deborah said, her eyes widening with interest.

"You're really stressed out—"

"And how," Deborah agreed.

"I wondered if you'd like to borrow Mr. Everett for a few hours now and then. He'd be more than willing to spell you during lunch, or if you wanted to catch up on your paperwork."

Deborah's hand flew to her throat. "Oh, Tricia, that is so nice of you to offer—but I couldn't afford to pay—"

"I'm not asking you to. I'd be glad to help you—and so would Mr. Everett."

Deborah's hand moved up to cover her mouth, and she looked like she was about to cry. "It's so sweet of you, but I just can't accept."

"Why?" Tricia asked, trying not to feel hurt.

Deborah seemed at a loss for words. "I just can't."

Tricia swallowed her disappointment. "Why don't you think about it for a few days? Or just give a holler when you feel overwhelmed?"

Deborah nodded. "I will. I promise." She cleared her throat, and looked for an escape. "I need another cup of coffee. You want one?" she asked.

Tricia shook her head.

"I'll be back," Deborah said, patted Tricia's arm, and took off in the direction of the refreshment table.

Tricia let her gaze travel back to Captain Baker. He caught her eye and gave her a hesitant smile. Despite the way her conversation with Deborah had ended, she found herself smiling back—then caught sight of Russ watching her. The smile instantly evaporated. Captain Baker took a step forward, then stopped, looking at something behind Tricia. She turned, and saw Stoneham's librarian, Lois Kerr, approaching.

"Tricia, I'm so pleased you made it. I hear I have you to thank for our latest donation."

"Me?"

"Yes, Livvie Roth called the library yesterday afternoon. She's donated the entire surviving stock from History Repeats Itself to the library, to use as we see fit. We'll have quite a World War Two collection, and anything that we can't use will go in our next book sale. Of course, some of the more valuable pieces we'll try to sell to collectors, but it looks like it'll generate quite a bit of revenue for us. Thank you so much for suggesting us to Mrs. Roth."

"You're very welcome. Do you know if she plans to attend this morning? When I last spoke with her, she was undecided."

"I believe she said she was going to try to make it. Frannie has asked me to make the announcement about the donation."

"It'll be quite a tribute to Jim," Tricia agreed.

Frannie approached. "Lois—Tricia, I'm so glad you both could come."

Tricia gave Frannie a brief hug. "I'm glad to be here—for you, and for Jim," she whispered. She pulled back.

"If you'll excuse me," Lois said, "I'm going to warm up my coffee."

"We'll be starting in just a few minutes," Frannie warned. Lois gave her a brief wave and headed for the coffee urn.

"That's a lovely outfit you have on," Tricia said.

A blush rose on Frannie's cheeks, and she looked down at herself. "Do you think? I bought it when I thought. . . ." Tears filled her eyes. "Last fall, Jim and I talked about getting married. But that's all that came of it—talk. I guess I was foolish to buy it. And then when Jim was killed, I figured I'd never get the chance to look pretty for him. Then I thought—well, why not wear it today, in his honor?"

Tricia nodded, trying not to see it as the pathetic gesture it was.

"Of course, I haven't told anyone but you about our hopes and plans, and I'm sure I can trust you not to say a word. Not even to Angelica."

Tricia said nothing, and hoped she could get to Angelica before she mentioned it to Frannie. She gave the room a once-over.

"I see the Dexter sisters are here," Tricia said.

Frannie let out a frustrated sigh and pursed her lips.

"Those old biddies. They didn't know Jim. They wanted a chance to speak—to urge everyone to sign their petition to reestablish a Stoneham police force. I told them no, but they wouldn't leave, and are circulating the room asking people to sign. I'd give them a piece of my mind, but my mama taught me to respect my elders."

Tricia saw a man adding his signature to the petition. She figured she ought to change the subject, before Frannie exploded in anger. "I spoke to Bob Kelly this morning. He said he didn't feel well enough to make it."

Frannie shrugged. "I'm not surprised. He's kept a low profile since Jim's death. If he hadn't been in the building when it blew, I'm sure people would assume he was behind Jim's death."

"You sound like you've changed your mind about him."

"There don't seem to be any other viable suspects," Frannie said, with a pointed look at Captain Baker. He just stared back.

Frannie looked at her watch. "I guess I'd better get things moving along. These dear people—as well as you and I— need to get their shops open in another hour or so. If you'll excuse me." Frannie crossed the room, but paused to speak to Chauncey Porter. He held a sheet of paper—his eulogy, no doubt. He nodded, and then Frannie stepped over to the refreshment table, picked up one of the glass punch cups and a spoon, and moved to the front of the room. Chauncey picked up the easel and poster, and set it beside Frannie. Tricia cringed as Frannie tapped the spoon on the glass. So much for keeping her feelings and aspirations a secret. Was Frannie determined to employ every wedding tradition at this wake?

"May I have your attention, please?" Frannie called.

The voices died down, and everyone stepped closer to the front of the room.

"It's with deep sadness that we're here today, to bid our friend Jim Roth good-bye." She sighed, looked like she was about to cry, but then forced a smile. "I met Jim when he joined the Chamber of Commerce just five years ago. He was a great asset to the organization, as well as being the kindest, sweetest man you'd ever want to meet," she continued. "Jim could be counted on to make great suggestions, and he always paid his dues on time. In addition, he—he. . . ." She seemed to struggle to find something else to say. "He was a wonderful man."

A soft smattering of applause followed. Frannie waited for quiet to return before speaking again. "Jim's good friend and Main Street neighbor, Chauncey Porter, will give the eulogy."

Chauncey stepped up to the microphone, tapped it twice, and said, "Test, test." A titter of laughter went through the waiting audience. Chauncey retrieved a pair of reading glasses from the breast pocket of his suit jacket, settled them on his nose, and glanced down at his speech.

"Friends, we're here today to say good-bye to our neighbor, our fellow Chamber member, and a friend to us all. Jim Roth was all those things, but he was much, much more. Jim could be counted on to pitch in at Chamber meetings, bringing good ideas to help his fellow members and strengthen the organization, as well as helping out at the many charity events the Chamber sponsored."

Tricia frowned. She hadn't remembered Jim doing any of those things. Perhaps he'd been more active before she'd come to Stoneham.

"Jim's knowledge of history was vast—he was a veritable font of information. He was the perfect man to own a shop like History Repeats Itself, sharing what he knew about events of the past—from prehistoric days, right through the Cold War, to the conflicts in the Middle East. He may have missed his calling, for I believe he would've made a wonderful teacher. He would've made history fun for the kids of Stoneham High—or any other place of education."

All around Tricia, heads nodded in agreement. Someone blew their nose, and there were several pairs of damp eyes as tears were brushed away. Head bent, her eyes covered by the wad of tissues in her hand, Frannie quietly sobbed. Russ scribbled in his steno pad, no doubt gathering material for Jim's obit.

As Tricia looked around the room, she noticed Livvie Roth standing in the open doorway, listening to the tribute for her son. She gave Mrs. Roth a tentative smile and a brief wave, but the old woman's eyes were riveted on Chauncey.

"But perhaps Jim Roth's greatest legacy was the lives he saved in battle," Chauncey continued. "Those of you who knew Jim well will remember his exciting tales of fighting in the jungles of Vietnam. Yes, Jim was also a decorated war hero. Once, in a heated firefight, he single-handedly saved the lives of seven men in his battalion. He was awarded a number of medals, which he proudly displayed in his shop. The Bronze Star, the Silver Star, and, of course, the Purple Heart for being wounded in battle.

"We will miss Jim. His winning smile, his friendly ways, and most of all his big heart. Farewell, dear friend. May you rest in peace." Chauncey folded his notes, placed them in his suit pocket, and stepped away from the microphone.

Frannie took a shuddering breath and composed herself before she stepped back to the microphone. "Thank you,

Chauncey. That was lovely. And now, I believe Lois Kerr, Stoneham's librarian, would like to say a few words about Jim and another of his legacies."

Lois stepped forward, but before she could say a word, a voice from the back of the room pierced the quiet. "I have a few things to say, as well."

Everyone turned as Livvie Roth entered the conference room, threading her way through the crowd. Clad in a stunningly loud, magenta floral dress, she seemed ill-dressed for a memorial service, and the dark expression covering her face was menacing enough to frighten small animals and children. This was not at all the sometimes sweet, little old lady Tricia had met previously.

Livvie stepped up to the microphone. She took a few moments to look each and every person in the room in the eye. "I, too, came here today to tell you about my son." Mrs. Roth's hard gaze raked her audience once again. "I heard what Ms. Armstrong said, that he was a kind and decent man. I listened with interest to Mr. Porter's tall tales. But I'm here to tell you that James Winston Roth was a liar and a cad. He treated me, his own mother, like a servant. He took my money, kept me homebound, and even drove my car—not allowing me its use. He could never have become a teacher. Jim never even graduated high school. He learned much of what he knew about history from comic books and the Military Channel. He was a terrible businessman. His store was on the brink of bankruptcy through bad management and his gambling habit. Even Gamblers Anonymous couldn't keep him away from the craps tables. Did you know about that?"

No one said a word, or even nodded. Several guests looked embarrassed. Had they known Jim from GA meetings? Tricia felt like a rubbernecker at a crash site, but she, too, could not look away.

"Worst of all, James lied about his military record," Mrs. Roth continued. "He had none! He was declared Four-F by the Selective Service, and often bragged that if he hadn't been found ineligible to serve, he would have escaped to Canada to dodge the draft. Those medals he displayed on the walls of his store were bought at an estate sale!"

Tricia looked around and saw mouths hanging open in shock and dismay.

"And you," Mrs. Roth said with disgust, staring at Frannie. "When I heard it was you who'd set up this farce of a service, I was livid. How dare you prance around here in a wedding dress, talking about James as though he had any use for you?"

All eyes roved to Frannie, who stood stock still at the front of the room.

"This pitiable woman desperately wanted to believe James was going to marry her," Mrs. Roth said with scorn. "Did she tell you he'd dumped her just days before his death?"

Captain Baker's eyes narrowed. Frannie's eyes widened in horror, and her jaw dropped.

"Yes," Mrs. Roth continued, "that was the kind of man James Roth was. Dishonest, deceitful, and a bully to the end. It is the saddest thing a mother can say about her child, but the world is better off without him."

And with that, she gave Frannie a parting glare and stepped away from the microphone. The mourners moved back, giving her plenty of space as she stalked out of the conference room.

A deadly silence followed her departure. The guests looked at each other in shared shock, all trying not to look at Frannie. For a terribly long moment, Frannie stood there, dumbfounded, and then she burst into tears. Grace, who was the closest, rushed to her side, but was pushed away as Frannie bolted from the room. Ginny ran after her, with Russ right on her heels.

Tricia sidled up to Captain Baker and whispered, "Looks like you've now got three suspects."

SEVENTEEN

 Tricia had never seen a room clear out so fast. Within seconds of Frannie's humiliated escape, most of the rest of the mourners grabbed their serving plates and scattered. Even the Dexter sisters gave up their petition quest and filed out after the others. Only Tricia, Mr. Everett, Grace, and Captain Baker remained to take in the chaos.

Ginny quickly returned. "I thought maybe Frannie had run to the bathroom to have a good cry, but I couldn't find her. I looked in the parking lot, and her car's gone." She shook her head. "Boy, Mrs. Roth's announcements were a bit of a shocker, weren't they?"

"It certainly doesn't sound like she'll miss him," Tricia agreed.

"But do you think it's possible she might have killed her own son?" Ginny pressed.

"That's infanticide," Grace said, appalled.

"Jim was no baby," Ginny said with a smirk.

Tricia frowned. "I have to admit Mrs. Roth is one strange duck. She'd started redecorating her home—removing Jim's presence—before he'd even had a chance to be missed. That alone doesn't make her look good."

"Why didn't you mention that before?" Baker asked.

She shrugged. "I guess I didn't want her to look heart-less. Then again . . . I entertained the thought she might've been poisoning Jim."

"Poison?" It was Mr. Everett's turn to be appalled.

"That first day I met her, she kind of creeped me out. She offered me a lemon bar cookie that had a strange, al-most glowing yellow color. It reminded me of antifreeze. And then, not two days later, I saw a gallon jug of the stuff in her garage."

"Many people store antifreeze. It doesn't make them criminals," Grace said.

Tricia turned to Captain Baker. "Did the medical exam-iner's office do any toxicology tests on what was left of Jim?"

Baker looked uncertain. "They weren't able to scrape up much—although I can certainly ask. But they wouldn't have been looking for that kind of evidence, so there's a possibility they didn't do more than a DNA test to prove he'd died in the blast."

"Tricia, you can't be serious," Grace chided. "No mother would kill her only child, no matter how bad a boy he was." Tricia knew Grace spoke from experience, but there was plenty of evidence to the contrary.

"It depends on how abusive he was. She said Jim was a lifelong bully," Ginny said.

"But that's not the impression he gave his customers,

or his friends at the Chamber of Commerce," Tricia said in Jim's defense. "There's got to be some middle ground."

"He lied about his military service," Mr. Everett said, aghast.

"Don't forget," Ginny said, "we've now got another suspect: Frannie. 'Hell hath no fury like a woman scorned,'" she quoted.

"Oh, dear," Mr. Everett murmured. "Oh, dear, oh, dear."

"I never knew they were dating. Do you think it's true that Jim dropped her just days before he died?" Grace asked.

"Then why would she go to all the trouble of arranging this memorial service?" Ginny asked.

"To avert suspicion," Baker answered. "I'll be having a talk with both Mrs. Roth *and* Ms. Armstrong." He nodded in Tricia's direction. "If you'll excuse me."

They watched him as he left the silent conference room.

Nobody had mentioned Bob Kelly, or that he'd been conspicuous by his absence from the memorial service. He certainly hadn't sounded unwell when Tricia had spoken to him earlier.

Tricia glanced at her watch. "We'd better go, too. I need to open the store in less than an hour."

"I'll see you there," Mr. Everett said, and took Grace's hand. He nodded a good-bye to Ginny, and Grace gave a halfhearted wave.

Ginny sighed. "I wonder if Frannie will show up at the Cookery."

"Oh, dear. I hadn't thought of that."

"I could sub for her today," Ginny offered.

"But it's your only day off."

"I can use the money," Ginny admitted. After all, she'd done it before. And Angelica wouldn't be pleased if the Cookery lost a day's revenue.

"Thanks, Ginny. I'll walk with you to your car," Tricia said, and picked up her own plate from the long, empty table. All that remained was the solitary pseudo-wedding cake, which hadn't even been cut.

"Shouldn't one of us take that picture of Jim?" Ginny asked.

Tricia glanced back at the giant, smiling picture of Jim, taken in happier times, that was still on the easel. "I don't know anyone who'd want it. Not his mother— and at this point, I shouldn't think Frannie would want it, either."

The bright, warming sunshine was a stark difference from the gloom that had fallen inside the inn's conference room. The flowering crabapple tree outside the entrance reminded Tricia that no matter what, life went on.

The parking lot was decidedly empty now that the mourners had left, and Tricia remembered her earlier conversation with a worried Eleanor. Could the inn really be shut down if they couldn't find an investor?

"I'll meet you at Haven't Got a Clue. It'll save time if I need to open the Cookery," Ginny said, and headed for her car.

Tricia opened her car door, but before she could get inside, her cell phone chirped for attention. Since the car had been sitting in the hot sun, she stood outside it and took the call, recognizing Angelica's number. "Hello."

"Trish, are you still at the memorial service?"

"Just leaving. Boy, did you miss the fireworks. Chauncey

Porter gave the eulogy, and then Jim's mother burst in to refute everything Chauncey said—including the fact that Jim lied about his military career."

"I always miss the good stuff," Angelica said, but she didn't sound all that enthralled.

"Where are you?" Tricia asked.

"In a parking lot in Bennington, Vermont. I've been trying to call Bob and still haven't been able to reach him. Did he show up at the service?"

"As a matter of fact, he didn't. But I spoke to him this morning. He said he wasn't well, but I suspect he was more interested in making a buck."

"Why?"

"Someone's already bought the lot where History Repeats Itself used to be," Tricia said.

"You're kidding! Who'd want that?" Angelica asked. "The cost of redevelopment would be astronomical."

"That's what I thought. But don't you think it bodes well for Stoneham?"

"I guess."

"Aren't you going to ask who bought it?" Tricia asked.

"Do I care?"

"A development company called Nigela Ricita Associates."

"And that's important because?" Angelica countered.

"Nobody's ever heard of it. And guess what—the Brookview Inn might go up for sale."

"You're kidding!" Angelica sounded more interested in that tidbit. "But it's always done so well."

"Not lately, thanks to the construction across the street."

"That's too bad, but let's get back to Bob. He's not answering his home phone number, his cell, or the line at the realty office. Trish, I'm really getting worried."

"Why?"

"Because it's not like Bob to ignore a call on his office phone."

"Does he have caller ID? You said he's been avoiding you."

"Bob's too cheap for caller ID."

Suddenly, the sun didn't feel quite so warm on Tricia's back.

"Trish, will you please go over to Bob's house and check up on him?"

"Ange!" Tricia protested, "I've got to open the store in less than an hour."

"Bob only lives two blocks from your store. It'll take you five minutes. *Please?*"

Tricia sighed. "Oh, all right."

"And call me when you get there," Angelica pressed.

"Okay." She remembered Frannie's frantic and tearful exit from the service. "Um, you might want to give Frannie a call—to make sure she intends to open the Cookery this afternoon."

"Why wouldn't she open?"

"Mrs. Roth trashed not only her son, but Frannie, too. She said Jim had dumped Frannie just days before his death, and kind of hinted she might have killed him."

"You're kidding."

"No. Frannie ran from the room in tears." Tricia made a quick sweep of the nearly empty lot. "I suppose she might've gone home, if only just to change clothes. Uh, she was kind of dressed like a bride."

"Why does everything juicy have to happen when I'm out of town?" Angelica demanded.

"But Captain Baker, who was also at the service, said he intended to talk to her."

"Tell me more. On second thought—don't. Get over to Bob's. You can fill me in on everything else that happened later. Luckily, Sundays aren't your busiest day at the shop."

"What about your signing?"

"I don't have to be there until one. There's still time. Now get going to Bob's."

"All right," Tricia said testily. "I'll call you later." And she folded her phone, tossing it into her purse. She got into the car, started it, and hit the air-conditioning button, then pulled out of the lot and headed for Bob's house.

As usual for a Sunday morning in Stoneham, traffic was light, and as Angelica predicted, it took her only five minutes to arrive at Bob's home, where she pulled up behind his car. The neighborhood looked half asleep. Only one of the neighbors was visible—a man mowing his lawn several houses away.

Tricia got out of her car, walked up the path, and climbed the steps to the porch. She rang the bell and waited. A bird called out from the bushes at the end of the porch. Tricia looked down and noticed a crushed cigarette butt lying next to one of the white plastic chairs. Bob didn't smoke, and though he might have cheap lawn furniture, he kept the place neat and tidy.

Tricia frowned, glanced at her watch, and sighed. "Come on, Bob." She pressed the bell again, heard the muffled chime from inside. The neighbor made another circuit around his yard, and the skin on the back of Tricia's neck prickled. The broken window had been repaired, and she stepped over to peer inside.

Bob's living room was a shambles. Furniture had been

tipped over, books and papers lay scattered across the living room rug, and the pictures on the wall were askew. Tricia could see broken crockery in the hall leading to the kitchen. And on the far side of the room, lying in front of the fireplace, was a body—Bob.

EIGHTEEN

Tricia rapped on the glass as hard as she dared. "Bob! Bob!" she called, but the figure on the rug did not move. She dived for the door handle and yanked at it, but of course it was locked.

She thought of Jim Roth—and how someone had messed with his gas meter—and what had happened when a spark ignited it.

She stepped away from the house, took out her cell phone, and punched in 9-1-1.

"I'd advise you to stand as far away from the house as possible, ma'am," the dispatcher cautioned in as dispassionate a voice as Tricia had ever heard.

"But what if he's suffocating?"

"You won't help him if you die in the explosion, too."

Within in a minute, wailing sirens broke the midmorning quiet. Thank goodness the Stoneham Fire Department was only a couple of blocks away. Its bright red pumper truck pulled up in front of Bob's house, with the rescue unit right behind. And bringing up the rear was Russ's junky old pickup truck. He jumped out and met Tricia on the sidewalk across the street from Bob's house. "I heard the call on my police scanner."

Of course.

"What's the story here?" Russ demanded.

Tricia ignored him as Fire Chief Farrar hurried over to join them. "Man down?"

"Yes, in the living room. There may be a gas leak. It looks like Bob's lying on the floor, unconscious."

He nodded, and headed for the house.

The other firefighters were already converging on the porch, dressed in protective gear and masks, and armed with hatchets. They thought to do what Tricia hadn't: look under the welcome mat for the key. They found it, opened the door, and cautiously went inside.

Tricia found herself clenching her fists, her nails digging into her palms as she waited for something to happen. Russ put a protective arm around her, and she angrily shrugged it off.

"I only meant to be reassuring," Russ said, but again Tricia ignored him.

Finally, after what seemed like hours, but was probably less than two minutes, two firefighters dragged an unconscious Bob from the house, shuffled down the steps, and laid him on the ground. Tricia ran across the street, with Russ in hot pursuit.

She stood by helplessly as one of the firefighters took off his mask and covered Bob's face. In a few moments, Bob roused and was coughing—a very good sign.

The Stoneham volunteer ambulance pulled to the curb, its lights flashing, and in moments the paramedics had exited the vehicle and relieved the firefighters.

Fire Chief Farrar trundled down the porch steps and waved Tricia and Russ aside, giving the paramedics more room to work. "Ms. Miles, Russ. I thought you'd like to know someone *had* tampered with the gas meter. We're airing the place out now."

"Will Bob be okay?"

He nodded. "They'll take him to St. Joseph's Hospital in Milford, just to make sure. It's a good thing you showed up when you did. You undoubtedly saved his life."

"How about that meter?" Russ asked. "Same as at History Repeats Itself?"

The chief hesitated, and instead of answering Russ's question, said, "We shut off the gas. Now it's up to the Sheriff's Department to determine if there're any fingerprints. My guess is no. But maybe Mr. Kelly saw something and can give them an inkling of who they should go after."

And maybe he couldn't. Or more likely—wouldn't.

"Can we talk to Bob?" Russ asked.

Bob sat on the grass, his mouth and nose still covered by an oxygen mask, talking with the paramedics and, from the muffled sound of it, insisting he did not need to go to the hospital.

"I guess, but don't interfere with the EMTs," Chief Farrar said, and waved at one of his men that he'd be right there. "If you'll excuse me."

Tricia and Russ walked across Bob's lawn until they stood in front of him. Bob moved the mask aside. "Don't tell Angelica about this, Tricia. Otherwise, she'll be calling me day and night, and I don't want her to worry."

"She might not worry so much if you actually answered her calls."

He glared at her for a second, then put the mask back up to his face and closed his eyes.

"What happened?" Russ asked.

Bob shook his head, and again removed the mask. "I was taking a nap. I guess I must have smelled the gas, and tried to get up. That's all I remember."

Tricia scowled. She knew a lie when she heard one. The house was a shambles. No one could have slept through that kind of destruction.

The paramedics helped Bob onto the gurney, and this time he didn't protest. "We're ready to roll," the female EMT said, ushering Tricia and Russ out of her path.

"Give me a call if you want a ride back from the hospital," Russ volunteered.

Bob gave a feeble wave, and closed his eyes once more.

Tricia and Russ followed as the EMTs rolled the gurney across the grass and loaded Bob into the back of the ambulance. A minute or two later, they pulled away from the curb—with no lights or siren.

"Poor Bob's having a string of bad luck," Russ commented. "I'm beginning to wonder if the intended victim wasn't Jim Roth at all."

"You mean you've only *now* come to that conclusion?" Tricia asked, even though she'd come to the same conclusion only seconds before.

Russ bristled indignantly. "And what was your first clue?"

"The night someone tried to break into Bob's house, of course. And the fact that he wouldn't talk about his conversation with Jim Roth. He also had a security system installed. Everyone's been so preoccupied with Jim's death, they haven't looked at the big picture."

"Everyone but you?" he asked skeptically.

Tricia shrugged. "The question is, when is Captain Baker going to get around to making the connection?"

"Why don't you just tell him? You seem to have his ear on a regular basis."

"I don't know why you're jealous of my friendship with him. *You* dumped *me*, remember?"

"That was a mistake. I've been trying to win you back ever since."

"I don't *want* to be *won*. And for another thing, I may forgive—but I never forget." And with that, Tricia turned and stalked back to her car. This time Russ did not follow.

Once in her car, Tricia retrieved her purse from the passenger seat and rummaged through it until she found her phone. Then she punched in Captain Baker's private number. He wasn't likely to answer if he was questioning Frannie or Mrs. Roth, or had gone home to change into his uniform, but she felt she should at least tell him about this latest development. Voice mail answered after three rings.

"Grant, it's Tricia Miles. I don't know how tuned in you are to emergency calls, but someone tampered with Bob Kelly's gas meter—the same as what happened at History Repeats Itself. They've taken him to St. Joseph's Hospital in Milford. Maybe you need to have more than just a friendly chat with Bob. Otherwise, he's going to end up in the morgue—just as dead as Jim Roth."

It was after twelve o'clock when Tricia made it back to Haven't Got a Clue, where she found not only Mr. Everett standing outside the door, but Ginny, too. "Where've you been?" Ginny scolded. "Frannie never showed up at the Cookery."

"A number of customers came by, but we had to turn them away," Mr. Everett said. "We were getting worried about you."

"I'm sorry. I got a call from Angelica. She wanted me to go check on Bob Kelly. It's a good thing I did," she said, and explained how she'd found Bob.

"Wow," Ginny breathed. "Was there an explosion? Is he okay?"

"No explosion, and he'll be fine."

"You'll have to tell me more, but first we'd better get these stores open," Ginny said. As usual, she had her priorities straight.

Tricia unlocked Haven't Got a Clue, and Mr. Everett entered. He immediately reversed the CLOSED sign to OPEN and turned on the lights, while she and Ginny headed for the Cookery. No sooner had they opened the cookbook store's door than a couple of customers arrived. "We saw Angelica Miles on TV last night. She said she owned this store, and that her new book was available. Do you have signed copies?" one woman asked.

"We sure do," Ginny answered, and ushered the woman to a stock of copies by the register.

Tricia left Ginny to help Angelica's fans while she readied the cash register and made sure the tape in the credit card machine was full. After that, she rang up the sale of Angelica's cookbooks while Ginny bagged them. Neither of them spoke until after the women had left the shop.

"Can I put this cutout somewhere else?" Ginny asked. "Having Angelica looking over my shoulder all day will drive me nuts."

"That's what Frannie said. She put it outside. But someone keeps doing stuff to it."

"Stuff?"

"Dressing it up. Putting goofy glasses on it. If you put it outside, try to catch whoever is messing with it before they deface it."

Ginny shrugged. "Whatever you say."

"Oh, gosh, I promised Ange I'd buy a copy of her book. I'd better do that now," Tricia said, and grabbed a copy.

"Better take one of the unsigned ones," Ginny advised. "If customers are actually traveling to Stoneham to get them, we want to keep them happy."

"You're right. Ange can always sign mine later," Tricia said. Ginny handed her a copy of the book from a box behind the counter. Tricia paid for it, gave Ginny a good-bye nod, and headed back for her own store.

Though she hadn't really expected Frannie to show up for work, she had hoped she'd get a call. Once back inside Haven't Got a Clue, Tricia checked for messages, but there were none. It was time to consult Angelica's emergency phone list once again.

Leaving Mr. Everett and Miss Marple in charge, Tricia headed for her loft to call Frannie. This wasn't a conversation she wanted to share with her customers.

Tricia settled on one of the kitchen's island stools, and punched in Frannie's number. She answered on the second ring. "Hello?" It was more of a question than a greeting.

"Frannie? It's Tricia. I was calling to see if you're all right."

"No. But. . . . Oh, dear, I didn't open the Cookery. Oh, Tricia, I'm so sorry. And I'm sorry I didn't call. I've just been too upset," Frannie said, and from her wobbly voice, it sounded like she'd been crying. Tricia got up and wandered into her living room, thanking those who followed Alexander Graham Bell for inventing the wireless phone.

"It's okay. Ginny can cover for you for a few hours. Do you think you'll be able to make it in later today?"

"Nooooo." Frannie started crying again.

"It's okay," Tricia said at least five times before she could get Frannie to answer again. "Ginny's willing to stay until closing. Do you think you'll make it in tomorrow?"

Tricia heard the sound of Frannie blowing her nose— loudly—several times. "I'll try."

Tricia sighed. Perhaps that was the best she could expect right now. "Do you need company?" she asked, desperately hoping the answer was no. She really needed to attend to her own store.

"Thank you, but no. Penny and I will be okay." Penny was Frannie's orange-and-white cat.

Tricia moved into her bedroom, and stopped at the bank of windows that overlooked Main Street. "Maybe I could bring you something later—from the Bookshelf Diner?"

"Oh, no, I don't want to put you to any trouble. I'm just so embarrassed. And to make it worse, Captain Baker followed me home from the Brookview after Jim's . . . wake . . . and practically interrogated me. I think he actually believes I might've *killed* Jim. *Me!* I loved him. You have to believe me!" And Frannie started crying again.

Tricia cast about, desperate to find something to say to distract Frannie. Her gaze landed on the sign across the street. "Uh, did you know a development company bought the empty lot across the street?" Tricia asked. She wasn't about to mention the name of Frannie's dead lover's store.

Frannie sniffed. "No. But I haven't had time to think of much of anything, what with everything else that's going on."

"It was bought by a development company by the name of Nigela Ricita Associates."

Frannie sniffed again. "I've heard that name before."

"Oh?"

"But I can't remember where."

"Well, if you think of it, please let me know."

Frannie blew her nose again.

"Do you think you'll be in to work at the Cookery tomorrow?" Tricia asked again.

"I may have to wear a bag over my head but, yes, I'll be there bright and early."

"Thank you. I'll be here at the store for the rest of the day, and have no plans for the evening, so if you need someone to talk to—"

"Thank you, Tricia. You're a good friend."

"I'll see you tomorrow," Tricia said, added a good-bye, and pushed down the phone's rest buttons. There was another phone call she needed to make. She glanced at her watch. Angelica's signing was for one o'clock, and it wasn't yet one thirty. She'd still be tied up. And was it a good idea to tell her about Bob when she had more driving to do later in the day? Learning about Bob's hospitalization might be too distracting.

Tricia hung up the receiver and decided to put off being the bearer of bad news. After all, there was probably nothing Angelica could do for Bob. And her attentions of late hadn't been all that welcome. Then again, Tricia could just leave a message telling Angelica she'd checked up on Bob and would call later. That way Angelica wouldn't worry, at least not too much, and would be able to carry on with her day's agenda. Tricia picked up the receiver once more and dialed.

With that chore out of the way, she returned to Haven't Got a Clue.

Booked for Lunch stayed open an extra hour on Sundays, and Tricia anticipated another visit from Darcy with the café's cash and receipts, so she was surprised when it was Jake who showed up at her door a little after four that afternoon. Clearly, he didn't want to be there, and tossed the blue bank bag onto the cash desk. "Here you go, Toots."

Toots?

"Where's Darcy?" Tricia asked.

"She had other things to do. Like I do," he said, and turned for the door.

"Wait—what other things?"

He paused. "How would I know? I'm not her keeper. And you're not mine."

"Jake, please. We need to get along while Angelica's gone."

"No, we don't."

"Let me rephrase that. It's in our best interests to get along while Angelica is gone."

"If you say so." Jake opened the door, and the bell's cheerful tinkle made quite a contrast with the man's sullen demeanor. He let the door slam shut behind him.

"Oh, dear," Mr. Everett said. Tricia hadn't seen him approach from the side shelves. "He certainly is a disagreeable person."

"Yes, and we may have to put up with him until Angelica finishes her book tour."

"How long is that?"

Tricia sighed. Another three weeks."

"Oh, dear," Mr. Everett said again, shook his head, and went back to straightening the bookshelves.

An hour later, Tricia tallied up the day's results. Though they hadn't been terribly busy, between them, Tricia and Mr. Everett had sold fourteen books during the four-plus hours they'd been open, none of them from the discount shelf and five of them by Agatha Christie.

Tricia turned the OPEN sign to CLOSED while Mr. Everett finished the last of his dusting. "Another good day," he said, returning his lamb's wool duster to the storage area in the back of the store.

"Not bad for a Sunday," Tricia agreed. "Do you have any plans for the evening?"

"Grace wanted to go out to dinner, but now that the Brookview isn't serving on weekends. . . ." He didn't look brokenhearted, and Tricia suspected it meant one less disagreement about money—and who should pay for what.

"I'll be off now," Mr. Everett said. "I shall see you on Tuesday."

"Have a nice evening and have a good day off," Tricia said, and closed the door behind him. She didn't bother to lock it, since Ginny would be arriving in minutes with the Cookery's daily receipts.

Tricia looked out the window and saw a well-dressed man standing with his back toward the street, looking over the lot where History Repeats Itself had once stood. He held a clipboard and seemed to be making notes. She grabbed her keys, locked the door, and headed across the road. The man looked up as Tricia approached.

"Hello, my name is Tricia Miles." She held out her hand. "I own Haven't Got a Clue, the mystery bookstore across the street."

"How do you do?" said the young man, with the hint of an Italian accent. "I am Antonio Barbero. Very nice to meet you." And he kissed the back of Tricia's hand.

She stifled the urge to giggle. Antonio had to be at least ten years younger than her.

"Are you here representing the new owner?" Tricia asked.

"*Sì*. Nigela Ricita Associates." He offered no other information.

"I was surprised this lot was bought so quickly," Tricia said, hoping to draw the man out.

"Our company is interested in expanding our operations in New England. We were fortunate to find this property."

Not so fortunate for the man who'd died only five days before, but Tricia decided not to voice that opinion.

"As your new neighbor, I'd like to invite you to my store for a cup of coffee. Do you have a few minutes to spare?"

The man consulted his watch and then looked up, giving Tricia a dazzling smile. "*Sì. Grazie.*" She led him across the street, unlocked the door, and ushered him into Haven't Got a Clue. He looked the place over and seemed to like what he saw. "Is very nice."

"Thank you. The coffee is over here," she said, gesturing to the coffee station.

Ginny entered Haven't Got a Clue, clutching the blue bank bag. "The Cookery's all buttoned up for the night," she called, and stopped dead as her gaze zeroed in on Tricia's guest. Her eyes widened until Tricia thought Ginny's pupils might burst, and Tricia wondered if she was witnessing love at first sight.

"Antonio Barbero, this is my assistant, Ginny Wilson. Ginny, meet Antonio."

Ginny staggered forward as Antonio made a small bow. He took Ginny's hand, and when he kissed it, his gaze was riveted on hers. "*Buona sera, signorina.*"

Ginny giggled. "Nice to meet you, uh, Antonio." And she giggled again.

"Antonio represents the company that's buying the lot across the street."

Ginny giggled yet again. Really, it was embarrassing to witness her downward spiral into utter girlishness. "Why don't you take a seat in the readers' nook, and I'll pour you that cup of coffee, Antonio," Tricia said.

The man finally relinquished Ginny's hand and seemed to shake himself back to sense. "*Sì, grazie.*"

"*Siete benvenuto,*" Tricia said and waved a hand in the direction of the comfy chairs.

Antonio started off in that direction, and Ginny grabbed Tricia's arm, whispering, "I didn't know you could speak Italian."

"Just enough to get by," Tricia said, manufacturing a smile, and stepped behind the counter, grabbing the coffeepot. "I'm afraid it's not espresso, but we've never had any complaints about our coffee."

"I'm sure it will be beautiful—like the ladies in this shop," Antonio said, and Ginny nearly swooned.

Oh, she was so, *so* young, Tricia lamented, and poured coffee into one of the Haven't Got a Clue tall cardboard coffee cups. "Do you take cream and sugar?" she asked, but he shook his head. She crossed the room to join him, handed him the cup, and took the adjacent seat.

"Tell us about your employer," Tricia said, dying to hear the dirt but trying to sound nonchalant.

Antonio crossed his legs, showing off the sharp creases in his black trousers. "We are new in this country," he said, "looking for opportunities for investment. We think New Hampshire and New England in general have great potential for tourist development. I hope you won't think badly of us for that."

"No," Tricia agreed, "the more the merrier. Will your employer be coming to Stoneham to see the property?"

Antonio shook his head. "Is not necessary. I take care of things for the *signora.*"

Ah, a married woman, Tricia thought, or at least an

older woman. Then again, how many young women had the money for this type of investment? And it didn't sound as though Ms. Ricita had to worry about her financial standings—or was she just as enamored of Antonio as Ginny was?

"What other opportunities are you pursuing?" Tricia asked.

Antonio took a sip of coffee before answering. "Hotels and restaurants. My employer wishes to branch out."

"The Brookside Inn on the other side of the village may be looking for an investor," Tricia suggested.

"Is a nice place?" Antonio asked.

"The best in town. Head south out of town and you can't miss it. I'd be happy to make some calls for you."

"That would be very generous of you. *Grazie.*"

"What will you do with the property across the street?" Ginny asked.

"It will be used for retail, although my employer has not yet decided what to open. Perhaps antiques. Perhaps another bookstore. We must study the situation."

"Will you be staying in the area?" Ginny asked hopefully.

"I am currently based in Manhattan, but it may become necessary for me to relocate as my employer develops properties in New England. I am told is very beautiful here in autumn."

"It's the prettiest place on Earth," Ginny agreed. "Maybe I could show you around sometime."

Antonio smiled. "Perhaps." He lifted his cup to Tricia. "I'm afraid I must be on my way. I have appointments in Nashua later this evening."

"Your boss must be a slave driver, making you work on Sunday," Ginny said.

"Not at all. I enjoy my work, as I'm sure you must."

Again, Ginny giggled, her cheeks going pink once more.

"If you'll give me your card, I'll make those calls and get back to you," Tricia said.

"*Grazie.*" Antonio took a gold business card holder from the inside pocket of his sports coat and extracted two cards. One he gave to Tricia, and the other to Ginny, who looked like she was about to bust.

Once again, Antonio kissed their hands, and with a wave he said, "*Ciao,*" and was gone.

Ginny let out a loud breath. "I think I'm in love. That is the most gorgeous man I've ever met."

"Retract your tongue, girl, you're positively drooling."

Ginny laughed, and again her cheeks flushed. She remembered the bank bag, and handed it to Tricia.

"How did things go at the Cookery?" Tricia asked.

"Not a bad day," Ginny said, and dug into her purse for the keys to the Cookery. "But the cutout dresser struck again. I must've been helping a customer, and when I looked out about an hour ago, someone had put a black beret on the cutout's head, and a pair of pink woolly gloves on its hands."

Tricia sighed. "And you didn't see who did it?"

Ginny shook her head. "I brought it in at closing. It took me nearly ten minutes to get those gloves off, and then I thought—why did I try to save them? I should have just cut them off."

Tricia sighed and closed the blinds on the shop's door. "If nothing else, we at least know a little about the firm that's bought the lot across the street. I think I'll do a Google search when I get upstairs."

"You know, during a lull at the Cookery, I wondered why *you* didn't buy the lot," Ginny said.

"Me?" Tricia asked.

"Sure. It would've been a great investment. Eventually it would have paid for itself. If you rebuilt, you could either rent it out or move Haven't Got a Clue to that location."

Tricia peered through the store's main display window, studying the empty lot. If it had been one building over, the narrow lot would have been perfect for Angelica to expand Booked for Lunch—allowing her to serve a bigger crowd al fresco, at least during the summer months. In winter, she didn't even bother to open the café on Sundays. Of course, if the Brookside Inn continued with its no-brunch Sundays, maybe it would pay Angelica to stay open during the winter. Then again, she didn't get much time off, juggling two successful businesses and a budding writing career.

"I'm surprised the lot sold so quickly," Ginny said, and turned away from the window.

"Me, too. But it just goes to prove that being a book town has put Stoneham on the map. Obviously someone thinks rebuilding here would be worthwhile. That's especially comforting to know after the most recent economic downturn."

"It sure is. Well, gotta go."

"Thanks for helping out at the Cookery."

"No problem," Ginny called, and headed for the door.

"Wait—we should talk about visiting Billie Hanson at the bank tomorrow."

"Can't right now," Ginny said, and opened the door. "Meeting a friend in ten minutes for dinner. See you tomorrow." And out the door she went.

Tricia frowned. Was Ginny avoiding the whole subject

of the mortgage? Didn't she understand what allowing the debt to mount was doing to her credit rating?

As she reached for the cord of the display window's blinds, Tricia saw a Sheriff's Department cruiser coming up Main Street. It pulled up outside of Haven't Got a Clue, and Captain Baker got out of the driver's side. He retrieved his high-crowned hat and put it on before heading for Tricia's door. This was certainly her evening for visitors. Noticing the CLOSED sign, Baker knocked.

Tricia stepped over to the door and opened it. "My, you seem to be making a habit of visiting me after hours."

"I wish I could say this was a personal visit, but I'm afraid it's business."

"Bob Kelly?' Tricia asked.

Baker nodded. Obviously he'd gotten her message. "I thought you might like to know St. Joseph's Hospital is holding Mr. Kelly overnight for observation."

"That's not unusual, is it? I mean, he could've been asphyxiated."

"Tricia, the gas meter at the back of his house had been tampered with, just like what happened at History Repeats Itself."

"What are you driving at?"

"Chief Farrar and I concur; we believe Mr. Kelly may have been responsible. It's possible he tried to kill himself."

Tricia's mouth dropped. "I don't think I heard you right."

"Yes, you did."

"Bob—attempt suicide? No way." Tricia shook her head. "He just sewed up a deal to sell the empty lot on Main Street. Believe me, Bob loves money more than anything else. He'd never kill himself."

"According to several members of the Chamber of Commerce, Mr. Kelly has seemed depressed for the past couple of weeks. And if he was responsible for killing Jim Roth, he may have had reason to—"

"Look, I may not be Bob's best friend and advocate, but he wouldn't kill anybody. He's never been in any trouble with the law—why start now?"

"Who says he's never been in trouble?" Baker asked reasonably.

Was it possible? Though Tricia had known Bob for just over two years, she knew virtually nothing about his past—except that he'd come from a home where food was sometimes scarce. Did Angelica know much more about him? Tricia would have to ask. And yet, Angelica hadn't wanted to talk about Jake's criminal past—would she be as tight-lipped about Bob's past as well?

Still, if Tricia trusted one thing about Bob, it was that he'd go to any lengths to save his own hide.

"I don't believe it. Bob would never risk his life to further a business deal. He owned the building. He could've been killed in that blast," Tricia pointed out. "And now he's made a deal to sell the property."

"Someone wants that lot?"

"Yes, and until the building was destroyed, Bob was one of them. He's got a lock on most of the property on Main Street. Renting out that real estate is the major source of his income." Tricia shook her head again. "Besides, someone ransacked Bob's house."

"He could have done that himself."

"I don't believe it."

"Tricia, there's no gas stove—just a furnace. The wrench used to loosen the connection on the pipe was on Kelly's kitchen counter."

"So? If someone did this to him, they might've left it there as a misleading clue. Did you look for fingerprints?"

"It was wiped clean."

"Was there a suicide note? Was it signed?"

"We found a typed letter on the kitchen counter. Mr. Kelly has denied writing it."

"Well, of course he would. You should be able to determine if the note came from Bob's computer printer."

"Only if we confiscate all his home and office equipment. We're not ready to do that now—but it's an option."

"Do you seriously consider him a suspect?"

Baker didn't blink. "Yes. So much so, that we intend to present our evidence to the district attorney, possibly as early as tomorrow."

"You can't be serious."

"I'm deadly serious."

"But you have at least two other suspects."

"Who?"

"Jim Roth's mother. You have to admit her behavior at the memorial this morning was outrageous."

"She may have had a motive, but not the opportunity. She has an iron-clad alibi."

"Who?"

"Her"—the captain paused, looked uncomfortable—"gentleman friend."

"They could be lying."

Baker didn't answer. Instead, he asked, "Who's your other suspect?"

It pained Tricia to say it. "Frannie Armstrong."

"Possible motive, but no opportunity. Your sister swears she was working at the Cookery Wednesday afternoon and never left the premises."

Tricia's mouth dropped open in disbelief. Angelica had

been cooking in her apartment for most of that day. She wouldn't have known if Frannie ducked out for five or ten minutes. Had Angelica lied to Baker to protect Frannie?

"Now, I'd appreciate it if you'd keep this information about Mr. Kelly to yourself," Baker said.

"Even from my sister?" Tricia asked.

"Especially from your sister."

Tricia laughed. "Do you have any siblings?"

"I've got a brother."

"Not a sister." She waved a hand in the air. "Then you just wouldn't understand."

"Be that as it may, I don't want you talking about this—to anyone. Do I make myself clear?"

"Then why did you tell me in the first place?"

For the first time since she'd met him, Captain Baker seemed unsure of himself. He touched the brim of his hat. "I'll be leaving now. Until next time."

He reached for the door handle, turned it, and left the store.

Tricia watched as he got into his cruiser and took off, heading north once again.

She lowered the blinds, grabbed the phone's receiver, and dialed.

Angelica picked up on the fourth ring.

NINETEEN

 "Why did you have to call right now?" Angelica complained. "I've just run a bath. This lovely little bed-and-breakfast has one of those deep, old-fashioned claw-footed tubs. It must hold a million gallons. I intend to soak for at least an hour."

"You'll probably pull the plug and let it run out when I tell you the latest," Tricia said, and wished she'd used her cell phone so she could settle down in Haven't Got a Clue's readers' nook. This call could become yet another marathon event. "I did as you asked, and went over to Bob's house."

"So you mentioned in your message. I hope he wasn't as obstinate as he's been lately."

"Actually, he was unconscious when I got there," Tricia said, keeping her voice neutral.

"Good grief. I hope you're joking," Angelica said, her distress evident over the miles.

"Someone tampered with his gas meter."

226

"Just like Jim's! Oh, Tricia, is he okay?"

"They took him to St. Joseph's in Milford. He's going to be okay. But they kept him overnight for observation. He's on suicide watch."

"What? That's ridiculous. If Bob was going to kill himself, he would've done it when the market crashed in two thousand and eight."

"I know. But what's worse, Captain Baker thinks Bob might've killed Jim Roth."

"Oh sure—and blew up his own building? Give me a break."

"Which is exactly what I told the captain." Tricia considered asking Angelica about her vouching for Frannie on Wednesday afternoon, but figured she'd already dumped enough trouble in her sister's lap. And she wasn't about to mention the cutout being decked out in fun wear.

Angelica sighed. "I guess I'd better let the water out of the tub, check out, and head home."

"What about your book tour?"

"Bob needs me," she said, sounding resigned.

"Right now, he needs a good lawyer more than he needs you. Maybe I should call my lawyer, Roger Livingston."

"He doesn't deal with criminal cases. You'd better let me handle this. I'll call him for a referral. Do you think they're letting Bob take calls at the hospital?"

"There's only one way to find out."

"Pull out the phone book, will you? I'll go scout up a pen and some paper."

By the time Tricia found the number, Angelica was ready to take down the information.

"Are you really coming home?" Tricia asked.

"That depends on what I hear from the hospital, Bob, and the attorney."

"I'm sorry, Angelica. I know you've worked hard for this tour—"

"Yes, and I hate to disappoint all those people who'll be showing up at the bookstores, just dying for me to autograph their copies of my book." She sighed dramatically.

"Well, I have one piece of good news for you—something I forgot to tell you this morning. Someone in Stoneham bought the winning Powerball lottery ticket. The prize is twenty million dollars."

"And how does that affect me?" Angelica asked.

"I just thought you might like to know."

"Only if they spend a good portion of it at the Cookery and Booked for Lunch." Angelica sighed once more. "I'll call you later. Thanks for everything you've done over the last few days, Trish. I don't know what I'd do without you. I love you."

Tricia's mouth dropped. She'd never heard Angelica actually say those three words before. She swallowed. "I love you, too. Call me."

"I will. 'Bye."

"'Bye."

Tricia replaced the receiver, feeling empty inside. Miss Marple jumped down from the shelf behind the counter, rubbed her head against Tricia's arm, and gave a sympathetic "*Yow.*"

Tricia gazed around Haven't Got a Clue. Usually, she felt more at home in the store than she did in her loft. But now she felt restless.

"*Yow!*" Miss Marple insisted, purring hopefully and head butting Tricia's arm, which was now covered in long, gray cat hair.

"It's not time for your dinner yet." Then, as she thought about it, Tricia realized the only things she had in her fridge were blueberry muffins and leftover pizza, neither of which sounded appealing. "I think I'll drive to Milford to get supplies."

"*Yow!*"

"You know you don't like riding in the car. Besides, they have a no-animals policy," Tricia said. She grabbed the lint roller she kept under the counter.

"*Yow!*" Miss Marple said more emphatically.

"Yes, I will buy you more kitty cookies. And afterward, I'll sit on the couch and read, and you can sit on my lap and get cat hair all over my slacks. Won't that be fun?"

"*Yow!*" Miss Marple agreed.

Tricia replaced the roller and snagged her purse from under the cash desk. "You're in charge while I'm gone," she said, and locked the door behind her.

As Tricia headed up the sidewalk toward the municipal parking lot to retrieve her car, she felt a prickle on the back of her neck. She looked to her left and saw Russ standing in the window of his office, watching her. Was he really planning on stalking her? She quickened her pace, and when she got in her car, she locked the door, feeling shaken.

"I am not afraid of him—I am *not* afraid of him," she said, but her hand was shaking as she tried to put the key into the ignition.

By the time she'd arrived at the grocery store, less than ten minutes later, Tricia was berating herself for allowing Russ to upset her. She had too many other things on her mind to let him have that kind of power over her.

Tricia left her car in the parking lot, making sure she locked it, and entered the store. Grocery shopping had to be one of the most boring aspects of life, at least for her, but at that moment she was grateful for the distraction. Usually she kept to the outside aisles of the store, where the healthier products were located, but today she felt like wandering the aisles. Who knew there were so many variations on the basic baked bean? Pit barbeque, bourbon and brown sugar, Southern style . . . .

Tricia shook her head and rounded the corner into the baking aisle. Her second muffin experience had been much more satisfying than the first, bolstering her confidence. As she studied the wall of boxed cake, cookie, and brownie mixes, she wondered if maybe she'd been too ambitious by starting to bake from scratch. Maybe she should stick to prepackaged mixes, for which all you needed was water, oil, or an egg.

She was standing there, considering a carrot cake mix when *Bang!* Her cart slammed into her stomach. She glanced up, irritated to see Darcy Gebhard standing before her.

"Oops!" Darcy said, and giggled.

Tricia exhaled a breath, counted to ten, and then forced a smile. "Darcy. What are you doing here?"

"Shopping. Everybody's got to do it sometime."

Yes, and wasn't it Tricia's good fortune that Darcy ran into her? No! She glanced down at her empty cart, wishing she had a list to consult—anything to occupy her attention. Then maybe Darcy might take the hint and move on. No such luck.

"I found out why Jake went to jail," Darcy said. "Want to know?"

Okay, that got Tricia's attention. She raised an eyebrow, but didn't want to appear too eager.

"Attempted murder," Darcy said, a gleam in her eye.

Tricia swallowed, but when she spoke, she kept her voice steady. "It turns out Angelica knows all about Jake's past."

"I wish I had. I probably never would have taken the job. Who wants to work with a murderer?"

"You said it was attempted murder."

"Just because the guy didn't die doesn't mean Jake didn't do his best to try to kill him."

"What were the circumstances?" Tricia asked.

"I thought you said Angelica knows all about it." Darcy said.

"*She* does. *I* don't."

Darcy shrugged. "Oh. Well, it seems he went berserk and almost beat a guy to death. Too bad he recovered, else Jake would still be in jail."

Tricia couldn't believe what she'd just heard. Okay, it wasn't right for someone to nearly kill someone, no matter what the circumstances, but to wish the victim had died was appalling.

"Maybe when Angelica has finished with her book tour, you might want to think about finding another job somewhere else," Tricia suggested.

"I've been trying to get more hours at my other job—I waitress at a much fancier joint at night—but things have been slow, which is why I took the job at Booked for Lunch. I like the hours, and the tips aren't bad, either. But I'll probably only stay through the summer. I don't want to be on the road all that much come winter. I'm thinking of heading south again."

"Is that where you're originally from?" Tricia asked, then wanted to smack herself in the head. If she wanted to end this conversation, she'd have to stop asking questions.

Darcy shook her head. "Massachusetts. I came to New Hampshire because a boyfriend of mine lived here. Boy, that was a mistake."

"Yes, well—I don't want to hold you up," Tricia said, hoping she could put an end to their unwanted chat.

"Don't worry, I've got plenty of time. No one's going to be waiting up for me," Darcy said, and laughed.

Tricia could see why. "Well, I really must get going. It was great to see you."

"Yeah, you, too," Darcy said, and finally pushed her cart forward. "See you."

Tricia exhaled a breath, grateful to be rid of Darcy, and turned her attention back to the mixes on the shelf in front of her. Maybe she'd try one for lemon squares. She had to admit, despite the garish color, Mrs. Roth's lemon bars had tasted pretty good. If she made them from a mix, and they turned out well, she could put them out for the customers—which is what she should have done with the muffins she and Angelica had baked the night before.

She tossed the box into her cart and headed down the aisle. When she got to the end, she could see the parking lot through the big windows at the front of the store. And out in the parking lot, standing by his junky pickup truck, was Russ Smith.

TWENTY

 Tricia felt the blood drain from her face. So much for telling herself she wasn't afraid of Russ. The thing was, on the drive to the store, she'd kept looking in the rearview mirror, checking to make sure he hadn't followed her. And now—there he was. Or was it just that after spending the better part of a year with her, he knew her habits? She often shopped on Sunday evenings after closing Haven't Got a Clue. No matter, there he was, and Tricia felt trapped.

She thought about her options. Confronting him—not a good idea; what if he became violent?—and calling for help. The problem was, calling for help meant calling some other male friend, and right now that amounted to Mr. Everett, who was hardly a threat to Russ, or Bob Kelly—who was in the hospital under suicide watch—not a good candidate to play knight in shining armor. That left . . . Grant Baker . . . and it was likely his presence would only infuriate Russ, making the situation even more precarious.

A woman pushed her grocery cart around Tricia, who realized she must have been blocking the aisle for more than a minute. Another cart approached. "Are you okay, Tricia?" Darcy Gebhard asked. She looked from Tricia to the parking lot beyond. "Is that geeky guy with the glasses bothering you?"

"I'm afraid he is."

Darcy looked back at Russ. "He's the editor of the local weekly, isn't he?"

Tricia nodded.

"I'm just about finished here. Let me check out my stuff, and then I'll go have a talk with him," Darcy said.

"No, don't. Until yesterday, I would've said he wasn't violent. I can't say that anymore."

"Yeah, I heard he slugged an off-duty sheriff's deputy in the Bookshelf Diner last night."

"Word gets around."

"And how." Darcy patted Tricia's arm. "Don't worry, honey. As a waitress, I've defused this kind of situation lots of times."

Tricia didn't believe that for a moment, especially after what happened at the diner the day Jake bugged out early— but she hung back and waited, cell phone in hand, really to punch in 9-1-1 as Darcy pushed her cart of groceries out of the store and toward Russ.

She found herself gripping the cart's handle as she watched and waited. Russ kept looking toward the store, listening as Darcy talked. Eventually he nodded, got into his truck, and drove off. Tricia abandoned her cart—and the box of lemon bar mix—and headed for the exit. Darcy met her halfway.

"What did you say to him?" Tricia asked, almost too anxious to hear the answer.

Darcy shrugged. "I asked him to think about the consequences of going to jail for longer than just a night. How it would affect his business. That it might drive away advertising. I've always found hitting people in their wallets works best—at least in most situations."

"Thank you," Tricia said, and she meant it.

"Glad I could be of help. I guess I'll see you tomorrow when I bring over the café's receipts."

"Yeah. Thanks again, Darcy."

"No problem," she said.

This time, the phrase didn't make Tricia cringe—much.

Tricia wasn't sure if she should continue her shopping mission, but the truth was she needed at least the basics: coffee, milk, and cat food. She saw no sign of Russ in the grocery store's parking lot, nor when she parked her car in Stoneham's municipal lot. Tricia held her key ring in one hand, with the store key in her fist—ready to use it as a weapon if necessary. She wasn't going to act like one of those loony heroines in a bad mystery who walked into a dark alley, an attic, or a basement where a bad guy was waiting in the shadows. If Russ came at her, she was ready. She got out of her car, grabbed her groceries, and looked around. Still no sign of Russ.

Tricia walked briskly toward Haven't Got a Clue. It was only after she was inside the store with the door locked that the panic began to abate.

Miss Marple yawned and stretched, then jumped down from one of the readers' nook's chairs. *"Yow!"* she said, with a *what took you so long* attitude.

"You don't want to know," Tricia told the cat.

She needed something to divert her attention, and the day's events were certainly fodder for that, considering the three suspects in Jim's murder: Bob, Frannie, and Mrs. Roth, none of whom seemed capable of murder.

Ah, but could one of them have *hired* someone to do their dirty work? And who?

Baker had hinted that Bob might not have had a squeaky clean past. But how would Mrs. Roth or Frannie connect with someone with a criminal background? It would have to be someone in Stoneham with a dubious background.

Then it came to her: Jake Masters. He was a felon convicted of attempted murder. Something Darcy had said earlier came back to Tricia: If he could almost beat a man to death, what else was Jake capable of doing?

As one of Angelica's employees, Frannie had probably met Jake at least a couple of times. Ginny had quoted "hell hath no fury," and Frannie was definitely a woman scorned.

And how about Mrs. Roth? Could she have run into Jake at Booked for Lunch, or had she gone to dinner with her gentleman friend at La Parisienne? That seemed the least likely scenario.

Tricia thought back to something she'd seen on Bob's porch: a crushed cigarette butt. Jake smoked. Could he have had a reason to want Bob dead? He was loyal to Angelica, and she and Bob hadn't been getting along all that well, but that was Bob's fault—not that dealing with Angelica couldn't get a bit aggravating. Still, could Jake have acted on his own, thinking he'd be doing Angelica a favor by getting rid of Bob? If so, why mess with the gas meter at History Repeats Itself? Bob spent hours alone at his realty office—and at his home, where the gas meter had been tampered with.

Tricia wondered if the cigarette butt would still be on Bob's porch. She could call Darcy to see what brand Jake smoked—or look behind Booked for Lunch. No doubt Jake tossed his butts into the alley. It was dark now, but she could check out Bob's porch first thing in the morning, and if she found the butt, compare it with what she found behind Angelica's café.

With her mind whirling about the possibilities of Jake as bad guy, Tricia found she was too wound up to read a current or classic mystery, and instead spent the rest of the evening in the living room with Miss Marple on her lap as she reread Angelica's cookbook. Tricia had proofread the manuscript for *Easy-Does-It Cooking*, which had seemed rather dull at the time. This time, though, she found the pictures of home-cooked meals and the lovely photo styling had a calming effect on her. And she was surprised at how much of Angelica had been infused into the writing, which she also found oddly comforting.

All too soon it was bedtime. Tricia slunk into the bedroom without turning on a light, closed the blinds, and peeked out. No sign of Russ. But then, the west side of Main Street was bathed in shadows. He could be hiding in one of the shop doorways, watching for her lights to go on. Well, she wouldn't give him the satisfaction. She undressed for bed in the bathroom, and climbed into bed—a bed she had, on occasion, shared with Russ. Now the thought of his touch left her shaken.

After her trouble at the market, Tricia was surprised she'd fallen asleep so easily. But twenty minutes later, the ringing phone demanded her attention. Was it Russ? Was he calling to badger her? This phone didn't have caller ID. Tricia picked it up on the fourth ring. "Hello?" she said cautiously, expecting dead air.

"I'm downstairs. Can I come up?" Angelica asked, her voice sounding shaky.

"Oh, sure. What's wrong?" Tricia answered, still sleepy.

"I'll explain when I get up there," Angelica said, and hung up.

Miss Marple was quite indignant when Tricia hauled herself out of bed, reached for her robe, and staggered toward the kitchen. By the time she got there, Angelica was already opening the door. With one look at Angelica's ashen face, Tricia flew across the room to embrace her. The hug was intense. Funny, two years ago they might have exchanged air kisses that meant nothing. Now, they clung to one another, and the sentiment was real—and treasured.

"Are you okay?" Tricia asked. "What happened?"

"I had a scare on the road," Angelica answered. "Boy, I could sure use a nice cup of tea."

"Tea, I've got. Come, sit down," Tricia said, and ushered her sister to one of the stools at the kitchen island. "Are you sure you wouldn't like something stronger?"

Angelica thought about it and nodded. "Stronger is probably better. Have you got any gin?"

Tricia nodded and reached for the cabinet door, removing a bottle of Bombay Sapphire. She found a bottle of tonic water in her pantry, and reached for a tall glass.

"Make it a short one—and not too much ice," Angelica said.

Miss Marple arrived, looking sleepy-eyed and annoyed, walked up to the island, stretched and yawned, and then jumped onto Angelica's lap. Angelica petted the cat's head. A year ago she probably would have tossed her aside, but now she seemed content to encourage Miss Marple's purrs. Maybe one day soon Angelica would be ready to accept another pet. Cat . . . dog . . . it didn't matter. Angelica had so much love to give, and not enough places to give it.

Tricia put ice in the glass, poured two fingers of gin, topped the glass with tonic, found a spoon, and stirred the drink. "Sorry, I don't have any limes." She handed the drink to Angelica, who took a deep gulp.

"I'll have a cup of tea with you as soon as this stuff takes effect," Angelica said.

Tricia moved to the counter and filled the electric kettle with water. "What do you want? Earl Grey? Orange pekoe? Herb tea?"

"Whatever you want."

"Orange pekoe it is," Tricia said.

Miss Marple rubbed her head against Angelica's shoulder, leaving stray gray hairs, but instead of scolding her, Angelica bent down to kiss the cat's head. Miss Marple's back end flew into the air and she purred even louder, nuzzling Angelica's chin.

"Are you up to telling me what happened?" Tricia asked as she opened her cupboard, grabbed her shamrock-decorated teapot, and placed it on the counter.

Angelica heaved a loud, dramatic sigh. "I checked out of the B and B and started for home. It was an uneventful drive until I was halfway between Nashua and Milford, when these bright lights came up behind me at an appalling speed. I figured I'd better get out of the way, and swerved to the right. The car zoomed right past me, bashed into the guardrail, straightened out, and kept going."

"They didn't even stop to assess the damage?"

"No. I was going to call the Sheriff's Department, but I figured what could they do? I didn't get the make of the car or see the license plate, and I was so tired, I didn't want the hassle of waiting."

"The Nashua or Milford cops would've been there in a flash."

"Oh. I hadn't thought of that. I'm used to dealing with the county Mounties—and I just couldn't be bothered."

Another reason for Stoneham to reestablish its own police force.

"Angelica, this is the second incident you've had since you've been on the road. You said you had your tires slashed."

"That was the second," she admitted sheepishly, "if you count nearly getting creamed in front of the hospital last Wednesday night. Tonight's was the fifth incident."

"Good grief, Ange, what else haven't you told me?" Tricia demanded.

"Someone keyed the words *fat bitch* along the side of my car. I wonder how much that will cost to get rid of," she said, wearily.

"And what was number four?"

"Two broken headlights."

"Oh, Ange," Tricia admonished.

"I didn't want to worry you."

"I've now gone past worry all the way to terrified."

"Until tonight, I figured these were just isolated incidents," Angelica explained. "Or at least I wanted to believe that."

"It sounds to me like someone's after you," Tricia said.

"It could just be a string of bad luck. Either that, or a literary critic would rather take it out on me personally. I'll be glad when I'm done with my book tour and can sleep in my own bed every night. In fact, I think I'm going to try to come home more often."

"But it sounds like these incidents were *meant* to keep

you off the road. Maybe you should cancel—or at least postpone—the rest of your tour."

"And piss off every independent bookseller in New England who put time, effort, and money into promoting my signings? I know how I'd feel if an author canceled on me at the last minute." Angelica gulped the rest of her drink, getting cat hair on the glass, which was wet with condensation. "Now, please, can we change the subject?"

"For the moment," Tricia said, exasperated. She struggled to remember what had originally brought Angelica home. "When we last talked, you said you were going to find Bob a lawyer," Tricia said.

"Your Mr. Livingston was very helpful. He dispatched a criminal lawyer to St. Joseph's and apparently has sprung Bob from the place. At this point, I'm merely paying his bill, and unless Bob starts talking, I'm not privy to attorney-client confidentiality."

"That doesn't seem fair."

"Well, it's the law," Angelica said, resigned. She bent down and pressed another kiss on Miss Marple's head. The cat basked in the attention. Tricia tried, but didn't succeed, in suppressing a smile.

"What happens next?" Tricia asked, and took two bone china mugs from the cupboard.

"I don't know," Angelica said, and sighed. "I still haven't heard from Bob, but I'm hoping I can salvage tomorrow night's signing." She shook her head, gently put Miss Marple down on the floor, and stood. "I'm way too rattled to go to bed. I need to bake. What have you got on hand?"

"Not much more than I had last night."

Angelica frowned. "It's enough to make a coffee cake. Do you like coffee cake?"

"I love it," Tricia said. She wasn't sure she did, but right now Angelica needed positive reinforcement. Tricia took out the brown and white sugars, flour, baking powder, butter, and eggs, and arranged them on the counter while Angelica found an eight-inch-square baking pan.

"I'll have to adjust the recipe for this size pan, but it'll taste just as good as one done in a Bundt pan," Angelica said, and turned to take the vegetable spray from a cupboard.

The kettle whistled, and Tricia made the tea, then got out of the way, letting Angelica take over. "Turn the oven on to three fifty, will you?" Angelica asked.

Tricia did so, and then poured them both a cup of tea. "For what it's worth, I don't think Bob is a murderer." She placed Angelica's cup before her on the counter, but Angelica was too preoccupied to notice.

"Of course he's not. But that means someone else is," Angelica said as she measured flour into a bowl.

Tricia blew on the steaming tea to cool it. "I'm beginning to think it might be Russ," Tricia said in jest.

"Really?" Angelica asked, intrigued, as she added baking powder to the bowl of flour.

"No." Tricia wasn't going to mention her thoughts about Jake—at least not yet. "But we almost had another run-in this evening. It was Darcy who saved me."

"Darcy?" Angelica asked, and Tricia told her what had happened at the grocery store. "Don't worry. We'll find a way to deal with Russ," Angelica said. "But right now, Bob is my main priority." She put a stick of butter into a small bowl, put it in the microwave, set the the timer, and hit the Start button.

"Speaking of Bob, don't you find it suspicious that this Nigela Ricita Associates shows up and buys the empty lot the day after it's put on the market?" Tricia asked.

"I've been thinking about that. That it might actually be a good investment. Except for Jim, most of the booksellers were able to weather the financial meltdown without too much trouble."

"But that building was a prime piece of real estate," Tricia stressed.

The microwave *dinged*, and Angelica removed the bowl of melted butter. "Are you suggesting someone blew up the building to get Bob to sell?" Angelica asked.

"Stranger things have happened."

"I don't believe it. It's too far-fetched. And who's to say the property would be put up for sale? Although, if it had been the Armchair Tourist that had gone up instead, I could've expanded my operations at Booked for Lunch and had a place for al fresco dining."

"You're being terribly morbid."

"I'm being realistic," Angelica said, and cracked an egg into a bowl.

"I must admit I had the same idea," Tricia said.

"And you call *me* morbid?" Angelica said in a huff. "Tell me more about the new buyer," she said, grabbing a fork from the silverware drawer and beating the egg.

"I didn't meet the buyer—just her representative. Antonio Barbero."

"Barbero—wasn't that the horse that broke its leg at the Kentucky Derby?"

"That was Barbaro—and it was at the Preakness. Believe me, there was nothing horsey about Antonio. Ginny's quite smitten with him."

Angelica waved a hand in dismissal. "She'll get over him." She thought about it for a moment. "She probably won't. You'd think after what Brian did, she'd be off men forever."

"Rod cheating on you didn't make you swear off men."

"More's the pity. At least Ginny never married her scoundrel." Angelica mixed brown sugar with a little flour.

"True, but she's still facing credit problems that will dog her for years." •

"Oh, yeah, how's that mortgage thing going?" Angelica asked, and poured the wet ingredients into the dry, stirring the mixture.

"Ginny's been stalling. I don't understand it."

"Maybe she came to her senses. It's not good for an employee to be so beholden to a boss. It wouldn't be in her best interest in the long run."

"Are you saying you think I'd take advantage of her sense of loyalty?"

"You, never. But she should always be open to opportunities, and let's face it, ringing up mysteries isn't going to get her that shop she wants."

No, it wouldn't. And neither would hanging on to the little cottage in the woods.

"Eventually, Ginny's going to need to look for something that's going to pay far more than even you can afford to give her. Or she's going to have to marry well." Angelica laughed. "Look what marrying well has done for me."

"I wouldn't be surprised if she's already thinking about marrying Antonio Barbero," Tricia said, and sipped her tea.

Angelica shook her head. "Poor Ginny's been alone for almost eight months, and let's face it, the prospects of her finding someone here in Stoneham are slim. This guy probably seems heaven sent. That is, until he disappoints her."

Tricia laughed. "She just met him, and already he's breaking her heart?"

Angelica shrugged, and poured the batter into the prepared pan and sprinkled the brown sugar mixture over the top. "I've been down that road too many times myself. I know the signs."

That was too depressing a subject to dive into yet again. Tricia changed the subject. "What are your plans for the morning?"

Angelica popped the coffee cake into the oven and set the timer. "Talk to Bob. Talk to the lawyer. And no doubt talk to Captain Baker. Or at least argue with him."

"I'm a bit concerned about something you've already told him."

Angelica picked up the dirty bowls and measuring equipment and set them in the sink. "What's that?"

"That you could vouch for Frannie the afternoon Jim died."

"Why are you concerned?" Angelica asked, running warm water into the bowls.

"Because you spent most of the day cooking for your launch party."

"Don't remind me of that fiasco," Angelica said.

"I'm serious, Ange. What if this whole thing ends up in court? Can you swear on a Bible that Frannie never left the Cookery?"

Angelica opened her mouth to answer but said nothing, and turned back to the sink.

"Aha!"

"Don't 'aha' me. Frannie wouldn't leave the store unattended. I can swear to that."

"It's not the same thing, and you know it."

"What am I supposed to do? Let my boyfriend or my employee go to jail? Somebody killed Jim Roth, and I don't think it was either Bob or Frannie."

"That leaves Jim's mother."

Angelica nodded vigorously. "You said she made a spectacle of herself at the memorial service. If she hated him so much, surely she had a motive to kill him."

"Captain Baker says she's got an alibi—her boyfriend."

"Who could've lied," Angelica countered.

"Like you did about Frannie?"

Angelica's gaze narrowed. "I didn't lie. I made an educated assumption. And who's to say there isn't someone else out there who had a motive to kill Jim?"

"If there is, he or she hasn't come forward."

"And who wants to advertise themselves as a murderer?" Angelica asked.

"My point exactly." Tricia again thought about, and rejected, the idea of mentioning her suspicions about Jake. She and Angelica were actually getting along, and she didn't want to spoil it.

Angelica chewed on her thumbnail. "We've got to build a case against Mrs. Roth."

Tricia laughed. "And how are we supposed to do that?"

"I don't know. You're the one who reads all those mysteries."

"And police procedurals," Tricia added.

"Then, go to it!" Angelica cried, exasperated.

"I can't. I have a business to run."

"You have two employees who can take care of it while you take a few hours to help your friends stay out of prison." Tricia shook her head doubtfully. "Look," Angelica continued, "all you have to do is establish reasonable doubt."

"How do you know about that?"

"I've watched a lot of TV shows about lawyers."

"It's not that easy," Tricia countered.

"Frannie can help you. She's got an entire spy network

out there, thanks to her years working at the Chamber of Commerce."

That was true. Hadn't Frannie already told Tricia about Mrs. Roth booking a cruise with money she expected to receive from Jim's insurance policy? "Okay, that's a possibility. But I'll look like a hypocrite if I hand Jim's mother the money I've been collecting for her, and then have the police come after her as a murderer. And there's no guarantee she is."

"Reasonable doubt," Angelica repeated again, "that's all you have to establish."

Suddenly, Tricia wished she had recently reread some Erle Stanley Gardner books. She was no Paul Drake, and Angelica was certainly no Della Street—let alone Perry Mason. She shook her head. "This doesn't feel right."

"And what if Mrs. Roth is the murderer, and you let either Bob or Frannie go to jail? Then how would you feel?"

Terrible. "All right. I'll try to think of something."

Angelica let out a pent-up breath and reached out to touch Tricia's arm. "Thank you."

Tricia gave her sister a weak smile. She had the feeling she was going to find it much harder to fall asleep the next time her head hit the pillow.

TWENTY-ONE

Tricia awoke to low-hanging clouds heavy with rain, leaving her feeling depressed and anxious about Russ, about Bob, about just about everything. The weatherman's prediction for more of the same didn't lift her spirits, either, causing her to worry even more about Angelica going back on the road that morning.

Four miles on the treadmill, a shower, and coffee later, Tricia packed up Angelica's coffee cake and she and Miss Marple went down the stairs. Miss Marple was ready to start work, and looked puzzled as Tricia grabbed her umbrella and raincoat from a peg at the back of the store before she deposited the coffee cake on the coffee station's counter and started for the door. "I've got an errand to run," she told the cat. "Mind the store while I'm gone."

Miss Marple just blinked as Tricia pulled the door closed behind her.

Tricia decided to walk the two blocks to Bob's house,

figuring that parking at the curb in front would only bring attention to her and her mission.

Without a backward glance, she marched up the walk in front of Bob's house and quietly climbed the steps to his porch, hoping not to alert Bob to her presence.

So far, so good.

She swept her gaze along the gray-painted wooden floor, but didn't see the cigarette butt that had been there days before. Rats! Had Bob taken a broom to the porch? Tricia peered around the wicker love seat and chairs, wishing the day had been brighter. She was about to give up when she saw the butt in the far left corner. It must've been kicked or blown there.

Relieved, she withdrew a small pair of tweezers and a plastic snack bag from her slacks pocket. She sealed the bag and pulled a marker from her other pocket, writing a large numeral 1 on the bag. She blew on the ink to make sure it had dried before stowing the bag in her left pocket.

Her heart was pounding as she descended the stairs and started to purposefully walk back down to the street, fighting the urge to break into a run. But no one seemed to have seen her, and no one challenged her.

Within minutes, Tricia was back on Main Street, and turned for the alley that ran behind the west side of Stoneham's main thoroughfare. She'd never walked that way before, and took note of how shabby the backs of the stores looked. Behind each building stood one or two Dumpsters, and Tricia's fingers tightened around the handle of her umbrella as she approached the rear of Booked for Lunch. Had it only been eight months ago she'd found the body of her former college roommate in a garbage tote behind Angelica's café?

She put that image out of her mind and concentrated

on her task. Sure enough, the concrete apron outside the café was littered with soggy cigarette butts. She withdrew the tweezers and the second snack bag from her pocket, snagged a couple of sample butts, and sealed the bag's zip lock. Stuffing the bag into her pocket, she decided to wait until she got back to Haven't Got a Clue to compare the butts.

The damage to the back of the Armchair Tourist was evident from where she stood. As Chauncey had said, the back of his store was boarded over with plywood. She wondered if he'd find a large puddle in the back of his store when he opened for the day.

The concrete slab behind the now-empty lot was pitted and cracked, no doubt from debris that had hit after the explosion. It was eerie to look up and see gray sky where less than a week before a building had stood.

Although the rubble had been cleared, the ground was left uneven with potholes filled with rainwater. It wouldn't be smart to cut through, but Tricia decided not to retrace her steps. That would take her back to the north end of Main Street, and Russ's office. Instead, she continued south until she reached the end of the block, crossed the street, and doubled back to Haven't Got a Clue with more than half an hour to spare before opening.

After hanging up her coat and soggy umbrella, Tricia headed for the cash desk and the old-fashioned phone that sat upon it. But before she dialed Captain Baker's number, she placed the plastic bags containing the cigarette butts on the counter for a comparison. They were exact matches. Of course, she wasn't sure if all cigarettes had the same filters and paper casings. That would be up to a trained investigator to decide. In the meantime, she had collected evidence that might put a killer in jail. Could there be anything more satisfying than to help see justice done?

Tricia picked up the receiver and dialed, and was surprised when Baker answered on the third ring.

"Grant? It's Tricia Miles. I have a theory about who killed Jim Roth."

"Oh?" he said, sounding mildly interested. His boss, Sheriff Wendy Adams, had never been this polite when Tricia had offered her views or suggestions in a criminal investigation.

"Now, don't laugh—but what would you say the possibility was that one of the suspects hired someone to get rid of Jim Roth?"

A long silence followed that statement. For a moment, Tricia thought the line might have gone dead. Finally, Baker spoke. "Why would you think that?"

"They all seem to have alibis."

"Seem to have?" Baker repeated.

Had the captain already figured out that Angelica had fudged about Frannie's alibi? She decided to ignore that possibility and plunged on. "If Bob Kelly, Frannie Armstrong, or Livvie Roth didn't kill Jim Roth, then someone else had to have done it."

"That makes sense," he said reasonably, if not enthusiastically.

"And there's already someone here in Stoneham who is a convicted felon—convicted of attempted murder. Suppose this person was paid to get rid of Jim."

"Would you be talking about the short-order cook in your sister's restaurant? The one you asked me to check up on?"

"I would."

"And what makes you think Jake Masters killed Jim Roth?"

"I've collected some evidence."

"What evidence?" Baker asked sharply. "Please don't tell me you moved this evidence from where you found it. That you touched it. That—"

"Of course I didn't touch it with my hands. I used tweezers."

"But you *did* move it."

"Well, yes—"

"Which would taint it."

"Oh, dear," Tricia said, realizing he was right. And why hadn't she thought of that before she'd donned her trench coat and played Columbo?

"Tricia, why didn't you call me before you decided to play detective?"

"I figured you might not be interested in what I had to say. After all, your boss—"

"Is not me—and when are you going to get that through your head?"

Silence seemed to be the best reply to that question.

"What was this possible evidence that is now unusable?"

"Cigarette butts. I remembered seeing one on Bob Kelly's porch on Sunday morning, after Jim Roth's memorial gathering. Bob doesn't smoke, which means someone who does smoke was at his house. Possibly someone who didn't belong there. Like the person who tried to break into Bob's house on Friday and whoever tried to kill him on Sunday. I got to thinking about Jake and all the smoke breaks he takes at Booked for Lunch, and wondered if there'd be a match."

"So you picked up that butt and then compared it to the butts behind your sister's café?"

"They're the same."

"Just because Kelly had a visitor who smoked, and Jake Masters smokes, in no way ties him to the murder of Jim Roth. Something you haven't considered is motive."

"I have. Jake is extremely loyal to Angelica. Bob has not been treating her very well of late, and—"

"Isn't it more likely that your sister would try to kill Kelly?"

"Of course not! Angelica was at the Cookery at the time of the explosion. She was out of town when someone tried to break into Bob's house and when someone tried to kill him by tampering with his gas meter."

"And why wouldn't your sister hire this guy to do these things?"

"My sister is not a murderer—she wouldn't hire someone to commit a murder; she's—"

"Just as viable a suspect as Kelly, Anderson, and old lady Roth."

Good grief. Not only had Tricia created reasonable doubt, but reasonable suspicion—against her own sister!

Another long silence followed. Tricia's fingers clenched the heavy receiver in a death grip as she fought back six kinds of panic. What had she done? Was there a way to fix it?

Finally, Baker spoke. "As it turns out, I checked up on this guy Masters."

"And?"

"Yes, he is a convicted felon. However, he was a model prisoner. He learned food service when he was in prison. He works two jobs, reports to his parole officer, and has not gotten so much as a parking ticket since he was released from jail two years ago."

"Oh." It was all Tricia could think to say.

"Look, why don't we pretend you never made this call?" Baker said.

"That might be a very good idea," Tricia agreed, feeling incredibly stupid.

"Tricia," Baker said, his tone sympathetic, "I don't want you to feel you can't come to me with these kinds of theories."

Very charitable of him. "But?"

"Please, please, in future, leave the evidence collection to professionals. Say those cigarette butts could've been linked to the person behind all these crimes; your interfering would make them inadmissible in court."

"I wasn't sure you'd be interested, and now I feel stupid. I've read enough police procedurals and legal thrillers to know better. I guess I got carried away."

"I understand," Baker said. And he really seemed to.

"You won't mention this to Sheriff Adams, will you?" Tricia asked, trying to blot out the memories of how that insufferable woman had embarrassed her in the past.

"I won't," Baker promised. "Now, why don't you go back to bookselling, and I'll go back to—"

"Eating doughnuts and drinking coffee?" Tricia asked.

"That's exactly what I was going to say," Baker said, and Tricia could hear the amusement in his voice. "And I'll keep you posted on how the investigation is going if you promise not to—"

"Interfere?" Tricia supplied.

"I was going to say put yourself in harm's way. Do you think you can do that?"

"Yes," she said contritely.

"Okay. Have a good day."

"You, too," Tricia said, and hung up.

Miss Marple regarded her from her perch behind the register.

"Okay, so I blew it. Don't rub it in," Tricia said.

Miss Marple merely gave a bored *"Yow."*

Mondays were Mr. Everett's day off, and Ginny arrived a full twenty minutes ahead of opening, a few minutes after Tricia had ended her call with Captain Baker.

By the time Ginny had made a fresh batch of coffee, Tricia had set up the cash register, and joined Ginny at the coffee station for a fortifying cup. Ginny looked suspiciously at the coffee cake that sat on the station's counter. "Did you bake it?"

Tricia shook her head. "Angelica did—last night."

"I thought I saw her car in the municipal lot. This must have been another unexpected visit. Wasn't she supposed to be out on the road for at least another week?"

"Until Friday," Tricia confirmed.

Ginny picked up a square of coffee cake, sniffed it, apparently decided it smelled okay, and took a bite, leaving a trail of brown sugar crumbs tumbling down on the carpet. "Mmm. No doubt about it—your sister can bake." She brushed more sugar from the top of her apron. "What's on tap for today?" Ginny asked, and bent to gather up the crumbs on the floor.

"I need to be out of the store for a while today. Errands to run," Tricia said with an unconvincing laugh. "Do you mind?"

"Of course not."

"I may not be able to fit in our visit to Billie Hanson at the bank."

"Oh, that's okay. You do what you have to do. There's always tomorrow," Ginny said with a nervous laugh.

Tricia could no longer hide her disappointment. "Ginny, what aren't you telling me about this mortgage deal?"

Ginny looked away, and Tricia couldn't help but notice her lower lip was trembling. "Tricia, I've had several days to think about it, and I've decided. . . ." Ginny sighed, tears filling her blue eyes. "As much as I love and want to keep my house, I can't let you pay it off for me."

"Why not?" Tricia asked, hurt and a little confused.

"I thought about what I want out of life, and more than anything—more than keeping my house—I want to start my own business. Much as I love it, the house is a burden on me right now. I can't keep it and move forward with my life. And moving forward means starting my own business—being my own boss."

"You've seen what Deborah Black has been going through. Are you sure you want to put yourself in that position?"

"I feel bad for Deborah. She wouldn't feel so overwhelmed if her husband wasn't so selfish and would help her a little. I'm not interested in another relationship where I have to do all the work. If I can't find a man who wants to be my partner in all aspects of my life—including my work—then I'll just have to be alone."

Tricia's disappointment multiplied. "I see," she said, and perhaps she did. She'd gotten over the old 'feather the nest' syndrome when she'd married Christopher and made their first home together. But all the while, the thought of opening her own bookstore one day stayed in the back of her mind. And it took the death of her marriage before that could happen. What could she have accomplished if she'd put her dreams of entrepreneurship first, instead of wasting ten years of marriage with someone who'd ultimately chosen to leave her?

"I hope you don't think I'm being ungrateful," Ginny continued. "Nobody's ever done anything so nice for me. But I think in the long run, I'll be happier if I work toward my life goals first—and then, when I can afford it, I'll buy myself the nicest house around." She managed a weak laugh. "In fact, maybe in five or ten years, I'll buy back my little house. Stranger things have happened."

"Yes," Tricia agreed, "they have." She forced a smile—and a positive attitude. "What will you do in the meantime?"

"A friend of mine in Milford has been looking for a roommate. It's a two-bedroom apartment. She works nights, I work days. It sounds like it could be the perfect arrangement. And I can even have a pet if I want." Miss Marple's ears perked up at that—a coincidence?

"That sounds great," Tricia said, still working to keep her disappointment at bay.

Ginny nodded, and the awkward moment seemed to stretch. Finally, Ginny cleared her throat. "Is there anything you want me to do while you're running your errands?"

Tricia cast about the store, trying to come up with something. "Uh, I forgot to vacuum last night."

"I'll do it," Ginny volunteered, "and I'll put the carpet sweeper behind the coffee station. As long as we still have coffee cake available to customers, we're going to need it."

"Okay," Tricia said, and gathered up her umbrella, her purse with the check made out to Livvie Roth in it, gave Ginny a wave, and headed out the door for the municipal parking lot.

In the parking lot, Tricia unlocked her car, got in, and stared through the raindrop-laden windshield. Angelica was right. It hadn't been a good idea to offer to hold Ginny's mortgage—and Ginny had been smart to turn it down. Things might have become awkward. Still, for some reason Tricia felt sad.

She stabbed the key into the ignition and started the car, remembering her promise to Captain Baker not to interfere, and Angelica's admonition to find reasonable doubt against Mrs. Roth. To whom should she feel more loyal?

There was only one answer to that.

It took only a few minutes to reach the Roth home. She opened the car door, stuck the umbrella out and pushed the button that opened it, then got out of the car, feeling damp and decidedly grumpy.

Mrs. Roth opened the door. "Tricia. What a . . . nice . . . surprise." Her tone didn't match the sentiment. The two women stared at one another for several long, uncomfortable seconds before Mrs. Roth said, "Won't you come in?" and beckoned Tricia inside.

The redecorating had continued since Tricia had last been in the little house. A hooked area rug, festooned with ivy leaves, covered most of the living room's wall-to-wall carpet. Several lamps were lit, giving the room a cozy glow that made it a pleasant place to be on a rainy summer's day, so different from what Tricia had seen less than a week before.

"I'm sorry I didn't call first," Tricia apologized. "I'm glad I caught you in. I brought you something." She handed Mrs. Roth the envelope containing the check.

Livvie Roth frowned. "What's this?"

"Something from the Stoneham booksellers and some of Jim's other friends," Tricia said.

Mrs. Roth hesitated before she opened the envelope, removed the check, and stared at the figure on it. "Oh, my."

She looked up at Tricia in dismay. "I couldn't possibly accept this. Not after what I said about James at his memorial yesterday."

Tight-lipped, Tricia said nothing.

The old lady shook her head, tears filling her eyes, and wandered farther into the living room, where she settled on the love seat. "After yesterday, you must think me a monster." She shook her head, but when she faced Tricia once more, her gaze was filled with determination. "For the first time since I met Harold Roth, more than sixty years ago, I am finally my own person."

"I don't understand," Tricia said.

Mrs. Roth stared at the check in her hand. "I was only nineteen years old, an unschooled, impetuous girl who listened to the tales of a lonely GI. When he asked me to marry him, I leapt at the opportunity to leave my little village in the heart of England to sail off to America." She looked up at Tricia. "Sadly, this country wasn't at all what I'd expected."

"Why is that?" Tricia asked.

"I'd been led to believe everyone led a grand life, like in the Mickey Rooney–Judy Garland movies, but Harold wasn't descended from aristocrats. Instead, he brought me to the heart of America's rust belt—Pittsburgh, Pennsylvania. The air was bad, our home was a rental, dirty and decrepit. And when he lost his job at the steel mill, we moved from city to city. By then James had come along, and we needed a steady income. So when Harold couldn't find a job, I had to support us. I worked as a waitress, as a department store salesclerk, and even as an usher in a movie theater."

She laughed, but it held no mirth. "Harold never laid a hand on me, but he never gave me any affection, either. I can't say I mourned when he died twenty years ago. Since then it was just James and me. I tried to push him out of the nest, but he wasn't one to take chances—not when he had someone to take care of him."

"But he opened a store here in Stoneham. I understand he was the first bookseller to open on Main Street," Tricia said.

"That was Bob Kelly's doing," Mrs. Roth said bitterly. "He talked James into it—told him there was money to be made. That was all James had to hear, and the next thing I knew, he'd signed a lease. And of course he expected me to provide the funds to stock the store."

"I assume Jim must've had some income before that?"

"Certainly. He always worked in retail—never a well-paying job. And he wasted what little wages he earned on gambling and loose women."

Tricia tried not to smile at that. Frannie was hardly what Tricia thought of as "loose."

Mrs. Roth continued. "Several years ago, I finally convinced him to join Gamblers Anonymous, and for a year or two he did well. He worked to pay off his debts, and even put a little money aside. And then, when the economy went bad, he started buying lottery tickets. Three months ago, he was at it again full tilt."

Frannie hadn't mentioned that Jim gambled. Did she even know?

Mrs. Roth sighed. "Look at me, I'm almost eighty years old, and for the first time in my adult life I have the opportunity to be happy. Lawrence and I may have only a few weeks, months, or maybe a year or two together, but we're determined to have the time of our lives."

"Is that why you're taking a cruise?" Tricia asked.

Mrs. Roth frowned. "How do you know about that?"

Tricia swallowed but didn't answer.

Mrs. Roth's frown deepened. "That Armstrong woman,

I'll bet. She seems to know what's happening with every-one in Stoneham." She waved a hand in dismissal. "So be it. Yes, Lawrence and I are going on a cruise. And why shouldn't we? I can afford it—and it's the first holiday I've ever had. Would Frannie begrudge me even that?"

"I can't speak for Frannie, but I can for myself. I hope you find peace and happiness, Mrs. Roth. It sounds like you deserve it."

Mrs. Roth nodded, and handed the check back to Tricia. "I can't take this money. I'm sure there are more deserving souls. Perhaps it could do something for the good people of Stoneham who aren't as fortunate as you and me."

"The Stoneham Food Shelf can always use donations."

"James didn't have much use for charity—it would be lovely that something good could come as a result of his death, something to help others in some way."

Tricia accepted the check. "I'll pay a visit to Libby Hirt at the Food Shelf on my way back to my store. I'm sure she'll be very grateful."

"You do that, dear."

Mrs. Roth led Tricia to the door. "Thank you for helping me these last few days. It's good to know James had a few good friends—even if he never knew or appreciated it."

Mrs. Roth closed the door. Although the rain had eased to just a drizzle, a troubled Tricia opened her umbrella any-way, and slowly headed back to her car. Reasonable doubt? She had no doubt at all—there was no way she'd ever be convinced Livvie Roth had killed her own son.

That left her with either Bob or Frannie in the role of murderer, something she couldn't believe or accept.

There was only one other possibility. Someone else killed Jim Roth. And either Frannie or Bob had to know who that person was.

Frannie had been forthcoming about her relationship with Jim. Okay, not how and when it had ended, but that she'd *had* a relationship with him. Then again, it was only Tricia she'd confided in about her affair with Jim. She hadn't been happy when Tricia had told Captain Baker about it, and she'd been mortified when Mrs. Roth had told the Chamber membership about it. Why? There had to be more to the story than Frannie had told her.

Tricia lowered her umbrella and got in her car, setting the damp bumbershoot on the passenger-side floor. She put the key in the ignition but didn't start the car. Something Mrs. Roth said niggled at her brain. Jim had started gambling again—some three months ago. What had caused him to resume his addiction? Had his and Frannie's relationship started to crumble at about the same time? She'd said they'd been talking about marriage some three months before all that. What had happened to change that?

Tricia started the car, checked the mirrors, and pulled out into the street. There was only one person who could answer those questions for her: Frannie.

Some days the rain brought people out to shop. That Monday morning wasn't one of them. Tricia parked her car in the municipal lot, opened her umbrella once again, headed for the Cookery, and didn't pass another soul on the street.

As Tricia suspected, the Cookery was devoid of customers. The demented Angelica cutout stood behind the counter, no doubt because of the inclement weather. A red-eyed Frannie sat behind the counter with what she'd called a comfort read—an old Nancy Drew book she'd bought at Haven't Got a Clue the day before Jim's death, *The Clue of the Broken Locket*. It had been a bargain because it had lost its dust jacket, and Frannie had probably bought it to help her through the days after being dumped.

"Tricia," Frannie said in greeting, and put an *Easy-Does-It Cooking* bookmark between the pages to mark her place. "What brings you out in the rain?"

"I've just been to see Jim's mother."

Frannie's lips pursed, and she slammed the book onto the counter. "If I never see that horrible old witch again, it'll be too—"

Tricia held up a hand to stave off the flow of vitriol. "Frannie, please listen to what I have to say. It's important."

"Oh, all right," Frannie acquiesced, but with bad grace.

"Mrs. Roth said Jim had had a gambling problem in the past, but that he had licked it. Or she thought he had, until about three months ago. Was that about the same time your relationship with Jim changed?"

Frannie looked away. "That's kind of an embarrassing question, Tricia."

"Don't take this the wrong way, Frannie, but wouldn't you rather tell me than Captain Baker?"

"But you'll have to tell him about it, and then he'll come to me for confirmation anyway."

"That's true. But maybe by then it won't hurt so much to talk about it."

Frannie bit her lip, and considered Tricia's words. She sighed. "I guess you're right." It took her a few moments to compose herself. "Back in March, Jim did start acting funny."

"Funny? How?" Tricia asked.

"He started ignoring my calls. He started being busy during 'our time.'"

"When was that?"

"Friday evenings. He used to come to my house on Fridays. We'd have dinner and then we'd. . . ." She let the sentence trail off. She didn't need to spell it out for Tricia.

"Did you suspect he might be seeing someone else?"

"Maybe. I didn't want to confront him in case . . . in case he dumped me."

"Oh, Frannie," Tricia said, and felt the same sympathy she did for every other friend—and Angelica—who'd confessed to her that their significant other had strayed. She was lucky her ex-husband Christopher had never cheated on her. That hadn't stopped him from leaving her to find peace in a life of solitude in the Colorado Rockies, and it had hurt just as much.

"Do you think he was gambling?" Tricia said, sidestepping the fidelity issue.

Frannie nodded. "Jim got all his mail at his store. Two weeks ago, I sneaked a peek at his VISA bill and saw the Foxwoods Casino in Connecticut listed. He'd closed the shop and gone out of town for a day last month, supposedly on a buying trip. Or at least that's what he told me." Her bottom lip trembled. "There was also an item from the Milford Florist Shop. He didn't send me any flowers, and his mother's birthday is in August."

"Is that all your evidence?"

"Getting dumped pretty much confirmed it."

"What did Jim say? That he'd found someone else?" Tricia pressed.

Frannie shrugged. "More or less. I was certainly surprised to learn that his mother knew about us."

Tricia didn't want to go into that territory. "If Jim was seeing someone else, is there a chance this woman might have had a reason for killing him?"

Frannie looked up sharply. "But why?"

"Maybe she was just as unhappy knowing Jim hadn't broken off with you—until just days before his death."

"Maybe," Frannie admitted. "But he didn't have to dump me. I was prepared to . . . to share him."

"Oh, Frannie, did you really want to be with someone who cheated on you?"

"Who else has even looked at me in the last twenty years?" Frannie said with a sob. "I'm tired of being alone, Tricia. Apart from getting my cat, Penny, being with Jim— even on a part-time basis—has been the best part of my life these last two years."

At least a cat won't betray you, Tricia thought, but didn't voice that opinion.

They needed to move on from that subject. "What else do you know about Jim's life away from History Repeats Itself?"

"Not much. He watched the Military Channel. He read a lot. And he went to Gamblers Anonymous meetings."

Tricia's eyes widened. "Even though he'd started gambling again?"

Frannie nodded.

"Where? And when?" Tricia asked.

"Tuesday evenings, in a church in Nashua. He wouldn't say exactly where. I think that's where he met that other woman. And by the looks of that credit card bill, he'd started gambling again. Maybe his mother was afraid he'd bleed her dry—and that murder would get him out of her hair. You could tell by the way she spoke about him at the memorial that she hated him."

"I wouldn't say hate. More profound disappointment."

"You won't find me crying tears for her."

No, Tricia was sure she wouldn't.

"You must have some other clue about this mysterious woman who was seeing Jim."

"Tricia, I just don't know. Why don't you ask Bob Kelly?"

"Why?"

"Because Jim said Bob knew the woman, too—a long time ago."

"If that was true, why hasn't Bob said anything to Captain Baker about it?"

Frannie shrugged. "I'm not sure that Bob even knew about her and Jim."

And how many other women had Bob had a serious relationship with during his adult life? Five? Ten? More? Who said it had to be an adult relationship? Bob had gone to high school in Stoneham. Had he been a teenaged lothario? Try as she might, Tricia couldn't imagine that.

The bell over the door rang as a soggy customer entered the Cookery. "Welcome," Frannie greeted with a smile. "Let me know if you need any help."

The woman nodded, and moseyed along the north bookshelves.

Frannie cleared her throat and changed the subject. "Did you hear they're going to announce the winner of the Powerball lottery this evening at the convenience store up by the highway?"

Tricia shook her head.

"Should be a big crowd. I'm going. I mean—what else have I got to do on a Monday night? How about you?"

Tricia shook her head. "It's not my kind of thing."

"Suit yourself."

Tricia looked at her watch. "I'd better get going."

"Do you want me to bring the day's receipts over tonight?"

Tricia felt weary just thinking of her long to-do list. She really did need to make a bank run for herself and Angelica, along with everything else on her to-do list. "Yes, please."

"Okay. See you later, then," Frannie said, and moved away from the counter, heading in the direction of her customer. "What kind of cooking do you like to do?"

Tricia exited the Cookery, but felt in no hurry to return to Haven't Got a Clue. She really should go see Bob, but had to make the banking a priority. Angelica had hinted Bob had been withdrawn for months leading up to Jim's death. Tricia didn't believe Bob was responsible for the explosion, but he was definitely hiding something. Something he didn't want anyone to know about. He hadn't told Angelica, the person he was closest to, nor Captain Baker, and presumably he'd been just as tight-lipped with his new lawyer. How was Tricia going to get him to open up and tell her whatever it was he'd been hiding?

Was there a possibility that Bob and Jim had both been cheating—and with the same woman?

There was only one way to find out: confront Bob with the evidence. The only problem was, she didn't have any.

TWENTY-TWO

 Before Tricia could get her deposit slips filled out, a Granite State tourist bus drove down Main Street and let off forty or more potential customers, the bulk of whom seemed to land on Haven't Got a Clue's doorstep. Without Mr. Everett, there was no way Ginny could keep up with the onslaught on her own, and Tricia resigned herself to staying put for the time being.

By the time the crowd had thinned and the sun had come out, Tricia seized the opportunity to try to track down Bob. There was no answer at his house, his business, or his cell phone. And Betsy Dittmeyer at the Chamber of Commerce told Tricia she hadn't seen or heard from Bob. Could he have skipped town? Not likely—not when all his assets were tied up in Stoneham. She'd have to try again later. In the meantime, she needed to get some money into Haven't Got a Clue's checking account so she could pay bills.

"I've got to go to the bank," Tricia told Ginny, and dumped

her own and Angelica's blue bank pouches into a sturdy Haven't Got a Clue shopping bag. She grabbed her purse and flew out the door. She hadn't gone two feet when she saw Russ Smith standing outside of the Cookery, his Nikon camera slung around his neck, snapping pictures of Angelica's life-sized cutout. This time, it was decked out in a colorful paper Hawaiian lei and a grass hula skirt. There could be only one citizen in all of Stoneham who owned such attire.

Tricia marched up to Russ, startling him. "What do you think you're doing?"

"Taking pictures. What else?"

"Why?" she demanded.

"Because it's funny. I've got pictures of all the goofy getups this thing has worn."

"And what do you intend to do with them? Put them in your cheap little rag?"

"Hey, that's my paper—my pride and joy—you're talking about."

"I don't care what you call it—especially when you're trying to make a laughingstock of my sister."

Russ jabbed his index finger at the cutout. "*This* is news."

"No, wars are news. This is—"

"Advertising," Russ finished for her. "When I print the pictures, they'll be worth thousands in free PR for Angelica."

"I forbid you to use those pictures."

Russ shook his head. "The First Amendment is on my side, sweetheart. But"—he softened his voice—"I might reconsider my full-page treatment if a certain author's sister were to grant me certain favors. . . ."

Tricia's anger smoldered. "You are despicable. I don't know what I ever saw in you."

Russ raised an eyebrow and stared at her for a moment, then he took more photos of the cutout.

Tricia turned, yanked open the door to the Cookery, and stomped inside.

Frannie was at the cash desk with a customer, preventing Tricia from exploding on the spot. Frannie acknowledged her presence with a nervous smile, but continued to chatter with the woman.

Tricia waited impatiently as Frannie and the woman talked, Talked, TALKED for at least another minute. At last the woman seemed to realize Tricia was there. "Oh, I've monopolized your time something terrible," she told Frannie. "I'll let you help this other person now."

"Oh, no," Frannie called as the woman turned to leave, "Tricia isn't a customer. She's just Tricia."

"Thanks a lot," Tricia said.

But the woman waved good-bye and headed out the door.

Once she was gone, Frannie gave another nervous laugh. "What was it you wanted?"

"To know why you lied to me."

"Lie? Me?" Frannie said innocently.

"Yes, about the sombrero, the goofy glasses, and the cat's cradle."

"I didn't lie to you. At the time I didn't know who decorated Angelica's cutout."

"And now you do?" Tricia demanded.

"It turns out some of the other merchants were playing a game decorating the cutout. The first time, it was Deborah Black. She had parts of her husband's Halloween costume in the back of her store and on a whim decided to decorate the cutout. The next day, it was Joyce Widman over at Have a Heart. And then Nikki took a stab at it."

"And today it was you."

Frannie's nervous laugh was beginning to bug Tricia. "Yeah. But it's all for a good cause. Russ Smith has taken pictures of all of them. He said he'll give the Cookery and Angelica's book a full-page spread in the next issue of the *Stoneham Weekly News*."

"That's what he said, but he's angry at me and now he's going to take it out on Angelica—to make her a laughing-stock in front of the whole village."

Frannie waved her hands frantically. "No, no—it's not like that. I called Angelica and let her know about it. She's fine with it. She said there's no such thing as bad publicity."

Tricia could do nothing but stand there and seethe. Frannie continued, "It's brilliant. Since the cutout went outside, it's attracted a lot of attention. We've almost sold out the first two cases of *Easy-Does-It Cooking*, and I've had to reorder the book. Angelica will get writer's cramp from signing all those copies."

"What do you have planned for the cutout's next costume?" Tricia asked, still finding it hard to keep the anger out of her voice.

"That'll be up to Alexa over at the Coffee Bean. All the booksellers are going to take a turn. Russ is hoping he can interest another paper in the story and pictures. I'm surprised he didn't mention it to you."

"We're no longer friends," Tricia said through gritted teeth.

"Tricia, life is too short to carry grudges. I'm alone now, and I hate it. You've still got a chance to reconcile with Russ—"

Tricia's anger boiled over, but somehow she managed not to explode. "I'm going to the bank," she said in a strangled voice, turned on her heel, and left the Cookery. Thank goodness Russ had already disappeared, for Tricia was almost certain she would have cheerfully strangled him on the spot.

It had taken several hours for Tricia's temper to cool completely. It helped to look out Haven't Got a Clue's big display window and see the lovely hanging baskets on the lampposts. She had no green thumb but wondered if she should pay a visit to The Milford Nursery to find something low-maintenance and pretty for the shop—maybe an orchid or two, in homage to Nero Wolfe.

Tricia was lost in thought when Jake walked in the door at two forty-five with the blue bank bag in one hand, and an attitude that spelled trouble. Thankfully, there were no customers near the cash desk when he tossed the bag on the counter.

Tricia's ire flared again. "Do you have to be so rude?"

"When it comes to dealing with you, I have to work at it," Jake said.

"Look, just because I worry about my sister hiring an ex-con doesn't make me public enemy number one. I think you had that title wrapped up when you went to jail for attempted murder."

"I admit trying to kill the scumbag who raped my nine-year-old niece wasn't the smartest thing to do, but I—"

"Nine years old?" Tricia repeated, incredulous.

"Yeah. Things like that tend to rile me. Otherwise, I'm usually a pretty easygoing guy. Pity you're too biased to give someone like me a second chance. Thank goodness there are people like your sister around. You could take a lesson from her."

But I'm the GOOD sister, Tricia wanted to shout, and immediately felt like a heel. She took a breath to calm herself. "What did you do to the guy who hurt your niece?"

"I beat him to a pulp. He got three years in jail for raping Emily. I got nine. What kind of justice is that, oh Lady of Mystery?"

Tricia wasn't sure how to answer that question. She swallowed. "You have to understand, Angelica is my sister. I care about her."

"Like I cared about my niece?"

How far would I go to protect someone I loved? Tricia asked herself. She wasn't sure how to answer that question, either.

"Look, I know you don't approve of what I did thirteen years ago," Jake began. "In retrospect, I don't approve of it, either. But I'm not the same person I was then—and I suspect you could probably say that about yourself, too."

Yes. She could.

"I'm sorry we got off on the wrong foot," he apologized. "I wouldn't do anything to hurt your sister, her business, or the entire village of Stoneham. It doesn't matter whether you believe me, I just needed to tell you that. Now, I'll get out of your hair," he said, and turned for the door.

"Wait," Tricia called after him. Jaw set, Jake turned back to face her. She felt a flush rising from her neck to her cheeks. "I'm . . . I'm sorry."

For a long—very long—moment, Jake just stood there. Then he said, quietly, "I accept your apology."

Tricia's flush deepened. She swallowed. "Maybe we should start all over again." She took a deep, calming breath and thrust her hand in Jake's direction. "Hello, I'm Tricia. Welcome to Haven't Got a Clue."

Jake looked at her offered hand for what seemed like

eons, then he stepped forward and clasped it—not too
hard—and they shook on it. "I'm Jake Masters. Nice to
meet you."

The door to Haven't Got a Clue opened, making the bell
overhead tinkle, and Darcy Gebhard entered. "What's taking you so long?" she asked Jake, irritated.

Jake withdrew his hand from Tricia's, looking
embarrassed.

"Hi, Darcy," Tricia said.

"Oh, hi. Everything work out okay for you at the grocery store the other night?"

"Yes, thanks to you."

"Good. We'd better get going, Jake," Darcy said.

Tricia looked at the two of them quizzically.

"Her car's in the shop. I'm giving her a lift," Jake said.

"Yeah, he's a regular taxi driver," Darcy said. She didn't
sound all that appreciative, considering Jake was doing her
a favor. Tricia frowned. How ironic that five minutes ago
she wouldn't have cared, but now that she knew a bit more
about Jake, Darcy's attitude annoyed her.

"Let's go," Darcy said, and opened the door.

"See you," Jake said, and followed her.

Ginny wandered up to the cash desk. "What was that
all about?"

"Nothing." It was all too complicated to explain.

It was after five by the time Tricia had a chance to dial
Bob's various telephone numbers. Not surprisingly, only
recorded messages greeted her. She left messages on all
three, but doubted she'd hear from Bob anytime soon. He
could be stubborn when he wanted—which was most of
the time.

The rest of the afternoon dragged. Ginny disappeared to the stock room to work on the inventory, and Tricia and Miss Marple were left alone to handle the last few stragglers who came in looking for something to read—and not finding it.

Ginny reappeared just a few minutes before the store's official closing, looking triumphant. "I've got all the boxes unpacked and the books shelved, so we're just about caught up on the inventory."

"Sounds like a cause for celebration. How about I treat you to dinner at the Bookshelf Diner?" Tricia said.

"The winner of the New Hampshire Powerball lottery is going to be announced this evening at the convenience store. I'd really like to find out who it is. Could we go there first and then have dinner? It'll only be half an hour delay," Ginny said.

"Why not?" Tricia agreed. "It's not like I have a date or anything else to keep me home."

Ginny ran the vacuum over the carpet while Tricia tallied up the day's receipts and locked them in the safe. A contrite Frannie showed up just after seven with the Cookery's receipts. Tricia made no mention of their previous discussion, and could hardly object when Ginny invited Frannie to accompany them to the convenience store. Ginny made a show of jingling her keys and offered to do the driving honors.

The convenience store's parking lot was maxed out, and Ginny parked her car on the side of the road, behind a long line of others. "We'll have to hoof it," she said, and opened the driver's-side door. Tricia and Frannie followed her down the road and into the store, which was packed with people. Tricia recognized many Chamber of Commerce members, and of course the Dexter twins with their ever-present petition. Tricia had lived in Stoneham for two years, and had never met them until a few days before—now they seemed to be everywhere.

The elusive Bob was also in attendance, looking uncomfortable in one of his green Kelly Real Estate jackets. Tricia'd have to corner him after the announcement. She was surprised to see a keyed-up Grace and the ever-placid Mr. Everett standing on the sidelines. Grace gave Tricia a quick wave. Russ stood among the throng of TV reporters and cameramen, his Nikon dangling from his neck once again, and clutching a steno pad. (Did he buy them by the case?) He gave Tricia a tentative smile, but she turned away without acknowledging him.

"This has to be the biggest day in Stoneham history," Frannie said, and dug into her purse. "I'm glad I always carry my camera with me." She took it out and turned it on, ready to take a shot. She looked up, and waved to someone in the crowd. "Look—there's Julia Overline," a member of Haven't Got a Clue's readers' group. "I need to talk to her about tomorrow's meeting. I'll be back," Frannie said, and threaded her way through the crowd.

"That's the first time I've seen Frannie smile since Jim Roth's death," Tricia told Ginny, who nodded in agreement.

The air practically crackled with the crowd's pent-up excitement.

"Boy, looks like half the town is out tonight to meet the Powerball winner," Ginny said. "Who do you think it is?" she asked Tricia.

"Probably someone we don't even know."

"Wouldn't it be weird if it's the person responsible for Jim Roth's death? They say the ticket was bought last Wednesday—the day he died," Ginny said.

Weird indeed.

Two twenty-something young women, dressed in matching tight blue, star-spangled dresses, simpered for the cameras. They held a big cardboard check made out for twenty million dollars. The Pay To line was hidden by a large piece of paper.

A forty-something man in a suit stepped up to a microphone, and the TV cameras swung in his direction to capture the big announcement. He tapped on the microphone. "Testing, one, two, three." Then he cleared his throat. "Uh, ladies and gents, I'm Gordon Swingle from the New Hampshire Lottery Commission, and I'm pleased to be here tonight to announce the latest winner of the New Hampshire Powerball. The winning ticket contained the following numbers: four, six, nine, eight, eleven, twenty-eight, and thirty-one."

"Hey," Ginny said with delight, "two of those numbers are my birthday."

"Mine, too," Tricia said. "Talk about a coincidence."

"It's my pleasure to introduce the Powerball winners. Let's give a big hand to William and Grace Everett, from right here in Stoneham. Come on, folks, step right up." He waved at the lucky couple.

The crowd erupted in cheers. "Holy cow!" Ginny screamed, grabbed Tricia's arm, and jumped up and down.

Mr. Everett—a millionaire!

Grace's smile was radiant, but Mr. Everett looked uncomfortable with all the fuss. A jubilant Grace clutched his hand and pulled him toward the makeshift podium.

"Twenty million dollars! Twenty million dollars!" Ginny chanted over and over.

Twenty million dollars. Tricia couldn't seem to get a handle on the amount and the identity of the lucky winners.

"Why is it always old people who win these things?" a male voice behind Tricia groused. "They'll never be able to spend it all before they die."

Tricia resisted the temptation to glare at the idiot behind her.

"Was there any significance to the numbers you played?" Gordon Swingle asked Mr. Everett, shoving a microphone in his face.

"Yes. They are the birthdays of my wife, my employer, and my coworker."

"See," Ginny whispered to Tricia, "I told you so!"

"And how often do you play the New Hampshire Powerball?"

"This was my first time," Mr. Everett admitted.

Swingle waggled his eyebrows for the press. "See, folks, it *can* be done. First-time players can win big!" He turned back to Mr. Everett. "And do you intend to keep playing?"

"Certainly not," Mr. Everett said with some force. "I don't approve of gambling."

"Then why did you decide to play Powerball?" Swingle asked, looking annoyed.

Mr. Everett looked down at his shoes. "Very odd circumstances." He said no more on the subject, but Tricia had a feeling Grace's paying off his debts had been at the heart of it. And playing the lottery had to be the desperate measure he'd spoken of the previous week.

"What are you going to do with this windfall?" Swingle asked. Mr. Everett looked downright annoyed at this invasion of his privacy, but Grace jumped right in to answer for him. "We're going on a cruise! And we're going to buy all our friends lovely gifts, and give a sizable amount to charity."

"Will you move to a mansion?" one of the reporters asked.

"Heavens, no," Grace answered. "We're staying right here in Stoneham. And my husband is going to continue working at Haven't Got a Clue, Stoneham's mystery bookshop."

"Free publicity for the store," Ginny whispered, still excited.

"I'm just glad I don't have to find another employee," Tricia said. "Nobody could replace you *or* Mr. Everett."

A reporter shoved a microphone in front of Bob. "What do you think of Stoneham's biggest lottery winners?"

"William and Grace are a wonderful asset to our community. I couldn't be happier."

"And what about that explosion on Stoneham's Main Street last Wednesday? I understand you own the property—that you were in the store at the time of the blast."

Bob glowered and growled, "No comment." He pushed away, heading for the exit. Tricia struggled to get through the crowd to follow. "Bob! Wait!" she called, but he paid no attention and kept going.

Once outside, Tricia looked from left to right and finally saw Bob across the busy road, hurrying for his car. She waited for traffic to allow, and crossed the road to follow. "Bob! Wait!"

Finally, Bob stopped and turned. "Will you stop hounding me."

Tricia was taken aback by his tone.

"Angelica has been worried sick about you. Have you at least had the courtesy to talk to her?"

"We spoke."

"This morning?"

Bob nodded.

"And?"

"What we said is none of your business. And if Angelica hasn't already told you, she probably won't."

That was true. Years ago, Tricia and Angelica might have kept secrets from each other, but no more. And Angelica had a schedule to adhere to—no time to make a phone call, although she might spill all at the end of the day. Tricia would just have to wait.

"Is there anything else?" Bob asked, anger coloring his voice.

"Yes. Frannie Armstrong said you might know the name of the woman Jim Roth was seeing."

"Why would I know that?"

"Frannie couldn't say. Just that Jim had mentioned you and this woman were acquainted."

Bob's face went slack, the pallor behind his burns more distinct. "What did you say?"

"If you know who Jim was seeing, it could be the missing piece of the puzzle—you might know who killed him."

"Good Lord," Bob breathed, and stumbled toward his car.

"Bob—if you know something, you've got to call the Sheriff's Department. Please, call Captain Baker."

"I can handle this," he said.

"Is that the person who's been harassing you, Bob? Did this woman try to kill you, too?"

Bob turned, his face screwed into a mask of fury. "For once in your life, will you just try and stay out of things?" He turned, unlocked his car, and jumped in. Tricia ran to the car and beat her fists against the driver's-side window.

"Bob, wait!"

But he started the car, revved it, and peeled out, scraping the bumper of the car in front.

"Bob!" Tricia hollered, but he paid no mind and zoomed down the road.

Was he about to confront Jim's killer, or would he be the next victim?

TWENTY-THREE

 Tricia dug through her purse to find her car keys, then remembered Ginny had driven her and Frannie to the convenience store. She snatched her cell phone and stabbed in Grant Baker's personal number but, as expected, got only his voice mail. She left a message as she walked back to the store to get Ginny. "Grant, this is Tricia Miles. You'd better put out an APB on Bob Kelly. He's gone after Jim Roth's killer. It's too complicated to explain—but he feels Jim was killed by a woman, a mutual acquaintance. Please call me back as soon as you get this message."

She paused at the convenience store's door. Inside everyone was still celebrating. She turned her back on the merrymakers and punched in 9-1, then paused before she hit the last digit. What was she going to tell the dispatcher?

Tricia closed her phone, shoved it back in her purse, and yanked open the convenience store's door, searching for Ginny.

A crowd of people encircled Grace and Mr. Everett. Reporters with microphones pelted them with questions, and the cameras continued to roll. Ginny stood on the edge of the crowd, teetering on tiptoe. Tricia threaded her way through the crowd and grabbed Ginny's arm. The poor girl nearly stumbled while trying to right herself.

"What's up?" she demanded.

Tricia started pulling Ginny toward the door. "We have to leave. Now!"

"Where are we going?" Ginny demanded

"To follow Bob."

"Why?"

Tricia pushed through the double glass doors. "I'll tell you on the way."

"What about Frannie?"

"She'll have to find her own way home. Come on."

Finally Ginny seemed to understand the urgency of the situation, and hurried down the road to retrieve her car, with Tricia dogging her footsteps. Ginny pressed the unlock button on her key fob and the women jumped into the car.

"You'll have to turn around. Bob headed back into Stoneham," Tricia said.

"Where do you think he'd go? His house?" Ginny asked, and started the car.

"Maybe. We should probably start there."

"Why are we chasing Bob?"

"It's a long story, but he may know who killed Jim Roth—and more important, why."

"Oh, boy," Ginny cried with glee. "I always wanted to go on one of these adventures with you. Usually Angelica gets all the fun."

"This is not fun. Bob is—and maybe we could be, too—facing a life-and-death situation."

"Who are we chasing?"

"That's the problem. I don't know!"

Ginny frowned, and looked at the gas indicator on the dashboard. "We've been at this for almost an hour now, Tricia, riding up and down the streets of Stoneham. Bob isn't here."

Tricia exhaled an exasperated breath. "You're right. I'm sorry. Take me back to Haven't Got a Clue and drop me off. You may as well go home. And I'll give you some money for gas. I appreciate you driving me around in circles."

"Hey, you promised me dinner at the Bookshelf Diner," Ginny reminded her, and to prove it, her stomach growled loudly.

Tricia sighed again. Yes, she had promised Ginny dinner, but after all the worry while they'd been driving around, she'd lost her appetite.

Ginny pulled into the municipal parking lot and turned off the engine. "Ooh, look at that gorgeous Jaguar," she said, pointing toward a maroon car parked at the north end of the lot, far from other cars that might dent its doors. A sleek, chrome cat adorned the hood of the vehicle.

"Who do you suppose that belongs to?" Ginny asked as they got out of her aging Focus.

"I have no idea," Tricia said, and couldn't care less. "Come on, let's go to the diner" *and get this over with*, she added to herself.

They crossed the street and entered the Bookshelf Diner. "At last, a customer!" called Eugenia, the evening waitress, and then she recognized Tricia and Ginny and scowled. "What do *you* want?"

"What do you think?" Ginny said, sarcastically. "We came here to eat. And if you have a problem with that, I suggest you ask the manager to step in." She turned to Tricia, her tone dramatically sweeter. "Where would you like to sit, Tricia?"

The diner was completely empty. Was everyone still at the convenience store celebrating the announcement of the Powerball winners? "Anywhere," Tricia answered. She'd forgotten Eugenia would be on duty. The bad blood that had passed between her and Ginny the previous fall was obviously still there. Tricia followed Ginny to the second booth in, and took her seat, facing into the restaurant.

"May we have menus, please?" Ginny asked, unable to keep the contempt out of her voice as she spoke to Eugenia.

Eugenia tossed a couple of menus on the table and stalked off.

"I'm sorry I suggested we come here," Tricia apologized. "I'd forgotten about your situation with Eugenia."

"I haven't, and I make a point of coming in at least once a week just to annoy her."

"Ginny!" Tricia admonished.

"Well, after what she put me—put all of us—through last fall. . . ." She let the sentence drop, and concentrated on her menu.

"Order anything you want," Tricia said, and let her gaze fall on the salad portion of the menu.

"I'm starved. Would it be okay if I ordered a steak dinner?"

"The sky's the limit," Tricia assured Ginny, frowning as she read and reread the words "Cobb salad." All of a sudden, resentment filled her. She was sick to death of salad. She'd eaten salads for years. She'd run a million miles on her treadmill in an effort to keep what Angelica teased as her *girlish figure*, and for what? To please some man? Christopher had dumped her for a life of solitude. Russ had turned out to be a major jerk, and Grant Baker was too preoccupied with his ex-wife's illness to spend quality time with her.

Angelica had never been what Tricia would call svelte, and yet she'd never hurt for male companionship.

Grant had been right. Life was short. Start with dessert.

Tricia closed her menu and set it on the table.

Ginny, too, looked up, but it wasn't Tricia she gazed at. Tricia turned and saw Antonio Barbero standing outside the window. He caught sight of them and waggled his fingers in a wave.

Ginny's smile lit up her face, and her eyes widened. "Ohmigod," she said through her teeth, like a ventriloquist. "Do you think he might come in?"

Tricia smiled. "Let's ask him." She beckoned Antonio to enter the diner.

"Here he comes!" Ginny nearly squealed, still doing her Sherri Lewis imitation.

"*Buona sera, signorina e signora.*" He reached out to kiss Ginny's hand. She giggled like a schoolgirl.

"Would you like to join us?" Tricia asked.

Antonio smiled. "It would be my pleasure." Ginny slid over, and he sat down beside her—close beside her. Ginny's fair skin blushed bright pink, and Tricia fought the urge to laugh.

"Why don't we start with a glass of wine? Would you like red or white?" Tricia asked Antonio.

"Red. Like lovely Ginny's hair." If anything, Ginny's blush grew even deeper.

Tricia looked up. Eugenia stood at the back of the diner, scowling. Tricia waved, and Eugenia pushed herself away from the wall, stalking toward their table. "Yes?" she asked defiantly.

"Three glasses of the house red."

But Eugenia was too busy staring at Antonio to write down the order. "Who're you?"

"Antonio Barbero, from Nigela Ricita Associates. Pleased to meet you"—he read her name tag— "Eugenia."

Tricia stifled a laugh. He said the word as though it might be the name of a disease. Ginny giggled yet again.

It was Eugenia's turn to blush. "Three glasses of red, coming up." Somehow she managed to keep the surliness out of her tone. She turned and walked slowly back to the kitchen, her hips swaying.

"Would you like to look at my menu, Antonio?" Ginny asked, her voice almost an octave higher than usual. She cleared her throat and handed it to him.

"I love American diners. The food is so disgustingly fattening, yet so wonderfully delicious. So much so, I rarely eat in them."

"You must be starved for real Italian cooking," Tricia said.

He shook his head. "No, no. I cook for myself. One day I would like to cook for you two ladies, as well. You are my first friends here in Stoneham and have made me feel so welcome."

Ginny said nothing. Tricia wasn't sure she was actually breathing—she looked ready to explode. Obviously, she wasn't going to be able to carry her share of the conversational load. "What brings you back to town?" Tricia asked Antonio.

"I want to check out the site before my architect comes tomorrow."

"Surely the sale won't go through until after the insurance company settles with the current owner."

"Oh, *sì*, I know. But my employer wants to be ready to start construction the day after we close on the property."

"What's the hurry?" Ginny asked, and then added, "not that there's anything wrong with that."

"Time is money," Antonio answered. "I will be on the site every day, overseeing the construction."

"Every day?" Ginny asked eagerly. "And when do you think that will be?"

"Hopefully in the fall. My employer has many friends in the insurance business. I'm sure she can speed up the process. The *polizia* have already signed off on the cause of the explosion that destroyed the old building." He shook his head. "My employer wants the new building to have the same character—to blend in with the rest of the street. Of course, it will have many upgrades: insulation, up-to-date HVAC systems. But the *turisti* will not know it was not there for one hundred years."

Eugenia arrived with a tray, placed paper napkins on the table, and set the glasses down. She did so with care, and this time when she spoke, her voice held respect. "What may I get you, sir?"

Antonio waved a hand to take in Ginny and Tricia. "Ladies first."

"I'll have the house salad with raspberry vinaigrette," Ginny said politely. So much for a big steak dinner.

"Tricia?" Antonio said.

"I'll have the strawberry shortcake—with extra whipped cream, thank you."

"Tricia?" Ginny asked, amazed at her choice.

"Life is short. Eat dessert first," she said simply.

Antonio frowned, looking like he might have missed something.

"And you?" Eugenia asked, her voice soft—almost soothing—as she clenched her pencil, poised to write down his order. She hadn't written down either Tricia's or Ginny's request.

"Steak, medium rare. Baked potato. And salad." Antonio collected Tricia's menu and handed them both to Eugenia." *Grazie.*"

Eugenia looked almost as love-struck as Ginny. She gave a little laugh and said, "No problem," making Tricia cringe.

Ginny waited for Eugenia to retreat before speaking again. "Do you think you'll be moving to Stoneham anytime soon?"

Tricia resisted the urge to shake her head, keeping her teeth clenched. *Don't be so obvious,* she wanted to warn Ginny, who gazed at Antonio with cow eyes. Either Antonio didn't notice, or he had chosen to overlook it. He shook his head. "Not until later this summer. I have much business to take care of before I can relocate. And I wish to thank you, Ms. Miles, for giving me the number of the manager at the Brookview Inn. We are speaking tomorrow about a possible alliance. My employer is very interested in investigating the possibilities."

"You wouldn't buy the inn outright?" Tricia asked.

"At this point, we are only talking about possibilities. Who knows if we will come to an agreement? I was just telling Bob Kelly—"

"You've spoken with Bob?" Tricia asked. "When?"

"About twenty minutes ago."

"We spent the last hour looking for him," Ginny said.

"I'm surprised he took your call. He's been ignoring all mine," Tricia said. "Did he say where he was or where he was going?"

Antonio shook his head.

"Just that he had business out of town. A mission of mercy, I think he called it."

Tricia instantly thought of Angelica. If someone was after Bob, could they be after Angelica as well? She thought of all the little accidents and mishaps Angelica had experienced since Wednesday evening, and suddenly they seemed even more sinister.

"I have to go," Tricia said, grabbed her purse, and struggled to get out of the booth. She paused only long enough to dig into her wallet for two twenty-dollar bills. "You two have fun."

"Tricia, where are you going?" Ginny asked, concerned.

"I just remembered something I have to do. I'll see you in the morning, Ginny," she said, gave a quick wave, and hurried for the door.

"*Ciao*," Antonio called after her.

Once outside, Tricia pulled out her cell phone and hit autodial for Angelica's phone. It went to voice mail on the fourth ring. "It's Angelica. I'm not available right now. Leave me a message, and I'll get back to you."

"Ange, it's Tricia. No time to explain, but someone may be after you—the same person who killed Jim Roth. Call me as soon as you get this message, and don't trust anyone! I mean no one—not even Bob! Call me!"

Tricia flipped the phone shut and broke into a jog, heading for Haven't Got a Clue, her thoughts racing. Where was Angelica's next signing? She couldn't remember. She had printed out her whole book tour itinerary, and a copy was taped to the fridge and another was under the counter at Haven't Got a Clue.

Tricia was breathless by the time she reached Haven't Got a Clue. She fumbled with her keys, unlocked the door, and burst inside. Miss Marple was sitting on the sales counter and rose with a sharp *"Yow!"*

"No time now," Tricia told the cat, and practically skidded around the cash desk. "I've got to warn Angelica!" She pawed through the stuff littering the shelf under the counter and found the printed sheet, then ran her finger down the page until she found Monday night's signing in Woodstock. The old rotary phone on the counter was too slow, so she punched in the number on her cell phone.

"Crazy Hermit Bookstore, Martha here. How can I help you?"

"Angelica Miles is supposed to sign her cookbook tonight at your store."

"That's right."

"This is an emergency. I need to speak with her right away."

"I'm sorry, but the signing ended about half an hour ago. Ms. Miles has already left the store."

"Did she say where she was going? To her hotel?"

"I think she said she was driving home."

"Oh, dear."

"I wish I could help you more."

"Thank you. You've already been a big help." Tricia folded her phone. What should she do now? If whoever killed Jim and had already gone after Bob was gunning for Angelica, too, she would be the most vulnerable on the road. In fact, every time the person attacked, he or she had targeted Angelica's car—or targeted Angelica with his or her own car.

Tricia's mind raced. Angelica had said that whoever chased her on the road the night before had hit a guardrail. Darcy's car was out of commission and she needed a ride from Jake. Could she have been chasing Angelica?

That didn't seem likely. Angelica had never mentioned that Darcy knew anyone in Stoneham prior to her taking the waitressing job at Booked for Lunch. But then, why would Angelica discuss her employee in great detail? She certainly hadn't mentioned Jake's past.

Darcy had been an acceptable, if annoying, employee. Angelica trusted her with the cash receipts.

Which hadn't been adding up.

And it had been Jake who'd brought the receipts over for the past two days—not Darcy.

And what about that order of chicken Angelica had known nothing about? Darcy had seemed nervous when Tricia wrote out the check for the deliveryman. Jake had been watching from the café's small kitchen, and had said nothing. Could he and Darcy be in on all this together?

Tricia didn't want to believe that. Not with all the faith Angelica had put in Jake.

She pawed through the papers to find Angelica's list of emergency numbers and came across Darcy's phone number. She dialed it, but there was no answer—not even voice mail.

She glanced at the clock. By now Jake would be at his second job at La Parisienne in Nashua. Unless that was a fabrication, too. But, no, Captain Baker confirmed he worked there. She was getting herself all shook up and confused. She looked up that number on Angelica's list and dialed.

"La Parisienne, this is Patty. We have a one-hour wait for seating. Can I take your reservation?"

"Patty? My name is Tricia Miles. I'm a friend of the sous-chef—Jake Masters—" That was a bald-faced lie. "I need to speak to him—it's an emergency."

"Kitchen help can't take calls during working hours. Let

me take your number, and Jake can return your call on his break."

"Did you hear me—this is an emergency! Someone's life could be at stake. Now, please let me talk to Jake."

Patty exhaled an impatient breath. "Hold on."

Tricia heard the thud of the phone being put down. In the background she could hear the buzz of voices in the tiny, crowded dining room.

The minutes ticked by. Finally, Jake came on the phone. "Hello?"

"Jake, it's Tricia Miles—"

"Are you trying to get me fired? We're up to our armpits in customers, and—"

"What's going on with Darcy?"

"Look, I'm going to hang up—"

"Jake, I think she might be out to get Angelica. Did she tell you what her car was in the shop for?"

There was a pause, and again Tricia could hear La Parisienne's patrons in the background—laughing, the clinking of glasses and silverware. "She said she hit a guardrail. The front end was out of alignment. She also had a big dent in the right front quarter panel, but was going to get that fixed another time." That was consistent with Angelica's description.

"What was with that shipment of chicken that was delivered last Thursday? Angelica didn't know anything about it."

"Ahhh," he groaned, which didn't sound encouraging. "The thing is . . . there was no shipment. Darcy and the deliveryman split the money."

"Why didn't you tell me what was going on?"

"I don't know you. I was waiting for Angelica to come back."

"You have her number. You could've called her."

"Look, now wasn't the time to rat on Darcy over a couple hundred bucks' worth of chicken. I mean—we need her right now to keep the place open while Angelica's on her book tour." He said the words "book tour" as though it was a frivolous waste of time. "Believe me, I've documented everything Darcy's done. I'm sure you noticed I've brought over the receipts for the past two days. I saw her being light-fingered with the till—and pocketing some of the receipts. I need that job. I don't want to see Booked for Lunch close because of that stinking little bitch's gambling debts."

Gambling debts! Frannie suspected Jim had met some little hussy at a Gamblers Anonymous meeting in Nashua. Darcy *lived* in Nashua.

"Jake, tell me everything you know about Darcy. I think she's already killed one man. She may be after Angelica, too. I need your help to keep my sister safe."

"I don't know what to tell you, Tricia."

"Did she know Jim Roth, the man killed in the explosion last week?"

"Of course. We'd see him outside the shop when he'd take his smoke breaks."

"Does Darcy smoke?"

"Same brand as me."

Maybe those cigarette butts might still come in handy—Tricia was glad she hadn't yet tossed them. But she still had other questions that needed answering. "Did Angelica leave a copy of her itinerary with you at the café?"

"Sure, but—"

"When was the last time you saw it?"

Jake hesitated. "I don't remember. Friday—maybe Saturday. I can't be sure."

Darcy had been adamant about leaving work on time—

time enough to race around half of New England chasing after Angelica? Slashing her tires? Smashing her headlights? Keying the paint on her car? Why? Had Bob refused to dump Angelica for Darcy?

"I've got Darcy's number," Jake said. "I'll give her a call, but I don't think—"

"I've already tried calling her. There was no answer. I called the bookstore where Angelica was signing, but she'd already left for home. Bob Kelly went off to intercept her, but there's a lot of highway between Woodstock, Vermont, and Stoneham."

"Call the Sheriff's Department. Don't you have a friend on the force?"

"I've already got a call in to Captain Baker, but so far he hasn't gotten back to me."

"Call the dispatcher. He or she should be able to track him down, especially if he's the lead investigator on the Roth homicide."

Damn! Why hadn't Tricia thought of that?

"I'll do it right now."

"And I'll make a few calls to see what I can find out— and hope like hell I don't lose my job over this."

"Will you call me back?"

"Give me your number." He took it down and hung up— with no good-bye, no nothing. Tricia wasn't about to berate him on his phone etiquette, and instead punched in 9-1-1.

TWENTY-FOUR

"I'm sorry, ma'am, but you shouldn't be calling Emergency Services to track down a member of the Sheriff's Department," the 9-1-1 operator said.

"But this is an emergency! Who else am I supposed to call at a time like this?" Tricia tried to explain for the third time.

"Misuse of an emergency—"

"Oh, never mind," Tricia said and flipped her phone shut.

There was only one thing to do—try to intercept Angelica along the way.

And what if Angelica had deviated from her Mapquest printout?

Tricia grabbed her purse and keys and headed for the door. She ran to the municipal parking lot, but with every step she thought better of her haphazard plan. There were hundreds of miles of highway between where Angelica might be and where Tricia was now. The old finding-a-needle-in-a-haystack analogy fit this situation perfectly. And Tricia had promised Captain Baker she would not put herself in harm's way. The logical thing to do was to stay put, be available by phone, and hope and pray Angelica would be okay.

Tricia turned and started back for Haven't Got a Clue. She'd make a big pot of coffee. Maybe she'd call Deborah to wait with her . . . not that Deborah could get away. Her husband probably wouldn't want to forgo a Red Sox game to watch the baby. She could call Ginny, but she might still be with Antonio Barbero, and if she was, wouldn't appreciate being interrupted.

Thank goodness for Miss Marple. She'd been a true companion through some of the lowest times of Tricia's life.

As she slowly walked back to her store, Tricia sorted through her keys, pausing in front of the Cookery. Something caught her eye, and she looked at the door. The little CLOSED sign that hung on a chain was gently swinging— as though someone had just looked out the blind-covered window.

But no one should be inside the Cookery.

Tricia had last seen Frannie at the convenience store. She'd probably gotten a ride back into the village, and if so, her home, not the Cookery, would've been her destination. She had no reason to be inside the store at this hour.

Angelica's car was not in the parking lot, and Tricia and Frannie were the only other people who had the keys to the Cookery.

Don't put yourself in harm's way.

Tricia opened her phone, dialed Captain Baker's number once more, and listened to it ring and ring and ring before voice mail kicked in. She waited for the tone. "Grant, it's Tricia. Please call me back on my cell phone as soon as possible. Please!"

She folded her phone and put it in her slacks pocket.

What constituted "harm's way," anyway? Surely not opening a door and peeking inside her sister's shop.

Tricia sorted through her keys once more, came up with the one that opened the Cookery, and placed it in the lock. She opened the door slowly. The inside of the shop was dim. Frannie had apparently forgotten to flip on the switch for the security lighting before leaving.

Or someone had flipped the switch off.

Tricia's hand tightened on the door handle. She felt like one of those bimbos in a mystery novel, the ones who walked into darkened alleys, basements, or attics where an armed serial killer lurked. If she walked inside, she might be in harm's way. Or she might just find that Frannie had forgotten to turn on the security lights.

She took a step forward. The light switch was just inside on the left. She needed to turn the lights on so Angelica wouldn't walk into the darkened store.

She took another step forward, squinting as her gaze swept across the empty shop. The store was eerily silent. Angelica's life-sized cutout, still clad in the hula skirt and paper lei, stood just ahead of her on the right.

She took another step forward and reached for the switch.

A sudden movement to her right startled Tricia as the Angelica cutout rushed toward her.

She stumbled off balance as the cutout shoved her to the ground. The door slammed, and Tricia crawled backward crablike, farther into the store.

"Stop it! Stop!" she hollered.

The cutout stopped moving. It was then that Tricia saw the lacquered nails and silver rings on the fingers holding the cutout upright.

"What are you doing here, Darcy?"

Darcy poked her head around the left side of the cutoff. "Looks just like Angelica, doesn't it? Demented. Delusional. Soon to be departed."

For some reason, Tricia wasn't afraid of dumpy little Darcy—despite what she suspected the woman had done. She struggled to her feet. "You didn't answer my question."

"Duh! I'm waiting for Angelica."

"How did you get in?"

"Through the door. How else?"

"How did you get through the *locked* door?"

"I have a key. I have a copy of *all* Angelica's keys. I've been in her bedroom. She's got a lot of nail polish. Why doesn't she get her nails done professionally? *She* can afford it more than I can."

Tricia could imagine all Angelica's nail polish bottles spilled or smashed on her rugs and bedspread. A malicious little prank pulled by a malicious little slob.

"We could dance around what you're doing here, but why waste time? Why are you jealous of Angelica, and why have you been stalking her?"

Darcy's grin was wolfish. "Stalking her? Me? I'm not a stalker, I'm a fan. I've been to at least half of her book signings."

"But you didn't go inside the bookstores. Instead, you waited outside, slashing her tires, breaking her headlights, and keying the paint on her car. Calling Angelica a fat bitch by ruining the paint on her driver's door doesn't sound like the work of a fan to me. And have you looked in the mirror lately, Darcy? You might benefit from a diet yourself."

"Shut up, bitch! Skinny broads like you always have an edge over people like me. You get all the breaks."

"Hard work got me my breaks." That and a nice fat inheritance, plus a generous divorce settlement—but she wasn't about to go into that.

Tricia bent down to pick up her purse, but Darcy spoke up. "Uh-uh-uh! Leave that stuff on the floor."

"I have a call in to Captain Baker of the Sheriff's Department. He'll be here any minute now, looking to talk to me about—of all things—you."

"You're lying."

Tricia shrugged, hoping Darcy wouldn't notice the sweat that had broken out on her forehead.

"While we wait, we can talk about Bob Kelly and Jim Roth—and why you've already killed once, and tried to kill again."

"I'm not one of the blabbermouths in those stupid mysteries you read—the ones who go on and on confessing their guilt. And I don't need to, because I've done nothing wrong."

The woman was either in denial or had no scruples, but maybe Tricia could buy some time by talking through the points that had been coalescing in her mind. "Let's talk about Jim Roth. Why did you want him dead?"

"Why would I want him dead? I didn't know him."

"There are only so many meetings of Gamblers Anonymous in Nashua. I'm sure the Sheriff's Department will be able to prove the two of you attended meetings together."

"There's a reason they're *anonymous*—nobody snitches," Darcy said with a sneer.

"The two of you were dating. I'll bet the surveillance

cameras at Foxwoods Casino caught the two of you together. Jim used his credit card, proving he was there."

Darcy's sneer wavered.

"What happened? Did he reconsider his promise to drop
Frannie?"

"That skinny hag," Darcy grated. "She's at least fifteen
years older than me."

"And what about Bob Kelly? The two of you had been
together in the past, but his taste in women had improved
over the years. He'd long ago given up bologna for Angus
steak."

Darcy's mouth twisted into a frown. She might not be
blabbing about her motives, but her expression was con-
firming everything Tricia said. She pushed on.

"But while you were dating Jim, you were two-timing
him with Bob."

"So much for Angus beef," Darcy said, and the sneer
was back.

"But then he realized what you were and what he stood
to lose with Angelica, so he broke it off. Now you had no
one, and a crappy job waiting tables in a hick town. Not
much of a life," Tricia said.

"You don't know anything," Darcy muttered.

"You were so angry," Tricia went on, "that when you
saw Bob and Jim together last Wednesday at History Repeats Itself, you decided to take action. Not something overt
that might cast suspicion your way, so you went behind the
store and loosened the connection on his gas meter. You
knew Jim would eventually come outside for a cigarette,
and then—*boom!*"

"There was no boom! It hardly made a noise at all. It
was the glass shattering and the ceiling falling in that made
all the noise."

"I didn't see you in the crowd on the sidewalk, but you had to be there. You had to see the ambulance take Bob to the hospital in Nashua. When you learned he wasn't badly hurt, you decided to expand your little reign of terror, and include Angelica in your plan for revenge."

Darcy didn't comment.

"You tried to run her over outside the hospital that night. That was your first attempt to get rid of her."

"Pure conjecture," Darcy said.

Tricia hadn't thought Darcy's vocabulary was that evolved. "You made sure you left work on time or early every day so you could chase all over New England after Angelica. You let Bob know what you were doing, but he didn't believe you because Angelica didn't tell him about the incidents."

Darcy's mouth had pursed once more.

"Why did you try to kill Bob? Or were you just trying to scare him into taking you back? Not a very clever plan, but then, were you ever able to acquire your GED?"

"That's it," Darcy said, finally losing her temper. "Get in that chair." She pointed to the only upholstered chair Angelica had provided for her customers.

"Going to tie me up?" Tricia asked. "With what?"

Darcy's mouth dropped open, but then abruptly shut again.

"You're right—I don't need to tie you up. I have a gun," Darcy said, and withdrew it from the pocket of her slacks. It looked like a toy, barely bigger than the size of her hand. But Tricia knew even a small handgun could do deadly damage if the shooter hit the target in just the right place.

"I don't think you'll shoot me," Tricia bluffed, keeping her voice level, but her gaze was riveted on the chrome-plated gun barrel.

Darcy's smile was positively evil. "What have I got to lose?"

Something moved behind the shop door's blinds, momentarily diverting Tricia's attention.

"That's the oldest trick in the book," Darcy said, employing yet another cliché, "and I'm not falling for it."

Then, in a clash of shattering glass and splintering wood, the door burst open, but instead of Captain Baker, it was Bob Kelly who plunged into the shop. Darcy barely had time to react before Bob tackled her like a Patriots linebacker.

Darcy went sprawling, but quickly rolled onto her back.

The gun exploded, and Tricia felt a searing pain along her left bicep. She fell to her knees with a yelp of pain as Bob knocked the gun from Darcy's hand and sat atop her, holding her wrists to keep her from punching him.

"Stop struggling," Bob ordered, as Darcy started to laugh.

"This is just like old times, isn't it, Bobby? Remember the times you'd tie me up before we had sex? Remember the times you had me spank you?"

"Bob!" Tricia cried, incredulous. "I'm shot!"

"Pull up your sleeve," Bob ordered.

Tricia did as she was told, expecting to find a neat bullet hole and lots of blood, but instead the wound was more like a deep scrape—and boy, did it hurt.

"I'm not as young as I used to be, Tricia," Bob said with some urgency. "I'd appreciate it if you'd get on the damn phone and call the Sheriff's Department. Then run outside and see if you can flag down someone to help us!"

"Oh, good idea!" Tricia extricated her phone from her slacks pocket and opened it, but before she could dial 9-1-1, she saw a Sheriff's Department cruiser pulled up outside.

In seconds, Captain Baker stood in the doorway, his service revolver in hand. "What's going on here?"

"Bob just captured Jim Roth's killer," Tricia said. "Look at my arm. She tried to kill me, too!"

"I could use some help here," Bob said, still holding on to a struggling Darcy.

"Where's the gun?" Baker asked.

"Somewhere on the floor, by the side bookshelves," Tricia said, pointing.

Baker holstered his gun and advanced on Bob and Darcy, detaching his handcuffs from his belt. He bent down, attaching one of the cuffs to Darcy's left wrist.

"I didn't kill anybody," Darcy hollered. "These two dragged me inside the shop—Bob tried to rape me!"

"Oh, yeah, then how did Tricia get shot?" Baker asked.

"I was protecting myself," Darcy cried.

"You can tell me all about it down at the station," Baker said, as Bob climbed off his ex-lover and let the captain take over. His forehead and upper lip were covered in sweat, and his face was an ugly shade of purple.

"What's going on?" Tricia and Bob turned at the sound of a voice in the shop doorway. "Who kicked in my door?" Angelica demanded.

"That was me, Honey Bunch. Darcy was threatening to shoot Tricia."

"Threaten, hell," Tricia said. "She shot me! Look!"

Angelica hurried inside the shop, threw the light switch, and the shop was as bright as day. "Are you okay?" she demanded, and Tricia brandished the welt on her arm. Angelica inspected it. "Hmm—looks like it's only a flesh wound."

"Hey, what's happening?" came another voice at the open doorway. The room exploded in flashes of light as

Russ Smith depressed the shutter on his Nikon with lightning speed.

"Darcy killed Jim Roth, tried to kill me and Angelica, and shot Tricia," Bob said.

"All right," Russ cried, absolutely delighted. "Just in time for Friday's edition of the *Stoneham Weekly News*!"

Hands on hips, Angelica turned and gave Russ the loudest raspberry Tricia had ever heard.

Tricia glanced down at her throbbing arm and seconded the sentiment.

TWENTY-FIVE

After the paramedics had inspected Tricia's arm, applied antiseptic and a bandage, and left the scene, there wasn't much to do except wait for the emergency enclosure people to come and fix the Cookery's door. Darcy had already been dragged off to the county lockup, and several deputies had taken statements. Still, it was after midnight by the time Tricia made it back to Haven't Got a Clue and found that a sleepy Miss Marple had waited up for her.

Mr. Everett hadn't made it to work on Tuesday—he'd been too busy trying to duck the press and hordes of people who'd heard about his windfall and were looking for a handout. He and Grace had already had their phone number changed, and were giving it out only to trusted friends. But he assured Tricia he would make it to work on Wednesday.

Angelica had hit the road for yet another round of book signings, vowing to return on Friday. Tricia's belated birthday dinner was on hold because Angelica said she and Bob needed to hash out what—if any—of their relationship was still viable. Tricia didn't mind. Having dinner with Bob wasn't big on her list of things to do, anyway.

The Tuesday Night Book Club met as usual, but instead of talking about their featured read, the group was more interested in seeing Tricia's bullet wound and hearing the tale of how she was instrumental in the capture of Darcy Gebhard. Frannie was notably absent from the meeting.

By the time Wednesday morning rolled around, Tricia found herself feeling mildly depressed. After all, she was now officially one year older. She and Miss Marple came down to work early, and Tricia was just setting up for coffee when she heard a knock at the door. It was only nine fifteen—a whole forty-five minutes before the store was due to open. She peeked through the blinds and saw Ginny standing there. She unlocked the door and let Ginny inside.

"Happy birthday!" she cried, and gave Tricia an enthusiastic hug.

"I didn't know you knew," Tricia said.

Ginny's smile was genuine. "Angelica was afraid you'd be lonely on your birthday, so she made a point of telling both me and Mr. Everett."

"That was sweet of her. I wish she could be here today, but when you get to my age—"

"Like you're some old fogey?" Ginny asked, laughing.

"—you don't want to celebrate the same way you did when you were younger."

"So you've got no big plans for the day?"

"I'll probably just have a glass of wine later today. Although I had thought of splitting a precooked lobster with Miss Marple."

"Don't skimp on the melted butter," Ginny advised.

The door rattled, and Mr. Everett and Grace entered Haven't Got a Clue. "Good morning, and happy birthday, Ms. Miles," Mr. Everett said.

"Happy birthday, Tricia," Grace echoed.

"Thank you, and welcome back, Mr. Everett—or should I say Mr. Millionaire?" Tricia said, laughing.

Mr. Everett winced. "I'm certainly glad I can come back to work today, to get back to my *real* life. I wasn't made for celebrity," he said with disgust.

"I'm so pleased you decided to stay with us here at Haven't Got a Clue," Tricia said. "We need you, Mr. Everett."

"And I need the three of you," he admitted.

"Three?" Ginny asked.

"Don't forget Miss Marple," Mr. Everett said. "I'm sad to say that winning the lottery was the worst thing that could have happened to us."

"Why?" Ginny asked. "Are the people asking for hand-outs already out of control?"

"Yes," Grace admitted. "I didn't know there was such misery and misfortune in the world until we won that money. Yesterday we received over one hundred begging letters in the mail. That was less than twenty-four hours after it was announced we'd won."

"Speaking of letters," Ginny said, and pulled a much-folded envelope from the pocket of her slacks. "Tricia, I thought we agreed you wouldn't be paying off my mortgage," she said, sounding hurt.

Tricia frowned. "I don't know what you're talking about."

"I got a notice in the mail saying my mortgage had been paid in full."

Tricia held out her hands in mock surrender. "Believe me, I'd like to take credit, but—"

"I'm afraid that was me, Ginny," Mr. Everett said, his voice tinged with embarrassment.

"But why?" Ginny asked, her eyes wide.

"I have no children. I have no one to leave all that lottery money to. You and Ms. Miles, Miss Marple, and Grace are all I have. I wanted to repay you in some way for all the kindnesses you've shown me over the past year or so."

"Oh, Mr. Everett," Ginny said, her voice cracking, her eyes swimming with tears. She stepped up to him, wrapping her arms around him in a gentle hug. "I don't know what to say. 'Thank you' seems so inadequate."

He patted her back paternally. "I've also arranged to have the roof fixed and all new appliances delivered. Of course, I'll leave it up to you to decide what you want in your kitchen and laundry room."

Ginny pulled back. "Mr. Everett, that is way too kind of you. I can't accept—"

"Yes, you can," he said softly.

"But I—"

Tricia placed a hand on Ginny's arm, knowing how important it would be for her to accept Mr. Everett's generous gift. "Yes, you can."

"I haven't forgotten you or Miss Marple," Mr. Everett said, addressing Tricia.

Tricia shook her head. "We don't need anything, Mr. Everett, but it's so kind of you to think of us."

"I bought a case of Miss Marple's favorite kitty snacks. They're in the trunk of my car. I was hoping I could borrow the shop's dolly to bring them in."

Tricia laughed. "Of course you can." Then she addressed her cat. "Say 'thank you,' Miss Marple."

Miss Marple said, *"Yow!"*

Grace and Ginny laughed, but Mr. Everett turned a somber face to Tricia. "As for you, Ms. Miles, I owe you the most."

"Me? I don't understand."

"During the first six months you were in business, you never chased me out of your store, even though I sat in your readers' nook for hours and read your books, drank your coffee, and brought you no income. Then, you gave me work, when everyone else had written me off as just an old man. You brought value back to my life, and you saved my darling Grace from a terrible existence, when everyone thought she suffered from dementia. I can never, ever repay you for all your kindnesses."

Tricia swallowed the lump that had formed in her throat. She didn't know what to say, so she simply said, "Thank you."

"I'm sorry, but I could think of nothing to get you," the old man apologized.

"Mr. Everett, your friendship is worth more than millions to me." She stepped forward and kissed his cheek.

Mr. Everett and Grace beamed.

"What will you do with the rest of the money?" Ginny asked.

"Grace would like us to make a sizable donation to the Stoneham Food Shelf, which we will do. Grace has taken it upon herself to investigate each request we receive, and if it has merit, we will grant it. Of course, our priority will be the people of southern New Hampshire, but I believe there will be plenty of money to go to other worthy causes, as well."

"It's a wonderful thing you're doing, Mr. Everett," Tricia said. "I commend you."

A Milford Florist Shop truck pulled up outside of Haven't Got a Clue, capturing their attention. The driver got out, opened the back of his van, and pulled out a box, checking a clipboard before he shut the door and advanced toward the shop. "Delivery," he called, "for Ms. Tricia Miles."

"That's me," Tricia said, delighted, and took the box.

"Ooh, open it," Ginny said eagerly.

"Give me a chance," Tricia placated, and slid the pink ribbon from the box, removed the lid, and peeled back the green tissue. Nestled inside were six perfect calla lilies.

"Read the card," Ginny urged. "Who are they from?"

Tricia removed the envelope, withdrew a card, and frowned. *Happy birthday, darling*. It was signed "Russ."

"Russ?" Ginny repeated, appalled. "But—"

At that moment, the shop door opened once again, and a smiling Angelica glided in. "Happy birthday, darling sister," she called.

Tricia dropped the card into the box as Angelica advanced, embraced her, and planted a big wet kiss on Tricia's cheek.

"Ange, what are you doing here?" Tricia asked, pulling back.

"You didn't really think I'd leave you alone on your birthday, did you?"

"But your itinerary said—"

"I lied!" Angelica said, and everyone laughed.

The deliveryman was back with another white box. "Will you sign for this one, too?"

Feeling a little overwhelmed, Tricia took his pen and added her signature to another sheet. The deliveryman went back outside as Tricia slid the peach-colored ribbon from the box and placed them both on the counter. Again she peeled back the florist's tissue. This time, there were a dozen perfect calla lilies inside. "What does the card say?" Grace asked.

"To darling Tricia. From your big sister." She turned to Angelica. "Oh, Ange, thank you, they're beautiful."

Angelica noticed the already-open box on the coffee station's counter, and frowned. "Apparently I'm not the only one who remembered your favorite flower."

"No," Ginny said, her voice flat. "I'd better see if I can scout up a vase—or two." She headed for the back of the store just as the door opened once more. This time it was Bob Kelly, who held a white envelope in his hand.

"Hello, Tricia. Happy birthday." He handed her the card.

"Thank you, Bob."

Angelica bristled. "Hello, Bob. What brings you here?"

"Tricia's birthday, of course. You did tell me you'd planned on surprising her today."

"Did I? Why did you pay attention to that and nothing else I've said for the past month or so?"

"I had a *lot* on my mind," he admitted.

"How about your other body parts?" Angelica asked coldly.

Bob's cheeks flushed a dark red. Mr. Everett and Grace looked nearly as embarrassed.

Bob cleared his throat. "I know I've abused your trust, Angelica. I'll do anything I can to regain it."

Angelica looked away. "How's that vase coming, Ginny?" she called.

"Angelica, please don't treat me with such indifference," Bob pleaded.

"Oh, you mean I shouldn't emulate your behavior of the last two months? Remind me why."

Bob lowered his voice. "Angelica, you know how much you mean to me."

"Oh? And what did Darcy mean to you?"

Bob glowered. "Nothing. Nothing at all."

"That's not what Darcy told Captain Baker."

"You'd believe her over me?" Bob asked, sounding hurt.

"Let me think about it for all of two seconds." She looked at the ceiling and nodded her head twice. "Yes!"

Bob chewed at his bottom lip, looking uncomfortable. Much as she didn't like him, Tricia actually felt a little sorry for him. Okay, on a scale of one to ten, she gave him a one point five worth of pity. Then she recalled he'd saved her life two days before and upped it to two.

The little bell over the door captured their attention as the floral deliveryman once again entered, this time carrying a long white box with a royal blue ribbon. Again he handed the box to Tricia and offered her the clipboard.

"Goodness, another one?"

He nodded, she signed, and off he went again.

Everyone leaned in to watch as Tricia opened the box. She pulled back the tissue, and inside was—no surprise!—six more magnificent calla lilies. She opened the small white envelope and read the card. "Thank you for welcoming me to your village and your country. Happy birthday. Antonio Barbero, Nigela Racita Associates."

"Didn't you just meet that guy?" Angelica asked.

"Yes. Ginny must've told him it was my birthday today. We were going to have dinner Monday night, but—oh, well, it's a long story. I'm more interested in hearing what else Bob has to say about Darcy."

"What about her?" he asked warily.

"I'm assuming Darcy was an old flame. How did you two get reacquainted?" Tricia asked.

"At a meeting of Chamber of Commerce presidents. It was held in Nashua back in February. Darcy was the hostess at the restaurant. We had a few drinks after the meeting, and I . . . kind of drove her home."

"How does one *kind of* drive someone home?" Angelica asked pointedly.

"And then what happened?" Tricia asked.

"We had a few more drinks and talked and . . . then I woke up in her bed the next morning," Bob admitted sheepishly.

"Fancy that," Angelica said.

"I was so hungover, I don't even know if we . . . you know."

"Had sex?" Angelica supplied.

Bob wouldn't look her in the eye.

"How did Darcy come to work for Angelica?" Tricia asked.

"I must have told her Booked for Lunch was looking for a waitress."

"Did you tell her about *us* at the same time?" Angelica asked.

"I . . . don't know."

"Surely there were plenty of waitressing jobs in Nashua at the time," Grace suggested.

"Darcy told me she had another job working evenings," Tricia said, "but she needed the money. To pay off gambling debts, perhaps?"

Bob shrugged. "I guess."

"Did she hit you up for money?" Angelica asked.

Bob squirmed. "Not exactly—at least not at first. She said she was more interested in reestablishing a relationship. I told her I wasn't interested. I told her that you and I were a couple, but she hounded me anyway."

"And, of course, you succumbed to her charms; after all, you're just a weak man," Angelica said with scorn.

"I did not sleep with that woman!" Bob declared.

"Haven't we heard that before? And just what did you do instead of sleeping with her?" Angelica wanted to know.

"I kept a low profile," Bob explained. "She was forty-one and she wanted to get married to somebody—*anybody!* When I made it clear I wasn't interested in her, she set her sights on Jim Roth."

"Jake said she knew Jim after taking smoke breaks at the same time he did," Tricia said.

"She started showing up at his Gamblers Anonymous meetings, too," Bob said. "That was after she saw his house and his business. She figured he was a successful businessman."

"And when she found out the truth?" Tricia asked.

"Let's just say she didn't take the news well. She was angry with me for rebuffing her advances, and she was angry with Jim when she found out he was seeing someone else."

"But Jim broke up with Frannie," Grace said.

"Yes, but he wouldn't leave his mother," Bob explained. "Darcy was furious—and for some reason, she blamed me! When she saw the two of us together at History Repeats Itself, she decided to get rid of both of us—just out of spite."

"There's something I don't understand," Tricia said, changing the subject. "When Russ and I got to your house the night you said someone tried to break in, you said you were pretty sure it was a man. Why didn't you level with us that it was Darcy?"

"And admit I was afraid of a woman? Get real, Tricia."

"You could have saved yourself—and the Sheriff's Department—a lot of trouble."

"Don't lecture me," Bob snapped.

"Don't you speak to my sister like that," Angelica admonished. "Especially on her birthday!"

Bob hung his head. "I'm sorry, Tricia."

"I don't know if I ever can forgive you, Bob," Angelica said. "You know how I feel about cheaters. I've been married to four of them."

"I'm sorry, Angelica. I didn't mean for it to happen," Bob said, embarrassed.

"I've heard that four times too many," Angelica said and sniffed loudly.

Bob eyed Tricia and the others. "Angelica, don't you think we should be discussing this in private?"

Angelica crossed her arms over her chest. "Why? Do you have anything else to hide?"

Tricia wished she could just fade into the woodwork, glad it was Bob and not she who was pinned by Angelica's baleful stare. Still, why did they have to have this conversation in Haven't Got a Clue? The saving grace was that the store hadn't yet opened for the day.

Tricia took a step back and signaled to Mr. Everett and Grace. "We'll just leave you two alone—"

"You'll do nothing of the kind," Angelica said, turning her laserlike glare on Tricia. Angelica meant business. She turned back to Bob. "You're going to have to work very hard to get back into my good graces."

"Anything you want, Cupcake."

"Cupcake?" Tricia repeated.

Angelica swung her angry gaze back to Tricia. *Oops!* Apparently there were some things that transcended even Angelica's birthday goodwill.

Ginny returned with two clear glass vases filled with water. "Would you like me to arrange the flowers?" she asked Tricia.

"That would be lovely. Thank you, Ginny."

Before Ginny could get started, the florist's deliveryman was back again, with yet another long white box. The ribbon on this one was pale yellow. He handed it to Tricia.

"Not another one?"

"Apparently you're very popular, ma'am."

Once again, Tricia slid the ribbon from the box and opened it. Inside were another dozen perfect calla lilies.

"Who are they from?" Angelica asked.

Tricia read the card. "Sorry we couldn't be there on your special day. Love, Mother and Daddy." Oh, well, at least they'd made an effort.

"Goodness, I'm going to have to go home and rustle up another couple of vases," Angelica said, but before she could do so, the door opened again, and Russ stepped inside, his camera dangling around his neck.

"Happy birthday, Tricia!"

"Hello, Russ," Tricia said, unable to muster any enthusiasm.

"I saw the florist's truck and—" He frowned at the sight of the four florist's boxes on the coffee station's counter. "Oh. Gee . . . I guess my gift wasn't as original as I thought."

"Thank you for thinking of me, Russ," Tricia said coolly. No way was he getting a hug and a kiss for remembering her birthday—not after the way he'd been acting of late.

The door rattled, and it was the deliveryman with still another long white florist's box. "Please sign here," he said and handed Tricia his clipboard for a fifth time.

"Aren't you getting writer's cramp by now?" Angelica asked. "I didn't sign my name that much at some of my book events."

Tricia ignored her sarcasm. This time the ribbon was

mauve, which went perfectly with her sweater set. She opened the box and found another six magnificent calla lilies.

"And this time they're from—?" Ginny prompted eagerly, while trying to force one more lily into the first vase.

Tricia read the card. "Happy birthday. Grant."

"Baker!" Russ cried, clearly annoyed.

Tricia wasted less than two seconds of her day to glare at him before she removed one of the lovely flowers from the box. How had Captain Baker known calla lilies were her favorite, let alone her birth date? Tricia glanced at Angelica, who seemed to find the tin ceiling of infinite interest.

The door opened again—the deliveryman, back for a sixth time.

"No more," Tricia cried.

"'Fraid so," the man said and laughed, once again proffering the pen and invoice for Tricia to sign. The ribbon was deep purple. Tricia tugged it from the box and opened it. Six more calla lilies. She read the card. "Happy birthday. Love, Ginny and Mr. E." Tricia turned to her employees. "Oh, thank you so much. You two are the greatest." She leapt forward to capture them both in a hug.

"About time that guy brought our flowers in," Ginny said, just a little exasperated.

Russ looked hurt. "I gave you the same gift, but I didn't get a hug."

Tricia looked down her nose at him. "I said 'thank you.'"

The door opened once more. The deliveryman. Again. With yet a seventh box of flowers. This time the ribbon was scarlet. He offered Tricia the pen and clipboard one more time, and Tricia signed.

"Why didn't you just deliver them all at once?" Ginny asked.

The man smiled and winked. "Don't you think it was more fun this way?"

"I do," Tricia said and accepted the latest box. "Is this the last one?"

"I sure hope so," Angelica said. "This place is beginning to look like a funeral parlor."

"I'm afraid so," the deliveryman confirmed. "I think your friends and family have wiped out the entire East Coast's stock of lilies."

Tricia accepted the box and set it on the counter. "Let me give you something for your trouble," she said, and headed for the cash register.

The deliveryman backed toward the door and tipped his cap. "It's not necessary, ma'am. Hope your day is happy!"

"Thank you."

Tricia heard the door close, but she was too absorbed in removing the satin ribbon from the box. Again, she pulled back the tissue and again found a dozen perfect calla lilies.

"Ahhh," Ginny cooed.

Tricia read the card, which wasn't signed. *Don't forget what my last note said*. Tricia frowned. For a moment, the message didn't register. And then she reached up to finger the chain around her neck, and thought about the calla lily locket Christopher had sent, and the note that went with it: *To remind you of the one you love the most*. She frowned. Why would he send flowers from Miss Marple?

"Who's it from?" Angelica asked.

"I'm not sure," Tricia lied.

Grace appeared with a tray filled with Haven't Got a Clue cardboard coffee cups, passing them to those assembled. "It's time for a birthday toast," she said.

"It would be better with champagne," Russ commented, but accepted a cup anyway. He raised his cup and was about to speak when Angelica silenced him with one of her icy glares. Russ lowered his cup.

Angelica raised hers. "To my dear sister, Tricia. Many happy returns of the day!"

"Hear, hear!" the others cried in agreement, and raised their cups, too. Miss Marple rubbed against Tricia's ankles.

For the first time in a long, long time, Tricia felt truly loved—and it felt pretty darned good.

ANGELICA'S RECIPES

HACIENDA (SOFT) TACOS

3 cups coarsely chopped or shredded (pulled)
    poached chicken
1 onion, chopped
1/2 green pepper, chopped
1 1/2 teaspoons salt
1/8 teaspoon pepper
1 1/2 to 2 teaspoons chili powder (according to taste)
1 (8-ounce) can tomato sauce
1/2 cup water
12 corn (or flour) 8- or 9-inch tortillas
1 tomato, chopped
3/4 cup grated or shredded Cheddar cheese
1 cup lettuce cut into strips
Your favorite bottled salsa

In large skillet, mix together chicken, onion, green pepper, salt, pepper, chili powder, tomato sauce, and water. Cook covered over low heat for about 15 minutes, then uncovered for 5 to 10 minutes, until excess liquid is gone. Oven heat the tortillas and fill lower 3/4 with chicken mixture, and the remainder with the tomatoes, cheese, and lettuce. Top with a spoonful of the salsa.

Makes 12 tacos/6 servings.

Coconut Cake

> 3 cups sifted cake flour (sift before measuring)
> 2 teaspoons baking powder
> 1/4 teaspoon salt
> 1 cup (2 sticks) unsalted butter, at room temperature
> 1 pound powdered sugar
> 4 egg yolks, well beaten
> 1 cup milk
> 1 teaspoon vanilla extract
> 1 cup shredded coconut
> 4 egg whites, well beaten

Measure the sifted cake flour into a bowl. Add baking powder and salt. Sift these ingredients at least 2 times. In a mixing bowl, cream butter and gradually add sugar. Continue creaming until light and fluffy. Add the beaten egg yolks and beat well. Add flour mixture alternately with the milk, beating well after each addition. Stir in vanilla and coconut. Gently fold in egg whites. Bake in three greased 8-inch round pans at 350°

for about 30 minutes, or until a wooden toothpick inserted in the center comes out clean.

Makes three 8-inch layers.

COCONUT ICING

> 1 cup (2 sticks) unsalted butter, at room
>   temperature
> 2 1/2 cups confectioners' sugar
> 1/3 cup coconut milk, at room temperature*
> 1 1/2 teaspoons vanilla extract
> 1/8 teaspoon salt
> 1 1/2 cups sweetened flaked coconut

You can substitute regular milk for the coconut milk, then substitute coconut extract for vanilla extract.

Using an electric mixer, beat butter in large bowl until smooth. Add sugar, coconut milk, vanilla, and salt. Beat on medium-low speed until blended, scraping down the sides of the bowl. Increase speed to medium-high, and beat until light and fluffy.

Frost the cake. Gently press coconut onto the sides of the cake, and sprinkle the top with coconut, too.

Serves 6–8.

Blueberry Muffins

1 egg
1/2 cup milk
1/4 cup unsalted butter, melted
1 1/2 cups all-purpose flour
1/2 cup sugar
2 teaspoons baking powder
1/4 teaspoon salt
1 cup fresh blueberries or well-drained frozen blue-
   berries (thawed)

Heat oven to 400°. Grease the bottoms of 12 medium muffin cups or line them with paper baking cups. Beat egg; stir in milk and melted butter. Mix in remaining ingredients just until flour is dampened. Batter should be lumpy.

Fill muffin cups 2/3 full. Bake 20 to 25 minutes or until golden brown. Immediately remove from pan.

Makes 12 muffins.

Cinnamon Coffee Cake

1 1/2 cups all-purpose flour
3/4 cup sugar
2 1/2 teaspoons baking powder

1/4 teaspoon salt
1/4 cup unsalted butter
1/4 cup milk
1 egg

Heat oven to 375°. Grease 9x1½-inch round layer pan or 8x8x2-inch square pan. Blend all ingredients except topping. Beat vigorously for 30 seconds. Spread batter in pan. Sprinkle topping over batter. Bake 25 to 30 minutes, or until wooden toothpick inserted in the center comes out clean. Serve warm.

TOPPING:

1/3 cup brown sugar (firmly packed)
1/4 cup all-purpose flour
1/2 teaspoon cinnamon
3 tablespoons firm unsalted butter

Mix all ingredients until they resemble coarse crumbs.

VARIATIONS:

Add 1/2 cup chopped walnuts and/or 1/2 cup raisins to cake batter.

9 servings.

Mrs. Roth's Lemon Bars

  1 cup flour
  1/2 cup unsalted butter, softened
  1/4 cup confectioners' sugar

Preheat oven to 350°. Mix these ingredients and press into an ungreased 8x8-inch square pan, building up the edges. Bake 15-20 minutes, or until just starting to brown.

  2 eggs
  1 cup granulated sugar
  1/2 teaspoon baking powder
  1/4 teaspoon salt
  2 teaspoons grated lemon peel (about one lemon's worth)
  2 tablespoons lemon juice (about one lemon's worth)

Reduce oven temperature to 300°. Beat the above ingredients together until they're light and fluffy (about 3 minutes). Pour over the crust while it is still hot. Bake until no indentation remains when you touch lightly in the center, about 25 minutes. When cool, cut into squares. Dust with a bit more confectioners' sugar.

Mrs. Roth liked to add a dab of yellow paste food coloring to her lemon bars, but they don't need it (and I don't recommend it).

If you liked CHAPTER & HEARSE,
you'll love the new Victoria Square Mysteries
by Lorraine Bartlett.
Turn the page for a preview of . . .

A CRAFTY
KILLING

Coming February 2011
from Berkley Prime Crime!

Ezra Hilton lay sprawled at the bottom step of the staircase, facedown in a puddle of his own congealed blood. He'd probably broken his long, proud nose when he hit Artisans Alley's carpet-covered concrete floor, Katie Bonner decided. She wondered if McKinlay Mill's funeral director could make Ezra look presentable for a viewing.

Katie took a ragged breath and cursed her practicality. But that would be what Ezra would've wanted. At least, that's what she *thought* he would have wanted.

"Are you okay, ma'am?" asked the lanky, uniformed deputy, Schuler by the nametag on his breast pocket.

"No. But I guess that's to be expected. Mr. Hilton was my husband's business partner. My business partner, now, I guess. My husband died in a car accident last winter," she explained unnecessarily. She didn't add that they'd been separated at the time. It was still too painful to revisit those memories.

After putting two fingers through the left leg of her panty hose that morning, Katie knew it was going to be one of those days. She'd had no idea it was going to be *this* bad. Not that the death of a seventy-five-year-old man should have come as a shock. But Ezra had been such a lively old coot. And dying so soon after Chad . . .

"Did Mr. Hilton have any enemies?" the deputy asked.

"Enemies?" Katie repeated. "Ezra? Of course not."

The deputy looked toward the cash desks at the front of the store. "The cash register's empty. The drawer was open when we got here. Do you know how much would've been in the till?"

Katie blinked, open-mouthed. "No. We could run the total, though—"

The deputy caught her by the arm before she could move more than a foot in that direction. "We'll wait for the tech team to dust for prints."

"Oh, of course." Then it dawned on her just what the deputy was saying. "You can't think someone—" She had to swallow before voicing the impossible. "—that someone killed him?"

Schuler looked back down at the dead man. "Looks like blunt trauma to the back of the head," he said without emotion. "The M.E. will have to determine the time of death."

Katie looked down at the still form on the floor and the rusty patch of dried blood staining the snowy hair on the back of Ezra's head. Tears stung her eyes and a lump rose in her throat. "Robbery?" she ventured.

"Most likely," the deputy agreed.

Katie had to take a shaky breath before she could speak again. "Thursdays are typically slow in this business." Not that she knew from personal experience. Her late husband had told her that on more than one occasion. "There couldn't have been more than a couple hundred dollars in the drawer."

"People have been murdered for a lot less," Schuler said. "The side door was unlocked. Could someone have had an appointment with Mr. Hilton after hours?"

"I don't know. I have a regular job. I'm not part of the day-to-day routine here at Artisans Alley. I was on my way to work when I saw the patrol cars in the lot and figured I should stop in to see what was up."

Schuler nodded. "Is there any chance Mr. Hilton kept an appointment calendar?"

"I could look," Katie said and took a step to her left, in the direction of Ezra's office.

Again Schuler held her back. "We'll wait until our chief investigator gets here."

Katie's gaze returned to the still figure on the floor. Ezra dying peacefully in his sleep wouldn't have been a shock, but murder? Katie searched the pockets of her suit jacket, found a balled-up tissue, and wiped her nose.

She wasn't the only one who needed a hanky. A woman older than she sat on a Victorian horsehair sofa in the dreary, cluttered booth across the way, wiping away tears as she answered another uniformed deputy's questions.

"Did she find him?" Katie asked, with a nod in the stranger's direction.

Schuler nodded. "Do you know her?"

Katie shook her head.

"Her name is Mary Elliott. She says she's the co-owner of the tea shop across the Square."

Though her face was twisted with grief, the woman conveyed an aura of mature elegance that her pastel blue jogging suit couldn't disguise. The shoulder-length blonde hair in a loose ponytail at her neck accentuated the firm lines of her neck and chin. She had to be at least twenty years older than Katie's thirty, but she carried it well. Two spilled cups of take-out coffee stained the rug near Artisans Alley's side door. The woman must have dropped them upon finding the body.

Embarrassed to witness the other woman's flood of emotion, Katie brushed a piece of fuzz from her drab gray wool skirt, the pleated one that always made her feel pudgy, and studied the toes of her scruffy sneakers. She'd change out of them once—if ever—she made it to work.

Shouldn't she be crying, too? Ezra was her business partner, for God's sake. But she couldn't break down. At least not yet. She'd shed far too many tears in the last year. Instead, Katie rummaged through her purse for a peppermint. She unwrapped it, popped it into her mouth, and immediately crunched it, the sharp, sweet flavor instantly delivering what was to her, comfort. She tucked the wrapper into her pocket.

Outside, a car door slammed. A man appeared in the open doorway, carrying what looked like a big green tackle box. He had to be the medical examiner, Katie realized, and he was closely followed by a plainclothes cop, his badge pinned to the lapel of his raincoat. Was that a lab team and a crime photographer behind them?

"Do you need me?" Katie asked Schuler, glancing down at Ezra's polished Florsheims. "I'll need to make some calls in the office. And I'll look for Ezra's calendar, too."

"Oh, no," the deputy warned. "You'll have to make your calls from another phone. This entire building is now considered a crime scene. We don't know if anything else was taken."

"Okay. I'll be in my car—the blue Ford Focus in the lot."

Again Schuler nodded, and left her to confer with the other police personnel.

Katie turned, hugging herself against the morning chill as she headed back to her little sedan. She really should call her boss, Josh, first, but decided against it; she wasn't up to an argument. Why couldn't he have gone to Syracuse on business today and not yesterday?

Katie settled herself behind the car's steering wheel, grabbed the small address book from her purse, and hunted for attorney Seth Landers's name. As McKinlay Mill's only lawyer, Seth knew just about everyone in the village. He'd handled the legalities when Chad bought into Artisans Alley, and he'd advised Katie after Chad's death. Katie and Chad hadn't filed any paperwork on their separation. Maybe she'd been in denial, hoping they'd reconcile. It hadn't mattered in the long run.

Katie dialed the lawyer's number, grateful she'd taken her cell phone from the charger before starting out this morning, and got through to his secretary, who quickly transferred her to the lawyer.

"Seth, I've got some bad news. Ezra Hilton is dead."

"Dead? Oh, I'm sorry to hear that," he said calmly. "In his sleep?"

"No! A robbery at Artisans Alley. It looks like someone snuck up on him from behind, hit him over the head, and killed him."

"Good grief." She heard him take a breath. "When did this happen?"

"Probably last night. One of the other merchants in the Square found him."

"Katie, did you know Ezra named you executor of his estate?"

"Me? But I hardly knew him," she cried.

"You were his partner," Seth said.

"On paper only." Executor of Ezra's estate? She exhaled, raking her fingers through the hair curling around her collar, the enormity of that responsibility only just beginning to dawn on her. She reached into her purse for another peppermint, unwrapped it, and crunched. "Is there anyone I should notify? Any relatives?" she asked around the shards of candy.

"Just a nephew in Rochester. If you want, I can take care of that for you."

"Yes, thank you." The last thing Katie wanted to do was dump that kind of news on some poor, unsuspecting survivor. "Did Ezra leave any"—she closed her eyes and swallowed—"funeral instructions with you?"

"I'll have to pull his will from the files, but I think so. I'll call Mr. Collier at the funeral home to make sure."

"Thank you," she breathed. She looked through the car's windshield, taking in the rambling old wooden structure that was Artisans Alley. "What should I do about the Alley?"

"You're already a limited partner, so there's nothing to keep you from conducting business as usual. The estate still has to go through probate, but it's in your best interest to keep Artisans Alley open—if that's what you want."

Seth's tone on that last part of the sentence gave her pause, but she plowed on. "How long will probate take?"

"Anywhere from six months to a couple of years, depending on the complexity of the estate."

"Swell. Do I have to remind you I've already got a real job?"

"Now you have two," Seth said.

"What should I do next?"

"Can you sign the Alley's checks?"

"Yes. Ezra added my name to the bank accounts and I signed a signature card right after Chad died."

"Then you're in business. It wouldn't hurt to talk to Ezra's accountant, too."

"Thank you, Seth. I already feel better just talking to you."

"I'm glad to help in any way. Where can I reach you?"

"My cell phone, and maybe Ezra's number at Artisans Alley, if they let me back in. I won't know until later today." She gave him the numbers.

"I'll get back to you on what Ezra wanted in the way of a funeral. Knowing the old man, I'll bet he set that up in advance. He was very much a no-nonsense kind of guy."

"If you say so," Katie said. She'd barely known the man.

Seth said good-bye, and Katie folded the phone closed. Before she could put it away, she noticed a solidly built woman with short-cropped gray hair and oversized glasses charge across the parking lot, heading straight for her car. Katie cranked open her window, trying not to prejudge a woman who would willingly go out in public dressed in a garish purple polyester pantsuit left over from the seventies.

"I just heard Ezra Hilton died," the woman barked. "Are you the new owner?"

"Uh—I guess so," Katie answered, startled by the newcomer's directness.

"Edie Silver," she said, extending a beefy hand. "I'm a crafter. I crochet and paint, and I make the most gorgeous silk flower arrangements you'll ever see, if I do say so myself. Will you be renting booth space to crafters? Mr. Hilton never would." Her voice vibrated with disapproval.

"I don't know."

"If crafters are coming in, I want to be at the top of the list. Take down my name, will you?"

Dazed, Katie pawed through her purse to find a small spiral notebook and a pen, and then dutifully copied down the information.

"When will you be making a decision?" the woman badgered.

"I don't know."

"I'll call Artisans Alley in a day or so for your decision." With a curt nod, Edie stalked back toward the fringe of the crowd that had gathered in front of the Square's tony wine and cheese shop, The Perfect Grape.

Katie stared after her, appalled. Ezra's body had only been discovered within the hour and already the vultures were circling. She placed her phone in her purse and nearly jumped as a slight, well-dressed woman—on the high side of fifty—suddenly appeared in front of her still-opened window.

"Am I disturbing you?" the woman asked and bent low, the remnants of a Brooklyn accent tingeing her voice. Her dyed-black pageboy emphasized her pale face.

"Uh . . . no," Katie said.

"I'm Gilda Ringwald." She offered her hand. "I own Gilda's Gourmet Baskets, across the Square."

Katie took it, surprised at the strength of the woman's handshake. "I'm Katie Bonner. Have we met before?"

"Briefly. At dear Chad's wake. Such a nice young man," she said and shook her head, her expression somber.

Those days after Chad's death were a blur, but Katie did remember writing a thank-you note for a lovely gift basket filled with luscious chocolates and fattening cookies that had arrived at the apartment.

"The whole Square has already heard about poor Ezra's

passing. Naturally, we're all in shock. He was the Merchants Association's driving force, you know. I don't know how we'll manage without him. I expect you'll be in charge of Artisans Alley's affairs, won't you?"

"For now," Katie admitted.

"You're not going to close the Alley, are you?" Gilda asked, an edgy note coloring her tone.

"For today, at least. Long term . . . I don't know."

Gilda nodded over the roof of Katie's car. "There's already a crew from Channel Nine rolling tape. I'll speak to them on behalf of the merchants." She sighed, clasping her hands. "Ezra would've jumped at the chance for this kind of publicity. For the Alley and the Square, I mean."

She was right about that. And Ezra's PR efforts had paid off. He'd turned a decrepit warehouse into an artists cooperative. On the strength of his labors, the surrounding houses had been converted to boutiques and specialty shops like Gilda's Gourmet Baskets.

The result was Victoria Square—a budding tourist destination on the cusp of becoming truly successful. With decent marketing, its gaslights and the charming gingerbread facades on the buildings could bring in visitors on their way to Niagara Falls, some eighty miles west, as well as customers from nearby Rochester, New York.

"Artisans Alley is our anchor," Gilda continued, her voice firm. "The rest of us need it to pull in shoppers and keep us afloat."

That was a rather cold assessment of the situation. Had Gilda forgotten that a man had been killed?

"The Merchants Association will probably call an emergency meeting in the next day or so," Gilda continued. "I hope you'll come."

"I'll try." Katie caught sight of the dashboard clock,

realizing she still hadn't called her boss to explain her absence.

As though taking the hint, Gilda straightened. "I'll let you know about the meeting. In the meantime, I'm so sorry about Ezra. I just hope his death isn't a fatal blow to Victoria Square, too."

The woman turned on her heel and walked back to her store. With no one else coming her way, Katie realized she could no longer avoid the inevitable, flipped open her phone again, and punched in her work number. It rang once, twice.

"Kimper Insurance, Josh Kimper speaking."

"Josh, it's Katie—"

"Where the hell are you?" he bellowed, so loud she had to hold the phone away from her ear. "Do you realize there's no coffee and I've got a client meeting in five minutes?"

"Sorry, Josh, but my late husband's business partner was killed overnight. As minority owner, I'll have to take care of things at Artisans Alley here in McKinlay Mill for at least today."

"I don't appreciate a last-minute call like this, Katie," Josh barked.

Katie bit back her anger. "I'm sure Ezra didn't plan on being murdered."

"Murdered?"

"The police think it may have happened during a robbery attempt last night."

"That's too bad," he said, with no hint of sympathy. "But you can't let this affect *your* life."

Katie knew Josh meant he didn't want Ezra's murder to affect *his* life.

Josh Kimper's abrasive personality alone qualified him

as the boss from hell. He'd given Katie a job as office manager when she'd been desperate for work with flexible hours while finishing her graduate degree. Four years later Josh liked to remind her of it on a daily—if not hourly—basis. Since Chad's death, he'd gotten used to her putting in fifty- and sometimes sixty-hour weeks. Katie had preferred immersing herself in office routine rather than facing her empty apartment—her empty life. And, she wasn't ashamed to admit, she needed the overtime money.

A good salary was Josh's carrot to keep her at the agency. She made much less than Josh, of course, but then he was the talent, as he so often liked to tell her. That left Katie with the drudgery.

"The coffee's in the cabinet. I brought in homemade chocolate chip cookies yesterday. They're in the jar on the counter. Put them on a plate, lay out napkins, and everything will be fine."

"You'd better be in tomorrow," Josh grated. "We can't let the filing go for more than a day."

You could always do it yourself, she thought, but held her tongue. "I'll tell you my plans as soon as I know them."

"And I'm not paying you for today, either," he said.

"Then I'll take a day of vacation. I still have more than a week left."

"And you always wait until it's inconvenient to take it. You'd better be here tomorrow," Josh ordered and hung up.

Eyes narrowed, Katie stuck out her tongue at the phone.

"Do you always end your conversations that way?" came an amused male voice from outside her still-opened window.

Chagrined, Katie stabbed the phone's power button

and forced a smile for Deputy Schuler. "Only on days like today."

"This is Detective Ray Davenport, our lead investigator." Schuler stepped away, revealing the stocky, balding man Katie had seen earlier. She eyed the ratty raincoat. Was he trying to channel an old Columbo rerun?

Davenport nodded at her. "Ma'am."

Or maybe he was channeling Joe Friday.

Katie studied the detective's nondescript face, wondering if his no-nonsense demeanor was a defense mechanism he'd erected to shield him from the results of the violence he saw on a regular basis. Or could it be he was just grumpy? But then, grumpy was an apt description of her current emotional state.

"What can I do for you, detective?" Katie asked, trying to be helpful.

The older man opened a worn notebook and took a pen from the inside pocket of his raincoat. "Did the deceased—uh, Mr. Hilton—have any family?"

Deceased. It made it sound so . . . permanent. Then again, it was.

"Apparently Ezra had a nephew. His lawyer is contacting him," Katie said.

"And that man's name is?" Davenport prompted.

"Sorry, I don't know." She gave him Seth's name and phone number, which he dutifully jotted down.

"Did Mr. Hilton always close the place by himself?"   •

Katie lifted her hands from her lap and shrugged. "I don't know."

Davenport frowned. "Who might've seen the deceased last, ma'am?"

"I—"

"Don't tell me—you don't know," Davenport supplied,

slapping his notebook closed. "Would you have a list of all the vendors who rent space at Artisans Alley? We'll want to talk to everyone to see if they saw something or can tell if anything else was taken from the building."

"I'm sure there's a list somewhere in the office. I just don't know where to put my hands on it. Ezra was pretty much a one-man show—from handling the paperwork, to arranging publicity, to manning the register if need be. From the looks of it, he may have spread himself far too thin."

"And that," the detective said with a penetrating gaze, "could be what got him killed."

THE *NEW YORK TIMES* BESTSELLING
BOOKTOWN MYSTERIES FROM

LORNA BARRETT

CONTINUES WITH

BOOKPLATE SPECIAL

Bookstore owner Tricia Miles has put up—and
put up with—her uninvited college roommate
for weeks. In return, Pammy has stolen one
hundred dollars. But the day she's kicked out,
Pammy's found dead in a Dumpster, leaving
loads of questions unanswered.

penguin.com

ALSO FROM *NEW YORK TIMES*
BESTSELLING AUTHOR

Lorna Barrett

Bookmarked for Death

To celebrate her bookstore's anniversary, Tricia Miles hosts a book signing for bestselling author Zoë Carter. But the event takes a terrible turn when the author is found dead in the washroom. Before long, both police and reporters are demanding the real story. So far, the author's assistant/niece is the only suspect. And with a sheriff who provides more obstacles than answers, Tricia will have to take matters into her own hands—and read between the lines to solve this mystery...

M508T0310

MURDER IS BINDING

FROM *NEW YORK TIMES* BESTSELLING AUTHOR

Lorna Barrett

The streets of Stoneham, New Hampshire, are lined with bookstores... and paved with murder.

When she moved to Stoneham, city slicker Tricia Miles was met with nothing but friendly faces. And when she opened her mystery bookstore, she was met with friendly competition. But when she finds Doris Gleason dead in her own cookbook store, killed with a kitchen knife, the atmosphere seems more cutthroat than cordial. Someone wanted to get their hands on the rare cookbook that Doris had recently purchased—and the locals think that someone is Tricia. To clear her name, Tricia will take a page out of one of her own mysteries—and hunt down someone who isn't killing by the book.

penguin.com